The Lady of Blossholme by H. Rider Haggard

Sir Henry Rider Haggard, KBE was born on June 22nd, 1856 at Bradenham in Norfolk, England.

After his education he was pushed towards an Army career but failed the entrance exam. Next Haggard was positioned to work for the British Foreign Office but he seems not to have sat that exam. Using family connections, he was sent to Southern Africa by his father in search of a further opportunity of a career.

Haggard spent six years there before a return to England and marriage. He had begun to write and publish some non-fiction in Africa but it was only after studying Law in the hope it might prove to be the proper career his father wanted for him that Haggard began to write fiction, using his African experiences as the basis.

His first fiction was published in 1885 and the following year King Solomon's Mines was published. It was a phenomenal success. His career was set.

Haggard wrote well and wrote often. He managed to sympathise with the local populations even though they were exploited and manipulated by Europeans intent on amassing fortunes in money, people and resources. His writing career covered the great sprint to Empire of several European powers and both reflects and criticizes these events through his well-loved characters including Allan Quatermain and Ayesha.

In his later years Haggard pursued much in the way social reform as well as standing for Parliament and writing a great many letters to The Times.

Henry Rider Haggard died on May 14th, 1925 at the age of 68. His ashes were buried at Ditchingham Church.

Index of Contents
Chapter I - Sir John Foterell
Chapter II - The Murder by the Mere
Chapter III - A Wedding
Chapter IV - The Abbot's Oath
Chapter V - What Passed at Cranwell
Chapter VI - Emlyn's Curse
Chapter VII - The Abbot's Offer
Chapter VIII - Emlyn Calls Her Man
Chapter IX - The Blossholme Witchings
Chapter X - Mother Megges and the Ghost
Chapter XI - Doomed
Chapter XII - The Stake
Chapter XIII - The Messenger
Chapter XIV - Jacob and the Jewels
Chapter XV - The Devil at Court

Chapter XVI - The Voice in the Forest
Chapter XVII - Between Doom and Honour
Chapter XVIII - Out of the Shadows
H. Rider Haggard – A Short Biography
H. Rider Haggard – A Concise Bibliography

Chapter I

Sir John Foterell

Who that has ever seen them can forget the ruins of Blossholme Abbey, set upon their mount between the great waters of the tidal estuary to the north, the rich lands and grazing marshes that, backed with woods, border it east and south, and to the west by the rolling uplands, merging at last into purple moor, and, far away, the sombre eternal hills! Probably the scene has not changed very much since the days of Henry VIII, when those things happened of which we have to tell, for here no large town has arisen, nor have mines been dug or factories built to affront the earth and defile the air with their hideousness and smoke.

The village of Blossholme we know has scarcely varied in its population, for the old records tell us this, and as there is no railway here its aspect must be much the same. Houses built of the local grey stone do not readily fall down. The folk of that generation walked in and out of the doorways of many of them, although the roofs for the most part are now covered with tiles or rough slates in place of reeds from the dike. The parish wells also, fitted with iron pumps that have superseded the old rollers and buckets, still serve the place with drinking-water as they have done since the days of the first Edward, and perhaps for centuries before.

Although their use, if not their necessity, has passed away, not far from the Abbey gate the stocks and whipping-post, the latter arranged with three sets of iron loops fixed at different heights and of varying diameters to accommodate the wrists of man, woman, and child, may still be found in the middle of the Priests' Green. These stand, it will be remembered, under a quaint old roof supported on rough, oaken pillars, and surmounted by a weathercock which the monkish fancy has fashioned to the shape of the archangel blowing the last trump. His clarion or coach-horn, or whatever instrument of music it was he blew, has vanished. The parish book records that in the time of George I a boy broke it off, melted it down, and was publicly flogged in consequence, the last time, apparently, that the whipping-post was used. But Gabriel still twists about as manfully as he did when old Peter, the famous smith, fashioned and set him up with his own hand in the last year of King Henry VIII, as it is said to commemorate the fact that on this spot stood the stakes to which Cicely Harflete, Lady of Blossholme, and her foster-mother, Emlyn, were chained to be burned as witches.

So it is with everything at Blossholme, a place that Time has touched but lightly. The fields, or many of them, bear the same names and remain identical in their shape and outline. The old farmsteads and the few halls in which reside the gentry of the district, stand where they always stood. The glorious tower of the Abbey still points upwards to the sky, although bells and roof are gone, while half-a- mile away the parish church that was there before it—having been rebuilt indeed upon Saxon foundations in the days of William Rufus—yet lies among its ancient elms. Farther on, situate upon the slope of a vale down which runs a brook through meadows, is the stark ruin of the old Nunnery that was subservient to the proud Abbey on the hill, some of it now roofed in with galvanised iron sheets and used as cow- sheds.

It is of this Abbey and this Nunnery and of those who dwelt around them in a day bygone, and especially of that fair and persecuted woman who came to be known as the Lady of Blossholme, that our story has to tell.

It was dead winter in the year 1535—the 31st of December, indeed. Old Sir John Foterell, a white-bearded, red-faced man of about sixty years of age, was seated before the log fire in the dining-hall of his great house at Shefton, spelling through a letter which had just been brought to him from Blossholme Abbey. He mastered it at length, and when it was done any one who had been there to look might have seen a knight and gentleman of large estate in a rage remarkable even for the time of the eighth Henry. He dashed the document to the ground; he drank three cups of strong ale, of which he had already had enough, in quick succession; he swore a number of the best oaths of the period, and finally, in the most expressive language, he consigned the body of the Abbot of Blossholme to the gallows and his soul to hell.

"He claims my lands, does he?" he exclaimed, shaking his fist in the direction of Blossholme. "What does the rogue say? That the abbot who went before him parted with them to my grandfather for no good consideration, but under fear and threats. Now, writes he, this Secretary Cromwell, whom they call Vicar-General, has declared that the said transfer was without the law, and that I must hand over the said lands to the Abbey of Blossholme on or before Candlemas! What was Cromwell paid to sign that order with no inquiry made, I wonder?"

Sir John poured out and drank a fourth cup of ale, then set to walking up and down the hall. Presently he halted in front of the fire and addressed it as though it were his enemy.

"You are a clever fellow, Clement Maldon; they tell me that all Spaniards are, and you were taught your craft at Rome and sent here for a purpose. You began as nothing, and now you are Abbot of Blossholme, and, if the King had not faced the Pope, would be more. But you forget yourself at times, for the Southern blood is hot, and when the wine is in, the truth is out. There were certain words you spoke not a year ago before me and other witnesses of which I will remind you presently. Perhaps when Secretary Cromwell learns them he will cancel his gift of my lands, and mayhap lift that plotting head of yours up higher. I'll go remind you of them."

Sir John strode to the door and shouted; it would not be too much to say that he bellowed like a bull. It opened after a while, and a serving-man appeared, a bow-legged, sturdy-looking fellow with a shock of black hair.

"Why are you not quicker, Jeffrey Stokes?" he asked. "Must I wait your pleasure from noon to night?"

"I came as fast as I could, master. Why, then, do you rate me?"

"Would you argue with me, fellow? Do it again and I will have you tied to a post and lashed."

"Lash yourself, master, and let out the choler and good ale, which you need to do," replied Jeffrey in his gruff voice. "There be some men who never know when they are well served, and such are apt to come to ill and lonely ends. What is your pleasure? I'll do it if I can, and if not, do it yourself."

Sir John lifted his hand as though to strike him, then let it fall again.

"I like one who braves me to my teeth," he said more gently, "and that was ever your nature. Take it not ill, man; I was angered, and have cause to be."

"The anger I see, but not the cause, though, as a monk came from the Abbey but now, perhaps I can hazard a guess."

"Aye, that's it, that's it, Jeffrey. Hark; I ride to yonder crows'- nest, and at once. Saddle me a horse."

"Good, master. I'll saddle two horses."

"Two? I said one. Fool, can I ride a pair at once, like a mountebank?"

"I know not, but you can ride one and I another. When the Abbot of Blossholme visits Sir John Foterell of Shefton he comes with hawk on wrist, with chaplains and pages, and ten stout men-at-arms, of whom he keeps more of late than a priest would seem to need about him. When Sir John Foterell visits the Abbot of Blossholme, at least he should have one serving-man at his back to hold his nag and bear him witness."

Sir John looked at him shrewdly.

"I called you fool," he said, "but you are none except in looks. Do as you will, Jeffrey, but be swift. Stop. Where is my daughter?"

"The Lady Cicely sits in her parlour. I saw her sweet face at the window but now staring out at the snow as though she thought to see a ghost in it."

"Um," grunted Sir John, "the ghost she thinks to see rides a grand grey mare, stands over six feet high, has a jolly face, and a pair of arms well made for sword and shield, or to clip a girl in. Yet that ghost must be laid, Jeffrey."

"Pity if so, master. Moreover, you may find it hard. Ghost-laying is a priest's job, and when maids' waists are willing, men's arms reach far."

"Be off, sirrah," roared Sir John, and Jeffrey went.

Ten minutes later they were riding for the Abbey, three miles away, and within half-an-hour Sir John was knocking, not gently, at its gate, while the monks within ran to and fro like startled ants, for the times were rough, and they were not sure who threatened them. When they knew their visitor at last they set to work to unbar the great doors and let down the drawbridge, that had been hoist up at sunset.

Presently Sir John stood in the Abbot's chamber, warming himself at the great fire, and behind him stood his serving-man, Jeffrey, carrying his long cloak. It was a fine room, with a noble roof of carved chestnut wood and stone walls hung with costly tapestry, whereon were worked scenes from the Scriptures. The floor was hid with rich carpets made of coloured Eastern wools. The furniture also was rich and foreign-looking, being inlaid with ivory and silver, while on the table stood a golden crucifix, a miracle of art, and upon an easel, so that the light from a hanging silver lamp fell on it, a life-sized picture of the Magdalene by some great Italian painter, turning her beauteous eyes to heaven and beating her fair breast.

Sir John looked about him and sniffed.

"Now, Jeffrey, would you think that you were in a monk's cell or in some great dame's bower? Hunt under the table, man; sure, you will find her lute and needlework. Whose portrait is that, think you?" and he pointed to the Magdalene.

"A sinner turning saint, I think, master. Good company for laymen when she was sinner, and good for priests now that she is saint. For the rest, I could snore well here after a cup of yon red wine," and he jerked his thumb towards a long-necked bottle on a sideboard. "Also, the fire burns bright, which is not to be wondered at, seeing that it is made of dry oak from your Sticksley Wood."

"How know you that, Jeffrey?" asked Sir John.

"By the grain of it, master—by the grain of it. I have hewn too many a timber there not to know. There's that in the Sticksley clays which makes the rings grow wavy and darker at the heart. See there."

Sir John looked, and swore an angry oath.

"You are right, man; and now I come to think of it, when I was a little lad my old grandsire bade me note this very thing about the Sticksley oaks. These cursed monks waste my woods beneath my nose. My forester is a rogue. They have scared or bribed him, and he shall hang for it."

"First prove the crime, master, which won't be easy; then talk of hanging, which only kings and abbots, 'with right of gallows,' can do at will. Ah! you speak truth," he added in a changed voice; "it is a lovely chamber, though not good enough for the holy man who dwells in it, since such a saint should have a silver shrine like him before the altar yonder, as doubtless he will do when ere long he is old bones," and, as though by chance, he trod upon his lord's foot, which was somewhat gouty.

Round came Sir John like the Blossholme weathercock on a gusty day.

"Clumsy toad!" he yelled, then paused, for there within the arras, that had been lifted silently, stood a tall, tonsured figure clothed in rich furs, and behind him two other figures, also tonsured, in simple black robes. It was the Abbot with his chaplains.

"Benedicite!" said the Abbot in his soft, foreign voice, lifting the two fingers of his right hand in blessing.

"Good-day," answered Sir John, while his retainer bowed his head and crossed himself. "Why do you steal upon a man like a thief in the night, holy Father?" he added irritably.

"That is how we are told judgment shall come, my son," answered the Abbot, smiling; "and in truth there seems some need of it. We heard loud quarrelling and talk of hanging men. What is your argument?"

"A hard one of oak," answered old Sir John sullenly. "My servant here said those logs upon your fire came from my Sticksley Wood, and I answered him that if so they were stolen, and my reeve should hang for it."

"The worthy man is right, my son, and yet your forester deserves no punishment. I bought our scanty store of firing from him, and, to tell truth, the count has not yet been paid. The money that should have discharged it has gone to London, so I asked him to let it stand until the summer rents come in. Blame him not, Sir John, if, out of friendship, knowing it was naught to you, he has not bared the nakedness of our poor house."

"Is it the nakedness of your poor house"—and he glanced round the sumptuous chamber—"that caused you to send me this letter saying that you have Cromwell's writ to seize my lands?" asked Sir John, rushing at his grievance like a bull, and casting down the document upon the table; "or do you also mean to make payment for them—when your summer rents come in?"

"Nay, son. In that matter duty led me. For twenty years we have disputed of those estates which, as you know, your grandsire took from us in a time of trouble, thus cutting the Abbey lands in twain, against the protest of him who was Abbot in those days. Therefore, at last I laid the matter before the Vicar-General, who, I hear, has been pleased to decide the suit in favour of this Abbey."

"To decide a suit of which the defendant had no notice!" exclaimed Sir John. "My Lord Abbot, this is not justice; it is roguery that I will never bear. Did you decide aught else, pray you?"

"Since you ask it—something, my son. To save costs I laid before him the sundry points at issue between us, and in sum this is the judgment: Your title to all your Blossholme lands and those contiguous, totalling eight thousand acres, is not voided, yet it is held to be tainted and doubtful."

"God's blood! Why?" asked Sir John.

"My son, I will tell you," replied the Abbot gently. "Because within a hundred years they belonged to this Abbey by gift of the Crown, and there is no record that the Crown consented to their alienation."

"No record," exclaimed Sir John, "when I have the indentured deed in my strong-box, signed by my great-grandfather and the Abbot Frank Ingham! No record, when my said forefather gave you other lands in place of them which you now hold? But go on, holy priest."

"My son, I obey you. Your title, though pronounced so doubtful, is not utterly voided; yet it is held that you have all these lands as tenant of this Abbey, to which, should you die without issue, they will relapse. Or should you die with issue under age, such issue will be ward to the Abbot of Blossholme for the time being, and failing him, that is, if there were no Abbot and no Abbey, of the Crown."

Sir John listened, then sank back into a chair, while his face went white as ashes.

"Show me that judgment," he said slowly.

"It is not yet engrossed, my son. Within ten days or so I hope—But you seem faint. The warmth of this room after the cold outer air, perhaps. Drink a cup of our poor wine," and at a motion of his hand one of the chaplains stepped to the sideboard, filled a goblet from the long-necked flask that stood there, and brought it to Sir John.

He took it as one that knows not what he does, then suddenly threw the silver cup and its contents into the fire, whence a chaplain recovered it with the wood-tongs.

"It seems that you priests are my heirs," said Sir John in a new, quiet voice, "or so you say; and, if that is so, my life is likely to be short. I'll not drink your wine, lest it should be poisoned. Hearken now, Sir Abbot. I believe little of this tale, though doubtless by bribes and other means you have done your best to harm me behind my back up yonder in London. Well, to-morrow at the dawn, come fair weather or come foul, I ride through the snows to London, where I too have friends, and we will see, we will see. You are a clever man, Abbot Maldon, and I know that you need money, or its worth, to pay your men-at-arms and satisfy the great costs at which you live—and there are our famous jewels—yes, yes, the old Crusader jewels. Therefore you have sought to rob me, whom you ever hated, and perchance Cromwell has listened to your tale. Perchance, fool priest," he added slowly, "he had it in his mind to fat this Church goose of yours with my meal before he wrings its neck and cooks it."

At these words the Abbot started for the first time, and even the two impassive chaplains glanced at each other.

"Ah! does that touch you?" asked Sir John Foterell. "Well, then, here is what shall make you smart. You think yourself in favour at the Court, do you not? because you took the oath of succession which braver men, like the brethren of the Charterhouse, refused, and died for it. But you forget the words you said to me when the wine you love had a hold of you in my hall—"

"Silence! For your own sake, silence, Sir John Foterell!" broke in the Abbot. "You go too far."

"Not so far as you shall go, my Lord Abbot, ere I have done with you. Not so far as Tower Hill or Tyburn, thither to be hung and quartered as a traitor to his Grace. I tell you, you forget the words you spoke, but I will remind you of them. Did you not say to me when the guests had gone, that King Henry was a heretic, a tyrant, and an infidel whom the Pope would do well to excommunicate and depose? Did you not, when I led you on, ask me if I could not bring about a rising of the common people in these parts, among whom I have great power, and of those gentry who know and love me, to overthrow him, and in his place set up a certain Cardinal Pole, and for the deed promise me the pardon and absolution of the Pope, and much advancement in his name and that of the Spanish Emperor?"

"Never," answered the Abbot.

"And did I not," went on Sir John, taking no note of his denial, "did I not refuse to listen to you and tell you that your words were traitorous, and that had they been spoken otherwhere than in my house, I, as in duty bound by my office, would make report of them? Aye, and have you not from that hour striven to undo me, whom you fear?"

"I deny it all," said the Abbot again. "These be but empty lies bred of your malice, Sir John Foterell."

"Empty words, are they, my Lord Abbot! Well, I tell you that they are all written down and signed in due form. I tell you I had witnesses you knew naught of who heard them with their ears. Here stands one of them behind my chair. Is it not so, Jeffrey?"

"Aye, master," answered the serving-man. "I chanced to be in the little chamber beyond the wainscot with others waiting to escort the Abbot home, and heard them all, and afterward I and they put our marks upon the writing. As I am a Christian man that is so, though, master, this is not the place that I should have chosen to speak of it, however much I might be wronged."

"It will serve my turn," said the enraged knight, "though it is true that I will speak of it louder elsewhere, namely, before the King's Council. To-morrow, my Lord Abbot, this paper and I go to London, and then you shall learn how well it pays you to try to pluck a Foterell of his own."

Now it was the Abbot's turn to be frightened. His smooth, olive-coloured cheeks sank in and went white, as though already he felt the cord about his throat. His jewelled hand shook, and he caught the arm of one of his chaplains and hung to it.

"Man," he hissed, "do you think that you can utter such false threats and go hence to ruin me, a consecrated abbot? I have dungeons here; I have power. It will be said that you attacked me, and that I did but strive to defend myself. Others can bring witness besides you, Sir John," and he whispered some words in Latin or Spanish into the ear of one of his chaplains, whereon that priest turned to leave the room.

"Now it seems that we are getting to business," said Jeffrey Stokes, as, lying his hand upon the knife at his girdle, he slipped between the monk and the door.

"That's it, Jeffrey," cried Sir John. "Stop the rat's hole. Look you, Spaniard, I have a sword. Show me to your gate, or, by virtue of the King's commission that I hold, I do instant justice on you as a traitor, and afterward answer for it if I win out."

The Abbot considered a moment, taking the measure of the fierce old knight before him. Then he said slowly—

"Go as you came, in peace, O man of wrath and evil, but know that the curse of the Church shall follow you. I say that you stand near to ill."

Sir John looked at him. The anger went out of his face, and, instead, upon it appeared something strange—a breath of foresight, an inspiration, call it what you will.

"By heaven and all its saints! I think you are right, Clement Maldon," he muttered. "Beneath that black dress of yours you are a man like the rest of us, are you not? You have a heart, you have members, you have a brain to think with; you are a fiddle for God to play on, and however much your superstitions mask and alter it, out of those strings now and again will come some squeak of truth. Well, I am another fiddle, of a more honest sort, mayhap, though I do not lift two fingers of my right hand and say, 'Benedicite, my son,' and 'Your sins are forgiven you'; and just now the God of both of us plays His tune in me, and I will tell you what it is. I stand near to death, but you stand not far from the gallows. I'll die an honest man; you will die like a dog, false to everything, and afterwards let your beads and your masses and your saints help you if they can. We'll talk it over when we meet again elsewhere. And now, my Lord Abbot, lead me to your gate, remembering that I follow with my sword. Jeffrey, set those carrion crow in front of you, and watch them well. My Lord Abbot, I am your servant; march!"

Chapter II

The Murder by the Mere

For a while Sir John and his retainer rode in silence. Then he laughed loudly.

"Jeffrey," he called, "that was a near touch. Sir Priest was minded to stick his Spanish pick-tooth between our ribs, and shrive us afterwards, as we lay dying, to salve his conscience."

"Yes, master; only, being reasonable, he remembered that English swords have a longer reach, and that his bullies are in the Ford ale- house seeing the Old Year out, and so put it off. Master, I have always told you that old October of yours is too strong to drink at noon. It should be saved till bed-time."

"What do you mean, man?"

"I mean that ale spoke yonder, not wisdom. You have showed your hand and played the fool."

"Who are you to teach me?" asked Sir John angrily. "I meant that he should hear the truth for once, the slimy traitor."

"Perhaps, perhaps; but these be bad days for Truth and those who court her. Was it needful to tell him that to-morrow you journey to London upon a certain errand?"

"Why not? I'll be there before him."

"Will you ever be there, master? The road runs past the Abbey, and that priest has good ruffians in his pay who can hold their tongues."

"Do you mean that he will waylay me? I say he dare not. Still, to please you, we will take the longer path through the forest."

"A rough one, master; but who goes with you on this business? Most of us are away with the wains, and others make holiday. There are but three serving-men at the hall, and you cannot leave the Lady Cicely without a guard, or take her with you through this cold. Remember there's wealth yonder which some may need more even than your lands," he added meaningly. "Wait a while, then, till your people return or you can call up your tenants, and go to London as one of your quality should, with twenty good men at your back."

"And so give our friend the Abbot time to get Cromwell's ear, and through him that of the King. No, no; I ride to-morrow at the dawn with you, or, if you are afraid, without you, as I have done before and taken no harm."

"None shall say that Jeffrey Stokes is afraid of man or priest or devil," answered the old soldier, colouring. "Your road has been good enough for me this thirty years, and it is good enough now. If I warned you it was not for my own sake, who care little what comes, but for yours and that of your house."

"I know it," said Sir John more kindly. "Take not my words ill, my temper is up to-day. Thank the saints! here is the hall at last. Why! whose horse has passed the gates before us?"

Jeffrey glanced at the tracks which the moonlight showed very clearly in the new-fallen snow.

"Sir Christopher Harflete's grey mare," he said. "I know the shoeing and the round shape of the hoof. Doubtless he is visiting Mistress Cicely."

"Whom I have forbidden to him," grumbled Sir John, swinging himself from the saddle.

"Forbid him not," answered Jeffrey, as he took his horse. "Christopher Harflete may yet be a good friend to a maid in need, and I think that need is nigh."

"Mind your business, knave," shouted Sir John. "Am I to be set at naught in my own house by a chit of a girl and a gallant who would mend his broken fortunes?"

"If you ask me, I think so," replied the imperturbable Jeffrey, as he led away the horses.

Sir John strode into the house by the backway, which opened on to the stable-yard. Taking the lantern that stood by the door, he went along galleries and upstairs to the sitting-chamber above the hall, which, since her mother's death, his daughter had used as her own, for here he guessed that he would find her. Setting down the lantern upon the passage table, he pushed open the door, which was not latched, and entered.

The room was large, and, being lighted only by the great fire that burned upon the hearth and two candles, all this end of it was hid in shadow. Near to the deep window-place the shadow ceased, however, and here, seated in a high-backed oak chair, with the light of the blazing fire falling full upon her, was Cicely Foterell, Sir John's only surviving child. She was a tall and graceful maiden, blue-eyed, brown- haired, fair-skinned, with a round and child-like face which most people thought beautiful to look upon. Just now this face, that generally was so arch and cheerful, seemed somewhat troubled. For this there might be a reason, since, seated upon a stool at her side, was a young man talking to her earnestly.

He was a stalwart young man, very broad about the shoulders, clean-cut in feature, with a long, straight nose, black hair, and merry black eyes. Also, as such a gallant should do, he appeared to be making love with much vigour and directness, for his face was upturned pleading with the girl, who leaned back in her chair answering him nothing. At this moment, indeed, his copious flow of words came to an end, perhaps from exhaustion, perhaps for other reasons, and was succeeded by a more effective method of attack. Suddenly sinking from the stool to his knees, he took the unresisting hand of Cicely and kissed it several times; then, emboldened by his success, threw his long arms about her, and before Sir John, choked with indignation, could find words to stop him, drew her towards him and treated her red lips as he had treated her fingers. This rude proceeding seemed to break the spell that bound her, for she pushed back the chair and, escaping from his grasp, rose, saying in a broken voice—

"Oh! Christopher, dear Christopher, this is most wrong."

"May be," he answered. "So long as you love me I care not what it is."

"That you have known these two years, Christopher. I love you well, but, alas! my father will have none of you. Get you hence now, ere he returns, or we both shall pay for it, and I, perhaps, be sent to a nunnery where no man may come."

"Nay, sweet, I am here to ask his consent to my suit—"

Then at last Sir John broke out.

"To ask my consent to your suit, you dishonest knave!" he roared from the darkness; whereat Cicely sank back into her chair looking as though she would faint, and the strong Christopher staggered like a man pierced by an arrow. "First to take my girl and hug her before my very eyes, and then, when the mischief is done, to ask my consent to your suit!" and he rushed at them like a charging bull.

Cicely rose to fly, then, seeing no escape, took refuge in her lover's arms. Her infuriated father seized the first part of her that came to his hand, which chanced to be one of her long brown plaits of hair, and tugged at it till she cried out with pain, purposing to tear her away, at which sight and sound Christopher lost his temper also.

"Leave go of the maid, sir," he said in a low, fierce voice, "or, by God! I'll make you."

"Leave go of the maid?" gasped Sir John. "Why, who holds her tightest, you or I? Do you leave go of her."

"Yes, yes, Christopher," she whispered, "ere I am pulled in two."

Then he obeyed, lifting her into the chair, but her father still kept his hold of the brown tress.

"Now, Sir Christopher," he said, "I am minded to put my sword through you."

"And pierce your daughter's heart as well as mine. Well, do it if you will, and when we are dead and you are childless, weep yourself and go to the grave."

"Oh! father, father," broke in Cicely, who knew the old man's temper, and feared the worst, "in justice and in pity, listen to me. All my heart is Christopher's, and has been from a child. With him I shall have happiness, without him black despair; and that is his case too, or so he swears. Why, then, should you part us? Is he not a proper man and of good lineage, and name unstained? Until of late did you not ever favour him much and let us be together day by day? And now, when it is too late, you deny him. Oh! why, why?"

"You know why well enough, girl? Because I have chosen another husband for you. The Lord Despard is taken with your baby face, and would marry you. But this morning I had it under his own hand."

"The Lord Despard?" gasped Cicely. "Why, he only buried his second wife last month! Father, he is as old as you are, and drunken, and has grandchildren of well-nigh my age. I would obey you in all things, but never will I go to him alive."

"And never shall he live to take you," muttered Christopher.

"What matter his years, daughter? He is a sound man, and has no son, and should one be born to him, his will be the greatest heritage within three shires. Moreover, I need his friendship, who have bitter enemies. But enough of this. Get you gone, Christopher, before worse befall you."

"So be it, sir, I will go; but first, as an honest man and my father's friend, and, as I thought, my own, answer me one question. Why have you changed your tune to me of late? Am I not the same Christopher Harflete I was a year or two ago? And have I done aught to lower me in the world's eye or in yours?"

"No, lad," answered the old knight bluntly; "but since you will have it, here it is. Within that year or two your uncle whose heir you were has married and bred a son, and now you are but a gentleman of good name, and little to float it on. That big house of yours must go to the hammer, Christopher. You'll never stow a bride in it."

"Ah! I thought as much. Christopher Harflete with the promise of the Lesborough lands was one man; Christopher Harflete without them is another—in your eyes. Yet, sir, I hold you foolish. I love your daughter and she loves me, and those lands and more may come back, or I, who am no fool, will win others. Soon there will be plenty going up there at Court, where I am known. Further, I tell you this: I believe that I shall marry Cicely, and earlier than you think, and I would have had your blessing with her."

"What! Will you steal the girl away?" asked Sir John furiously.

"By no means, sir. But this is a strange world of ours, in which from hour to hour top becomes bottom, and bottom top, and there—I think I shall marry her. At least I am sure that Despard the sot never will, for I'll kill him first, if I hang for it. Sir, sir, surely you will not throw your pearl upon that muckheap. Better crush it beneath your heel at once. Look, and say you cannot do it," and he pointed to the pathetic figure of Cicely, who stood by them with clasped hands, panting breast, and a face of agony.

The old knight glanced at her out of the corners of his eyes, and saw something that moved him to pity, for at bottom his heart was honest, and though he treated her so roughly, as was the fashion of the times, he loved his daughter more than all the world.

"Who are you, that would teach me my duty to my bone and blood?" he grumbled. Then he thought a while, and added, "Hear me, now, Christopher Harflete. To-morrow at the dawn I ride to London with Jeffrey Stokes on a somewhat risky business."

"What business, sir?"

"If you would know—that of a quarrel with yonder Spanish rogue of an Abbot, who claims the best part of my lands, and has poisoned the ear of that upstart, the Vicar-General Cromwell. I go to take the deeds and prove him a liar and a traitor also, which Cromwell does not know. Now, is my nest safe from you while I am away? Give me your word, and I'll believe you, for at least you are an honest gentleman, and if you have poached a kiss or two, that may be forgiven. Others have done the same before you were born. Give me your word, or I must drag the girl through the snows to London at my heels."

"You have it, sir," answered Christopher. "If she needs my company she must come for it to Cranwell Towers, for I'll not seek hers while you are away."

"Good. Then one gift for another. I'll not answer my Lord of Despard's letter till I get back again—not to please you, but because I hate writing. It is a labour to me, and I have no time to spare to-night. Now, have a cup of drink and be off with you. Love-making is thirsty work."

"Aye, gladly, sir, but hear me, hear me. Ride not to London with such slight attendance after a quarrel with Abbot Maldon. Let me wait on you. Although my fortunes be so low I can bring a man or two—six or eight, indeed—while yours are away with the wains."

"Never, Christopher. My own hand has guarded my head these sixty years, and can do so still. Also," he added, with a flash of insight, "as you say, the journey is dangerous, and who knows? If aught went wrong, you might be wanted nearer home. Christopher, you shall never have my girl; she's not for you. Yet, perhaps, if need were, you would strike a blow for her even if it made you excommunicate. Get hence, wench. Why do you stand there gaping on us, like an owl in sunlight? And remember, if I catch you at more such tricks, you'll spend your days mumbling at prayers in a nunnery, and much good may they do you."

"At least I should find peace there, and gentle words," answered Cicely with spirit, for she knew her father, and the worst of her fear had departed. "Only, sir, I did not know that you wished to swell the wealth of the Abbots of Blossholme."

"Swell their wealth!" roared her father. "Nay, I'll stretch their necks. Get you to your chamber, and send up Jeffrey with the liquor."

Then, having no choice, Cicely curtseyed, first to her father and next to Christopher, to whom she sent a message with her eyes that she dared not utter with her lips, and so vanished into the shadows, where presently she was heard stumbling against some article of furniture.

"Show the maid a light, Christopher," said Sir John, who, lost in his own thoughts, was now gazing into the fire.

Seizing one of the two candles, Christopher sprang after her like a hound after a hare, and presently the pair of them passed through the door and down the long passage beyond. At a turn in it they halted, and once more, without word spoken, she found her way into those long arms.

"You will not forget me, even if we must part?" sobbed Cicely.

"Nay, sweet," he answered. "Moreover, keep a brave heart; we do not part for long, for God has given us to each other. Your father does not mean all he says, and his temper, which has been stirred to-day, will soften. If not, we must look to ourselves. I keep a swift horse or two, Cicely. Could you ride one if need were?"

"I have ever loved riding," she said meaningly.

"Good. Then you shall never go to that fat hog's sty, for I'll stick him first. And I have friends both in Scotland and in France. Which like you best?"

"They say the air of France is softer. Now, away from me, or one will come to seek us," and they tore themselves apart.

"Emlyn, your foster-mother, is to be trusted," he said rapidly; "also she loves me well. If there be need, let me hear of you through her."

"Aye," she answered, "without fail," and glided from him like a ghost.

"Have you been waiting to see the moon rise?" asked Sir John, glancing at Christopher from beneath his shaggy eyebrows as he returned.

"Nay, sir, but the passages in this old house of yours are most wondrous long, and I took a wrong turn in threading them."

"Oh!" said Sir John. "Well, you have a talent for wrong turns, and such partings are hard. Now, do you understand that this is the last of them?"

"I understand that you may say so, sir."

"And that I mean it, too, I hope. Listen, Christopher," he added, with earnestness, but in a kindly voice. "Believe me, I like you well, and would not give you pain, or the maid yonder, if I could help it. Yet I have no choice. I am threatened on all sides by priest and king, and you have lost your heritage. She is the only jewel that I can pawn, and for your own safety's sake and her children's sake, must marry well. Yonder Despard will not live long, he drinks too hard; and then your day may come, if you still care for his leavings—perhaps in two years, perhaps in less, for she will soon see him out. Now, let us talk no more of the matter, but if aught befalls me, be a friend to her. Here comes the liquor—drink it up and be off. Though I seem rough with you, my hope is that you may quaff many another cup at Shefton."

It was seven o'clock of the next morning, and Sir John, having eaten his breakfast, was girding on his sword—for Jeffrey had already gone to fetch the horses—when the door opened and his daughter entered the great hall, candle in hand, wrapped in a fur cloak, over which her long hair fell. Glancing at her, Sir John noted that her eyes were wide and frightened.

"What is it now, girl?" he asked. "You'll take your death of cold among these draughts."

"Oh! father," she said, kissing him, "I came to bid you farewell, and—and—to pray you not to start."

"Not to start? And why?"

"Because, father, I have dreamed a bad dream. At first last night I could not sleep, and when at length I did I dreamed that dream thrice," and she paused.

"Go on, Cicely; I am not afraid of dreams, which are but foolishness—coming from the stomach."

"Mayhap; yet, father, it was so plain and clear I can scarcely bear to tell it to you. I stood in a dark place amidst black things that I knew to be trees. Then the red dawn broke upon the snow, and I saw a little pool with brown rushes frozen in its ice. And there—there, at the edge of the pool, by a pollard willow with one white limb, you lay, your bare sword in your hand and an arrow in your neck, shot from behind, while in the trunk of the willow were other arrows, and lying near you two slain. Then cloaked men came as though to carry them away, and I awoke. I say I dreamed it thrice."

"A jolly good morrow indeed," said Sir John, turning a shade paler. "And now, daughter, what do you make of this business?"

"I? Oh! I make that you should stop at home and send some one else to do your business. Sir Christopher, for instance."

"Why, then I should baulk your dream, which is either true or false. If true, I have no choice, it must be fulfilled; if false, why should I heed it? Cicely, I am a plain man and take no note of such fancies. Yet I have enemies, and it may well chance that my day is done. If so, use your mother wit, girl; beware of Maldon, look to yourself, and as for your mother's jewels, hide them," and he turned to go.

She clasped him by the arm.

"In that sad case what should I do, father?" she asked eagerly.

He stopped and stared at her up and down.

"I see that you believe in your dream," he said, "and therefore, although it shall not stay a Foterell, I begin to believe in it too. In that case you have a lover whom I have forbid to you. Yet he is a man after my own heart, who would deal well by you. If I die, my game is played. Set your own anew, sweet Cicely, and set it soon, ere that Abbot is at your heels. Rough as I may have been, remember me with kindness, and God's blessing and mine be on you. Hark! Jeffrey calls, and if they stand, the horses will take cold. There, fare you well. Fear not for me, I wear a chain shirt beneath my cloak. Get back to bed and warm you," and he kissed her on the brow, thrust her from him and was gone.

Thus did Cicely and her father part—for ever.

All that day Sir John and Jeffrey, his serving-man, trotted forward through the snow—that is, when they were not obliged to walk because of the depth of the drifts. Their plan was to reach a certain farm in a glade of the woodland within two hours of sundown, and sleep there, for they had taken the forest path, leaving again for the Fens and Cambridge at the dawn. This, however, proved not possible because of the exceeding badness of the road. So it came about that when the darkness closed in on them a little before five o'clock, bringing with it a cold, moaning wind and a scurry of snow, they were obliged to shelter in a faggot-built woodman's hut, waiting for the moon to appear among the clouds. Here they fed the horses with corn that they had brought with them, and themselves also from their store of dried meat and barley cakes, which Jeffrey carried on his shoulder in a bag. It was a poor meal eaten thus in the darkness, but served to stay their stomachs and pass away the time.

At length a ray of light pierced the doorway of the hut.

"She's up," said Sir John, "let us be going ere the nags grow stiff."

Making no answer, Jeffrey slipped the bits back into the horses' mouths and led them out. Now the full moon had appeared like a great white eye between two black banks of cloud and turned the world to silver. It was a dreary scene on which she shone; a dazzling plain of snow, broken by patches of hawthorns, and here and there by the gaunt shape of a pollard oak, since this being the outskirt of the forest, folk came hither to lop the tops of the trees for firing. A hundred and fifty yards away or so, at the crest of a slope, was a round- shaped hill, made, not by Nature, but by man. None knew what that hill might be, but tradition said that once, hundreds or thousands of years before, a big battle had been fought around it in which a king was killed, and that his victorious army had raised this mound above his bones to be a memorial for ever.

The story was indeed that, being a sea-king, they had built a boat or dragged it thither from the river shore and set him in it with all the slain for rowers; also that he might be seen at nights seated on his horse in armour, and staring about him, as when he directed the battle. At least it is true that the mount was called King's Grave, and that people feared to pass it after sundown.

As Jeffrey Stokes was holding his master's stirrup for him to mount, he uttered an exclamation and pointed. Following the line of his outstretched hand, in the clear moonlight Sir John saw a man, who sat, still as any statue, upon a horse on the very point of King's Grave. He appeared to be covered with a long cloak, but above it his helmet glittered like silver. Next moment a fringe of black cloud hid the face of the moon, and when it passed away the man and horse were gone.

"What did that fellow there?" asked Sir John.

"Fellow?" answered Jeffrey in a shaken voice, "I saw none. That was the Ghost of the Grave. My grandfather met him ere he came to his end in the forest, none know how, for the wolves, of which there were plenty in his day, picked his bones clean, and so have many others for hundreds of years; always just before their doom. He is an ill fowl, that Ghost of the Grave, and those who clap eyes on him do wisely to turn their horses' heads homewards, as I would to-night if I had my way, master."

"What use, Jeffrey? If the sight of him means death, death will come. Moreover, I believe nothing of the tale. Your ghost was some forest reeve or herdsman."

"A forest reeve or herdsman who wanders about in a steel helm on a fine horse in snow-time when there are no trees to cut or cattle to mind! Well, have it as you will, master; only God save me from such reeves and herdmen, for I think they hail from hell."

"Then he was a spy watching whither we go," answered Sir John angrily.

"If so, who sent him? The Abbot of Blossholme? In that case I would sooner meet the devil, for this means mischief. I say that we had better ride back to Shefton."

"Then do so, Jeffrey, if you are scared, and I will go on alone, who, being on an honest business, fear not Satan or an abbot, either."

"Nay, master. Many a year ago, when we were younger, I stood by you on Flodden Field when Sir Edward, Christopher Harflete's father, was killed at our side, and those red-bearded Scotch bare-breeks pressed us hard, yet I never itched to turn my back, even after that great fellow with an axe got you down, and we thought that all was lost. Then shall I do so now?—though it is true that I fear yon goblin more than all the Highlanders beyond the Tweed. Ride on; man can die but once, and for my part I care not when it comes, who have little to lose in an ill world."

So without more words they started forward, peering about them as they went. Soon the forest thickened, and the track they followed wound its way round great trunks of primeval oaks, or the edges of bog-holes, or through brakes of thorns. Hard enough it was to find it at times, since the snow made it one with the bordering ground, and the gloom of the oaks was great. But Jeffrey was a woodman born, and from his childhood had known the shape of every tree in that waste, so that they held safely to their road. Well would it have been for them if they had not!

They came to a place where three other tracks crossed that which they rode upon, and here Jeffrey Stokes, who was ahead, held up his hand.

"What is it?" asked Sir John.

"It is the marks of ten or a dozen shod horses passed within two hours, since the last snow fell. And who be they, I wonder?"

"Doubtless travellers like ourselves. Ride on, man; that farm is not a mile ahead."

Then Jeffrey broke out.

"Master, I like it not," he said. "Battle-horses have gone by here, not chapmen's or farmers' nags, and I think I know their breed. I say that we had best turn about if we would not walk into some snare."

"Turn you, then," grumbled Sir John indifferently. "I am cold and weary, and seek my rest."

"Pray God that you may not find it when you are colder," muttered Jeffrey, spurring his horse.

They went on through the dead winter silence, that was broken only by the hoots of a flitting owl hungry for the food that it could not find, and the swish of the feet of a galloping fox as it looped past them through the snow. Presently they came to an open place ringed in by forest, so wet that only marsh-trees would grow there. To their right lay a little ice-covered mere, with sere, brown reeds standing here and there upon its face, and at the end of it a group of stark pollarded willows, whereof the tops had been cut for poles by those who dwelt in the forest farm near by. Sir John looked at the place and shivered a little—perhaps because the frost bit him. Or was it that he remembered his daughter's dream, which told of such a spot? At any rate, he set his teeth, and his right hand sought the hilt of his sword. His weary horse sniffed the air and neighed, and the neigh was answered from close at hand.

"Thank the saints! we are nearer to that farm than I thought," said Sir John.

As he spoke the words a number of men appeared galloping down on them from out of the shelter of a thorn-brake, and the moonlight shone on the bared weapons in their hands.

"Thieves!" shouted Sir John. "At them now, Jeffrey, and win through to the farm."

The man hesitated, for he saw that their foes were many and no common robbers, but his master drew his sword and spurred his beast, so he must do likewise. In twenty seconds they were among them, and some one commanded them to yield. Sir John rushed at the fellow, and, rising in his stirrups, cut him down. He fell all of a heap and lay still in the snow, which grew crimson about him. One came at Jeffrey, who turned his horse so that the blow missed, then took his weight upon the point of his sword, so that this man, too, fell down and lay in the snow, moving feebly.

The rest, thinking this greeting too warm for them, swung round and vanished again among the thorns.

"Now ride for it," said Jeffrey.

"I cannot," answered Sir John. "One of those knaves has hurt my mare," and he pointed to blood that ran from a great gash in the beast's foreleg, which it held up piteously.

"Take mine," said Jeffrey; "I'll dodge them afoot."

"Never, man! To the willows; we will hold our own there;" and, springing from the wounded beast, which tried to hobble after them, but could not, for its sinews were cut, he ran to the shelter of the trees, followed by Jeffrey on his horse.

"Who are these rogues?" he asked.

"The Abbot's men-at-arms," answered Jeffrey. "I saw the face of him I spitted."

Now Sir John's jaw dropped.

"Then we are sped, friend, for they dare not let us go. Cicely dreams well."

As he spoke an arrow whistled by them.

"Jeffrey," he went on, "I have papers on me that should not be lost, for with them might go my girl's heritage. Take them," and he thrust a packet into his hand, "and this purse also. There's plenty in it. Away—anywhere, and lie hid out of reach a while, or they'll still your tongue. Then I charge you on your soul, come back with help and hang that knave Abbot—for your Lady's sake, Jeffrey. She'll reward you, and so will God above."

The man thrust away purse and deeds in some deep pocket.

"How can I leave you to be butchered?" he muttered, grinding his teeth.

As the words left his lips he heard his master utter a gurgling sound, and saw that an arrow, shot from behind, had pierced him through the throat; saw, too, he who was skilled in war, that the wound was mortal. Then he hesitated no longer.

"Christ rest you!" he said. "I'll do your bidding or die;" and, turning his horse, he drove the rowels into its sides, causing it to bound away like a deer.

For a moment the stricken Sir John watched him go. Then he ran out of his cover, shaking his sword above his head—ran into the open moonlight to draw the arrows. They came fast enough, but ere ever he fell, for that steel shirt of his was strong, Jeffrey, lying low on his horse's neck, was safe away, and though the murderers followed hard they never caught him.

Nor, though they searched for days, could they find him at Shefton or elsewhere, for Jeffrey, who knew that all roads were blocked, and who dared not venture home, doubling like a hare across country, had won down to the water, where a ship lay foreign bound, and by dawn was on the sea.

Chapter III

A Wedding

About noon of the day after that upon which Sir John had come to his death, Cicely Foterell sat at her meal in Shefton Hall. Not much of the rough midwinter fare passed her lips, for she was ill at ease. The man she loved had been dismissed from her because his fortunes were on the wane, and her father had gone upon a journey which she felt, rather than knew, to be very dangerous. The great old hall was lonesome, also, for a young girl who had no comrades near. Sitting there in the big room, she bethought her how different it had been in her childhood, before some foul sickness, of which she knew not the name or nature, had swept away her mother, her two brothers, and her sister all in a single week, leaving her untouched. Then there were merry voices about the house where now was silence, and she alone, with naught bout a spaniel dog for company. Also most of the men were away with the wains laden with the year's clip of wool, which her father had held until the price had heightened, nor in this snow would they be back for another week, or perhaps longer.

Oh! her heart was heavy as the winter clouds without, and young and fair as she might be, almost she wished that she had gone when her brothers went, and found her peace.

To cheer her spirits she drank from a cup of spiced ale, that the manservant had placed beside her covered with a napkin, and was glad of its warmth and comfort. Just then the door opened, and her foster- mother, Mrs. Stower, entered. She was still a handsome woman in her prime, for her husband had been carried off by a fever when she was but nineteen, and her baby with him, whereon she had been brought to the Hall to nurse Cicely, whose mother was very ill after her birth. Moreover, she was tall and dark, with black and flashing eyes, for her father had been a Spaniard of gentle birth, and, it was said, gypsy blood ran in her mother's veins.

There were but two people in the world for whom Emlyn Stower cared—Cicely, her foster-child, and a certain playmate of hers, one Thomas Bolle, now a lay-brother at the Abbey who had charge of the cattle. The tale was that in their early youth he had courted her, not against her will, and that when, after her parents' tragic deaths, as a ward of the former Abbot of Blossholme, she was married to her husband, not with her will, this Thomas put on the robe of a monk of the lowest degree, being but a yeoman of good stock though of little learning.

Something in the woman's manner attracted Cicely's attention, and gave a hint of tragedy. She paused at the door, fumbling with its latch, which was not her way, then turned and stood upright against it, like a picture in its frame.

"What is it, Nurse?" asked Cicely in a shaken voice. "From your look you bear tidings."

Emlyn Stower walked forward, rested one hand upon the oak table and answered—

"Aye, evil tidings if they be true. Prepare your heart, my sweet."

"Quick with them, Emlyn," gasped Cicely. "Who is dead? Christopher?"

She shook her head, and Cicely sighed in relief, adding—

"Who, then? Oh! was that dream true?"

"Aye, dear; you are an orphan."

The girl's head fell forward. Then she lifted it, and asked—

"Who told you? Give me all the truth or I shall die."

"A friend of mine who has to do with the Abbey yonder; ask not his name."

"I know it, Emlyn; Thomas Bolle," she whispered back.

"A friend of mine," repeated the tall, dark woman, "told me that Sir John Foterell, your sire, was murdered last night in the forest by a gang of armed men, of whom he slew two."

"From the Abbey?" queried Cicely in the same whisper.

"Who knows? I think it. They say that the arrow in his throat was such as they make there. Jeffrey Stokes was hunted, but escaped on to some ship that had her anchor up."

"I'll have his life for it, the coward!" exclaimed Cicely.

"Blame him not yet. He met another friend of mine, and sent a message. It was that he did but obey his master's last orders, and, as he had seen too much and to linger here was certain death, if he lived, he would return from over-seas with the papers when the times are safer. He prayed that you would not doubt him."

"The papers! What papers, Emlyn?"

She shrugged her broad shoulders.

"How should I know? Doubtless some that your father was taking to London and did not desire to lose. His iron chest stands open in his chamber."

Now poor Cicely remembered that her father had spoken of certain "deeds" which he must take with him, and began to sob.

"Weep not, darling," said her foster-mother, smoothing Cicely's brown hair with her strong hand. "These things are decreed of God, and done with. Now you must look to yourself. Your father is gone, but one remains."

Cicely lifted her tear-stained face.

"Yes, I have you," she said.

"Me!" she answered, with a quick smile. "Nay, of what use am I? Your nursing days are over. What did you tell me your father said to you before he rode—about Sir Christopher? Hush! there's no time to talk; you must away to Cranwell Towers."

"Why?" asked Cicely. "He cannot bring my father back to life, and it would be thought strange indeed that at such a time I should visit a man in his own house. Send and tell him the tidings. I bide here to bury my father, and," she added proudly, "to avenge him."

"If so, sweet, you bide here to be buried yourself in yonder Nunnery. Hark, I have not told you all my news. The Abbot Maldon claims the Blossholme lands under some trick of law. It was as to them that your father quarrelled with him the other night; and with the land goes your wardship, as once mine went under this monk's charter. Before sunset the Abbot rides here with his men-at-arms to take them, and to set you for safe-keeping in the Nunnery, where you will find a husband called Holy Church."

"Name of God! is it so?" said Cicely, springing up; "and the most of the men are away! I cannot hold the Hall against that foreign Abbot and his hirelings, and an orphaned heiress is but a chattel to be sold. Oh! now I understand what my father meant. Order horses. I'll off to Christopher. Yet, stay, Nurse. What will he do with me? It may seem shameless, and will vex him."

"I think he will marry you. I think to-night you will be a wife. If not, I'll know the reason why," she added viciously.

"A wife! To-night!" exclaimed the girl, turning crimson to her hair. "And my father but just dead! How can it be?"

"We'll talk of that with Harflete. Mayhap, like you, he'll wish to wait and ask the banns, or to lay the case before a London lawyer. Meanwhile, I have ordered horses and sent a message to the Abbot to say you come to learn the meaning of these rumours, which will keep him still till nightfall; and another to Cranwell Towers, that we may find food and lodging there. Quick, now, and get your cloak and hood. I have the jewels in their case, for Maldon seeks them more even than your lands, and with them all the money I can find. Also I have bid the sewing-girl make a pack of some garments. Come now, come, for that Abbot is hungry and will be stirring. There is no time for talk."

Three hours later in the red glow of the sunset Christopher Harflete, watching at his door, saw two women riding towards him across the snow, and knew them while they were yet far off.

"It is true, then," he said to Father Roger Necton, the old clergyman of Cranwell, whom he had summoned from the vicarage. "I thought that fool of a messenger must be drunk. What can have chanced, Father?"

"Death, I think, my son, for sure naught else would bring the Lady Cicely here unaccompanied save by a waiting-woman. The question is—what will happen now?" and he glanced sideways at him.

"I know well if I can get my way," answered Christopher, with a merry laugh. "Say now, Father, if it should so be that this lady were willing, could you marry us?"

"Without a doubt, my son, with the consent of the parents;" and again he looked at him.

"And if there were no parents?"

"Then with the consent of the guardian, the bride being under age."

"And if no guardian had been declared or admitted?"

"Then such a marriage duly solemnized, being a sacrament of the Church, would hold fast until the crack of doom unless the Pope annulled it, and, as you know, the Pope is out of favour in this realm on this very matter of marriage. Let me explain the law to you, ecclesiastic and civil—"

But Christopher was already running towards the gate, so the old parson's lecture remained undelivered.

The two met in the snow, Emlyn Stower riding on ahead and leaving them together.

"What is it, sweetest?" he asked. "What is it?"

"Oh! Christopher," she answered, weeping, "my poor father is dead—murdered, or so says Emlyn."

"Murdered! By whom?"

"By the Abbot of Blossholme's soldiers—so says Emlyn, yonder in the forest last eve. And the Abbot is coming to Shefton to declare me his ward and thrust me into the Nunnery—that was Emlyn's tale. And so, although it is a strange thing to do, having none to protect me, I have fled to you—because Emlyn said I ought."

"She is a wise woman, Emlyn," broke in Christopher; "I always thought well of her judgment. But did you only come to me because Emlyn told you?"

"Not altogether, Christopher. I came because I am distraught, and you are a better friend than none at all, and—where else should I go? Also my poor father with his last words to me, although he was so angry with you, bade me seek your help if there were need—and—oh! Christopher, I came because you swore you loved me, and, therefore, it seemed right. If I had gone to the Nunnery, although the Prioress, Mother Matilda, is good, and my friend, who knows, she might not have let me out again, for the Abbot is her master, and not my friend. It is our lands he loves, and the famous jewels—Emlyn has them with her."

By now they were across the moat and at the steps of the house, so, without answering, Christopher lifted her tenderly from the saddle, pressing her to his breast as he did so, for that seemed his best answer. A groom came to lead away the horses, touching his bonnet, and staring at them curiously; and, leaning on her lover's shoulder, Cicely passed through the arched doorway of Cranwell Towers into the hall, where a great fire burned. Before this fire, warming his thin hands, stood Father Necton, engaged in eager conversation with Emlyn Stower. As the pair advanced this talk ceased, evidently because it was of them.

"Mistress Cicely," said the kindly-faced old man, speaking in a nervous fashion, "I fear that you visit us in sad case," and he paused, not knowing what to add.

"Yes, indeed," she answered, "if all I hear is true. They say that my father is killed by cruel men—I know not for certain why or by whom—and that the Abbot of Blossholme comes to claim me as his ward and immure me in Blossholme Priory, whither I would not go. I have fled here to escape him, having no other refuge, though you may think ill of me for this deed."

"Not I, my child. I should not speak against yonder Abbot, for he is my superior in the Church, though, mind you, I owe him no allegiance, since this benefice is not in his gift, nor am I a Benedictine. Therefore I will tell you the truth. I hold the man not honest. All is provender that comes to his maw; moreover, he is no Englishman, but a Spaniard, one sent here to work against the welfare of this realm; to suck its wealth, stir up rebellion, and make report of all that passes in it, for the benefit of England's enemies."

"Yet he has friends at Court, or so said my father."

"Aye, aye, such folks have ever friends—their money buys them; though mayhap an ill day is at hand for him and his likes. Well, your poor father is gone, God knows how, though I thought for long that would be his end, who ever spoke his mind, or more; and you with your wealth are the morsel that tempts Maldon's appetite. And now what is to be done? This is a hard case. Would you refuge in some other Nunnery?"

"Nay," answered Cicely, glancing sideways at her lover.

"Then what's to be done?"

"Oh! I know not," she said, bursting into a fit of weeping. "How can I tell you, who am mazed with grief and doubt? I had but a single friend—my father, though at times he was a rough one. Yet he loved me in his way, and I have obeyed his last counsel;" and, all her courage gone, she sank into a chair and rocked herself to and fro, her head resting on her hands.

"That is not true," said Emlyn in her bold voice. "Am I who suckled you no friend, and is Father Necton here no friend, and is Sir Christopher no friend? Well, if you have lost your judgment, I have kept mine, and here it is. Yonder, not two bowshots away, stands a church, and before me I see a priest and a pair who would serve for bride and bridegroom. Also we can rake up witnesses and a cup of wine to drink your health; and after that let the Abbot of Blossholme do his worst. What say you, Sir Christopher?"

"You know my mind, Nurse Emlyn; but what says Cicely? Oh! Cicely, what say you?" and he bent over her.

She raised herself, still weeping, and, throwing her arms about his neck, laid her head upon his shoulder.

"I think it is the will of God," she whispered, "and why should I fight against it, who am His servant?—and yours, Chris."

"And now, Father, what say you?" asked Emlyn, pointing to the pair.

"I do not think there is much to say," answered the old clergyman, turning his head aside, "save that if it should please you to come to the church in ten minutes' time you will find a candle on the altar, and a priest within the rails, and a clerk to hold the book. More we cannot do at such short notice."

Then he paused for a while, and, hearing no dissent, walked down the hall and out of the door.

Emlyn took Cicely by the hand, led her to a room that was shown to them, and there made her ready for her bridal as best she might. She had no fine dress in which to clothe her, nor, indeed, would there have been time to don it. But she combed out her beautiful brown hair, and, opening that box of Eastern jewels which were the great pride of the Foterells—being the rarest and the most ancient in all the countryside—she decked her with them. On her broad brow she set a circlet from which hung sparkling diamonds that had been brought, the story said, by her mother's ancestor, a Carfax, from the Holy Land, where once they were the peculiar treasure of a paynim queen, and upon her bosom a necklet of large pearls. Brooches and rings also she found for her breast and fingers, and for her waist a jewelled girdle with a golden clasp, while to her ears she hung the finest gems of all—two great pearls pink like the hawthorn-bloom when it begins to turn. Lastly she flung over her head a veil of lace most curiously wrought, and stood back with pride to look at her.

Now Cicely, who all this while had been silent and unresisting, spoke for the first time, saying—

"How came this here, Nurse?"

"Your mother wore it at her bridal, and her mother too, so I have been told. Also once before I wrapped it about you—when you were christened, sweet."

"Mayhap; but how came it here?"

"In the bosom of my robe. Not knowing when we should get home again, I brought it, thinking that perhaps one day you might marry, when it would be useful. And now, strangely enough, the marriage has come."

"Emlyn, Emlyn, I believe that you planned all this business, whereof God alone knows the end."

"That is why He makes a beginning, dear, that His end may be fulfilled in due season."

"Aye, but what is that end? Mayhap this is my shroud you wrap about me. In truth, I feel as though death were near."

"He is ever that," replied Emlyn unconcernedly. "But so long as he doesn't touch, what does it matter? Now hark you, sweetest, I've Spanish and gypsy blood in me with which go gifts, and so I'll tell you something for your comfort. However oft he snatches, Death will not lay his bony hand on you for many a long year—not till you are well-nigh as thin with age as he is. Oh! you'll have your troubles like all of us, worse than many, mayhap, but you are Luck's own child, who lived when the rest were taken, and you'll win through and take others on your back, as a whale does barnacles. So snap your fingers at death, as I do," and she suited the action to the word, "and be happy while you may, and when you're not happy, wait till your turn comes round again. Now follow me and, though your father is murdered, smile as you should in such an hour, for what man wants a sad-faced bride?"

They walked down the broad oaken stairs into the hall where Christopher stood waiting for them. Glancing at him shyly, Cicely saw that he was clad in mail beneath his cloak, and that his sword was girded at his side, also that some men with him were armed. For a moment he stared at her glittering beauty confused, then said—

"Fear not this hint of war in love's own hour," and he touched his shining armour. "Cicely, these nuptials are strange as they are happy, and some might try to break in upon them. Come now, my sweet lady;" and bowing before her he took her by the hand and led her from the house, Emlyn walking behind them and the men with torches going before and following after.

Outside it was freezing sharply, so that the snow crunched beneath their feet. In the west the last red glow of sunset still lingered on the steely sky, and over against it the great moon rose above the round edge of the world. In the bushes of the garden, and the tall poplars that bordered the moat, blackbirds and fieldfares chattered their winter evening song, while about the grey tower of the neighbouring church the daws still wheeled.

The picture of that scene whereof at the time she seemed to take no note, always remained fixed in the mind of Cicely: the cold expanse of snow, the inky trees, the hard sky, the lambent beams of the moon, the dull glow of the torches caught and reflected by her jewels and her lover's mail, the midwinter sound of birds, the barking of a distant hound, the black porch of the church that drew nearer, the little oblong mounds which hid the bones of hundreds who in their day had passed it as infants, as bridegrooms and as brides, and at last as cold, white things that had been men and women.

Now they were in the nave of the old fane where the cold struck them like a sword. The dim lights of the torches showed them that, short as had been the time, the news of this marvellous marriage had spread about, for at least a score of people were standing here and there in knots, or a few of them seated on the oak benches near the chancel. All these turned to stare at them eagerly as they walked towards the altar where stood the priest in his robes, and since his sight was dim, behind him the old clerk with a stable-lantern held on high to enable him to read from his book.

They reached the carven rood-screen, and at a sign knelt down. In a clear voice the clergyman began the service; presently, at another sign, the pair rose, advanced to the altar-rails and again knelt down. The moonlight, flowing through the eastern window, fell full on both of them, turning them to cold, white statues, such as those that knelt in marble upon the tomb at their side.

All through the holy office Cicely watched these statues with fascinated eyes, and it seemed to her that they and the old crusaders, Harfletes of a long-past day who lay near by, were watching her with a wistful and kindly interest. She made certain answers, a ring that was somewhat too small was thrust upon her finger—all the rest of her life that ring hurt her at times, but she would have never it moved, and then some one was kissing her. At first she thought it must be her father, and remembering, nearly wept till she heard Christopher's voice calling her wife, and knew that she was wed.

Father Roger, the old clerk still holding the lantern behind him, writing something in a little vellum book, asking her the date of her birth and her full name, which, as he had been present at her christening, she thought strange. Then her husband signed the book, using the altar as a table, not very easily for he was no great scholar, and she signed also in her maiden name for the last time, and the priest signed, and at his bidding Emlyn Stower, who could write well, signed too. Next, as though by an afterthought, Father Roger called several of the congregation, who rather unwillingly made their marks as witnesses. While they did so he explained to them that, as the circumstances were uncommon, it was well that there should be evidence, and that he intended to send copies of this entry to sundry dignities, not forgetting the holy Father at Rome.

On learning this they appeared to be sorry that they had anything to do with the matter, and one and all of them melted into the darkness of the nave and out of Cicely's mind.

So it was done at last.

Father Necton blew on his little book till the ink was dry, then hid it away in his robe. The old clerk, having pocketed a handsome fee from Christopher, lit the pair down the nave to the porch, where he locked the oaken door behind them, extinguished his lantern and trudged off through the snow to the ale-house, there to discuss these nuptials and hot beer. Escorted by their torch-bearers Cicely and Christopher walked silently arm-in-arm back to the Towers, whither Emlyn, after embracing the bride, had already gone on ahead. So having added one more ceremony to its countless record, perhaps the strangest of them all, the ancient church behind them grew silent as the dead within its graves.

The Towers reached, the new-wed pair, with Father Roger and Emlyn, sat down to the best meal that could be prepared for them at such short notice; a very curious wedding feast. Still, though the company was so small it did not lack for heartiness, since the old clergyman proposed their health in a speech full of Latin words which they did not understand, and every member of the household who had assembled to hear him drank to it in cups of wine. This done, the beautiful bride, now blushing and now pale, was led away to the best chamber, which had been hastily prepared for her. But Emlyn remained behind a while, for she had words to speak.

"Sir Christopher," she said, "you are fast wed to the sweetest lady that ever sun or moon shone on, and in that may hold yourself a lucky man. Yet such deep joys seldom come without their pain, and I think that this is near at hand. There are those who will envy you your fortune, Sir Christopher."

"Yet they cannot change it, Emlyn," he answered anxiously. "The knot that was tied to-night may not be unloosed."

"Never," broke in Father Roger. "Though the suddenness and the circumstances of it may be unusual, this marriage is a sacrament celebrated in the face of the world with the full consent of both parties and of the Holy Church. Moreover, before the dawn I'll send the record of it to the bishop's registry and elsewhere, that it may not be questioned in days to come, giving copies of the same to you and your lady's foster-mother, who is her nearest friend at hand."

"It may not be loosed on earth or in heaven," replied Emlyn solemnly, "yet perchance the sword can cut it. Sir Christopher, I think that we should all do well to travel as soon as may be."

"Not to-night, surely, Nurse!" he exclaimed.

"No, not to-night," she answered, with a faint smile. "Your wife has had a weary day, and could not. Moreover, preparation must be made which is impossible at this hour. But to-morrow, if the roads are open to you, I think we should start for London, where she may make complaint of her father's slaying and claim her heritage and the protection of the law."

"That is good counsel," said the vicar, and Christopher, with whom words seemed to be few, nodded his head.

"Meanwhile," went on Emlyn, "you have six men in this house and others round it. Send out a messenger and summon them all here at dawn, bidding them bring provision with them, and what bows and arms they have. Set a watch also, and after the Father and the messenger have gone, command that the drawbridge be triced."

"What do you fear?" he asked, waking from his dream.

"I fear the Abbot of Blossholme and his hired ruffians, who reck little of the laws, as the soul of dead Sir John knows now, or can use them as a cover to evil deeds. He'll not let such a prize slip between his fingers if he can help it, and the times are turbulent."

"Alas! alas! it is true," said Father Roger, "and that Abbot is a relentless man who sticks at nothing, having much wealth and many friends both here and beyond the seas. Yet surely he would never dare—"

"That we shall learn," interrupted Emlyn. "Meanwhile, Sir Christopher, rouse yourself and give the orders."

So Christopher summoned his men and spoke words to them at which they looked very grave, but being true-hearted fellows who loved him, said they would do his bidding.

A while later, having written out a copy of the marriage lines and witnessed it, Father Roger departed with the messenger. The drawbridge was hoisted above the moat, the doors were barred, and a man set to watch in the gateway tower, while Christopher, forgetful of all else, even of the danger in which they were, sought the company of her who waited for him.

Chapter IV

The Abbot's Oath

On the following morning, shortly after it was light, Christopher was called from his chamber by Emlyn, who gave him a letter.

"Whence came this?" he asked, turning it over suspiciously.

"A messenger has brought it from Blossholme Abbey," she answered.

"Wife Cicely," he called through the door, "come hither if you will."

Presently she appeared, looking quaint and lovely in her long fur cloak, and, having embraced her foster-mother, asked what was the matter.

"This, my darling," he answered, handing her the paper. "I never loved book-learnings over-much, and this morn I seem to hate them; read, you who are more scholarly."

"I mistrust me of that great seal; it bodes us no good, Chris," she replied doubtfully, and paling a little.

"The message within is no medlar to soften by keeping," said Emlyn. "Give it me. I was schooled in a nunnery, and can read their scrawls."

So, nothing loth, Cicely handed her the paper, which she took in her strong fingers, broke the seal, snapped the silk, unfolded, and read. It ran thus—

"To Sir Christopher Harflete, to Mistress Cicely Foterell, to Emlyn Stower, the waiting-woman, and to all others whom it may concern.

"I, Clement Maldon, Abbot of Blossholme, having heard of the death of Sir John Foterell, Knt., at the cruel hands of the forest thieves and outlaws, sent last night to serve the declaration of my wardship, according to my prerogative established by law and custom, over the person and property of you, Cicely, his only child surviving. My messengers returned saying that you had fled from your home of Shefton Hall. They said further that it was rumoured that you had ridden with your foster-mother, Emlyn Stower, to Cranwell Towers, the house of Sir Christopher Harflete. If this be so, for the sake of your good name it is needful that you should remove from such company at once, as there is talk about you and the said Sir Christopher Harflete. I purpose, therefore, God permitting me, to ride this day to Cranwell Towers, and if you be there, as your lawful guardian and ghostly father, to command you, being an infant under age, to accompany me thence to the Nunnery of Blossholme. There I have determined, in the exercise of my authority, you shall abide until a fitting husband is found for you, unless, indeed, God should move your heart to remain within its walls as one of the brides of Christ.

"Clement, Abbot."

Now when the reading of this letter was finished, the three of them stood a little while staring at each other, knowing well that it meant trouble for them all, till Cicely said—

"Bring me ink and paper, Nurse. I will answer this Abbot."

So they were brought, and Cicely wrote in her round, girlish hand—

"My Lord Abbot,

"In answer to your letter, I would have you know that as my noble father (whose cruel death must be inquired of and avenged) bade me with his last words, I, fearing that a like fate would overtake me at the hands of his murderers, did, as you suppose, seek refuge at this house. Here, yesterday, I was married in the face of God and man in the church of Cranwell, as you may learn from the paper sent herewith. It is not, therefore, needful that you should seek a husband for me, since my dear lord, Sir Christopher Harflete, and I are one till death do part us. Nor do I admit that now, or at any time, you had or have right of wardship over my person or the lands and goods which I hold and inherit.

"Your humble servant,
"Cicely Harflete."

This letter Cicely copied out fair and sealed, and presently it was given to the Abbot's messenger, who placed it in his pouch and rode off as fast as the snow would let him.

They watched him go from a window.

"Now," said Christopher, turning to his wife, "I think, dear, we shall do well to ride also as soon as may be. Yonder Abbot is sharp-set, and I doubt whether letters will satisfy his appetite."

"I think so also," said Emlyn. "Make ready and eat, both of you. I go to see that the horses are saddled."

An hour later everything was prepared. Three horses stood before the door, and with them an escort of four mounted men, who were all having arms and beasts to ride that Christopher could gather at such short notice, though others of his tenants and servants had already assembled at the Towers in answer to his summons, to the number of twelve, indeed. Without the snow was falling fast, and although she tried to look brave and happy, Cicely shivered a little as she saw it through the open door.

"We go on a strange honeymoon, my sweet," said Christopher uneasily.

"What matter, so long as we go together?" she answered in a gay voice that yet seemed to ring untrue, "although," she added, with a little choke of the throat, "I would that we could have stayed here until I had found and buried my father. It haunts me to think of him lying somewhere in the snows like a perished ox."

"It is his murderers that I wish to bury," exclaimed Christopher; "and, by God's name, I swear I'll do it ere all is done. Think not, dear, that I forget your griefs because I do not speak much of them, but bridals and buryings are strange company. So while we may, let us take what joy we can, since the ill that goes before ofttimes follows after also. Come, let us mount and away to London to find friends and justice."

Then, having spoken a few words to his house-people, he lifted Cicely to her horse, and they rode out into the softly-falling snow, thinking that they had seen their last of the Towers for many a day. But this was not to be. For as they passed along the Blossholme highway, purposing to leave the Abbey on their left, when they were about three miles from Cranwell, suddenly a tall fellow, who wore a great sheepskin coat with a monk's hood to it and carried a thick staff in his hand, burst through the fence and stood in front of them.

"Who are you?" asked Christopher, laying his hand upon his sword.

"You'd know me well enough if my hood were back," he answered in a deep voice; "but if you want my name, it's Thomas Bolle, cattle-reeve to the Abbey yonder."

"Your voice proves you," said Christopher, laughing. "And now what is your business, lay-brother Bolle?"

"To get up a bunch of yearling steers that have been running on the forest-edge, living, like the rest of us, on what they can find, as the weather is coming on hard enough to starve them. That's my business, Sir Christopher. But as I see an old friend of mine there," and he nodded towards Emlyn, who was watching him from her horse, "with your leave I'll ask her if she has any confession to make, since she seems to be on a dangerous journey."

Now Christopher made as though he would push on, for he was in no mood to chat with cattle-reeves. But Emlyn, who had been eyeing the man, called out—

"Come here, Thomas, and I will answer you myself, who always have a few sins to spare for a priest's wallet, and need a blessing or two to warm me."

He strode forward, and, taking her horse by the bridle, led it a little way apart, and as soon as they were out of earshot fell into an eager conversation with its rider. A minute or so later Cicely, looking round—for they had ridden forward at a slow pace—saw Thomas Bolle leap through the other fence of the roadway and vanish at a run into the falling snow, while Emlyn spurred her horse after them.

"Stop," she said to Christopher; "I have tidings for you. The Abbot, with all his men-at-arms and servants, to the number of forty or more, waits for us under shelter of Blossholme Grove yonder, purposing to take the Lady Cicely by force. Some spy has told him of this journey."

"I see no one," said Christopher, staring at the Grove, which lay below them about a quarter of a mile away, for they were on the top of a rise. "Still, the matter is not hard to prove," and he called to the two best mounted of his men and bade them ride forward and make report if any lurked behind that wood.

So the men went off, while they remained where they were, silent, but anxious enough. Ten minutes or so later, before they could see them, for the snow was now falling quickly, they heard the sound of many horses galloping. Then the two men appeared, calling out as they came—

"The Abbot and all his folk are after us. Back to Cranwell, ere you be taken!"

Christopher thought for a moment, then, remembering that with but four men and cumbered by two women it was not possible to cut his way through so great a force, and admonished by that sound of advancing hoofs, he gave a sudden order. They turned about, and not too soon, for as they did so, scarce two hundred yards away, the first of the Abbot's horsemen appeared plunging towards them up the slope. Then the race began, and well for them was it that their horses were good and fresh, since before ever they came in sight of Cranwell Towers the pursuers were not ninety yards behind. But here on the flat their beasts, scenting home, answered nobly to whip and spur, and drew ahead a little. Moreover, those who watched within the house saw them, and ran to the drawbridge. When they were within fifty yards of the moat Cicely's horse stumbled, slipped, and fell, throwing her into the snow, then recovered itself and galloped on alone. Christopher reined up alongside of her, and, as she rose, frightened but unharmed, put out his long arm, and, lifting her to the saddle in front of him, plunged forward, while those behind shouted "Yield!"

Under this double burden his horse went but slowly. Still they reached the bridge before any could lay hands upon them, and thundered over it.

"Wind up," shouted Christopher, and all there, even the womenfolk, laid hands upon the cranks. The bridge began to rise, but now five or six of the Abbot's folk, dismounting, sprang at it, catching the end of it with their hands when it was about six feet in the air, and holding on so that it could not be lifted, but remained, moving neither up nor down.

"Leave go, you knaves," shouted Christopher; but by way of answer one of them, with the help of his fellows, scrambled on to the end of the bridge, and stood there, hanging to the chains.

Then Christopher snatched a bow from the hand of a serving-man, and the arrow being already on the string, again shouted—

"Get off at your peril!"

In answer the man called out something about the commands of the Lord Abbot.

Christopher, looking past him, saw that others of the company had dismounted and were running towards the bridge. If they reached it he knew well that the game was played. So he hesitated no longer, but, aiming swiftly, drew and loosed the bow. At that distance he could not miss. The arrow struck the man where his steel cap joined the mail beneath, and pierced him through the throat, so that he fell back dead. The others, scared by his fate, loosed their hold, so that now the bridge, relieved of the weight upon it, instantly rose up beyond their reach, and presently came home and was made fast.

As they afterwards discovered, this man, it may here be said, was a captain of the Abbot's guard. Moreover, it was he who had shot the arrow that killed Sir John Foterell some forty hours before, striking him through the throat, as it was fated that he himself should be struck. Thus, then, one of that good knight's murderers reaped his just reward.

Now the men ran back out of range, for they feared more arrows, while Christopher watched them go in silence. Cicely, who stood by his side, her hands held before her face to shut out the sight of death, let them fall suddenly, and, turning to her husband, said, as she pointed to the corpse that lay upon the blood-stained snow of the roadway—

"How many more will follow him, I wonder? I think that is but the first throw of a long game, husband."

"Nay, sweet," he answered, "the second; the first was cast two nights gone by King's Grave Mount in the forest yonder, and blood ever calls for blood."

"Aye," she answered, "blood calls for blood." Then, remembering that she was orphaned and what sort of a honeymoon hers was like to be, she turned and sought her chamber, weeping.

Now, while Christopher still stood irresolute, for he was oppressed by the sense of this man-slaying, and knew not what he should do next, he saw three men separate from the knot of soldiers and ride towards the Towers, one of whom held a white cloth above his head in token of parley. Then Christopher went up into the little gateway turret, followed by Emlyn, who crouched down behind the brick battlement, so that she could see and hear without being seen. Having reached the further side of the moat, he who held the white cloth threw back the hood of his long cape, and they saw that it was the Abbot of Blossholme himself, also that his dark eyes flashed and that his olive-hued face was almost white with rage.

"Why do you hunt me across my own park and come knocking so rudely at my doors, my Lord Abbot?" asked Christopher, leaning on the parapet of the gateway.

"Why do you work murder on my servant, Christopher Harflete?" answered the Abbot, pointing to the dead man in the snow. "Know you not that whoso sheds blood, by man shall his blood be shed, and that under our ancient charters, here I have the right to execute justice on you, as, by God's holy Name, I swear that I will do?" he added in a choked voice.

"Aye," repeated Christopher reflectively, "by man shall his blood be shed. Perhaps that is why this fellow died. Tell me, Abbot, was he not one of those who rode by moonlight round King's Grave lately, and there chanced to meet Sir John Foterell?"

The shot was a random one, yet it seemed that it went home; at least, the Abbot's jaw dropped, and some words that were on his lips never passed them.

"I know naught of the meaning of your talk," he said presently in a quieter voice, "or of how my late friend and neighbour, Sir John—may God rest his soul—came to his end. Yet it is of him, or rather of his, that we must speak. It seems that you have stolen his daughter, a woman under age, and by pretence of a false marriage, as I fear, brought her to shame—a crime even fouler than this murder."

"Nay, by means of a true marriage I have brought her to such small honour as may be the share of Christopher Harflete's lawful wife. If there be any virtue in the rites of Holy Church, then God's own hand has bound us fast as man can be tied to woman, and death is the only pope who can loose that knot."

"Death!" repeated the Abbot in a slow voice, looking up at him very curiously. For a little while he was silent, then went on, "Well, his court is always open, and he has many shrewd and instant messengers, such as this," and he pointed to the arrow in the neck of the slain soldier. "Yet I am a man of peace, and although you have murdered my servant, I would settle our cause more gently if I may. Listen now, Sir Christopher; here is my offer. Yield up to me the person of Cicely Foterell—"

"Of Cicely Harflete," interrupted Christopher.

"Of Cicely Foterell, and I swear to you that no violence shall be done to her, nor shall she be given to a husband till the King or his Vicar-General, or whatever court he may appoint, has passed judgment in this matter and declared this mock marriage of yours null and void."

"What!" broke in Christopher scoffingly; "does the Abbot of Blossholme announce that the powers temporal of this realm have right of divorce? Ere now I have heard him argue differently, and so have others, when the case of Queen Catherine was in question."

The Abbot bit his lip, but continued, taking no heed—

"Nor will I lay any complaint against you as to the death of my servant here, for which otherwise you should hang. That I will write down as an accident, and, further, compensate his family. Now you have my offer—answer."

"And what if I refuse this same generous offer to surrender her whom I hold dearer than a thousand lives?"

"Then, by virtue of my rights and authority, I will take her by force, Christopher Harflete, and if harm should happen to come to you, now or hereafter, on your own head be it."

At this Christopher's rage broke out.

"Do you dare to threaten me, a loyal Englishman, you false priest and foreign traitor," he shouted, "whom all men know to be in the pay of Spain, and using the cover of a monk's dress to plot against the land on which you fatten like a horse-leech? Why was John Foterell murdered in the forest two nights gone? You won't answer? Then I will. Because he rode to Court to prove the truth about you and your treachery, and therefore you butchered him. Why do you claim my wife as your ward? Because you wish to steal her lands and goods to feed your plots and luxury. You think you have bought friends at Court, and that for money's sake those in power there will turn a blind eye to your crimes. So it may be for a while; but wait, wait. All eyes are not blind yonder, nor all ears deaf. That head of yours shall yet be lifted higher than you think—so high that it sticks upon the top of Blossholme Towers, a warning to all who would sell England to her enemies. John Foterell lies dead with your knave's arrow in his throat, but Jeffrey Stokes is away with the writings. And now do your worst, Clement Maldon. If you want my wife, come take her."

The Abbot listened, listened intently, drinking in every ominous word. His swarthy face went white with fear, then turned black with rage. The veins upon his forehead gathered into knots; even from that distance Christopher could see them. He looked so evil that his countenance became twisted and ridiculous, and Christopher, noting it, burst into one of his hearty laughs.

The Abbot, who was not accustomed to mockery, whispered something to the two men who were with him, whereon they lifted the crossbows which they carried and pulled trigger. One quarel went wide and hit the wall of the house behind, where it stuck fast in the joints of the stud- work. But the other, better aimed, smote Christopher above the heart, causing him to stagger, but being shot from below and turned by the mail he wore glanced upwards over his left shoulder. The men, seeing that he was unhurt, pulled their horses round and galloped off, but Christopher, setting another arrow to the string of the bow he carried, drew it to his ear, covering the Abbot.

"Loose, and make an end of him," muttered Emlyn from her shelter behind the parapet. But Christopher thought a moment, then cried—

"Stay a while, Sir Abbot; I have more to say to you."

He took no heed who was also turning about.

"Stay!" thundered Christopher, "or I will kill that fine nag of yours;" then, as the Abbot still dragged upon the reins, he let the arrow fly. The aim was true enough. Right through the arch of the neck it sped, cutting the cord between the bones, so that the poor beast reared straight up and fell in a heap, tumbling its rider off into the snow.

"Now, Clement Maldon," cried Christopher, "will you listen, or will you bide with your horse and servant and hear no more till Judgment Day? If you do not guess it, learn that I have practised archery from my youth. Should you doubt, hold up your hand and I'll send a shaft between your fingers."

The Abbot, who was shaken but unhurt, rose slowly and stood there, the dead horse on one side and the dead man on the other.

"Speak," he said in a muffled voice.

"My Lord Abbot," went on Christopher, "a minute ago you tried to murder me, and, had not my mail been good, would have succeeded. Now your life is in my hand, for, as you have seen, I do not miss. Those servants of yours are coming to your help. Call to them to halt, or—" and he lifted the bow.

The Abbot obeyed, and the men, understanding, stayed where they were, at a distance, but within earshot.

"You have a crucifix upon your breast," continued Christopher. "Take it in your right hand now and swear an oath."

Again the Abbot obeyed.

"Swear thus," he said, Emlyn, who was crouched beneath the parapet, prompting him from time to time; "I, Clement Maldon, Abbot of Blossholme, in the presence of Almighty God in heaven, and of Christopher Harflete and others upon earth," and he jerked his head backwards towards the windows of the house, where all therein were gathered, listening, "make oath upon the symbol of the Rood. I swear that I abandon all claim of wardship over the body of Cicely Harflete, born Cicely Foterell, the lawful wife of Christopher Harflete, and all claim to the lands and goods that she may possess, or that were possessed by her father, John Foterell, Knight, or by her mother, Dame Foterell, deceased. I swear that I will raise no suit in any court, spiritual or temporal, of this or other realms against the said Cicely Harflete or against the said Christopher Harflete, her husband, nor seek to work injury to their bodies or their souls, or to the bodies or the souls of any who cling to them, and that henceforth they may live and die in peace from me or any whom I control. Set your lips to the Rood and swear thus now, Clement Maldon."

The Abbot hearkened, and so great was his rage, for he had no meek heart, that he seemed to swell like an angry toad.

"Who gave you authority to administer oaths to me?" he asked at length. "I'll not swear," and he cast the crucifix down upon the snow.

"Then I'll shoot," answered Christopher. "Come, pick up that cross."

But Maldon stood silent, his arms folded on his breast. Christopher aimed and loosed, and so great was his skill—for there were few archers in England like to him—that the arrow pierced Maldon's fur cap and carried it away without touching the shaven head beneath.

"The next shall be two inches lower," he said, as he set another on the string. "I waste no more good shafts."

Then, very slowly, to save his life, which he loved well enough, Maldon bent down, and, lifting the crucifix from the snow, held it to his lips and kissed it, muttering—

"I swear." But the oath he swore was very different to that which Christopher had repeated to him, for, like a hunted fox, he knew how to meet guile with guile.

"Now that I, a consecrated abbot, deeming it right that I should live on to fulfil my work on earth, have done your bidding, have I leave to go about my business, Christopher Harflete?" he asked, with bitter irony.

"Why not?" asked Christopher. "Only be pleased henceforth not to meddle with me and my business. To-morrow I wish to ride to London with my lady, and we do not seek your company on the road."

Then, having found his cap, the Abbot turned and walked back towards his own men, drawing the arrow from it as he went, and presently all of them rode away over the rise towards Blossholme.

"Now that is well finished, and I have an oath that he will scarcely dare to break," said Christopher presently. "What say you, Nurse?"

"I say that you are even a bigger simpleton than I took you to be," answered Emlyn angrily, as she rose and stretched herself, for her limbs were cramped. "The oath, pshaw! By now he is absolved from it as given under fear. Did you not hear me whisper to you to put an arrow through his heart, instead of playing boy's pranks with his cap?"

"I did not wish to kill an abbot, Nurse."

"Foolish man, what is the difference in such a matter between him and one of his servants? Moreover, he will only say that you tried to slay him, and missed, and produce the cap and arrow in evidence against you. Well, my talk serves nothing to mend a bad matter, and soon you will hear it straighter from himself. Go now and make your house ready for attack, and never dare to set a foot without its doors, for death waits you there."

Emlyn was right. Within three hours an unarmed monk trudged up to Cranwell Towers through the falling snow and cast across the moat a letter that was tied to a stone. Then he nailed a writing to one of the oak posts of the outer gate, and, without a word, departed as he had come. In the presence of Christopher and Cicely, Emlyn opened and read this second letter, as she had read the first. It was short, and ran—

"Take notice, Sir Christopher Harflete, and all others whom it may concern, that the oath which I, Clement Maldon, Abbot of Blossholme, swore to you this day, is utterly void and of none effect, having been wrung from me under the threat of instant death. Take notice, further, that a report of the murder which you have done has been forwarded to the King's grace and to the Sheriff and other officers of this county, and that by virtue of my rights and authority, ecclesiastical and civil, I shall proceed to possess myself of the person of Cicely Foterell, my ward, and of the lands and other property held by her father, Sir John Foterell, deceased, upon the former of which I have already entered on her behalf, and by exercise of such force as may be needful to seize you, Christopher Harflete, and to hand you over to justice. Further, by means of notice sent herewith, I warn all that cling to you and abet you in your crimes that they will do so at the peril of their souls and bodies.

"Clement Maldon, Abbot of Blossholme."

Chapter V

A week had gone by. For the first three days of that time little of note had happened at Cranwell Towers; that is, no assault was delivered. Only Christopher and his dozen or so of house-servants and small tenants discovered that they were quite surrounded. Once or twice some of them rode out a little way, to be hunted back again by a much superior force, which emerged from the copses near by or from cottages in the village, and even from the porch of the church. With these men they never came to close quarters, so that no lives were lost. In a fashion this was a disadvantage to them, since they lacked the excitement of actual fighting, the dread of which was ever present, but not its joy.

Meanwhile in other ways things went ill with them. Thus, first of all their beer gave out, and then such other cordials as they had, so that they were reduced to water to drink. Next their fuel became exhausted, for nearly all the stock of it was kept at the farmstead about a quarter of a mile away, and on the second day of the siege this stead was fired and burned with its contents, the cattle and horses being driven off, they knew not where.

So it came about at length they could keep only one fire, in the kitchen, and that but small, which in the end they were obliged to feed with the doors of the outhouses, and even with the floorings torn out of the attics, in order that they might cook their food. Nor was there much of this; only a store of salt meat and some pickled pork and smoked bacon, together with a certain amount of oatmeal and flour, that they made into cakes and bread.

On the fourth day, however, these gave out, so that they were reduced to a scanty diet of hung flesh, with a few apples by way of vegetables, and hot water to drink to warm them. At length, too, there was nothing more to burn, and therefore they must eat their meat raw, and grew sick on it. Moreover, a cold thaw set in, and the house grew icy, so that they moved about it with chattering teeth, and at night, ill-nurtured as they were, could scarce keep the life in them beneath all the coverings which they had.

Ah! how long were those nights, with never a blaze upon the hearth or so much as a candle to light them. At four o'clock the darkness came down, which did not lessen, for the moon grew low and the mists were thick, until day broke about seven on the following morning. And all this time, fearing attack, they must keep watch and ward through the gloom, so that even sleep was denied them.

For a while they bore up bravely, even the tenants, though news was shouted to these that their steads had been harried, and their wives and children hunted off to seek shelter where they might.

Cicely and Emlyn never murmured. Indeed, this new-made wife kept her dreadful honeymoon with a cheerful face, trudging through the black hours around the circle of the moat at her husband's side, or from window-place to window-place in the empty rooms, till at length they cast themselves down upon some bed to sleep a while, giving over the watch to others. Only Emlyn never seemed to sleep. But at length their companions did begin to murmur.

One morning at the dawn, after a very bitter night, they waited upon Christopher and told him that they were willing to fight for his sake and his lady's, but that, as there was no hope of help, they could no longer freeze and starve; in short, that they must either escape from the house or surrender. He listened to them patiently, knowing that what they said was true, and then consulted for a while with Cicely and Emlyn.

"Our case is desperate, dear wife. Now what shall we do, who have no chance of succour, since none know of our plight? Yield, or strive to escape through the darkness?"

"Not yield, I think," answered Cicely, choking back a sob. "If we yield certainly they will separate us, and that merciless Abbot will bring you to your death and me to a nunnery."

"That may happen in any case," muttered Christopher, turning his head aside. "But what say you, Nurse?"

"I say fight for it," answered Emlyn boldly. "It is certain that we cannot stay here, for, to be plain, Sir Christopher, there are some among us whom I do not trust. What wonder? Their stomachs are empty, their hands are blue, their wives and children are they know not where, and the heavy curse of the Church hangs over them, all of which things may be mended if they play you false. Let us take what horses remain and slip away at dead of night if we can; or if we cannot, then let us die, as many better folk have done before."

So they agreed to try their fortune, thinking that it was so bad it could not be worse, and spent the rest of that day in getting ready as best they could. The seven horses still stood in the stable, and although they were stiff from want of exercise, had been hay-fed and watered. On these they proposed to ride, but first they must tell the truth to those who had stood by them. So about three o'clock of the afternoon Christopher called all the men together beneath the gateway and sorrowfully set out his tale. Here, he showed them, they could bide no longer, and to surrender meant that his new-wed wife would soon be made a widow. Therefore they must fly, taking with them as many as there were horses for them to ride, if they cared to risk such a journey. If not, he and the two women would go alone.

Now four of the stoutest-hearted of them, men who had served him and his father for many years, stepped forward, saying that, evil as these seemed to be, they would follow his fortunes to the last. He thanked them shortly, whereon one of the others asked what they were to do, and if he proposed to desert them after leading them into this plight.

"God knows I would rather die," he replied, with a swelling heart; "but, my friends, consider the case. If I bide here, what of my wife? Alas! it has come to this: that you must choose whether you will slip out with us and scatter in the woods, where I think you will not be followed, since yonder Abbot has no quarrel against you; or whether you will wait here, and to-morrow at the dawn, surrender. In either event you can say that I compelled you to stand by us, and that you have shed no man's blood; also I will give you a writing."

So they talked together gloomily, and at last announced that when he and their lady went they would go also and get off as best they could. But there was a man among them, a small farmer named Jonathan Dicksey, who thought otherwise. This Jonathan, who held his land under Christopher, had been forced to this business of the defence of Cranwell Towers somewhat against his will, namely, by the pressure of Christopher's largest tenant, to whose daughter he was affianced. He was a sly young man, and even during the siege, by means that need not be described, he had contrived to convey a message to the Abbot of Blossholme, telling him that had it been in his power he would gladly be in any other place. Therefore, as he knew well, whatever had happened to others, his farm remained unharried. Now he determined to be out of a bad business as soon as he might, for Jonathan was one of those who liked to stand upon the winning side.

Therefore, although he said "Aye, aye," more loudly than his comrades, as soon as the dusk had fallen, while the others were making ready the horses and mounting guard, Jonathan thrust a ladder across the moat at the back of the stable, and clambered along its rungs into the shelter of a cattle-shed in the meadow, and so away.

Half-an-hour later he stood before the Abbot in the cottage where he had taken up his quarters, having contrived to blunder among his people and be captured. To him at first Jonathan would say nothing, but when at length they threatened to take him out and hang him, to save his life, as he said, he found his tongue and told all.

"So, so," said the Abbot when he had finished. "Now God is good to us. We have these birds in our net, and I shall keep St. Hilary's at Blossholme after all. For your services, Master Dicksey, you shall be my reeve at Cranwell Towers when they are in my hands."

But here it may be said that in the end things went otherwise, since, so far from getting the stewardship of Cranwell, when the truth came to be known, Jonathan's maiden would have no more to do with him, and the folk in those parts sacked his farm and hunted him out of the country, so that he was never heard of among them again.

Meanwhile, all being ready, Christopher at the Towers was closeted with Cicely, taking his farewell of her in the dark, for no light was left to them.

"This is a desperate venture," he said to her, "nor can I tell how it will end, or if ever I shall see your sweet face again. Yet, dearest, we have been happy together for some few hours, and if I fall and you live on I am sure that you will always remember me till, as we are taught, we meet again where no enemy has the power to torment us, and cold and hunger and darkness are not. Cicely, if that should be so and any child should come to you, teach it to love the father whom it never saw."

Now she threw her arms about him and wept, and wept, and wept.

"If you die," she sobbed, "surely I will do so also, for although I am but young I find this world a very evil place, and now that my father is gone, without you, husband, it would be a hell."

"Nay, nay," he answered; "live on while you may; for who knows? Often out of the worst comes the best. At least we have had our joy. Swear it now, sweet."

"Aye, if you will swear it also, for I may be taken and you left. In the dark swords do not choose. Let us promise that we will both endure our lives, together or separate, until God calls us."

So they swore there in the icy gloom, and sealed the oath with kisses.

Now the time was come at last, and they crept their way to the courtyard hand in hand, taking some comfort because the night was very favourable to their project. The snow had melted, and a great gale blew from the sou'-west, boisterous but not cold, which caused the tall elms that stood about to screech and groan like things alive. In such a wind as this they were sure that they would not be heard, nor could they be seen beneath that murky, starless sky, while the rain which fell between the gusts would wash out the footprints of their horses.

They mounted silently, and with the four men—for by now all the rest had gone—rode across the drawbridge, which had been lowered in preparation for their flight. Three hundred yards or so away their road ran through an ancient marl-pit worked out generations before, in which self-sown trees grew on either side of the path. As they drew near this place suddenly, in the silence of the night, a horse neighed ahead of them, and one of their beasts answered to the neigh.

"Halt!" whispered Cicely, whose ears were made sharp by fear. "I hear men moving."

They pulled rein and listened. Yes; between the gusts of wind there was a faint sound as of the clanking of armour. They strained their eyes in the darkness, but could see nothing. Again the horse neighed and was answered. One of their servants cursed the beast beneath his breath and struck it savagely with the flat of his sword, whereon, being fresh, it took the bit between its teeth and bolted. Another minute and there arose a great clamour from the marl-pit in front of them—a noise of shoutings, of sword-strokes, and then a heavy groan as from the lips of a dying man.

"An ambush!" exclaimed Christopher.

"Can we get round?" asked Cicely, and there was terror in her voice.

"Nay," he answered, "the stream is in flood; we should be bogged. Hark! they charge us. Back to the Towers—there is no other way."

So they turned and fled, followed by shouts and the thunder of many horses galloping. In two minutes they were there and across the bridge—the women, Christopher, and the three men who were left.

"Up with the bridge!" cried Christopher, and they leapt from their saddles and fumbled for the cranks; too late, for already the Abbot's horsemen pressed it down.

Then a fight began. The horses of the enemy shrank back from the trembling bridge, so their riders, dismounting, rushed forward, to be met by Christopher and his three remaining men, who in that narrow place were as good as a hundred. Wild, random blows were struck in the darkness, and, as it chanced, two of the Abbot's people fell, whereon a deep voice cried—

"Come back and wait for light."

When they had gone, dragging off their wounded with them, Christopher and his servants again strove to wind up the bridge, only to find that it would not stir.

"Some traitor has fouled the chains," he said in the quiet voice of despair. "Cicely and Emlyn, get you into the house. I, and any who will bide with me, stay here to see this business out. When I am down, yield yourself. Afterwards I think that the King will give you justice, if you can come to him."

"I'll not go," she wailed; "I'll die with you."

"Nay, you shall go," he said, stamping his foot, and, as he spoke, an arrow hissed between them. "Emlyn, drag her hence ere she is shot. Swift, I say, swift, or God's curse and mine rest on you. Unclasp your arms, wife; how can I fight while you hang about my neck? What! Must I strike you? Then, there and there!"

She loosed her grasp, and, groaning, fell back upon the breast of Emlyn, who half led, half carried her across the courtyard, where their scared horses galloped loose.

"Whither go we?" sobbed Cicely.

"To the central tower," answered Emlyn; "it seems safest there."

To this tower, whence the place took its name, they groped their way. Unlike the rest of the house, which for the most part was of wood, it was built of stone, being part of an older fabric dating from the Norman days. Slowly they stumbled up the steps till at length they reached the roof, for some instinct prompted them to find a spot whence they could see, should the stars break out. Here, on this lofty perch, they crouched them down and waited the end, whatever it might be—waited in silence.

A while passed—they never knew how long—till at length a sudden flame shot up above the roof of the kitchens at the rear, which the wind caught and blew on to the timbers of the main building, so that presently this began to blaze also. The house had been fired, by whom was never known, though it was said that the traitor, Jonathan Dicksey, had returned and done it, either for a bribe or that his own sin might be forgotten in this great catastrophe.

"The house burns," said Emlyn in her quiet voice. "Now, if you would save your life, follow me. Beneath this tower is a vault where no flame can touch us."

But Cicely would not stir, for by the fierce and ever-growing light she could see what passed beneath, and, as it chanced, the wind blew the smoke away from them. There, beyond the drawbridge, were gathered the Abbey guards, and there in the gateway stood Christopher and his three men with drawn swords, while in the courtyard the horses galloped madly, screaming in their fear. A soldier looked up and saw the two women standing on the top of the tower, then called out something to the Abbot, who sat on horseback near to him. He looked and saw also.

"Yield, Sir Christopher," he shouted; "the Lady Cicely burns. Yield, that we may save her."

Christopher turned and saw also. For a moment he hesitated, then wheeled round to run across the courtyard. Too late, for as he came the flames burst through the main roof of the house, and the timber front of it, blazing furiously, fell outwards, blocking the doorway, so that the place became a furnace into which none might enter and live.

Now a madness seemed to take hold of him. For a moment he stared up at the figures of the two women standing high above the rolling smoke and wrapping flame. Then, with his three men, he charged with a roar into the crowd of soldiers who had followed him into the courtyard, striving, it would seem, to cut his way to the Abbot, who lurked behind. It was a dreadful sight, for he and those with him fought furiously, and many went down. Presently, of the four only Christopher was left upon his feet. Swords and spears smote upon his armour, but he did not fall; it was those in front of him who fell. A great fellow with an axe got behind him and struck with all his might upon his helm. The sword dropped from Harflete's hand; slowly he turned about, looked upward, then stretched out his arms and fell heavily to earth.

The Abbot leapt from his horse and ran to him, kneeling at his side.

"Dead!" he cried, and began to shrive his passing soul, or so it seemed.

"Dead," repeated Emlyn, "and a gallant death!"

"Dead!" wailed Cicely, in so terrible a voice that all below heard it. "Dead, dead!" and sank senseless on Emlyn's breast.

At that moment the rest of the roof fell in, hiding the tower in spouts and veils of flame. Here they might not stay if they would live. Lifting her mistress in her strong arms, as she was wont to do when she was little, Emlyn found the head of the stair, so that when the wind blew the smoke aside for an instant, those below saw that both had vanished, as they thought withered in the fire.

"Now you can enter on the Shefton lands, Abbot," cried a voice from the darkness of the gateway, though in the turmoil none knew who spoke; "but not for all England would I bear that innocent blood!"

The Abbot's face turned ghastly, and though it was hot enough in that courtyard his teeth chattered.

"It is on the head of this woman-thief," he exclaimed with an effort, looking down on Christopher, who lay at his feet. "Take him up, that inquest may be held on him, who died doing murder. Can none enter the house? His pocket full of gold to him who saves the Lady Cicely!"

"Can any enter hell and live?" answered the same voice out of the smoke and gloom. "Seek her sweet soul in heaven, if you may come there, Abbot."

Then, with scared faces, they lifted up Christopher and the other dead and wounded and carried them away, leaving Cranwell Towers to burn itself to ashes, for so fierce was the heat that none could bide there longer.

Two hours had gone by. The Abbot sat in the little room of a cottage at Cranwell that he had occupied during the siege of the Towers. It was near midnight, yet, weary as he was, he could not rest; indeed, had the night been less foul and dark he would have spent the time in riding back to Blossholme. His heart was ill at ease. Things had gone well with him, it is true. Sir John Foterell was dead—slain by "outlawed men"; Sir Christopher Harflete was dead—did not his body lie in the neat-house yonder? Cicely, daughter of the one and wife to the other, was dead also, burned in the fire at the Towers, so that doubtless the precious gems and the wide lands he coveted would fall into his lap without further trouble. For, Cromwell being bribed, who would try to snatch them from the powerful Abbot of Blossholme, and had he not a title to them—of a sort?

And yet he was very ill at ease, for, as that voice had said—whose voice was it? he wondered, somehow it seemed familiar—the blood of these people lay on his head; and there came into his mind the text of Holy Writ which he had quoted to Christopher, that he who shed man's blood by man should his blood be shed. Also, although he had paid the Vicar-General to back him, monks were in no great favour at the English Court, and if this story travelled there, as it might, for even the strengthless dead find friends, it was possible that questions would be asked, questions hard to answer. Before Heaven he could justify himself for all that he had done, but before King Henry, who would usurp the powers of the very Pope, if the truth should chance to reach the royal ear—ah! that was another matter.

The room was cold after the heat of that great fire; his Southern blood, which had been warm enough, grew chill; loneliness and depression took hold of him; he began to wonder how far in the eyes of God above the end justifies the means. He opened the door of the place, and holding on to it lest the rough, wintry gale should tear it from its frail hinges, shouted aloud for Brother Martin, one of his chaplains.

Presently Martin arrived, emerging from the cattleshed, a lantern in his hand—a tall, thin man, with perplexed and melancholy eyes, long nose, and a clever face—and, bowing, asked his superior's pleasure.

"My pleasure, Brother," answered the Abbot, "is that you shut the door and keep out the wind, for this accursed climate is killing me. Yes, make up the fire if you can, but the wood is too wet to burn; also it smokes. There, what did I tell you? If this goes on we shall be hams by to-morrow morning. Let it be, for, after all, we have seen enough of fires to-night, and sit down to a cup of wine—nay, I forgot, you drink but water—well, then, to a bite of bread and meat."

"I thank you, my Lord Abbot," answered Martin, "but I may not touch flesh; this is Friday."

"Friday or no we have touched flesh—the flesh of men—up at the Towers yonder this night," answered the Abbot, with an uneasy laugh. "Still, obey your conscience, Brother, and eat bread. Soon it will be midnight, and the meat can follow."

The lean monk bowed, and, taking a hunch of bread, began to bite at it, for he was almost starving.

"Have you come from watching by the body of that bloody and rebellious man who has worked us so much harm and loss?" asked the Abbot presently.

The secretary nodded, then swallowing a crust, said—

"Aye, I have been praying over him and the others. At least he was brave, and it must be hard to see one's new-wed wife burn like a witch. Also, now that I come to study the matter, I know not what his sin was who did but fight bravely when he was attacked. For without doubt the marriage is good, and whether he should have waited to ask your leave to make it is a point that might be debated through every court in Christendom."

The Abbot frowned, not appreciating this open and judicial tone in matters that touched him so nearly.

"You have honoured me of late by choosing me as one of your confessors, though I think you do not tell me everything, my Lord Abbot; therefore I bare my mind to you," continued Brother Martin apologetically.

"Speak on then, man. What do you mean?"

"I mean that I do not like this business," he answered slowly, in the intervals of munching at his bread. "You had a quarrel with Sir John Foterell about those lands which you say belong to the Abbey. God knows the right of it, for I understand no law; but he denied it, for did I not hear it yonder in your chamber at Blossholme? He denied it, and accused you of treason enough to hang all Blossholme, of which again God knows the truth. You threatened him in your anger, but he and his servant were armed and won out, and next day the two of them rode for London with certain papers. Well, that night Sir John Foterell was killed in the forest, though his servant Stokes escaped with the papers. Now, who killed him?"

The Abbot looked at him, then seemed to take a sudden resolution.

"Our people, those men-at-arms whom I have gathered for the defence of our House and the Church. My orders to them were to seize him living, but the old English bull would not yield, and fought so fiercely that it ended otherwise—to my sorrow."

The monk put down his bread, for which he seemed to have no further appetite.

"A dreadful deed," he said, "for which one day you must answer to God and man."

"For which we all must answer," corrected the Abbot, "down to the last lay-brother and soldier—you as much as any of us, Brother, for were you not present at our quarrel?"

"So be it, Abbot. Being innocent, I am ready. But that is not the end of it. The Lady Cicely, on hearing of this murder—nay, be not wrath, I know no other name for it—and learning that you claimed her as your ward, flies to her affianced lover, Sir Christopher Harflete, and that very day is married to him by the parish priest in yonder church."

"It was no marriage. Due notice had not been given. Moreover, how could my ward be wed without my leave?"

"She had not been served with notice of your wardship, if such exists, or so she declared," replied Martin in his quiet, obstinate voice. "I think that there is no court in Europe which would void this open marriage when it learned that the parties lived a while as man and wife, and were so received by those about them—no, not the Pope himself."

"He who says that he is no lawyer still sets out the law," broke in Maldon sarcastically. "Well, what does it matter, seeing that death has voided it? Husband and wife, if such they were, are both dead; it is finished."

"No; for now they lay their appeal in the Court of Heaven, to which every one of us is summoned; and Heaven can stir up its ministers on earth. Oh! I like it not, I like it not; and I mourn for those two, so loving, brave, and young. Their blood and that of many more is on our hands—for what? A stretch of upland and of marsh which the King or others may seize to-morrow."

The Abbot seemed to cower beneath the weight of these sad, earnest words, and for a little while there was silence. Then he plucked up courage, and said—

"I am glad that you remember that their blood is on your hands as well as mine, since now, perhaps, you will keep them hidden."

He rose and walked to the door and the window to see that none were without, then returned and exclaimed fiercely—

"Fool, do you then think that these deeds were done to win a new estate? True it is that those lands are ours by right, and we need their revenues; but there is more behind. The whole Church of this realm is threatened by that accursed son of Belial who sits upon the throne. Why, what is it now, man?"

"Only that I am an Englishman, and love not to hear England's king called a son of Belial. His sins, I know, are many and black, like those of others—still, 'son of Belial!' Let his Highness hear it, and that name alone is enough to hang you!"

"Well, then, angel of grace, if it suits you better. At the least we are threatened. Against the law of God and man our blessed Queen, Catherine of Spain, is thrust away in favour of the slut who fills her place. Even now I have tidings from Kimbolton that she lies dying there of slow poison; so they say and I believe. Also I have other tidings. Fisher and More being murdered, Parliament next month will be moved to strike at the lesser monasteries and steal their goods, and after them our turn will come. But we will not bear it tamely, for ere this new year is out all England shall be ablaze, and I, Clement Maldon, I—I will light the fire. Now you have the truth, Martin. Will you betray me, as that dead knight would have done?"

"Nay, my Lord Abbot, your secrets are safe with me. Am I not your chaplain, and does not this wilful and rebellious King of ours work much mischief against God and His servants? Yet I tell you that I like it not, and cannot see the end. We English are a stiff-necked folk whom you of Spain do not understand and will never break, and Henry is strong and subtle; moreover, his people love him."

"I knew that I could trust you, Martin, and the proof of it is that I have spoken to you so openly," went on Maldon in a gentler voice. "Well, you shall hear all. The great Emperor of Germany and Spain is on our side, as, seeing his blood and faith, he must be. He will avenge the wrongs of the Church and of his royal aunt. I, who know him, am his agent here, and what I do is done at his bidding. But I must have more money than he finds me, and that is why I stirred in this matter of the Shefton lands. Also the Lady Cicely had jewels of vast price, though I fear greatly lest they should have been lost in the fire this night."

"Filthy lucre—the root of all evil," muttered Brother Martin.

"Aye, and of all good. Money, money—I must have more money to bribe men and buy arms, to defend that stronghold of Heaven, the Church. What matters it if lives are lost so that the immortal Church holds her own? Let them go. My friend, you are fearful; these deaths weigh upon your soul—aye, and on mine. I loved that girl, whom as a babe I held in my arms, and even her rough father, I loved him for his honest heart, although he always mistrusted me, the Spaniard—and rightly. The knight Harflete, too, who lies yonder, he was of a brave breed, but not one who would have served our turn. Well, they are gone, and for these blood-sheddings we must find absolution."

"If we can."

"Oh! we can, we can. Already I have it in my pouch, under a seal you know. And for our bodies, fear not. There is such a gale rising in England as will blow out this petty breeze. A question of rights, some arrows shot, a fire and lives lost—what of that when it agitates betwixt powers temporal and spiritual, and which of them shall hold the sceptre in this mighty Britain? Martin, I have a mission for you that may lead you to a bishopric ere all is done, for that's your mind and aim, and if you would put off your doubts and moodiness you've got the brain to rule. That ship, the Great Yarmouth, which sailed for Spain some days ago, has been beat back into the river, and should weigh anchor again to-morrow morning. I have letters for the Spanish Court, and you shall take them with my verbal explanations, which I will give you presently, for they would hang us, and may not be trusted to writing. She is bound for Seville, but you will follow the Emperor wherever he may be. You will go, won't you?" and he glanced at him sideways.

"I obey orders," answered Martin, "though I know little of Spaniards or of Spanish."

"In every town the Benedictines have a monastery, and in every monastery interpreters, and you shall be accredited to them all who are of that great Brotherhood. Well, 'tis settled. Go, make ready as best you can; I must write. Stay; the sooner this Harflete is under ground the better. Bid that sturdy fellow, Bolle, find the sexton of the church and help dig his grave, for we will bury him at dawn. Now go, go, I tell you I must write. Come back in an hour, and I will give you money for your faring, also my secret messages."

Brother Martin bowed and went.

"A dangerous man," muttered the Abbot, as the door closed on him; "too honest for our game, and too much an Englishman. That native spirit peeps beneath his cowl; a monk should have no country and no kin. Well, he will learn a trick or two in Spain, and I'll make sure they keep him there a while. Now for my letters," and he sat down at the rude table and began to write.

Half-an-hour later the door opened and Martin entered.

"What is it now?" asked the Abbot testily. "I said, 'Come back in an hour.'"

"Aye, you said that, but I have good news for you that I thought you might like to hear."

"Out with it, then, man. It's scarce now-a-days. Have they found those jewels? No, how could they? the place still flares," and he glanced through the window-place. "What's the news?"

"Better than jewels. Christopher Harflete is not dead. While I was praying over him he turned his head and muttered. I think he is only stunned. You are skilled in medicine; come, look at him."

A minute later and the Abbot knelt over the senseless form of Christopher where it lay on the filthy floor of the neat-house. By the light of the lanterns with deft fingers he felt his wounded head, from which the shattered casque had been removed, and afterwards his heart and pulse.

"The skull is cut, but not broken," he said. "My judgment is that though he may lie unsensed for days, if fed and tended this man will live, being so young and strong. But if left alone in this cold place he will be dead by morning, and perhaps he is better dead," and he looked at Martin.

"That would be murder indeed," answered the secretary. "Come, let us bear him to the fire and pour milk down his throat. We may save him yet. Lift you his feet and I will take his head."

The Abbot did so, not very willingly, as it seemed to Martin, but rather as one who has no choice.

Half-an-hour later, when the hurts of Christopher had been dressed with ointment and bound up, and milk poured down his throat, which he swallowed although he was so senseless, the Abbot, looking at him, said to Martin—

"You gave orders for this Harflete's burial, did you not?"

The monk nodded.

"Then have you told any that he needs no grave at present?"

"No one except yourself."

The Abbot thought a while, rubbing his shaven chin.

"I think the funeral should go forward," he said presently. "Look not so frightened; I do not purpose to inter him living. But there is a dead man lying in that shed, Andrew Woods, my servant, the Scotch soldier whom Harflete slew. He has no friends here to claim him, and these two were of much the same height and breadth. Shrouded in a blanket, none would know one body from the other, and it will be thought that Andrew was buried with the rest. Let him be promoted in his death, and fill a knight's grave."

"To what purpose would you play so unholy a trick, which must, moreover, be discovered in a day, seeing that Sir Christopher lives?" asked Martin, staring at him.

"For a very good purpose, my friend. It is well that Sir Christopher Harflete should seem to die, who, if he is known to be alive, has powerful kin in the south who will bring much trouble on us."

"Do you mean—? If so, before God I will have no hand in it."

"I said—seem to die. Where are your wits to-night?" answered the Abbot, with irritation. "Sir Christopher travels with you to Spain as our sick Brother Luiz, who, like myself, is of that country, and desires to return there, as we know, but is too ill to do so. You will nurse him, and on the ship he will die or recover, as God wills. If he recovers our Brotherhood will show him hospitality at Seville, notwithstanding his crimes, and by the time that he reaches England again, which may not be for a long while, men will have forgotten all this fray in a greater that draws on. Nor will he be harmed, seeing that the lady whom he pretends to have married is dead beyond a doubt, as you can tell him should he find his understanding."

"A strange game," muttered Martin.

"Strange or no, it is my game which I must play. Therefore question not, but be obedient, and silent also, on your oath," replied the Abbot in a cold, hard voice. "That covered litter which was brought here for the wounded is in the next chamber. Wrap this man in blankets and a monk's robe, and we will place him in it. Then let him be borne to Blossholme as one of the dead by brethren who will ask no questions, and ere dawn on to the ship Great Yarmouth, if he still lives. It lies near the quay not half-a-mile from the Abbey gate. Be swift now, and help me. I will overtake you with the letters, and see that you are furnished with all things needful from our store. Also I must speak with the captain ere he weighs anchor. Waste no more time in talking, but obey and be secret."

"I obey, and I will be secret, as is my duty," answered Brother Martin, bowing his head humbly. "But what will be the end of all this business, God and His angels know alone. I say that I like it not."

"A very dangerous man," muttered the Abbot, as he watched Martin go. "He also must bide a while in Spain; a long while. I'll see to it!"

Chapter VI

Emlyn's Curse

Just before the wild dawn broke on the morrow of the burning of the Towers, a corpse, roughly shrouded, was borne from the village into the churchyard of Cranwell, where a shallow grave had been dug for its last home.

"Whom do we bury in such haste?" asked the tall Thomas Bolle, who had delved the grave alone in the dark, for his orders were urgent, and the sexton was fled away from these tumults.

"That man of blood, Sir Christopher Harflete, who has caused us so much loss," said the old monk who had been bidden to perform the office, as the clergyman, Father Necton, had gone also, fearing the vengeance of the Abbot for his part in the marriage of Cicely. "A sad story, a very sad story. Wedded by night, and now buried by night, both of them, one in the flame and one in the earth. Truly, O God, Thy judgments are wonderful, and woe to those who lift hands against Thine anointed ministers!"

"Very wonderful," answered Bolle, as, standing in the grave, he took the head of the body and laid it down between his straddled feet; "so wonderful that a plain man wonders what will be the wondrous end of them, also why this noble young knight has grown so wondrously lighter than he used to be. Trouble and hunger in those burnt Towers, I suppose. Why did they not set him in the vault with his ancestors? It would have saved me a lonely job among the ghosts that haunt this place. What do you say, Father? Because the stone is cemented down and the entrance bricked up, and there is no mason to be found? Then why not have waited till one could be fetched? Oh, it is wonderful, all wonderful. But who am I that I should dare to ask questions? When the Lord Abbot orders, the lay-brother obeys, for he also is wonderful—a wonderful abbot.

"There, he is tidy now—straight on his back and his feet pointing to the east, at least I hope so, for I could take no good bearings in the dark; and the whole wonderful story comes to its wonderful end. So give me your hand out of this hole, Father, and say your prayers over the sinful body of this wicked fellow who dared to marry the maid he loved, and to let out the souls of certain holy monks, or rather of their hired rufflers, for monks don't fight, because they wished to separate those whom God—I mean the devil—had joined together, and to add their temporalities to the estate of Mother Church."

Then the old priest, who was shivering with cold, and understood little of this dark talk, began to mumble his ritual, skipping those parts of it which he could not remember. So another grain was planted in the cornfields of death and immortality, though when and where it should grow and what it should bear he neither knew nor cared, who wished to escape from fears and fightings back to his accustomed cell.

It was done, and he and the bearers departed, beating their way against the rough, raw wind, and leaving Thomas Bolle to fill in the grave, which, so long as they were in sight, or rather hearing, he did with much vigour. When they were gone, however, he descended into the hole under pretence of trampling the loose soil, and there, to be out of the wind, sat himself down upon the feet of the corpse and waited, full of reflections.

"Sir Christopher dead," he muttered to himself. "I knew his grandfather when I was a lad, and my grandfather told me that he knew his grandfather's great-grandfather—say three hundred years of them—and now I sit on the cold toes of the last of the lot, butchered like a mad ox in his own yard by a Spanish priest and his hirelings, to win his wife's goods. Oh! yes, it is wonderful, all very wonderful; and the Lady Cicely dead, burnt like a common witch. And Emlyn dead—Emlyn, whom I have hugged many a time in this very churchyard, before they whipped her into marrying that fat old grieve and made a monk of me.

"Well, I had her first kiss, and, by the saints! how she cursed old Stower all the way down yonder path. I stood behind that tree and heard her. She said he would die soon, and he did, and his brat with him. She said she would dance on his grave, and she did; I saw her do it in the moonlight the night after he was buried; dressed in white she danced on his grave! She always kept her promises, did Emlyn. That's her blood. If her mother had not been a gypsy witch, she wouldn't have married a Spaniard when every man in the place was after her for her beautiful eyes. Emlyn is a witch too, or was, for they say she is dead; but I can't think it, she isn't the sort that dies. Still, she must be dead, and that's good for my soul. Oh! miserable man, what are you thinking? Get behind me, Satan, if you can find room. A grave is no place for you, Satan, but I wish you were in it with me, Emlyn. You must have been a witch, since, after you, I could never fancy any other woman, which is against nature, for all's fish that comes to a man's net. Evidently a witch of the worst sort, but, my darling, witch or no I wish you weren't dead, and I'll break that Abbot's neck for you yet, if it costs me my soul. Oh! Emlyn, my darling, my darling, do you remember how we kissed in the copse by the river? Never was there a woman who could love like you."

So he moaned on, rocking himself to and fro on the legs of the corpse, till at length a wild ray from the red, risen sun crept into the darksome hole, lighting first of all upon a mouldering skull which Bolle had thrown back among the soil. He rose up and pitched it out with a word that should not have passed the lips of a lay-brother, even as such thoughts should not have passed his mind. Then he set himself to a task which he had planned in the intervals of his amorous meditations—a somewhat grizzly task.

Drawing his knife from its sheath, he cut the rough stitching of the grave-clothes, and, with numb hands, dragged them away from the body's head.

The light went out behind a cloud, but, not to waste time, he began to feel the face.

"Sir Christopher's nose wasn't broken," he muttered to himself, "unless it were in that last fray, and then the bone would be loose, and this is stiff. No, no, he had a very pretty nose."

The light came again, and Thomas peered down at the dead face beneath him; then suddenly burst into a hoarse laugh.

"By all the saints! here's another of our Spaniard's tricks. It is drunken Andrew the Scotchman, turned into a dead English knight. Christopher killed him, and now he is Christopher. But where's Christopher?"

He thought a little while, then, jumping out of the grave, began to fill it in with all his might.

"You're Christopher," he said; "well, stop Christopher until I can prove you're Andrew. Good-bye, Sir Andrew Christopher; I am off to seek your betters. If you are dead, who may not be alive? Emlyn herself, perhaps, after this. Oh, the devil is playing a merry game round old Cranwell Towers to-night, and Thomas Bolle will take a hand in it."

He was right. The devil was playing a merry game. At least, so thought others beside Thomas. For instance, that misguided but honest bigot, Martin, as he contemplated the still senseless form of Christopher, who, re-christened Brother Luiz, had been safely conveyed aboard the Great Yarmouth, and now, whether dead or living, which he was not sure, lay in the little cabin that had been allotted to the two of them. Almost did Martin, as he looked at him and shook his bald head, seem to smell brimstone in that close place, which, as he knew well, was the fiend's favourite scent.

The captain also, a sour-faced mariner with a squint, known in Dunwich, whence he hailed, as Miser Goody, because of his earnestness in pursuing wealth and his skill in hoarding it, seemed to feel the unhallowed influence of his Satanic Majesty. So far everything had gone wrong upon this voyage, which already had been delayed six weeks, that is, till the very worst period of the year, while he waited for certain mysterious letters and cargo which his owners said he must carry to Seville. Then he had sailed out of the river with a fair wind, only to be beaten back by fearful weather that nearly sank the ship.

Item: six of his best men had deserted because they feared a trip to Spain at that season, and he had been obliged to take others at hazard. Among them was a broad-shouldered, black-bearded fellow clad in a leather jerkin, with spurs upon his heels—bloody spurs—that he seemed to have found no time to take off. This hard rider came aboard in a skiff after the anchor was up, and, having cast the skiff adrift, offered good money for a passage to Spain or any other foreign port, and paid it down upon the nail. He, Goody, had taken the money, though with a doubtful heart, and given a receipt to the name of Charles Smith, asking no questions, since for this gold he need not account to the owners. Afterwards also the man, having put off his spurs and soldier's jerkin, set himself to work among the crew, some of whom seemed to know him, and in the storm that followed showed that he was stout-hearted and useful, though not a skilled sailor.

Still, he mistrusted him of Charles Smith, and his bloody spurs, and had he not been so short-handed and taken the knave's broad pieces would have liked to set him ashore again when they were driven back into the river, especially as he heard that there had been man-slaying about Blossholme, and that Sir John Foterell lay slaughtered in the forest. Perhaps this Charles Smith had murdered him. Well, if so, it was no affair of his, and he could not spare a hand.

Now, when at length the weather had moderated, just as he was hauling up his anchor, comes the Abbot of Blossholme, on whose will he had been bidden to wait, with a lean-faced monk and another passenger, said to be a sick religious, wrapped up in blankets and to all appearance dead.

Why, wondered that astute mariner Goody, should a sick monk wear harness, for he felt it through the blankets as he helped him up the ladder, although monk's shoes were stuck upon his feet. And why, as he saw when the covering slipped aside for a moment, was his crown bound up with bloody cloths?

Indeed, he ventured to question the Abbot as to this mysterious matter while his Lordship was paying the passage money in his cabin, only to get a very sharp answer.

"Were you not commanded to obey me in all things, Captain Goody, and does obedience lie in prying out my business? Another word and I will report you to those in Spain who know how to deal with mischief- makers. If you would see Dunwich again, hold your peace."

"Your pardon, my Lord Abbot," said Goody; "but things go so upon this ship that I grow afraid. That is an ill voyage upon which one lifts anchor twice in the same port."

"You will not make them go better, captain, by seeking to nose out my affairs and those of the Church. Do you desire that I should lay its curse upon you?"

"Nay, your Reverence, I desire that you should take the curse off," answered Goody, who was very superstitious. "Do that and I'll carry a dozen sick priests to Spain, even though they choose to wear chain shirts—for penance."

The Abbot smiled, then, lifting his hand, pronounced some words in Latin, which, as he did not understand them, Goody found very comforting. As they passed his lips the Great Yarmouth began to move, for the sailors were hoisting up her anchor.

"As I do not accompany you on this voyage, fare you well," he said. "The saints go with you, as shall my prayers. Since you will not pass the Gibraltar Straits, where I hear many infidel pirates lurk, given good weather your voyage should be safe and easy. Again farewell. I commend Brother Martin and our sick friend to your keeping, and shall ask account of them when we meet again."

I pray it may not be this side of hell, for I do not like that Spanish Abbot and his passengers, dead or living, thought Goody to himself, as he bowed him from the cabin.

A minute later the Abbot, after a few earnest, hurried words with Martin, began to descend the ladder to the boat, that, manned by his own people, was already being drawn slowly through the water. As he did so he glanced back, and, in the clinging mist of dawn, which was almost as dense as wool, caught sight of the face of a man who had been ordered to hold the ladder, and knew it for that of Jeffrey Stokes, who had escaped from the slaying of Sir John—escaped with the damning papers that had cost his master's life. Yes, Jeffrey Stokes, no other. His lips shaped themselves to call out something, but before ever a syllable had passed them an accident happened.

To the Abbot it seemed as though the whole ship had struck him violently behind—so violently that he was propelled headfirst among the rowers in the boat, and lay there hurt and breathless.

"What is it?" called the captain, who heard the noise.

"The Abbot slipped, or the ladder slipped, I know not which," answered Jeffrey gruffly, staring at the toe of his sea-boot. "At least he is safe enough in the boat now," and, turning, he vanished aft into the mist, muttering to himself—

"A very good kick, though a little high. Yet I wish it had been off another kind of ladder. That murdering rogue would look well with a rope round his neck. Still I dared do no more and it served to stop his lying mouth before he betrayed me. Oh, my poor master, my poor old master!"

Bruised and sore as he was—and he was very sore—within little over an hour Abbot Maldon was back at the ruin of Cranwell Towers. It seemed strange that he should go there, but in truth his uneasy heart would not let him rest. His plans had succeeded only far too well. Sir John Foterell was dead—a crime, no doubt, but necessary, for had the knight lived to reach London with that evidence in his pocket, his own life and those of many others might have paid the price of it, since who knows what truths may be twisted from a victim on the rack? Maldon had always feared the rack; it was a nightmare that haunted his sleep, although the ambitious cunning of his nature and the cause he served with heart and soul prompted him to put himself in continual danger of that fate.

In an unguarded moment, when his tongue was loosed with wine, he had placed himself in the power of Sir John Foterell, hoping to win him to the side of Spain, and afterwards, forgetting it, made of him a dreadful enemy. Therefore this enemy must die, for had he lived, not only might he himself have died in place of him, but all his plans for the rebellion of the Church against the Crown must have come to nothing. Yes, yes, that deed was lawful, and pardon for it assured should the truth become known. Till this morning he had hoped that it never would be known, but now Jeffrey Stokes had escaped upon the ship Great Yarmouth.

Oh, if only he had seen him a minute earlier; if only something—could it have been that impious knave, Jeffrey? he wondered—had not struck him so violently in the back and hurled him to the boat, where he lay almost senseless till the vessel had glided from them down the river! Well, she was gone, and Jeffrey in her. He was but a common serving-man, after all, who, if he knew anything, would never have the wit to use his knowledge, although it was true he had been wise enough to fly from England.

No papers had been discovered upon Sir John's body, and no money. Without doubt the old knight had found time to pass them on to Jeffrey, who now fled the kingdom disguised as a sailor. Oh! what ill chance had put him on board the same vessel with Sir Christopher Harflete?

Well, Sir Christopher would probably die; were Brother Martin a little less of a fool he would certainly die, but the fact remained that this monk, though able, in such matters was a fool, with a conscience that would not suit itself to circumstances. If Christopher could be saved, Martin would save him, as he had already saved him in the shed, even if he handed him over to the Inquisition afterwards. Still, he might slip through his fingers or the vessel might be lost, as was devoutly to be prayed, and seemed not unlikely at this season of the year. Also, the first opportunity must be taken to send certain messages to Spain that might result in hampering the activities of Brother Martin, and of Sir Christopher Harflete, if he lived to reach that land.

Meanwhile, reflected Maldon, other things had gone wrong. He had wished to proclaim his wardship over Cicely and to immure her in a nunnery because of her great possessions, which he needed for the cause, but he had not wished her death. Indeed, he was fond of the girl, whom he had known from a child, and her innocent blood was a weight that he ill could bear, he who at heart always shrank from the shedding of blood. Still, Heaven had killed her, not he, and the matter could not now be mended. Also, as she was dead, her inheritance would, he thought, fall into his hands without further trouble, for he—a mitred Abbot with a seat among the Lords of the realm—had friends in London, who, for a fee, could stifle inquiry into all this far-off business.

No, no, he must not be faint-hearted, who, after all, had much for which to be thankful. Meanwhile the cause went on—that great cause of the threatened Church to which he had devoted his life. Henry the heretic would fall; the Spanish Emperor, whose spy he was and who loved him well, would invade and take England. He would yet live to see the Holy Inquisition at work at Westminster, and himself—yes, himself; had it not been hinted to him?—enthroned at Canterbury, the Cardinal's red hat he coveted upon his head, and—oh, glorious thought!—perhaps afterwards wearing the triple crown at Rome.

Rain was falling heavily when the Abbot, with his escort of two monks and half-a-dozen men-at-arms, rode up to Cranwell. The house was now but a smoking heap of ashes, mingled with charred beams and burnt clay, in the midst of which, scarcely visible through the clouds of steam caused by the falling rain, rose the grim old Norman tower, for on its stonework the flames had beat vainly.

"Why have we come here?" asked one of the monks, surveying the dismal scene with a shudder.

"To seek the bodies of the Lady Cicely and her woman, and give them Christian burial," answered the Abbot.

"After bringing them to a most unchristian death," muttered the monk to himself, then added aloud, "You were ever charitable, my Lord Abbot, and though she defied you, such is that noble lady's due. As for the nurse Emlyn, she was a witch, and did but come to the end that she deserved, if she be really dead."

"What mean you?" asked the Abbot sharply.

"I mean that, being a witch, the fire may have turned from her."

"Pray God, then, that it turned from her mistress also! But it cannot be. Only a fiend could have lived in the heat of that furnace; look, even the tower is gutted."

"No, it cannot be," answered the monk; "so, since we shall never find them, let us chant the Burial Office over this great grave of theirs and begone—the sooner the better, for yon place has a haunted look."

"Not till we have searched out their bones, which must be beneath the tower yonder, whereon we saw them last," replied the Abbot, adding in a low voice, "Remember, Brother, the Lady Cicely had jewels of great price, which, if they were wrapped in leather, the fire may have spared, and these are among our heritage. At Shefton they cannot be found; therefore they must be here, and the seeking of them is no task for common folk. That is why I hurried hither so fast. Do you understand?"

The monk nodded his head. Having dismounted, they gave their horses to the serving-men and began to make an examination of the ruin, the Abbot leaning on his inferior's arm, for he was in great pain from the blow in the back that Jeffrey had administered with his sea-boot, and the bruises which he had received in falling to the boat.

First they passed under the gatehouse, which still stood, only to find that the courtyard beyond was so choked with smouldering rubbish that they could make no entry—for it will be remembered that the house had fallen outwards. Here, however, lying by the carcass of a horse, they found the body of one of the men whom Christopher had killed in his last stand, and caused it to be borne out. Then, followed by their people, leaving the dead man in the gateway, they walked round the ruin, keeping on the inner side of the moat, till they came to the little pleasaunce garden at its back.

"Look," said the monk in a frightened voice, pointing to some scorched bushes that had been a bower.

The Abbot did so, but for a while could see nothing because of the wreaths of steam. Presently a puff of wind blew these aside, and there, standing hand in hand, he beheld the figures of two women. His men beheld them also, and called aloud that these were the ghosts of Cicely and Emlyn. As they spoke the figures, still hand in hand, began to walk towards them, and they saw that they were Cicely and Emlyn indeed, but in the flesh, quite unharmed.

For a moment there was deep silence; then the Abbot asked—

"Whence come you, Mistress Cicely?"

"Out of the fire," she answered in a small, cold voice.

"Out of the fire! How did you live through the fire?"

"God sent His angel to save us," she answered, again in that small voice.

"A miracle," muttered the monk; "a true miracle!"

"Or mayhap Emlyn Stower's witchcraft," exclaimed one of the men behind; and Maldon started at his words.

"Lead me to my husband, my Lord Abbot, lest, thinking me dead, his heart should break," said Cicely.

Now again there was silence so deep that they could hear the patter of every drop of falling rain. Twice the Abbot strove to speak, but could not, but at the third effort his words came.

"The man you call your husband, but who was not your husband, but your ravisher, was slain in the fray last night, Cicely Foterell."

She stood quite quiet for a while, as though considering his words, then said, in the same unnatural voice—

"You lie, my Lord Abbot. You were ever a liar, like your father the devil, for the angel told me so in the midst of the fire. Also he told me that, though I seemed to see him fall, Christopher is alive upon the earth—yes, and other things, many other things;" and she passed her hand before her eyes and held it there, as though to shut out the sight of her enemy's face.

Now the Abbot trembled in his terror, he who knew that he lied, though at that time none else there knew it. It was as though suddenly he had been haled before the Judgment-seat where all secrets must be bared.

"Some evil spirit has entered into you," he said huskily.

She dropped her hand, pointing at him.

"Nay, nay; I never knew but one evil spirit, and he stands before me."

"Cicely," he went on, "cease your blaspheming. Alas! that I must tell it you. Sir Christopher Harflete is dead and buried in yonder churchyard."

"What! So soon, and all uncoffined, he who was a noble knight? Then you buried him living, and, living, in a day to come he shall rise up against you. Hear my words, all. Christopher Harflete shall rise up living and give testimony against this devil in a monk's robe, and afterwards—afterwards—" and she laughed shrilly, then suddenly fell down and lay still.

Now Emlyn, the dark and handsome, as became her Spanish, or perhaps gypsy blood, who all this while had stood silent, her arms folded upon her high bosom, leaned down and looked at her. Then she straightened herself, and her face was like the face of a beautiful fiend.

"She is dead!" she screamed. "My dove is dead. She whom these breasts nursed, the greatest lady of all the wolds and all the vales, the Lady of Blossholme, of Cranwell and of Shefton, in whose veins ran the blood of mighty nobles, aye, and of old kings, is dead, murdered by a beggarly foreign monk, who not ten days gone butchered her father also yonder by King's Grave—yonder by the mere. Oh! the arrow in his throat! the arrow in his throat! I cursed the hand that shot it, and to-day that hand is blue beneath the mould. So, too, I curse you, Maldonado, evil-gifted one, Abbot consecrated by Satan, you and all your herd of butchers!" and she broke into the stream of Spanish imprecations whereof the Abbot knew the meaning well.

Presently Emlyn paused and looked behind her at the smouldering ruins.

"This house is burned," she cried; "well, mark Emlyn's words: even so shall your house burn, while your monks run squeaking like rats from a flaming rick. You have stolen the lands; they shall be taken from you, and yours also, every acre of them. Not enough shall be left to bury you in, for, priest, you'll need no burial. The fowls of the air shall bury you, and that's the nearest you will ever get to heaven—in their filthy crops. Murderer, if Christopher Harflete is dead, yet he shall live, as his lady swore, for his seed shall rise up against you. Oh! I forgot; how can it, how can it, seeing that she is dead with him, and their bridal coverlet has become a pall woven by the black monks? Yet it shall, it shall. Christopher Harflete's seed shall sit where the Abbots of Blossholme sat, and from father to son tell the tale of the last of them—the Spaniard who plotted against England's king and overshot himself."

Her rage veered like a hurricane wind. Forgetting the Abbot, she turned upon the monk at his side and cursed him. Then she cursed the hired men-at-arms, those present and those absent, many by name, and lastly—greatest crime of all—she cursed the Pope and the King of Spain, and called to God in heaven and Henry of England upon earth to avenge her Lady Cicely's wrongings, and the murder of Sir John Foterell, and the murder of Christopher Harflete, on each and all of them, individually and separately.

So fierce and fearful was her onslaught that all who heard her were reduced to utter silence. The Abbot and the monk leaned against each other, the soldiers crossed themselves and muttered prayers, while one of them, running up, fell upon his knees and assured her that he had had nothing to do with all this business, having only returned from a journey last night, and been called thither that morning.

Emlyn, who had paused from lack of breath, listened to him, and said—

"Then I take the curse off you and yours, John Athey. Now lift up my lady and bear her to the church, for there we will lay her out as becomes her rank; though not with her jewels, her great and priceless jewels, for which she was hunted like a doe. She must lie without her jewels; her pearls and coronet, and rings, her stomacher and necklets of bright gems, that were worth so much more than those beggarly acres—those that once a Sultan's woman wore. They are lost, though perhaps yonder Abbot has found them. Sir John Foterell bore them to London for safe keeping, and good Sir John is dead; footpads set on him in the forest, and an arrow shot from behind pierced his throat. Those who killed him have the jewels, and the dead bride must lie without them, adorned in the naked beauty that God gave to her. Lift her, John Athey, and you monks, set up your funeral chant; we'll to the church. The bride who knelt before the altar shall lie there before the altar—Clement Maldonado's last offering to God. First the father, then the husband, and now the wife—the sweet, new-made wife!"

So she raved on, while they stood before her dumb-founded, and the man lifted up Cicely. Then suddenly this same Cicely, whom all thought dead, opened her eyes and struggled from his arms to her feet.

"See," screamed Emlyn; "did I not tell you that Harflete's seed should live to be avenged upon all your tribe, and she stands there who will bear it? Now where shall we shelter till England hears this tale? Cranwell is down, though it shall rise again, and Shefton is stolen. Where shall we shelter?"

"Thrust away that woman," said the Abbot in a hoarse voice, "for her witchcrafts poison the air. Set the Lady Cicely on a horse and bear her to our Nunnery of Blossholme, where she shall be tended."

The men advanced to do his bidding, though very doubtfully. But Emlyn, hearing his words, ran to the Abbot and whispered something in his ear in a foreign tongue that caused him to cross himself and stagger back from her.

"I have changed my mind," he said to the servants. "Mistress Emlyn reminds me that between her and her lady there is the tie of foster- motherhood. They may not be separated as yet. Take them both to the Nunnery, where they shall dwell, and as for this woman's words, forget them, for she was mad with fear and grief, and knew not what she said. May God and His saints forgive her, as I do."

Chapter VII

The Abbot's Offer

The Nunnery at Blossholme was a peaceful place, a long, grey-gabled house set under the shelter of a hill and surrounded by a high wall. Within this wall lay also the great garden—neglected enough—and the chapel, a building that still was beautiful in its decay.

Once, indeed, Blossholme Priory, which was older than the Abbey, had been rich and famous. Its foundress in the time of the first Edward, a certain Lady Matilda, one of the Plantagenets, who retired from the world after her husband had been killed in the Crusade, being childless, endowed it with all her lands. Other noble ladies who accompanied her there, or sought its refuge in after days, had done likewise, so that it grew in power and in wealth, till at its most prosperous time over twenty nuns told their beads within its walls. Then the proud Abbey rose upon the opposing hill, and obtained some royal charter that the Pope confirmed, under which the Priory of Blossholme was affiliated to the Abbey of Blossholme, and the Abbot of Blossholme became the spiritual lord of its religious. From that day forward its fortunes began to decline, since under this pretext and that the abbots filched away its lands to swell their own estates.

So it came about that at the date of our history the total revenue of this Nunnery was but £130 a year of the money of the day, and even of this sum the Abbot took tithe and toll. Now in all the great house, that once had been so full, there dwelt but six nuns, one of whom was, in fact, a servant, while an aged monk from the Abbey celebrated Mass in the fair chapel where lay the bones of so many who had gone before. Also on certain feasts the Abbot himself attended, confessed the nuns, and granted them absolution and his holy blessing. On these days, too, he would examine their accounts, and if there were money in hand take a share of it to serve his necessities, for which reason the Prioress looked forward to his coming with little joy.

It was to this ancient home of peace that the distraught Cicely and her servant Emlyn were conveyed upon the morrow of the great burning. Indeed, Cicely knew it well enough already, since as a child during three years or more she had gone there daily to be taught by the Prioress Matilda, for every head of the Priory took this name in turn to the honour of their foundress and in accordance with the provisions of her will. Happy years they were, as these old nuns loved her in her youth and innocence, and she, too, loved them every one. Now, by the workings of fate, she was borne back to the same quiet room where she had played and studied—a new-made wife, a new-made widow.

But of all this poor Cicely knew nothing till three weeks or more had gone by, when at length her wandering brain cleared and she opened her eyes to the world again. At the moment she was alone, and lay looking about her. The place was familiar. She recognized the deep windows, the faded tapestries of Abraham cutting Isaac's throat with a butcher's knife, and Jonah being shot into the very gateway of a castle where his family awaited him, from the mouth of a gigantic carp with goggle eyes, for the simple artist had found his whale's model in a stewpond. Well she remembered those delightful pictures, and how often she had wondered whether Isaac could escape bleeding to death, or Jonah's wife, with the outspread arms, withstand the sudden shock of her husband's unexpected arrival out of the interior of the whale. There also was the splendid fireplace of wrought stone, and above it, cunningly carved in gilded oak, gleamed many coats-of-arms without crests, for they were those of sundry noble prioresses.

Yes, this was certainly the great guest-chamber of the Blossholme Priory, which, since the nuns had now few guests and many places in which to put them, had been given up to her, Sir John Foterell's heiress, as her schoolroom. There she lay, thinking that she was a child again, a happy, careless child, or that she dreamed, till presently the door opened and Mother Matilda appeared, followed by Emlyn, who bore a tray, on which stood a silver bowl that smoked. There was no mistaking Mother Matilda in her black Benedictine robe and her white whimple, wearing the great silver crucifix which was her badge of office, and the golden ring with an emerald bezel whereon was cut St. Catherine being broken on the wheel—the ancient ring which every Prioress of Blossholme had worn from the beginning. Moreover, who that had ever seen it could forget her sweet, old, high-bred face, with the fine lips, the arched nose, and the quick, kind grey eyes!

Cicely strove to rise and to do her reverence, as had been her custom during those childish years, only to find that she could not, for lo! she fell back heavily upon her pillow. Thereon Emlyn, setting down the tray with a clatter upon a table, ran to her, and putting her arms about her, began to scold, as was her fashion, but in a very gentle voice; and Mother Matilda, kneeling by her bed, gave thanks to Jesus and His blessed saints—though why she thanked Him at first Cicely did not understand.

"Am I ill, reverend Mother?" she asked.

"Not now, daughter, but you were very ill," answered the Prioress in her sweet, low voice. "Now we think that God has healed you."

"How long have I been here?" she asked.

The Mother began to reckon, counting her beads, one for every day—for in such places time slips by—but long before she had finished Emlyn replied quickly—

"Cranwell Towers was burned three weeks yesternight."

Then Cicely remembered, and with a bitter groan turned her face to the wall, while the Mother reproached Emlyn, saying she had killed her.

"I think not," answered the nurse in a low voice. "I think she has that which will not let her die"—a saying that puzzled the Prioress at this time.

Emlyn was right. Cicely did not die. On the contrary, she grew strong and well in her body, though it was long before her mind recovered. Indeed, she glided about the place like a ghost in her black mourning robe, for now she no longer doubted that Christopher was dead, and she, the wife of a week, widowed as well as orphaned.

Then in her utter desolation came comfort; a light broke on the darkness of her soul like the moon above a tortured midnight sea. She was no longer quite alone; the murdered Christopher had left his image with her. If she lived a child would be born to him, and therefore she would surely live. One evening, on her knees, she whispered her secret to the Prioress Matilda, whereat the old nun blushed like a girl, yet, after a moment's silent prayer, laid a thin hand upon her head in blessing.

"The Lord Abbot declares that your marriage was no true marriage, my daughter, though why I do not understand, since the man was he whom your heart chose, and you were wed to him by an ordained priest before God's altar and in presence of the congregation."

"I care not what he says," answered Cicely in a stubborn voice. "If I am not a true wife, then no woman ever was."

"Dear daughter," answered Mother Matilda, "it is not for us unlearned women to question the wisdom of a holy Abbot who doubtless is inspired from on high."

"If he is inspired it is not from on high, Mother. Would God or His saints teach him to murder my father and my husband, to seize my heritage, or to hold my person in this gentle prison? Such inspirations do not come from above, Mother."

"Hush! hush!" said the Prioress, glancing round her nervously; "your woes have crazed you. Besides, you have no proof. In this world there are so many things that we cannot understand. Being an abbot, how could he do wrong, although to us his acts seem wrong? But let us not talk of these matters, of which, indeed, I only know from that rough- tongued Emlyn of yours, who, I am told, was not afraid to curse him terribly. I was about to say that whatever may be the law of it, I hold your marriage good and true, and its issue, should such come to you, pure and holy, and night by night I will pray that it shall be crowned with Heaven's richest blessings."

"I thank you, dear Mother," answered Cicely, as she rose and left her.

When she had gone the Prioress rose also, and, with a troubled face, began to walk up and down the refectory, for it was here that they had spoken together. Truly she could not understand, for unless all these tales were false—and how could they be false?—this Abbot, whom her high-bred English nature had always mistrusted, this dark, able Spanish monk was no saint, but a wicked villain? There must be some explanation. It was only that she did not understand.

Soon the news spread throughout the Nunnery, and if the sisters had loved Cicely before, now they loved her twice as well. Of the doubts as to the validity to her marriage, like their Prioress, they took no heed, for had it not been celebrated in a church? But that a child was to be born among them—ah! that was a joyful thing, a thing that had not happened for quite two hundred years, when, alas!—so said tradition and their records—there had been a dreadful scandal which to this day was spoken of with bated breath. For be it known at once this Nunnery, whatever may or may not have been the case with some others, was one of which no evil could be said.

Beneath their black robes, however, these old nuns were still as much women as the mothers who bore them, and this news of a child stirred them to the marrow. Among themselves in their hours of recreation they talked of little else, and even their prayers were largely occupied with this same matter. Indeed, poor, weak-witted, old Sister Bridget, who hitherto had been secretly looked down upon because she was the only one of the seven who was not of gentle birth, now became very popular. For Sister Bridget in her youth had been married and borne two children, both of whom had been carried off by the smallpox after she was widowed, whereon, as her face was seamed by this same disease, so that she had no hope of another husband, as her neighbours said, or because her heart was broken, as she said, she entered into religion.

Now she constituted herself Cicely's chief attendant, and although that lady was quite well and strong, persecuted her with advice and with noxious mixtures which she brewed, till Emlyn, descending on her like a storm, hunted her from the room and cast her medicines through the window.

That these sisters should be thus interested in so small a matter was not, indeed, wonderful, seeing that if their lives had been secluded before, since the Lady Cicely came amongst them they were ten times more so. Soon they discovered that she and her servant, Emlyn Stower, were, in fact, prisoners, which meant that they, her hostesses, were prisoners also. None were allowed to enter the Nunnery save the silent old monk who confessed them and celebrated the Mass, nor, by an order of the Abbot, were they suffered to go abroad upon any business whatsoever.

For the rest, as their only means of communication with those who dwelt beyond was the surly gardener, who was deaf and set there to spy on them, little news ever reached them. They were almost dead to the world, which, had they known it, was busy enough just then with matters that concerned them and all other religious houses.

At length one day, when Cicely and Emlyn were seated in the garden beneath a flowering hawthorn-tree—for now June had come and with it warm weather—of a sudden Sister Bridget hurried up saying that the Abbot of Blossholme desired their presence. At this tidings Cicely turned faint, and Emlyn rated Bridget, asking if her few wits had left her, or if she thought that name was so pleasant to her mistress that she should suddenly bawl it in her ear.

Thereon the poor old soul, who was not too strong-brained and much afraid of Emlyn since she had thrown her medicines out of the window, began to weep, protesting that she had meant no harm, till Cicely, recovering, soothed her and sent her back to say that she would wait upon his lordship.

"Are you afraid of him, Mistress?" asked Emlyn, as they prepared to follow.

"A little, Nurse. He has shown himself a man to be afraid of, has he not? My father and my husband are in his net, and will he spare the last fish in the pool—a very narrow pool?" and she glanced at the high walls about her. "I fear lest he should take you from me, and wonder why he has not done so already."

"Because my father was a Spaniard, and through him I know that which would ruin him with his friends, the Pope and the Emperor. Also, he believes that I have the evil eye, and dreads my curse. Still, one day he may try to murder me; who knows? Only then the secret of the jewels will go with me, for that is mine alone; not yours even, for if you had it they would squeeze it out of you. Meanwhile he will try to profess you a nun, but push him off with soft words. Say that you will think of it after your child is born. Till then he can do nothing, and, if Mother Matilda's fresh tidings are true, by that time perchance there will be no more nuns in England."

Now very quietly and by the side door they were entering the old reception-hall, that was only used for the entertainment of visitors and on other great occasions, and close to them saw the Abbot seated in his chair, while the Prioress stood before him, rendering her accounts.

"Whether you can spare it or no," they heard him say sharply, "I must have the half-year's rent. The times are evil; we servants of the Lord are threatened by that adulterous king and his proud ministers, who swear they will strip us to the shirt and turn us out to starve. I'm but just from London, and, although our enemy Anne Boleyn has lost her wanton head, I tell you the danger is great. Money must be had to stir up rebellion, for who can arm without it, and but little comes from Spain. I am in treaty to sell the Foterell lands for what they will fetch, but as yet can give no title. Either that stiff-necked girl must sign a release, or she must profess, for otherwise, while she lives, some lawyer or relative might upset the sale. Is she yet prepared to take her first vows? If not, I shall hold you much to blame."

"Nay," answered the Prioress; "there are reasons. You have been away, and have not heard"—she hesitated and looked about her nervously, to see Cicely and Emlyn standing behind them. "What do you there, daughter?" she asked, with as much asperity as she ever showed.

"In truth I know not, Mother," answered Cicely. "Sister Bridget told us that the Lord Abbot desired our presence."

"I bid her say that you were to wait him in my chamber," said the Prioress in a vexed voice.

"Well," broke in the Abbot, "it would seem that you have a fool for a messenger; if it is that pockmarked hag, her brain has been gone for years. Ward Cicely, I greet you, though after the sorrows that have fallen on you, whereof by your leave we will not speak, since there is no use in stirring up such memories, I grieve to see you in that worldly garb, who thought you would have changed it for a better. But ere you entered the holy Mother here spoke of some obstacle that stood between you and God. What is it? Perchance my counsel may be of service. Not this woman, as I trust," and he frowned at Emlyn, who at once answered, in her steady voice—

"Nay, my Lord Abbot, I stand not between her and God and His holiness, but between her and man and his iniquity. Still I can tell you of that obstacle—which comes from God—if you so need."

Now the old Prioress, blushing to her white hair, bent forward and whispered in the Abbot's ear words at which he sprang up as though a wasp had stung him.

"Pest on it! it cannot be," he said. "Well, well, there it is, and must be swallowed with the rest. Pity, though," he added, with a sneer on his dark face, "since many a year has gone by since these walls have seen a bastard, and, as things are, that may pull them down about your ears."

"I know such brats are dangerous," interrupted Emlyn, looking Maldon full in the eyes; "my father told me of a young monk in Spain—I forget his name—who brought certain ladies to the torture in some such matter. But who talks of bastards in the case of Dame Cicely Harflete, widow of Sir Christopher Harflete, slain by the Abbot of Blossholme?"

"Silence, woman. Where there is no lawful marriage there can be no lawful child—"

"To take that lawful inheritance that it lawfully inherits. Say, my Lord Abbot, did Sir Christopher make you his heir also?"

Then, before he could answer, Cicely, who had been silent all this while, broke in—

"Heap what insults you will on me, my Lord Abbot, and having robbed me of my father, my husband, and my heart, rob me of my goods also, if you can. In my case it matters little. But slander not my child, if one should be born to me, nor dare to touch its rights. Think not that you can break the mother as you broke the girl, for there you will find that you have a she-wolf by the ear."

He looked at her, they all looked at her, for in her eyes was something that compelled theirs. Clement Maldon, who knew the world and how a she-wolf can fight for its cub, read in them a warning which caused him to change his tone.

"Tut, tut, daughter," he said; "what is the good of vapouring of a child that is not and may never be? When it comes I will christen it, and we will talk."

"When it comes you will not lay a finger on it. I'd rather that it went unbaptized to its grave than marked with your cross of blood."

He waved his hand.

"There is another matter, or rather two, of which I must speak to you, my daughter. When do you take your first vows?"

"We will talk of it after my child is born. 'Tis a child of sin, you say, and I am unrepentant, a wicked woman not fit to take a holy vow, to which, moreover, you cannot force me," she replied, with bitter sarcasm.

Again he waved his hand, for the she-wolf showed her teeth.

"The second matter is," he went on, "that I need your signature to a writing. It is nothing but a form, and one I fear you cannot read, nor in faith can I," and with a somewhat doubtful smile he drew out a crabbed indenture and spread it before her on the table.

"What?" she laughed, brushing aside the parchment. "Have you remembered that yesterday I came of age, and am, therefore, no more your ward, if such I ever was? You should have sold my inheritance more swiftly, for now the title you can give is rotten as last year's apples, and I'll sign nothing. Bear witness, Mother Matilda, and you, Emlyn Stower, that I have signed and will sign nothing. Clement Maldon, Abbot of Blossholme, I am a free woman of full age, even though, as you say, I am a wanton. Where is your right to chain up a wanton who is no religious? Unlock these gates and let me go."

Now he felt the wolf's fangs, and they were sharp.

"Whither would you go?" he asked.

"Whither but to the King, to lay my cause before him, as my father would have done last Christmas-time."

It was a bold speech, but foolish. The she-wolf had loosed her hold to growl—to growl at a hunter with a bloody sword.

"I think your father never reached his Grace with his sack of falsehoods; nor might you, Cicely Foterell. The times are rough, rebellion is in the air, and many wild men hunt the woods and roads. No, no; for your own sake you bide here in safety till—"

"Till you murder me. Oh! it is in your mind. Do you remember the angel who spoke with me in the fire and told me my husband was not dead?"

"A lying spirit, then; no angel."

"I am not so sure," and again she passed her hand across her eyes, as she had done in that dreadful dawn at Cranwell. "Well, I prayed to God to help me, and last night that angel came again and spoke in my sleep. He told me to fear you not at all, my Lord Abbot; however sore my case and however near my death might seem, since God had shaped a stone to drop upon your head. He showed it me; it was like an axe."

Now the old Prioress held up her hands and gasped in horror, but the Abbot leapt from his seat in rage—or was it fear?

"Wanton, you named yourself," he exclaimed; "but I name you witch also, who, if you had your deserts, should die the death of a witch by fire. Mother Matilda, I command you, on your oath, keep this witch fast and make report to me of all her sorceries. It is not fitting that such a one should walk abroad to bring evil on the innocent. Witch and wanton, begone to your chamber!"

Cicely listened, then, without another word, broke into a little scornful laugh, and, turning, left the room, followed by the Prioress.

But Emlyn did not go; she stayed behind, a smile on her dark, handsome face.

"You've lost the throw, though all your dice were loaded," she said boldly.

The Abbot turned on her and reviled her.

"Woman," he said, "if she is a witch, you're the familiar, and certainly you shall burn even though she escape. It is you who taught her how to call up the devil."

"Then you had best keep me living, my Lord Abbot, that I may teach her how to lay him. Nay, threaten not. Why, the rack might make me speak, and the birds of the air carry the matter!"

His face paled; then suddenly he asked—

"Where are those jewels? I need them. Give me the jewels and you shall go free, and perchance your accursed mistress with you."

"I told you," she answered. "Sir John took them to London, and if they were not found upon his body, then either he threw them away or Jeffrey Stokes carried them to wherever he has gone. Drag the mere, search the forest, find Jeffrey and ask him."

"You lie, woman. When you and your mistress fled from Shefton a servant there saw you with the box that held those jewels in your hand."

"True, my Lord Abbot, but it no longer held them; only my mistress's love-letters, which she would not leave behind."

"Then where is the box, and where are those letters?"

"We grew short of fuel in the siege, and burned both. When a woman has her man she doesn't want his letters. Surely, Maldonado," she added, with meaning, "you should know that it is not always wise to keep old letters. What, I wonder, would you give for some that I have seen and that are not burned?"

"Accursed spawn of Satan," hissed the Abbot, "how dare you flaunt me thus? When Cicely was wed to Christopher she wore those very gems; I have it from those who saw her decked in them—the necklace on her bosom, the priceless rosebud pearls hanging from her ears."

"Oho! oho!" said Emlyn; "so you own that she was wed, the pure soul whom but now you called a wanton. Look you, Sir Abbot, we will fence no more. She wore the jewels. Jeffrey took nothing hence save your death-warrant."

"Then where are they?" he asked, striking his fist upon the table.

"Where? Why, where you'll never follow them—gone up to heaven in the fire. Thinking we might be robbed, I hid them behind a secret panel in her chamber, purposing to return for them later. Go, rake out the ashes; you might find a cracked diamond or two, but not the pearls; they fly in fire. There, that's the truth at last, and much good may it do to you."

The Abbot groaned. Like most Spaniards he was emotional, and could not help it; his bitterness burst from his heart.

Emlyn laughed at him.

"See how the wise and mighty of this world overshoot themselves," she said. "Clement Maldonado, I have known you for some twenty years, and when I was called the Beauty of Blossholme, and the Abbot who went before you made me the Church's ward, though I ever hated you, who hunted down my father, you had softer words for me than those you name me by to-day. Well, I have watched you rise and I shall watch you fall, and I know your heart and its desires. Money is what you lust for and must have, for otherwise how will you gain your end? It was the jewels that you needed, not the Shefton lands, which are worth little now-a-days, and will soon be worth less. Why, one of those pink pearls placed among the Jews would buy three parishes, with their halls thrown in. For the sake of those jewels you have brought death on some and misery on some, and on your own soul damnation without end, though had you but been wise and consulted me—why, they, or some of them, might have been yours. Sir John was no fool; he would have parted with a pearl or two, of which he did not know the value, to end a feud against the Church and safeguard his title and his daughter. And now, in your madness, you've burnt them—burnt a king's ransom, or what might have pulled down a king. Oh! had you but guessed it, you'd have hacked off the hand that put a torch to Cranwell Towers, for now the gold you need is lacking to you, and therefore all your grand schemes will fail, and you'll be buried in their ruin, as you thought we were in Cranwell."

The Abbot, who had listened to this long and bitter speech in patience, groaned again.

"You are a clever woman," he said; "we understand each other, coming from the same blood. You know the case; what is your counsel to me now?"

"That which you will not take, being foredoomed for your sins. Still I'll give it honestly. Set the Lady Cicely free, restore her lands, confess your evil doings. Fly the kingdom before Cromwell turns on you and Henry finds you out, taking with you all the gold that you can gather, and bribe the Emperor Charles to give you a bishopric in Granada or elsewhere—not near Seville, for reasons that you know. So shall you live honoured, and one day, after you have been dead a long while and many things are forgotten, perchance be beatified as Saint Clement of Blossholme."

The Abbot looked at her reflectively.

"If I sought safety only and old age comforts your counsel might be good, but I play for higher stakes."

"You set your head against them," broke in Emlyn.

"Not so, woman, for in any case that head must win. If it stays upon my shoulders it will wear an archbishop's mitre, or a cardinal's hat, or perhaps something nobler yet; and if it parts from them, why, then a heavenly crown of glory."

"Your head? Your head?" exclaimed Emlyn, with a contemptuous laugh.

"Why not?" he answered gravely. "You chance to know of some errors of my youth, but they are long ago repented of, and for such there is plentiful forgiveness," and he crossed himself. "Were it not so, who would escape?"

Emlyn, who had been standing all this while, sat herself down, set her elbows on the table and rested her chin upon her clenched hands.

"True," she said, looking him in the eyes; "none of us would escape. But, Clement Maldon, how about the unrepented errors of your age? Sir John Foterell, for instance; Sir Christopher Harflete, for instance; my Lady Cicely, for instance; to say nothing of black treason and a few other matters?"

"Even were all these charges true, which I deny, they are no sins, seeing that they would have been done, every one of them, not for my own sake, but for that of the Church, to overset her enemies, to rebuild her tottering walls, to secure her eternally in this realm."

"And to lift you, Clement Maldon, to the topmost pinnacle of her temple, whence Satan shows you all the kingdoms of the world, swearing that they shall be yours."

Apparently the Abbot did not resent this bold speech; indeed, Emlyn's apt illustration seemed to please him. Only he corrected her gently, saying—

"Not Satan, but Satan's Lord." Then he paused a while, looked round the chamber to see that the doors were shut and make sure that they were alone, and went on, "Emlyn Stower, you have great wits and courage—more than any woman that I know. Also you have knowledge both of the world and of what lies beyond it, being what superstitious fools call a witch, but I, a prophetess or a seer. These things come to you with your blood, I suppose, seeing that your mother was of a gypsy tribe and your father a high-bred Spanish gentleman, very learned and clever, though a pestilent heretic, for which cause he fled for his life from Spain."

"To find his dark death in England. The Holy Inquisition is patent and has a long arm. If I remember right, also it was this business of the heresy of my father that first brought you to Blossholme, where, after his vanishing and the public burning of that book of his, you so greatly prospered."

"You are always right, Emlyn, and therefore I need not tell you further that we had been old enemies in Spain, which is why I was chosen to hunt him down and how you come to know certain things."

She nodded, and he went on—

"So much for the heretic father—now for the gypsy mother. She died, by her own hand it is said, to escape the punishment of the law."

"No need to beat about the bush, Abbot; let's have truth between old friends. You mean, to escape being burnt by you as a witch, because she had the letters which were not burned and threatened to use them—as I do."

"Why rake up such tales, Emlyn?" he interposed blandly. "At least she died, but not until she had taught you all she knew. The rest of the history is short. You fell in love with old yeoman Bolle's son, or said you did—that same great, silly Thomas who is now a lay-brother at the Abbey—"

"Or said I did," she repeated. "At least he fell in love with me, and perhaps I wished an honest man to protect me, who in those days was young and fair. Moreover, he was not silly then. That came upon him after he fell into your hands. Oh! have done with it," she went on, in a voice of suppressed passion. "The witch's fair daughter was the Church's ward, and you ruled the Abbot of that time, and he forced me into marriage with old Peter Stower, as his third wife. I cursed him, and he died, as I warned him that he would, and I bore a child, and it died. Then with what was left to me I took refuge with Sir John Foterell, who ever was my friend, and became foster-mother to his daughter, the only creature, save one, that I have loved in this wide, wicked world. That's all the story; and now what more do you want of me, Clement Maldonado—evil-gifted one?"

"Emlyn, I want what I always wanted and you always refused—your help, your partnership. I mean the partnership of that brain of yours—the help of the knowledge that you have—no more. At Cranwell Towers you called down evil on me. Take off that ban, for I'll speak truth, it weighs heavy on my mind. Let us bury the past; let us clasp hands and be friends. You have the true vision. Do you remember that when you thought Cicely dead, you said that her seed should rise up against me, and now it seems that it will be so."

"What would you give me?" asked Emlyn curiously.

"I will give you wealth; I will give you what you love more—power, and rank too, if you wish it. The whole Church shall listen to you. What you desire shall be done in this realm—yes, and across the world. I speak no lie; I pledge my soul on it, and the honour of those I serve, which I have authority to do. In return all I ask of you is your wisdom—that you should read the future for me, that you should show me which way to walk."

"Nothing more?"

"Yes, two things—that you should find me those burned jewels and with them the old letters that were not burned, and that this child of the Lady Cicely shall not chance to live to take what you promised to it. Her life I give you, for a nun more or less can matter little."

"A noble offer, and in this case I am sure you will pay what you promise—should you live. But what if I refuse?"

"Then," answered the Abbot, dropping his fist upon the table, "then death for both of you—the witch's death, for I dare not let you go to work my ruin. Remember, I am master here, you are my prisoners. Few know that you live in this place, except a handful of weak-brained women who will fear to speak—puppets that must dance when I pull the string—and I'll see that no soul shall come near these walls. Choose, then, between death and all its terrors or life and all its hopes."

On the table there stood a wooden bowl filled with roses. Emlyn drew it to her, and taking the roses into her hands, threw them to the floor. Then she waited for the water to steady, saying—

"The riddle is hard; perhaps, if in truth I have such power, I shall find its answer here." Presently, as he gazed at her, fascinated, she breathed upon the water and stared into it for a long while. At length she looked up, and said—

"Death or Life; that was the choice you gave me. Well, Clement Maldonado, on behalf of myself and the Lady Cicely, and her husband Sir Christopher, and the child that shall be born, and of God who directs all these things, I choose—death."

There was a solemn silence. Then the Abbot rose, and said—

"Good! On your own head be it."

Again there was a silence, and, as she made no answer, he turned and walked towards the door, leaving her still staring into the bowl.

"Good!" she repeated, as he laid his hand upon the latch. "I have told you that I choose death, but I have not told you whose death it is I choose. Play your game, my Lord Abbot, and I'll play mine, remembering that God holds the stakes. Meanwhile I confirm the words I spoke in my rage at Cranwell. Expect evil, for I see now that it shall fall on you and all with which you have to do."

Then with a sudden movement she upset the bowl upon the table and watched him go.

Chapter VIII

Emlyn Calls Her Man

One by one the weeks passed over the heads of Cicely and Emlyn in their prison, and brought them neither hope nor tidings. Indeed, although they could not see its cords, they felt that the evil net which held them was drawing ever tighter. There were fear and pity as well as love in the eyes of Mother Matilda when she looked at Cicely, which she did only if she thought that no one observed her. The nuns also were afraid, though it was clear that they knew not of what. One evening Emlyn, finding the Prioress alone, sprang questions on her, asking what was in the wind, and why her lady, a free woman of full age, was detained there against her will.

The old nun's face grew secret. She answered that she did not know of anything unusual, and that, as regarded the detention, she must obey the commands of her spiritual superior.

"Then," burst out Emlyn, "I tell you that you do so at your peril. I tell you that whether my lady lives or dies, there are those who will call you to a strict account, aye, and those who will listen to the prayer of the helpless. Mother Matilda, England is not the land it was when as a girl they buried you in these mouldy walls. Where does God say that you have the right to hold free women like felons in a jail? Tell me."

"I cannot," moaned Mother Matilda, wringing her thin hands. "The right is very hard to find, this place is strictly guarded, and whatever I may think, I must do what I am bid, lest my soul should suffer."

"Your soul! You cloistered women think always of your miserable souls, but of those of other folk, aye, and of their bodies too, nothing. Then you'll not help me?"

"I cannot, I cannot, who am myself in bonds," she replied again.

"So be it, Mother; then I'll help myself, and when I do, God help you all," and with a contemptuous shrug of her broad shoulders she walked away, leaving the poor old Prioress almost in tears.

Emlyn's threats were bold as her own heart, but how could she execute even a tenth of them? The right was on their side, indeed, but, as many a captive has found in those and other days, right is no Joshua's trumpet to cause high walls to fall. Moreover, Cicely would not aid her. Now that her husband was dead she took interest in one thing only—his child who was to be.

For the rest she seemed to care nothing. Since she had no friends with whom she could communicate, and her wealth, as she understood, had been taken from her, what better place, she asked, could there be for that child to see the light than in this quiet Nunnery? When it was born and she was well again she would consider other matters. Meanwhile she was languid, and why was Emlyn always prating to her of freedom? If she were free, what should she do and whither should she go? The nuns were very kind to her; they loved her as she did them.

So she talked on, and Emlyn, listening, did not dare to tell her the truth: that here she feared for the life of her child, dreading lest that news might bring about the death of both of them. So she let her be, and fell back on her own wits.

First she thought of escape, only to abandon the idea, for her mistress was in no state to face its perils. Moreover, whither should they go? Then rescue came into her mind, but, alas! who would rescue them? The great men in London, perhaps, as a matter of policy, but great men are hard to come at, even for the free. If she were free she might find means to make them listen, but she was not, nor could she leave her lady at such a time. What remained, then? So to contrive that they should be set free.

Perhaps it might be done at a price—that of Cicely's jewels, of which she alone knew the hiding-place, and with them a deed of indemnity against her persecutors. Emlyn was not minded to give either. Moreover, she guessed that it might be in vain. Once outside those walls, they knew too much to be allowed to live. And yet within those walls Cicely's child would not be allowed to live—the child that was heir to all. What, then, could loose them and make them safe?

Terror, perhaps—such terror as that through which the Israelites escaped from bondage. Oh! if she could but find a Moses to call down the plagues of Egypt upon this Pharaoh of an Abbot—those plagues with which she had threatened him—but although she believed that they would fall (why did she believe it? she wondered), she was as yet impotent to fulfil.

Now Thomas Bolle! If only she could have words with that faithful Thomas Bolle, the fierce and cunning man whom they thought foolish!

This idea of Thomas Bolle took possession of Emlyn's mind—Thomas Bolle, who had loved her all his life, who would die to serve her. She strove in vain to get in touch with him. The old gardener was so deaf that he could not, or would not, understand. The silly Bridget gave the letter that she wrote to him to the Prioress by mistake, who burnt it before her eyes and said nothing. The monks who brought provisions to the Nunnery were always received by three of the sisters, set to spy on each other and on them, so that she could not come near to them alone. The priest who celebrated Mass was an old enemy of hers; with him she could do nothing, and no one else was allowed to approach the place except once or twice the Abbot, who was closeted for hours with the Prioress, but spoke to her no more.

Why, wondered Emlyn, should less than half-a-mile of space be such a barrier between her and Thomas Bolle? If he stood within twenty yards of her she could make him understand; why not, then, when he stood within five hundred? This idea possessed her; these limitations of nature made her mad. She refused to accept them. Night by night, lying brooding in her bed, while Cicely slept in peace at her side, she threw out her strong soul towards the soul of her old lover, Thomas Bolle, commanding him to listen, to obey, to come.

At first nothing happened. Afterwards she had a vague sense of being answered; although she could not see or hear him, she felt his presence. Then one afternoon, looking from an upper dormer window, she saw a scuffle going on outside the gateway, and heard angry voices. Thomas Bolle was trying to force his way in at the door, whence he was repelled by the Abbot's men who always watched there.

In the evening she gathered the truth from the nuns, who did not know that she was listening to what they said. It seemed that Thomas, whom they spoke of as a madman or as drunk, had tried to break into the Nunnery. When he was asked what he wanted, he answered that he did not know, but he must speak with Emlyn Stower. At this tidings she smiled to herself, for now she knew that he had heard her, and that in this way or in that he would obey her summons and come.

Two days later Thomas came—thus.

The September evening was fading into night, and Emlyn, leaving Cicely resting on her bed, which now she often did for a while before the supper-hour, had gone into the garden to enjoy the pleasant air. There she walked until she wearied of its sameness, then entered the old chapel by a side door and sat herself down to think in the chancel, not far from a life-sized statue of the Virgin, in painted oak, which stood here because of its peculiarities, for the back half of it seemed to be built into the masonry. Also the eye-sockets were empty, which suggested to the observant Emlyn either that they had once held jewels or that this was no likeness of the holy Mother, but rather one of the blind St. Lucy.

While Emlyn mused there quite alone—for at this hour none entered the place, nor would until the next morning—she thought that she heard strange noises, as of some one stirring, which came from the neighbourhood of the statue. Now many would have been scared and departed; but not so Emlyn, who only sat still and listened. Presently, without moving her head, she looked also. As it happened, the light of the setting sun, pouring through the west window, fell almost full upon the figure, and by it she saw, or thought she saw, that the eye-sockets were no longer empty; there were eyes in them which moved and flashed.

Now for a moment even Emlyn was frightened. Then she reasoned with herself, reflecting that a priest or one of the nuns was watching her from behind the statue, which they might do for as long as they pleased. Or perhaps this was a miracle, such as she had heard so much of but never seen. Well, why should she fear spies or miracles? She would sit where she was and see what happened. Nor had she long to wait, for presently a voice, a hoarse, manly voice, whispered—

"Emlyn! Emlyn Stower!"

"Yes," she answered, also in a whisper. "Who speaks?"

"Who do you think?" asked the voice, with a chuckle. "A devil, perhaps."

"Well, if it be a friendly devil I don't know that I mind, who need company in this lone place. So appear, man or devil," answered Emlyn stoutly. But in secret she crossed herself beneath her cape, for in those days folk believed in the appearance of devils for no good purposes.

The statue began to creak, then opened like a door, though very unwillingly, as though its hinges had been fixed for a long, long time and rusted in the damp, which was indeed the case. Inside of it, like a corpse in an upright coffin, appeared a figure, a square, strong figure, clad in a tattered monk's robe, surmounted by a large head with fiery red hair and beetling brows, beneath which shone two wild grey eyes. Emlyn, whose heart had stood still—for, after all, Satan is awkward company for a mortal woman—waited till it gave a jump in her breast and went on again as usual. Then she said quietly—

"What are you doing here, Thomas Bolle?"

"That is what I want to know, Emlyn. Night and day for weeks you have been calling me, and so I came."

"Yes, I have been calling you; but how did you come?"

"By the old monk's road. They have forgotten it long ago, but my grandfather told me of it when I was a boy, and at last a fox showed me where it ran. It's a dark road, and when first I tried it I thought I should be poisoned, but now the air is none so bad. It ran to the Abbey once, and may still, but my door and Mrs. Fox's is in the copse by the park wall, where none would ever look for it. If you would like a cub to play with, I will bring you one. Or perhaps you want something more than cubs," he added, with his cunning laugh.

"Aye, Thomas, I want much more. Man," she said fiercely, "will you do what I tell you?"

"That depends, Mistress Emlyn. Have I not done what you told me all my life, and for no reward?"

She moved across the chancel and sat herself down against him, pushing the image door almost to and speaking to him through the crack.

"If you have had no reward, Thomas," she said in a gentle voice, "whose fault was it? Not mine, I think. I loved you once when we were young, did I not? I would have given myself to you, body and soul, would I not? Well, who came between us and spoiled our lives?"

"The monks," groaned Thomas; "the accursed monks, who married you to Stower because he paid them."

"Yes, the accursed monks. And now our youth has gone, and love—of that sort—is behind us. I have been another man's wife, Thomas, who might have been yours. Think of it—your loving wife, the mother of your children. And you—they have tamed you and made you their servant, their cattle-herd, the strong fellow to fetch and carry, the half-wit, as they call you, who can still be trusted to run an errand and hold his tongue, the Abbey mule that does not dare to kick, the grieve of your own stolen lands—you, whose father was almost a gentleman. That's what they have done for you, Thomas; and for me, the Church's ward—well, I will not speak of it. Now, if you had your will, what would you do for them?"

"Do for them? Do for them?" gasped Thomas, worked up to fury by this recital of his wrongs. "Why, if I dared I'd cut their throats, every one, and grallock them like deer," and he ground his strong white teeth. "But I am afraid. They have my soul, and month by month I must confess. You remember, Emlyn, I warned you when you and the lady would have ridden to London before the siege. Well, afterward—I must confess it—the Abbot heard it himself, and oh! sore, sore was my penance. Before I had done with it my ribs showed through my skin and my back was like a red osier basket. There's only one thing I didn't tell them, because, after all, it is no sin to grub the earth off the face of a corpse."

"Ah!" said Emlyn, looking at him. "You're not to be trusted. Well, I thought as much. Good-bye, Thomas Bolle, you coward. I'll find me a man for a friend, not a whimpering, priest-ridden hound who sets a Latin blessing which he does not understand above his honour. God in heaven! to think I should ever have loved such a thing. Oh! I am shamed, I am shamed. I'll go wash my hands. Shut your trap and get you gone down your rat-run, Thomas Bolle, and, living or dead, never dare to speak to me again. Also forget not to tell your monks how I called you to my side—for that's witchcraft, you know, and I shall burn for it, and your soul gain benefit. God in heaven! to think that once you were Thomas Bolle," and she made as though to go away.

He stretched out his great arm and caught her by the robe, exclaiming—

"What would you have me do, Emlyn? I can't bear your scorn. Take it off me or I go kill myself."

"That's what you had best do. You'll find the devil a better master than a foreign abbot. Farewell for ever."

"Nay, nay; what's your will? Soul or no soul, I'll work it."

"Will you? Will you indeed? If so, stay a moment," and she ran down the chapel, bolting the doors; then returned to him, saying—

"Now come forth, Thomas, and since you are once more a man, kiss me as you used to do twenty years ago and more. You'll not confess to that, will you? There. Now, kneel before the altar here and swear an oath. Nay, listen to it before you swear, for it is wide."

Emlyn said the oath to him. It was a great and terrible oath. Under it he bound himself to be her slave and join himself with her in working woe to the monks of Blossholme, and especially to their Abbot, Clement Maldon, in payment of the wrongs that these had done to them both; in payment for the murder of Sir John Foterell and of Christopher Harflete, and of the imprisonment and robbery of Cicely Harflete, the daughter of the one and the wife of the other. He bound himself to do those things which she should tell him. He bound himself neither in the confessional nor, should it come to that, on the bed of torture or the scaffold to breathe a word of all their counsel. He prayed that if he did so his soul might pay the price in everlasting torment, and of all these things he took Heaven to be his witness.

"Now," said Emlyn, when she had finished setting out this fearful vow, "will you be a man and swear and thereby avenge the dead and save the innocent from death; or will you who have my secret be a crawling monk and go back to Blossholme Abbey and betray me?"

He thought a moment, rubbing his red head, for the thing frightened him, as well it might. The scales of the balance of his mind hung evenly, and Emlyn knew not which way they would turn. She saw, and put out all her woman's strength. Resting her hand upon his shoulder, she leaned forward and whispered into his ear.

"Do you remember, Thomas, how first we told our young love that spring day down in the copse by the water, and how sweet the daffodils bloomed about our feet—the daffodils and the wood-lilies? Do you remember how we swore ourselves each to each for all our lives, aye, and all the lives that were to come, and how for us two the earth was turned to heaven? And then—do you remember how that monk walked by—it was this Clement Maldon—and froze us with his cruel eyes, and said, 'What do you with the witch's daughter? She is not for you.' And—oh! Thomas, I can no more of it," and she broke down and sobbed, then added, "Swear nothing; get you gone and betray me, if you will. I'll bear you no malice, even when I die for it, for after more than twenty years of monkcraft, how could I hope that you would still remain a man? Come, get you gone swiftly, ere they take us together, and your fair fame is besmirched. Quick, now, and leave me and my lady and her unborn child to the doom Maldon brews for us. Alas! for the copse by the river; alas! for the withered lilies!"

Thomas heard; the big blue veins stood out upon his forehead, his great breast heaved, his utterance choked. At length the words came in a thick torrent.

"I'll not go, dearie; I'll swear what you will, by your eyes and by your lips, by the flowers on which we trod, by all the empty years of aching woe and shame, by God upon His throne in heaven, and by the devil in his fires in hell. Come, come," and he ran to the altar and clasped the crucifix that stood there. "Say the words again, or any others that you will, and I'll repeat them and take the oath, and may fiery worms eat me living for ever and ever if I break a letter of it."

With a little smile of triumph in her dark eyes Emlyn bent over the kneeling man and whispered—whispered through the gathering bloom, while he whispered after her, and kissed the Rood in token.

It was done, and they drew away from the altar back to the painted saint.

"So you are a man after all," she said, laughing aloud. "Now, man—my man—who, if we live through this, shall be my husband if you will—yes, my husband, for I'll pay, and be proud of it—listen to my commands. See you, I am Moses, and yonder in the Abbey sits Pharaoh with a hardened heart, and you are the angel—the destroying angel with the sword of the plagues of Egypt. To-night there will be fire in the Abbey—such fire as fell on Cranwell Towers. Nay, nay, I know; the church will not burn, nor all the great stone halls. But the dormitories, and the storehouses, and the hayricks, and the cattle-byres, they'll flame bravely after this time of drought, and if the wains are ashes, how will they draw in their harvest? Will you do it, my man?"

"Surely. Have I not sworn?"

"Then away to the work, and afterwards—to-morrow or next day—come back and make report. Just now I am much moved to solitary prayer, so wait till you see me here alone upon my knees. Stay! Wrap yourself in grave-clothes, for then if you are seen they will think you are a ghost, such as they say haunt this place. Fear not, by then I will have more work for you. Have you mastered it?"

He nodded his head. "All. All, especially your promise. Oh! I'll not die now; I'll live to claim it."

"Good. There's on account," and again she kissed him. "Go."

He reeled in the intoxication of his joy; then said—

"One word; my head swims; I forgot. Sir Christopher is not dead, or wasn't—"

"What do you mean?" she almost hissed at him. "In Christ's name be quick; I hear voices without."

"They buried another man for Christopher. I scraped him up and saw. Christopher was sent foreign, sore wounded, on the ship—pest! I have forgotten its name—the same ship that took Jeffrey Stokes."

"Blessings on your head for that tidings," exclaimed Emlyn, in a strange, low voice. "Away; they are coming to the door!"

The wooden figure creaked to and stared at her blandly, as it had stared for generations. For a moment Emlyn stood still, her hand upon her heart. Then she walked swiftly down the chapel, unlocked the door, and in the porch, just entering it, met the Prioress Matilda, another nun, and old Bridget, who was chattering.

"Oh! it is you, Mistress Stower," said Mother Matilda, with evident relief. "Sister Bridget here swore that she heard a man talking in the chapel when she came to shut the outer window at sunset."

"Did she?" answered Emlyn indifferently. "Then her luck's better than my own, who long for the sound of a man's voice in this home of babbling women. Nay, be not shocked, good Mother; I am no nun, and God did not create the world all female, or we should none of us be here. But, now you speak of it, I think there's something strange about that chapel. It is a place where some might fear to be alone, for twice when I knelt there at my prayers I have heard odd sounds, and once, when there was no sun, a cold shadow fell upon me. Some ghost of the dead, I suppose, of whom so many lie about. Well, ghosts I never feared; and now I must away to fetch my lady's supper, for she eats in her room to-night."

When she had gone the Prioress shook her head and remarked in her gentle fashion—

"A strange woman and a rough, but, my sisters, we must not judge her harshly, for she is of a different world to ours, and I fear has met with sorrows there, such as we are protected from by our holy office."

"Yes," answered the sister, "but I think also that she has met with the ghost that haunts the chapel, of which there are many records, and that once I saw myself when I was a novice. The Prioress Matilda—I mean the fourth of that name, she who was mixed up with Edward the Lame, the monk, and died suddenly after the—"

"Peace, sister; let us have no scandal about that departed—woman, who left the earth two hundred years ago. Also, if her unquiet spirit still haunts the place, as many say, I know not why it should speak with the voice of a man."

"Perhaps it was the monk Edward's voice that Bridget heard," replied the sister, "for no doubt he still hangs about her skirts as he did in life, if all tales are true. Well, Mistress Emlyn says that she does not mind ghosts, and I can well believe it, for she is a witch's daughter, and has a strange look in her eyes. Did you ever see such bold eyes, Mother? However it may be, I hate ghosts, and rather would I pass a month on bread and water than be alone in that chapel at or after sundown. My back creeps to think of it, for they say that the unhallowed babe walks too, and gibbers round the font seeking baptism—ugh!" and she shuddered.

"Peace, sister, peace to your goblin talk," said Mother Matilda again. "Let us think of holier things lest the foul fiend draw near to us."

That night, about one in the morning, the foul fiend drew very near to Blossholme, and he came in the shape of fire. Suddenly the nuns were aroused from their beds by the sound of bells tolling wildly. Running to the window-places, they saw great sheets of flame leaping from the Abbey roofs. They threw open the casements and stared out terrified. Sister Bridget was sent even to wake the deaf gardener and his wife, who lived in the gateway, and command them to go forth and learn what passed, and the meaning of the shouts they heard, for they feared that Blossholme was attacked by some army.

A long while went by, and Bridget returned with a confused tale, which, as it had been gathered by an imbecile from a deaf gardener, was not easy to understand. Meanwhile the shoutings went on and the fire at the Abbey burnt ever more fiercely, so that the nuns thought that their last hour had come, and knelt down to pray at the casement.

Just then Cicely and Emlyn appeared among them, and stared at the great fire.

Suddenly Cicely turned round, and, fixing her large blue eyes on Emlyn, said, in the hearing of them all—

"The Abbey burns. Why, Nurse, they told me that you said it would be so, yonder amid the ashes of Cranwell Towers. Surely you are foresighted."

"Fire calls for fire," answered Emlyn grimly, and the nuns around looked at her with doubtful eyes.

It was a very fierce fire, which appeared to have begun in the dormitories, whence, even at that distance, they saw half-clad monks escaping through the windows, some by means of bed-coverings tied together and some by jumping, notwithstanding the height. Presently the roof of the building fell in, sending up showers of glowing embers, which lit upon the thatch of the farm byres and sheds, and upon the ricks built and building in the stackyard, so that all these caught also, and before dawn were utterly consumed.

One by one the watchers in the Nunnery wearied of the lamentable sight, and muttering prayers, departed terrified to their beds. But Emlyn sat on at the open casement till the rim of the splendid September sun showed above the hills. There she sat, her head resting on her hand, her strong face set like that of a statue. Only her dark eyes, in which the flames were reflected, seemed to smile hardly.

"Thomas is a great tool," she muttered to herself at length, "and the first cut has bitten to the bone. Well, there shall be worse to come. You will live to beg Emlyn's mercy yet, Clement Maldonado."

Emlyn Calls Her Man

One by one the weeks passed over the heads of Cicely and Emlyn in their prison, and brought them neither hope nor tidings. Indeed, although they could not see its cords, they felt that the evil net which held them was drawing ever tighter. There were fear and pity as well as love in the eyes of Mother Matilda when she looked at Cicely, which she did only if she thought that no one observed her. The nuns also were afraid, though it was clear that they knew not of what. One evening Emlyn, finding the Prioress alone, sprang questions on her, asking what was in the wind, and why her lady, a free woman of full age, was detained there against her will.

The old nun's face grew secret. She answered that she did not know of anything unusual, and that, as regarded the detention, she must obey the commands of her spiritual superior.

"Then," burst out Emlyn, "I tell you that you do so at your peril. I tell you that whether my lady lives or dies, there are those who will call you to a strict account, aye, and those who will listen to the prayer of the helpless. Mother Matilda, England is not the land it was when as a girl they buried you in these mouldy walls. Where does God say that you have the right to hold free women like felons in a jail? Tell me."

"I cannot," moaned Mother Matilda, wringing her thin hands. "The right is very hard to find, this place is strictly guarded, and whatever I may think, I must do what I am bid, lest my soul should suffer."

"Your soul! You cloistered women think always of your miserable souls, but of those of other folk, aye, and of their bodies too, nothing. Then you'll not help me?"

"I cannot, I cannot, who am myself in bonds," she replied again.

"So be it, Mother; then I'll help myself, and when I do, God help you all," and with a contemptuous shrug of her broad shoulders she walked away, leaving the poor old Prioress almost in tears.

Emlyn's threats were bold as her own heart, but how could she execute even a tenth of them? The right was on their side, indeed, but, as many a captive has found in those and other days, right is no Joshua's trumpet to cause high walls to fall. Moreover, Cicely would not aid her. Now that her husband was dead she took interest in one thing only—his child who was to be.

For the rest she seemed to care nothing. Since she had no friends with whom she could communicate, and her wealth, as she understood, had been taken from her, what better place, she asked, could there be for that child to see the light than in this quiet Nunnery? When it was born and she was well again she would consider other matters. Meanwhile she was languid, and why was Emlyn always prating to her of freedom? If she were free, what should she do and whither should she go? The nuns were very kind to her; they loved her as she did them.

So she talked on, and Emlyn, listening, did not dare to tell her the truth: that here she feared for the life of her child, dreading lest that news might bring about the death of both of them. So she let her be, and fell back on her own wits.

First she thought of escape, only to abandon the idea, for her mistress was in no state to face its perils. Moreover, whither should they go? Then rescue came into her mind, but, alas! who would rescue them? The great men in London, perhaps, as a matter of policy, but great men are hard to come at, even for the free. If she were free she might find means to make them listen, but she was not, nor could she leave her lady at such a time. What remained, then? So to contrive that they should be set free.

Perhaps it might be done at a price—that of Cicely's jewels, of which she alone knew the hiding-place, and with them a deed of indemnity against her persecutors. Emlyn was not minded to give either. Moreover, she guessed that it might be in vain. Once outside those walls, they knew too much to be allowed to live. And yet within those walls Cicely's child would not be allowed to live—the child that was heir to all. What, then, could loose them and make them safe?

Terror, perhaps—such terror as that through which the Israelites escaped from bondage. Oh! if she could but find a Moses to call down the plagues of Egypt upon this Pharaoh of an Abbot—those plagues with which she had threatened him—but although she believed that they would fall (why did she believe it? she wondered), she was as yet impotent to fulfil.

Now Thomas Bolle! If only she could have words with that faithful Thomas Bolle, the fierce and cunning man whom they thought foolish!

This idea of Thomas Bolle took possession of Emlyn's mind—Thomas Bolle, who had loved her all his life, who would die to serve her. She strove in vain to get in touch with him. The old gardener was so deaf that he could not, or would not, understand. The silly Bridget gave the letter that she wrote to him to the Prioress by mistake, who burnt it before her eyes and said nothing. The monks who brought provisions to the Nunnery were always received by three of the sisters, set to spy on each other and on them, so that she could not come near to them alone. The priest who celebrated Mass was an old enemy of hers; with him she could do nothing, and no one else was allowed to approach the place except once or twice the Abbot, who was closeted for hours with the Prioress, but spoke to her no more.

Why, wondered Emlyn, should less than half-a-mile of space be such a barrier between her and Thomas Bolle? If he stood within twenty yards of her she could make him understand; why not, then, when he stood within five hundred? This idea possessed her; these limitations of nature made her mad. She refused to accept them. Night by night, lying brooding in her bed, while Cicely slept in peace at her side, she threw out her strong soul towards the soul of her old lover, Thomas Bolle, commanding him to listen, to obey, to come.

At first nothing happened. Afterwards she had a vague sense of being answered; although she could not see or hear him, she felt his presence. Then one afternoon, looking from an upper dormer window, she saw a scuffle going on outside the gateway, and heard angry voices. Thomas Bolle was trying to force his way in at the door, whence he was repelled by the Abbot's men who always watched there.

In the evening she gathered the truth from the nuns, who did not know that she was listening to what they said. It seemed that Thomas, whom they spoke of as a madman or as drunk, had tried to break into the Nunnery. When he was asked what he wanted, he answered that he did not know, but he must speak with Emlyn Stower. At this tidings she smiled to herself, for now she knew that he had heard her, and that in this way or in that he would obey her summons and come.

Two days later Thomas came—thus.

The September evening was fading into night, and Emlyn, leaving Cicely resting on her bed, which now she often did for a while before the supper-hour, had gone into the garden to enjoy the pleasant air. There she walked until she wearied of its sameness, then entered the old chapel by a side door and sat herself down to think in the chancel, not far from a life-sized statue of the Virgin, in painted oak, which stood here because of its peculiarities, for the back half of it seemed to be built into the masonry. Also the eye-sockets were empty, which suggested to the observant Emlyn either that they had once held jewels or that this was no likeness of the holy Mother, but rather one of the blind St. Lucy.

While Emlyn mused there quite alone—for at this hour none entered the place, nor would until the next morning—she thought that she heard strange noises, as of some one stirring, which came from the neighbourhood of the statue. Now many would have been scared and departed; but not so Emlyn, who only sat still and listened. Presently, without moving her head, she looked also. As it happened, the light of the setting sun, pouring through the west window, fell almost full upon the figure, and by it she saw, or thought she saw, that the eye-sockets were no longer empty; there were eyes in them which moved and flashed.

Now for a moment even Emlyn was frightened. Then she reasoned with herself, reflecting that a priest or one of the nuns was watching her from behind the statue, which they might do for as long as they pleased. Or perhaps this was a miracle, such as she had heard so much of but never seen. Well, why should she fear spies or miracles? She would sit where she was and see what happened. Nor had she long to wait, for presently a voice, a hoarse, manly voice, whispered—

"Emlyn! Emlyn Stower!"

"Yes," she answered, also in a whisper. "Who speaks?"

"Who do you think?" asked the voice, with a chuckle. "A devil, perhaps."

"Well, if it be a friendly devil I don't know that I mind, who need company in this lone place. So appear, man or devil," answered Emlyn stoutly. But in secret she crossed herself beneath her cape, for in those days folk believed in the appearance of devils for no good purposes.

The statue began to creak, then opened like a door, though very unwillingly, as though its hinges had been fixed for a long, long time and rusted in the damp, which was indeed the case. Inside of it, like a corpse in an upright coffin, appeared a figure, a square, strong figure, clad in a tattered monk's robe, surmounted by a large head with fiery red hair and beetling brows, beneath which shone two wild grey eyes. Emlyn, whose heart had stood still—for, after all, Satan is awkward company for a mortal woman—waited till it gave a jump in her breast and went on again as usual. Then she said quietly—

"What are you doing here, Thomas Bolle?"

"That is what I want to know, Emlyn. Night and day for weeks you have been calling me, and so I came."

"Yes, I have been calling you; but how did you come?"

"By the old monk's road. They have forgotten it long ago, but my grandfather told me of it when I was a boy, and at last a fox showed me where it ran. It's a dark road, and when first I tried it I thought I should be poisoned, but now the air is none so bad. It ran to the Abbey once, and may still, but my door and Mrs. Fox's is in the copse by the park wall, where none would ever look for it. If you would like a cub to play with, I will bring you one. Or perhaps you want something more than cubs," he added, with his cunning laugh.

"Aye, Thomas, I want much more. Man," she said fiercely, "will you do what I tell you?"

"That depends, Mistress Emlyn. Have I not done what you told me all my life, and for no reward?"

She moved across the chancel and sat herself down against him, pushing the image door almost to and speaking to him through the crack.

"If you have had no reward, Thomas," she said in a gentle voice, "whose fault was it? Not mine, I think. I loved you once when we were young, did I not? I would have given myself to you, body and soul, would I not? Well, who came between us and spoiled our lives?"

"The monks," groaned Thomas; "the accursed monks, who married you to Stower because he paid them."

"Yes, the accursed monks. And now our youth has gone, and love—of that sort—is behind us. I have been another man's wife, Thomas, who might have been yours. Think of it—your loving wife, the mother of your children. And you—they have tamed you and made you their servant, their cattle-herd, the strong fellow to fetch and carry, the half-wit, as they call you, who can still be trusted to run an errand and hold his tongue, the Abbey mule that does not dare to kick, the grieve of your own stolen lands—you, whose father was almost a gentleman. That's what they have done for you, Thomas; and for me, the Church's ward—well, I will not speak of it. Now, if you had your will, what would you do for them?"

"Do for them? Do for them?" gasped Thomas, worked up to fury by this recital of his wrongs. "Why, if I dared I'd cut their throats, every one, and grallock them like deer," and he ground his strong white teeth. "But I am afraid. They have my soul, and month by month I must confess. You remember, Emlyn, I warned you when you and the lady would have ridden to London before the siege. Well, afterward—I must confess it—the Abbot heard it himself, and oh! sore, sore was my penance. Before I had done with it my ribs showed through my skin and my back was like a red osier basket. There's only one thing I didn't tell them, because, after all, it is no sin to grub the earth off the face of a corpse."

"Ah!" said Emlyn, looking at him. "You're not to be trusted. Well, I thought as much. Good-bye, Thomas Bolle, you coward. I'll find me a man for a friend, not a whimpering, priest-ridden hound who sets a Latin blessing which he does not understand above his honour. God in heaven! to think I should ever have loved such a thing. Oh! I am shamed, I am shamed. I'll go wash my hands. Shut your trap and get you gone down your rat-run, Thomas Bolle, and, living or dead, never dare to speak to me again. Also forget not to tell your monks how I called you to my side—for that's witchcraft, you know, and I shall burn for it, and your soul gain benefit. God in heaven! to think that once you were Thomas Bolle," and she made as though to go away.

He stretched out his great arm and caught her by the robe, exclaiming—

"What would you have me do, Emlyn? I can't bear your scorn. Take it off me or I go kill myself."

"That's what you had best do. You'll find the devil a better master than a foreign abbot. Farewell for ever."

"Nay, nay; what's your will? Soul or no soul, I'll work it."

"Will you? Will you indeed? If so, stay a moment," and she ran down the chapel, bolting the doors; then returned to him, saying—

"Now come forth, Thomas, and since you are once more a man, kiss me as you used to do twenty years ago and more. You'll not confess to that, will you? There. Now, kneel before the altar here and swear an oath. Nay, listen to it before you swear, for it is wide."

Emlyn said the oath to him. It was a great and terrible oath. Under it he bound himself to be her slave and join himself with her in working woe to the monks of Blossholme, and especially to their Abbot, Clement Maldon, in payment of the wrongs that these had done to them both; in payment for the murder of Sir John Foterell and of Christopher Harflete, and of the imprisonment and robbery of Cicely Harflete, the daughter of the one and the wife of the other. He bound himself to do those things which she should tell him. He bound himself neither in the confessional nor, should it come to that, on the bed of torture or the scaffold to breathe a word of all their counsel. He prayed that if he did so his soul might pay the price in everlasting torment, and of all these things he took Heaven to be his witness.

"Now," said Emlyn, when she had finished setting out this fearful vow, "will you be a man and swear and thereby avenge the dead and save the innocent from death; or will you who have my secret be a crawling monk and go back to Blossholme Abbey and betray me?"

He thought a moment, rubbing his red head, for the thing frightened him, as well it might. The scales of the balance of his mind hung evenly, and Emlyn knew not which way they would turn. She saw, and put out all her woman's strength. Resting her hand upon his shoulder, she leaned forward and whispered into his ear.

"Do you remember, Thomas, how first we told our young love that spring day down in the copse by the water, and how sweet the daffodils bloomed about our feet—the daffodils and the wood-lilies? Do you remember how we swore ourselves each to each for all our lives, aye, and all the lives that were to come, and how for us two the earth was turned to heaven? And then—do you remember how that monk walked by—it was this Clement Maldon—and froze us with his cruel eyes, and said, 'What do you with the witch's daughter? She is not for you.' And—oh! Thomas, I can no more of it," and she broke down and sobbed, then added, "Swear nothing; get you gone and betray me, if you will. I'll bear you no malice, even when I die for it, for after more than twenty years of monkcraft, how could I hope that you would still remain a man? Come, get you gone swiftly, ere they take us together, and your fair fame is besmirched. Quick, now, and leave me and my lady and her unborn child to the doom Maldon brews for us. Alas! for the copse by the river; alas! for the withered lilies!"

Thomas heard; the big blue veins stood out upon his forehead, his great breast heaved, his utterance choked. At length the words came in a thick torrent.

"I'll not go, dearie; I'll swear what you will, by your eyes and by your lips, by the flowers on which we trod, by all the empty years of aching woe and shame, by God upon His throne in heaven, and by the devil in his fires in hell. Come, come," and he ran to the altar and clasped the crucifix that stood there. "Say the words again, or any others that you will, and I'll repeat them and take the oath, and may fiery worms eat me living for ever and ever if I break a letter of it."

With a little smile of triumph in her dark eyes Emlyn bent over the kneeling man and whispered—whispered through the gathering bloom, while he whispered after her, and kissed the Rood in token.

It was done, and they drew away from the altar back to the painted saint.

"So you are a man after all," she said, laughing aloud. "Now, man—my man—who, if we live through this, shall be my husband if you will—yes, my husband, for I'll pay, and be proud of it—listen to my commands. See you, I am Moses, and yonder in the Abbey sits Pharaoh with a hardened heart, and you are the angel—the destroying angel with the sword of the plagues of Egypt. To-night there will be fire in the Abbey—such fire as fell on Cranwell Towers. Nay, nay, I know; the church will not burn, nor all the great stone halls. But the dormitories, and the storehouses, and the hayricks, and the cattle- byres, they'll flame bravely after this time of drought, and if the wains are ashes, how will they draw in their harvest? Will you do it, my man?"

"Surely. Have I not sworn?"

"Then away to the work, and afterwards—to-morrow or next day—come back and make report. Just now I am much moved to solitary prayer, so wait till you see me here alone upon my knees. Stay! Wrap yourself in grave-clothes, for then if you are seen they will think you are a ghost, such as they say haunt this place. Fear not, by then I will have more work for you. Have you mastered it?"

He nodded his head. "All. All, especially your promise. Oh! I'll not die now; I'll live to claim it."

"Good. There's on account," and again she kissed him. "Go."

He reeled in the intoxication of his joy; then said—

"One word; my head swims; I forgot. Sir Christopher is not dead, or wasn't—"

"What do you mean?" she almost hissed at him. "In Christ's name be quick; I hear voices without."

"They buried another man for Christopher. I scraped him up and saw. Christopher was sent foreign, sore wounded, on the ship—pest! I have forgotten its name—the same ship that took Jeffrey Stokes."

"Blessings on your head for that tidings," exclaimed Emlyn, in a strange, low voice. "Away; they are coming to the door!"

The wooden figure creaked to and stared at her blandly, as it had stared for generations. For a moment Emlyn stood still, her hand upon her heart. Then she walked swiftly down the chapel, unlocked the door, and in the porch, just entering it, met the Prioress Matilda, another nun, and old Bridget, who was chattering.

"Oh! it is you, Mistress Stower," said Mother Matilda, with evident relief. "Sister Bridget here swore that she heard a man talking in the chapel when she came to shut the outer window at sunset."

"Did she?" answered Emlyn indifferently. "Then her luck's better than my own, who long for the sound of a man's voice in this home of babbling women. Nay, be not shocked, good Mother; I am no nun, and God did not create the world all female, or we should none of us be here. But, now you speak of it, I think there's something strange about that chapel. It is a place where some might fear to be alone, for twice when I knelt there at my prayers I have heard odd sounds, and once, when there was no sun, a cold shadow fell upon me. Some ghost of the dead, I suppose, of whom so many lie about. Well, ghosts I never feared; and now I must away to fetch my lady's supper, for she eats in her room to-night."

When she had gone the Prioress shook her head and remarked in her gentle fashion—

"A strange woman and a rough, but, my sisters, we must not judge her harshly, for she is of a different world to ours, and I fear has met with sorrows there, such as we are protected from by our holy office."

"Yes," answered the sister, "but I think also that she has met with the ghost that haunts the chapel, of which there are many records, and that once I saw myself when I was a novice. The Prioress Matilda—I mean the fourth of that name, she who was mixed up with Edward the Lame, the monk, and died suddenly after the—"

"Peace, sister; let us have no scandal about that departed—woman, who left the earth two hundred years ago. Also, if her unquiet spirit still haunts the place, as many say, I know not why it should speak with the voice of a man."

"Perhaps it was the monk Edward's voice that Bridget heard," replied the sister, "for no doubt he still hangs about her skirts as he did in life, if all tales are true. Well, Mistress Emlyn says that she does not mind ghosts, and I can well believe it, for she is a witch's daughter, and has a strange look in her eyes. Did you ever see such bold eyes, Mother? However it may be, I hate ghosts, and rather would I pass a month on bread and water than be alone in that chapel at or after sundown. My back creeps to think of it, for they say that the unhallowed babe walks too, and gibbers round the font seeking baptism—ugh!" and she shuddered.

"Peace, sister, peace to your goblin talk," said Mother Matilda again. "Let us think of holier things lest the foul fiend draw near to us."

That night, about one in the morning, the foul fiend drew very near to Blossholme, and he came in the shape of fire. Suddenly the nuns were aroused from their beds by the sound of bells tolling wildly. Running to the window-places, they saw great sheets of flame leaping from the Abbey roofs. They threw open the casements and stared out terrified. Sister Bridget was sent even to wake the deaf gardener and his wife, who lived in the gateway, and command them to go forth and learn what passed, and the meaning of the shouts they heard, for they feared that Blossholme was attacked by some army.

A long while went by, and Bridget returned with a confused tale, which, as it had been gathered by an imbecile from a deaf gardener, was not easy to understand. Meanwhile the shoutings went on and the fire at the Abbey burnt ever more fiercely, so that the nuns thought that their last hour had come, and knelt down to pray at the casement.

Just then Cicely and Emlyn appeared among them, and stared at the great fire.

Suddenly Cicely turned round, and, fixing her large blue eyes on Emlyn, said, in the hearing of them all—

"The Abbey burns. Why, Nurse, they told me that you said it would be so, yonder amid the ashes of Cranwell Towers. Surely you are foresighted."

"Fire calls for fire," answered Emlyn grimly, and the nuns around looked at her with doubtful eyes.

It was a very fierce fire, which appeared to have begun in the dormitories, whence, even at that distance, they saw half-clad monks escaping through the windows, some by means of bed-coverings tied together and some by jumping, notwithstanding the height. Presently the roof of the building fell in, sending up showers of glowing embers, which lit upon the thatch of the farm byres and sheds, and upon the ricks built and building in the stackyard, so that all these caught also, and before dawn were utterly consumed.

One by one the watchers in the Nunnery wearied of the lamentable sight, and muttering prayers, departed terrified to their beds. But Emlyn sat on at the open casement till the rim of the splendid September sun showed above the hills. There she sat, her head resting on her hand, her strong face set like that of a statue. Only her dark eyes, in which the flames were reflected, seemed to smile hardly.

"Thomas is a great tool," she muttered to herself at length, "and the first cut has bitten to the bone. Well, there shall be worse to come. You will live to beg Emlyn's mercy yet, Clement Maldonado."

Chapter IX

The Blossholme Witchings

On the afternoon of that day the Abbot came again to visit the Nunnery, and sent for Cicely and Emlyn. They found him alone in the guest-hall, walking up and down its length with a troubled face.

"Cicely Foterell," he said, without any form of greeting, "when last we met you refused to sign the deed which I brought with me. Well, it matters nothing, for that purchaser has gone back upon his bargain."

"Saying that he liked not the title?" suggested Cicely.

"Aye; though who taught you of titles and the ins and outs of law? But what need to ask—?" and he glowered at Emlyn. "Well, let it pass, for now I have a paper with me that you must sign. Read it if you will. It is harmless—only an instruction to the tenants of the lands your father held to pay their rents to me this Michaelmas, as warden of that property."

"Do they refuse, then, seeing that you hold it all, my Lord Abbot?"

"Aye, some one has been at work among them, and the stubborn churls will not without instruction under your hand and seal. The farms your father worked himself I have reaped, but last night every grain of corn and every fleece of wool were burned in the fire."

"Then I pray you keep account of them, my Lord, that you may pay me their value when we come to settle our score, seeing that I never gave you leave to shear my sheep and harvest my corn."

"You are pleased to be saucy, girl," he replied, biting his lip. "I have no time to bandy words—sign, and do you witness, Emlyn Stower."

Cicely took the document, glanced at it, then slowly tore it into four pieces and threw it to the floor.

"Rob me and my unborn child if you can and will, at least I'll be no thief's partner," she said quietly. "Now, if you want my name, go forge it, for I sign nothing."

The Abbot's face grew very evil.

"Do you remember, woman," he asked, "that here you are in my power? Do you not know that rebellious sinners such as you are can be shut in a dark dungeon and fed on the bread and water of affliction and beaten with the rods of penance? Will you do my bidding, or shall these things fall on you?"

Cicely's beautiful face flushed up, and for a moment her blue eyes filled with the tears of shame and terror. Then they cleared again, and she looked at him boldly and answered—

"I know that a murderer can be a torturer also. Why should not he who butchered the father scourge the daughter too? But I know also that there is a God who protects the innocent, though sometimes He is slow to lift His hand, and to Him I appeal, my Lord Abbot. I know, moreover, that I am Foterell and Carfax, and that no man or woman of my blood has ever yet yielded to fear or pain. I sign nothing," and, turning, she left the room.

Now the Abbot and Emlyn were alone. Suddenly, before she could speak, for her tongue was tied with rage, he began to rate and curse her and to threaten horrible things against her and her mistress, such things as only a cruel Spaniard could imagine. At length he paused for breath, and she broke in—

"Peace, wicked man, lest the roof fall on you, for I am sure that every cruel word you speak shall become a snake to strike you. Will you not take warning by what befell you last night, or must there be more such lessons?"

"Oho!" he answered; "so you know of that, do you? As I thought, your witchcraft was at work there."

"How can I help knowing what the whole sky blazoned? The fat monks of Blossholme must draw their girdles tight this winter. Those stolen lands bring no luck, it seems, and John Foterell's blood has turned to fire. Be warned, I say, be warned. Nay, I'll hear no more of your foul tongue. Lay a finger on that poor lady if you dare, and pay the price," and she too turned and went.

Ere he left the Nunnery the Abbot had an interview with Mother Matilda.

Cicely must be disciplined, he said; gently at first, afterwards with roughness, even to scourging, if need were—for her soul's sake. Also her servant Emlyn must be kept away from her—for her soul's sake, since without doubt she was a dangerous witch. Also, when the time of the birth of the child came on, he would send a wise woman to wait upon her, one who was accustomed to such cases—for her body's sake and that of her child. In the midst of the great trouble that had fallen upon them through the terrible fire at the Abbey, which had cost them such fearful loss, to say nothing of the lives of two of the servants and others burned and maimed, he had not much time to talk of such small things; but did she understand?

Then it was that Mother Matilda, the meek and gentle, brought pain and astonishment to the heart of the Lord Abbot, her spiritual superior.

She did not understand in the least. Such discipline as he suggested, whatever might be her faults and frailty, was, she declared with vigour, entirely unsuited to the case of the Lady Cicely, who, in her opinion, had suffered much for a small cause, and who, moreover, was about to become a mother, and therefore should be treated with every gentleness. For her part, she washed her hands of the whole business, and rather than enforce such commands would lay the case before the Vicar-General in London, who, she understood, was ready to look into such matters. Or at least she would set the Lady Harflete and her servant outside the gates and call upon the charitable to assist them. Of course, however, if his Lordship chose to send a skilled woman to wait upon her in her trouble, she could have no objection, provided that this woman were a person of good repute. But in the circumstances it was idle to talk to her of bread and water and dark cells and scourgings. Such things should never happen while she was Prioress. Before they did, she and her sisters would walk out of the Nunnery and leave the King's Courts to judge of the matter.

Now the state of the Abbot was very like to that of a terrier dog which, being accustomed to worry and torment a certain ewe-sheep, comes upon the same after it has lambed and finds a new creature—one that, instead of running in affright, turns upon it and, with head and hood and all its weight of mutton, butts, and leaps, and tramples. Then what chance has that dog against the terrible and unsuspected fury of the sheep, born, as it thought, for it to tear? Then what can it do but run, panting and discomfited, to its kennel? So it was with the Abbot at the onslaught of Mother Matilda in the defence of her lamb—Cicely. With Emlyn he had been prepared to exchange bite for bite—but Mother Matilda! his own pet quarry. It was too much. He could only go away, cursing all women and their infinite variety, on which no man might build. Who would have thought it of Mother Matilda, of all people on the earth!

So it came to pass that at the Nunnery, notwithstanding these terrible threats, things went on much as they had done before, since the times were such that even an all-powerful and remote Lord Abbot, with "right of gallows," could not drive matters to an extremity. Cicely was not shut into the dungeon and fed on bread and water, much less was she scourged. Nor was she separated from her nurse Emlyn, although it is true that the Prioress reproved her for her resistance to established authority, and when she had finished her lecture, kissed and blessed her, and called her "her sweet child, her dove and joy."

But if there was sameness at the Nunnery, at the Abbey there was constant change and excitement. Only three days after the fire the great flock of eight hundred lambs rushed one night over the Red Cliff on the fell, where, as all shepherds in that country know, there is a sheer drop of forty feet. Never was lamb's flesh so cheap in Blossholme and the country round as on the morrow of that night, while every hind within ten miles could have a winter coat for the skinning. Moreover, it was said and sworn to by the shepherds that the devil himself, with horns and hoofs, and mounted on a jackass, had been seen driving the same lambs.

Next the ghost of Sir John Foterell appeared, clad in armour, sometimes mounted and sometimes afoot, but always at night-time. First this dreadful spirit was perceived walking in the gardens of Shefton Hall, where it met the Abbot's caretaker—for the place was now shut up—as he went to set a springe for hares. He was a man advanced in years, yet few horses ever covered the distance between Shefton and Blossholme Abbey more quickly than he did that night.

Nor would he or any other return to his charge, so that henceforth Shefton was left as a dwelling for the ghost, which, as all might see from time to time, shone in the window-places like a candle. Moreover, the said ghost travelled far and wide, for on dark, windy nights it knocked upon the doors of those that in its lifetime had been its tenants, and in a hollow voice declared that it had been murdered by the Abbot of Blossholme and his underlings, who held its daughter in durance, and, under threats of unearthly vengeance, commanded all men to bring him to justice, and to pay him neither fees nor homage.

So much terror did this ghost cause that Thomas Bolle, the swift of foot, was set to watch for it, and returned announcing that he had seen it and that it called him by his name, whereon he, being a bold fellow and believing that it was but a man, sent an arrow straight through it, at which it laughed and forthwith vanished away. More; in proof of these things he led the Abbot and his monks to the very place, and showed them where he had stood and where the ghost stood—yes, and the arrow, of which all the feathers had been mysteriously burnt off and the wood seared as though by fire, sunk deep into a tree beyond. Then, as this thing had become a scandal and a dread, the Abbot, in his robes, solemnly laid the ghost, Thomas Bolle showing him exactly where it had passed.

This spirit being well and truly laid (like a foundation-stone), the Abbot and his monks returned homeward through the wood, but as they went a dreadful voice, which all recognized as that of Sir John Foterell, called these words from the shadows of an impenetrable thicket—for now the night was falling—

"Clement Maldonado, Abbot of Blossholme, I, whom thou didst murder, summon thee to meet me within a year before the throne of God."

Thereon all fled; yes, even the Abbot fled, or rather, as he said, his horse did, Thomas Bolle, who had lagged behind, outrunning them every one and getting home the first, saying Aves as he went.

After this, although the whole countryside hunted for it, Sir John's ghost was seen no more. Doubtless its work was done; but the Abbot explained matters differently. Other and worse things were seen, however.

One moonlight night a disturbance was heard among the cows, that bellowed and rushed about the field into which they had been turned after milking. Thinking that dogs had got amongst them, the herd and a watchman—for now no man would stir alone after sunset at Blossholme—went to see what was happening, and presently fell down half dead with fright. For there, leaning over the gate and laughing at them, was the foul fiend himself—the fiend with horns and tail, and in his hand an instrument like a pitchfork.

How the pair got home again, they never knew, but this is certain, that after that night no one could milk those cows; moreover, some of them slipped their calves, and became so wild that they must be slaughtered.

Next came rumours that even the Nunnery itself was haunted, especially the chapel. Here voices were heard talking, and Emlyn Stower, who was praying there, came out vowing that she had seen a ball of fire which rolled up and down the aisle, and in the centre of it a man's head, that seemed to try to talk to her, but could not.

Into this matter inquiry was held by the Abbot himself, who asked Emlyn if she knew the face that was in the ball of fire. She answered that she thought so. It seemed very like to one of his own guards, named Andrew Woods, or more commonly Drunken Andrew, a Scotchman whom Sir Christopher Harflete was said to have killed on the night of the great burning. At least his Lordship would remember that this Andrew had a broken nose, and so had the head in the fire, but, as it appeared to have changed a great deal since death, she could not be quite certain. All she was sure of was that it seemed to be trying to give her some message.

Now, recalling the trick that had been played with the said Andrew's body, the Abbot was silent. Only he asked shrewdly, if Emlyn had seen so terrible a thing there, how it came about that she was not afraid to be alone in the chapel, which he was informed she frequented much. She answered, with a laugh, that it was men she dreaded, not spirits, good or ill.

"No," he exclaimed, with a burst of rage, "you do not dread them, woman, because you are a witch, and summon them; nor shall we be free from these wizardries until the fire has you and your company."

"If so," replied Emlyn coolly, "I will ask dead Andrew for his message to you next time we meet, unless he chooses to deliver it to you himself."

So they parted, but that very night there happened the worst thing of all. It was about one in the morning when the Abbot, whose window was set open, was wakened by a voice that spoke with a Scotch accent and repeatedly called him by his name, summoning him to look out and see. He and others rose and looked, but could see nothing, for the night was very dark and rain fell. When the dawn came, however, their search was rewarded, for there, set upon a pinnacle of the Abbey church, and staring straight into the window of his Lordship's sleeping-room, from which it was but a few yards distant, was the dreadful head of Andrew Woods!

Furiously the Abbot asked who had done this horrible thing, but the monks, who were sure that it was the same being that had bewitched the cows, only shrugged their shoulders, and suggested that the grave of Andrew should be opened to see if he had lost his head. This was done at length, although, for his own reasons, the Abbot forbade it, talking of the violation of the dead.

Well, the grave was opened when Maldon was away on one of his mysterious journeys, and lo! no Andrew was there, but only a beam of oakwood stuffed out with straw to the shape of a man and sewn up in a blanket. For the real Andrew, or rather what was left of him, lay, it may be remembered, in another grave that was supposed to be filled by Sir Christopher Harflete.

From this day forward the whole countryside for fifty miles round rang with the tales of what were known as the Blossholme witchings, of which a proof was still to be seen by all men in the withered head of Andrew perched upon its pinnacle, whence none could be found to remove it for love or money. Only it was noted that the Abbot changed his sleeping-chamber, after which, except for a sickness which struck the monks—it was thought from the drinking of sour beer—these bedevilments were abated.

Indeed, at that time men had other things to think of, since the air was thick with rumours of impending change. The King threatened the Church, and the Church prepared to resist the King. There was talk of the suppression of the monasteries—some, in fact, had already been suppressed—and more talk of a rising of the faithful in the shires of York and Lincoln; high matters which called Abbot Maldon much away from home.

One day he returned weary, but satisfied, from a long journey, and amongst the news that awaited him found a message from the Prioress, over which he pondered while he ate his food. Also there was a letter from Spain, which he studied eagerly.

Some nine months had passed since the ship Great Yarmouth sailed, and during this time all that had been heard of her was that she had never reached Seville, so that, like every one else, the Abbot believed she had foundered in the deep seas. This was a sad event which he had borne with resignation, seeing that, although it meant the loss of his letters, which were of importance, she had aboard of her several persons whom he wished to see no more, especially Sir Christopher Harflete and Sir John Foterell's serving-man, Jeffrey Stokes, who was said to carry with him certain inconvenient documents. Even his secretary and chaplain, Brother Martin, could be spared, being, Maldon felt, a character better suited to heaven than to an earth where the best of men must be prepared sometimes to compromise with conscience.

In short, the vanishing of the Great Yarmouth was the wise decree of a far-seeing Providence, that had removed certain stumbling-blocks from his feet, which of late had been forced to travel over a rough and thorny road. For the dead tell no tales, although it was true that the ghost of Sir John Foterell and the grinning head of Drunken Andrew on his pinnacle seemed to be instances to the contrary. Christopher Harflete and Jeffrey Stokes at the bottom of the Bay of Biscay could bring no awkward charges, and left him none to deal with save an imprisoned and forgotten girl and an unborn child.

Now things were changed again, however, for the Spanish letter in his hand told him that the Great Yarmouth had not sunk, since two members of her crew who escaped—how, it was not said—declared that she had been captured by Turkish or other infidel pirates and taken away through the Straits of Gibraltar to some place unknown. Therefore, if he had survived the voyage, Christopher Harflete might still be living, and so might Jeffrey Stokes and Brother Martin. Yet this was not likely, for probably they would have perished in the fight, being hot-headed Englishmen, all three of them, or at the best have been committed to the Turkish galleys, whence not one man in a thousand ever returned.

On the whole, then, he had little cause to fear them, who were dead, or as good as dead, especially in the midst of so many more pressing dangers. All he had to fear, all that stood between him, or rather the Church, and a very rich inheritance was the girl in the Nunnery and an unborn child, and—yes, Emlyn Stower. Well, he was sure that the child would not live, and probably the mother would not live. As for

Emlyn, as she deserved, she would be burned for a witch, ere long too, now that he had time to see to it, and, if she survived her sickness, although he grieved for her, Cicely, her accomplice, should justly accompany her to the stake. Meanwhile, as Mother Matilda's message told him, this matter of the child was urgent.

The Abbot called a monk who was waiting on him and bade him send word to a woman known as Goody Megges, bidding her come at once. Within ten minutes she entered, having, as she explained, been warned to be close at hand.

This Goody Megges, who had some local repute as a "wise woman," was a person of about fifty years of age, remarkable for her enormous size, a flat face with small oblong eyes and a little, twisted mouth, which had caused her to be nicknamed "the Flounder." She greeted the Abbot with much reverence, curtseying till he thought she would fall backwards, and having received his fatherly blessing, sank into a chair, that seemed to vanish beneath her bulk.

"You will wonder why I summon you here, friend, since this is no place for the services of those of your trade," began the Abbot, with a smile.

"Oh, no, my Lord," answered the woman; "I've heard it is to wait upon Sir Christopher Harflete's wife in her trouble."

"I wish that I could call her by the honoured name of wife," said the Abbot, with a sigh. "But a mock-marriage does not make a wife, Mistress Megges, and, alas! the poor babe, if ever it should be born, will be but a bastard, marked from its birth with the brand of shame."

Now, the Flounder, who was no fool, began to take her cue.

"It is sad, very sad, your Holiness—no, that's wrong; but never mind, it will be right before all's done, and a good omen, I say, coming so sudden and chancy—your Lordship, I mean—not but what there's lots of the sort about here, as is generally the case round a—I mean everywhere. Moreover, they generally grow up bad and ungrateful, as I know well from my own three—not but what, of course, I was married fast enough. Well, what I was going to say was, that when things is so, sometimes it is a true blessing if the little innocents should go off at the first, and so be spared the finger of shame and the sniff of scorn," and she paused.

"Yes, Mistress Megges, or at least in such a case it is not for us to rail at the decree of Heaven—provided, of course, that the infant has lived long enough to be baptized," he added hastily.

"No, your Eminence, no. That's just what I said to that Smith girl last spring, when, being a heavy sleeper, I happened to overlie her brat and woke up to find it flat and blue. When she saw it she took on, bellowing like a heifer that has lost its first calf, and I said to her, 'Mary, this isn't me; it's Heaven. Mary, you should be very thankful, since my burden has rid you of your burden, and you can bury such a tiny one for next to nothing. Mary, cry a little if you like, for that's natural with the first, but don't come here flying in the face of Heaven with your railings, and gates, and posts—especially the rails, for Heaven hates 'em.'"

"Ah!" asked the Abbot, with mild interest, "and pray what did Mary do then?"

"Do, the graceless wench? Why, she said, 'Is it rails you're talking of, you pig-smothering old sow? Then here's a rail for you,' and she pulled the top bar off my own fence—for we were talking by the door—oak it was, and three by two—and knocked me flat—here's the scar of it on my head—singing out, 'Is that enough, or will you have the gate and the posts too?' Oh! If there's one thing I hate, it is railing, 'specially if made of hard oak and held edgeways."

So the wicked old hag babbled on, after her hideous fashion, while the Abbot stared at the ceiling.

"Enough of these sad stories of vice and violence. Such mischances will happen, and of course you were not to blame. Now, good Mistress Megges, will you undertake this case, which cannot be left to ignorant nuns? Though times are hard here, since of late many losses have fallen on our house, your skill shall be well paid."

The woman shuffled her big feet and stared at the floor, then looked up suddenly with a glance that seemed to bore to his heart like a bradawl, and asked—

"And if perchance the blessed babe should fly to heaven through my fingers, as in my time I have known dozens of them do, should I still get that pay?"

"Then," the Abbot answered, with a smile—a somewhat sickly smile—"then I think, mistress, you should have double pay, to console you for your sorrow and for any doubts that might be thrown upon your skill."

"Now that's noble trading," she replied, with an evil leer, "such as one might hope for from an Abbot. But, my Lord, they say the Nunnery is haunted, and I can't face ghosts. Man or woman, with rails or without 'em, Mother Flounder doesn't mind, but ghosts—no! Also Mistress Stower is a witch, and might lay a curse on me; and those nuns are full of crinks and cranks, and can pray an honest soul to death."

"Come, come, my time is short. What is it you want, woman? Out with it."

"The inn there at the ford—your Lordship, will need a tenant next month. It's a good paying house for those who know how to keep their mouths shut and to look the other way, and through vile scandal and evil slanderers, such as the Smith girl, my business isn't what it was. Now if I could have it without rent for the first two years, till I had time to work up the trade—"

The Abbot, who could bear no more of the creature, rose from his chair and said sharply—

"I will remember. Yes, I will promise. Go now; the reverent Mother is advised of your coming. And report to me night and morning of the progress of the case. Why, woman, what are you doing?" for she had suddenly slid to her knees and grasped his robes with her thick, filthy hands.

"Absolution, holy Lordship; I ask absolution and blessing—pax Meggiscum, and the rest of it."

"Absolution? There is nothing to absolve."

"Oh! yes, my Lord, there is plenty, though I am wondering who will absolve you for your half. Also there are rows of little angels that sometimes won't let me sleep, and that's why I can't stomach ghosts. I'd rather sup in winter on cold small ale and half-cooked pork than face even a still-born ghost."

"Begone!" said the Abbot, in such a voice that she scrambled to her feet and went, unblessed and unabsolved.

When the door had closed behind her he went to the window and flung it wide, although the night was foul.

"By all the saints!" he muttered, "that beastly murderess poisons the air. Why, I wonder, does God allow such filthy things to live? Cannot she ply her hell-trade less grossly? Oh! Clement Maldonado, how low are you sunk that you must use tools like these, and on such a business. And yet there is no other way. Not for myself, but for the Church, O Lord! The great plot thickens, and all men clamour to me, its head and spring, for money. Give me money, and within six months Yorkshire and the North will be up, and without a year Henry the Anti-Christ will be dead and the Princess Mary fast upon the throne, with the Emperor and the Pope for watchdogs. That stiff-necked Cicely must die and her babe must die, and then I'll twist the secret of the jewels out of the witch, Emlyn—on the rack, if need be. Those jewels—I've seen them so often; why, they would feed an army; but while Cicely or her brat lives where is my claim to them? So, alas! they must die, but oh! the hag is right. Who shall give me absolution for a deed I hate? Not for me, not for me, O my Patron, but for the Church!" and flinging himself to the floor before the holy image of his chosen Saint, he rested his head upon its feet and wept.

Chapter X

Mother Megges and the Ghost

Flounder Megges, with all the paraphernalia of her trade, was established as nurse to Cicely at the Nunnery. This establishment, it is true, had not been easy since Emlyn, who knew something of the woman's repute, and suspected more, resisted it with all her strength, but here the Prioress intervened in her gentle way. She herself, she explained, did not like this person, who looked so odd, drank so much beer and talked so fast. Yet she had made inquiries and found that she was extraordinarily skilled in matters of that nature. Indeed, it was said that she had succeeded in cases that were wonderfully difficult which the leech had abandoned as hopeless, though of course there had been other cases where she had not succeeded. But these, she was informed, were generally those of poor people who did not pay her well. Now in this instance her pay would be ample, for she, Mother Matilda, had promised her a splendid fee out of her private store, and for the rest, since no man doctor might enter there, who else was competent? Not she or the other nuns, for none of them had been married save old Bridget, who was silly and had long ago forgotten all such things. Not Emlyn even, who was but a girl when her own child was born, and since then had been otherwise employed. Therefore there was no choice.

To this reasoning Emlyn agreed perforce, though she mistrusted her of the fat wretch, whose appearance poor Cicely also disliked. Still, for very fear Emlyn was humble and civil to her, for if she were not, who could know if she would put out all her skill upon behalf of her mistress? Therefore she did her bidding like a slave, and spiced her beer and made her bed and even listened to her foul jests and talk unmurmuringly.

The business was over at length, and the child, a noble boy, born into the world. Had not the Flounder produced it in triumph laid upon a little basket covered with a lamb-skin, and had not Emlyn and Mother Matilda and all the nuns kissed and blessed it? Had it not also, for fear of accident (such was the fatherly forethought of the Abbot), been baptized at once by a priest who was waiting, under the names of John Christopher Foterell, John after its grandfather and Christopher after its father, with Foterell for a surname, since the Abbot would not allow that it should be called Harflete, being, as he averred, base-born?

So this child was born, and Mother Megges swore that of all the two hundred and three that she had issued into the world it was the finest, nine and a half pounds in weight at the very least. Also, as its voice and movements testified, it was lusty and like to live, for did not the Flounder, in sight of all the wondering nuns, hold it up hanging by its hands to her two fat forefingers, and afterwards drink a whole quart of spiced ale to its health and long life?

But if the babe was like to live, Cicely was like to die. Indeed, she was very, very ill, and perhaps would have passed away had it not been for a device of Emlyn's. For when she was at her worst and the Flounder, shaking her head and saying that she could do no more, had departed to her eternal ale and a nap, Emlyn crept up and took her mistress's cold hand.

"Darling," she said, "hear me," but Cicely did not stir. "Darling," she repeated, "hear me, I have news for you of your husband."

Cicely's white face turned a little on the pillow and her blue eyes opened.

"Of my husband?" she whispered. "Why, he is gone, as I soon shall be. What news of him?"

"That he is not gone, that he lives, or so I believe, though heretofore I have hid it from you."

The head was lifted for a moment, and the eyes stared at her with wondering joy.

"Do you trick me, Nurse? Nay, you would never do that. Give me the milk, I want it now. I'll listen. I promise you I'll not die till you have told me. If Christopher lives why should I die who only hoped to find him?"

So Emlyn whispered all she knew. It was not much, only that Christopher had not been buried in the grave where he was said to be buried, and that he had been taken wounded aboard the ship Great Yarmouth, of the fate of which ship fortunately she had heard nothing. Still, slight as they might be, to Cicely these tidings were a magic medicine, for did they not mean the rebirth of hope, hope that for nine long months had been dead and buried with Christopher? From that moment she began to mend.

When the Flounder, having slept off her drink, returned to the sick- bed, she stared at her amazed and muttered something about witchcraft, she who had been sure that she would die, as in those days so many women did who fell into hands like hers. Indeed, she was bitterly disappointed, knowing that this death was desired by her employer, who now after all might let the Ford Inn to another. Moreover, the child was no waster, but one who was set for life. Well, that at least she could mend, and if it were done quickly the shock might kill the mother. Yet the thing was not so easy as it looked, for there were many loving eyes upon that babe.

When she wished to take it to her bed at night Emlyn forbade her fiercely, and on being appealed to, the Prioress, who knew the creature's drunken habits and had heard rumours of the fate of the Smith infant and others, gave orders that it was not to be. So, since the mother was too weak to have it with her, the boy was laid in a little cot at her side. And always day and night one or more of the sweet-faced nuns stood at the head of that cot watching as might a guardian angel. Also it took only Nature's food since from the first Cicely would nurse it, so that she could not mix any drug with its milk that would cause it to sleep itself away.

So the days went on, bringing black wrath, despair almost, to the heart of Mother Megges, till at length there came the chance she sought. One fine evening, when the nuns were gathered at vespers, but as it happened not in the chapel, because since the tale of the hauntings they shunned the place after high noon, Cicely, whose strength was returning to her, asked Emlyn to change her garments and remake her bed. Meanwhile, the babe was given to Sister Bridget, who doted on it, with instructions to take it to walk in the garden for a time, since the rain had passed off and the afternoon was now very soft and pleasant. So she went, and there presently was met by the Flounder, who was supposed to be asleep, but had followed her, a person of whom the half-witted Bridget was much afraid.

"What are you doing with my babe, old fool?" she screeched at her, thrusting her fat face to within an inch of the nun's. "You'll let it fall and I shall be blamed. Give me the angel or I will twist your nose for you. Give it me, I say, and get you gone."

In her fear and flurry old Bridget obeyed and departed at a run. Then, recovering herself a little, or drawn by some instinct, she returned, hid herself in a clump of lilac bushes and watched.

Presently she saw the Flounder, after glancing about to make sure that she was alone, enter the chapel, carrying the child, and heard her bolt the door after her. Now Bridget, as she said afterwards, grew very frightened, she knew not why, and, acting on impulse, ran to the chancel window and, climbing on to a wheelbarrow that stood there, looked through it. This is what she saw.

Mother Megges was kneeling in the chancel, as she thought at first, to say her prayers, till she perceived, for a ray from the setting sun showed it all, that on the paving before her lay the infant and that this she-devil was thrusting her thick forefinger down its throat, for already it grew black in the face, and as she thrust muttering savagely. So horror-struck was Bridget that she could neither move nor cry.

Then, while she stood petrified, suddenly there appeared the figure of a man in rusty armour. The Flounder looked up, saw him and, withdrawing her finger from the mouth of the child, let out yell after yell. The man, who said nothing, drew a sword and lifted it, whereon the murderess screamed—

"The ghost! The ghost! Spare me, Sir John, I am poor and he paid me. Spare me for Christ's sake!" and so saying, she rolled on to the floor in a fit, and there turned and twisted until she lay still.

Then the man, or the ghost of a man, having looked at her, sheathed his sword and lifting up the babe, which now drew its breath again and cried, marched with it down the aisle. The next thing of which Bridget became aware was that he stood before her, the infant in his arms, holding it out to her. His face she could not see, for the vizor was down, but he spoke in a hollow voice, saying—

"This gift from Heaven to the Lady Harflete. Bid her fear nothing, for one devil I have garnered and the others are ripe for reaping."

Bridget took the child and sank down on to the ground, and at that moment the nuns, alarmed by the awful yells, rushed through the side door, headed by Mother Matilda. They too saw the figure, and knew the Foterell cognizance upon its helm and shield. But it waited not to speak to them, only passed behind some trees and vanished.

Their first care was for the infant, which they thought the man was stealing; then, after they were sure that it had taken no real hurt, they questioned old Bridget, but could get nothing from her, for all she did was to gibber and point first to the barrow and next to the chancel window. At length Mother Matilda understood and, climbing on to the barrow, looked through the window as Bridget had done. She looked, she saw, and fell back fainting.

An hour had gone by. The child, unhurt save for a little bruising of its tender mouth, was asleep upon its mother's breast. Bridget, having recovered, at length had told all her tale to every one of them save Cicely, who as yet knew nothing, for she and Emlyn did not hear the screams, their rooms being on the other side of the building. The Abbot had been sent for, and, accompanied by monks, arrived in the midst of a thunder-storm and pouring rain. He, too, had heard the tale, heard it with a pale face while his monks crossed themselves. At length he asked of the woman Megges. They replied that living or dead she was, as they supposed, still in the chapel, which none of them had dared to enter.

"Come, let us see," said the Abbot, and they went there to find the door locked as Bridget had said.

Smiths were sent for and broke it in while all stood in the pouring rain and watched. It was open at last, and they entered with torches and tapers, for now the darkness was dense, the Abbot leading them. They came to the chancel, where something lay upon the floor, and held down the torches to look. Then they saw that which caused them all to turn and fly, calling on the saints to protect them. In her life Mother Megges had not been lovely, but in the death that had overtaken her—!

It was morning. The Lord Abbot and his monks were assembled in the guest-chamber, and opposite to them were the Lady Prioress and her nuns, and with them Emlyn.

"Witchcraft!" shouted the Abbot, smiting his fist upon the table, "black witchcraft! Satan himself and his foulest demons walk the countryside and have their home in this Nunnery. Last night they manifested themselves—"

"By saving a babe from a cruel death and bringing a hateful murderess to doom," broke in Emlyn.

"Silence, Sorceress," shouted the Abbot. "Get thee behind me, Satan. I know you and your familiars," and he glared at the Prioress.

"What may you mean, my Lord Abbot?" asked Mother Matilda, bridling up. "My sisters and I do not understand. Emlyn Stower is right. Do you call that witchcraft which works so good an end? The ghost of Sir John Foterell appeared here—we admit it who saw that ghost. But what did the spirit do? It slew the hellish woman whom you sent among us and it rescued the blessed babe when her finger was down its throat to choke out its pure life. If that be witchcraft I stand by it. Tell us what did the wretch mean when she cried out to the spirit to spare her because she was poor and had been bribed for her iniquity?

Who bribed her, my Lord Abbot? None in this house, I'll swear. And who changed Sir John Foterell from flesh to spirit? Why is he a ghost to-day?"

"Am I here to answer riddles, woman, and who are you that you dare put such questions to me? I depose you, I set your house under ban. The judgment of the Church shall be pronounced against you all. Dare not to leave your doors until the Court is composed to try you. Think not you shall escape. Your English land is sick and heresy stalks abroad; but," he added slowly, "fire can still bite and there is store of faggots in the woods. Prepare your souls for judgment. Now I go."

"Do as it pleases you," answered the enraged Mother Matilda. "When you set out your case we will answer it; but, meanwhile, we pray that you take what is left of your dead hireling with you, for we find her ill company and here she shall have no burial. My Lord Abbot, the charter of this Nunnery is from the monarch of England, whatever authority you and those that went before you have usurped. It was granted by the first Edward, and the appointment of every prioress since his day has been signed by the sovereign and no other. I hold mine under the manual of the eighth Henry. You cannot depose me, for I appeal from the Abbot to the King. Fare you well, my Lord," and, followed by her little train of aged nuns, she swept from the room like an offended queen.

After the terrible death of the child-murderess and the restoration of her babe to her unharmed, Cicely's recovery was swift. Within a week she was up and walking, and within ten days as strong, or stronger, than ever she had been. Nothing more had been heard of the Abbot, and though all knew that danger threatened them from this quarter they were content to enjoy the present hour of peace and wait till it was at hand.

But in Cicely's awakened mind there arose a keen desire to learn more of what her nurse had hinted to her when she lay upon the very edge of death. Day by day she plied Emlyn with questions till at length she knew all; namely, that the tidings came from Thomas Bolle, and that he, dressed in her father's armour, was the ghost who had saved her boy from death. Now nothing would serve her but that she must see Thomas herself, as she said, to thank him, though truly, as Emlyn knew well, to draw from his own lips every detail and circumstance that she could gather concerning Christopher.

For a while Emlyn held out against her, for she knew the dangers of such a meeting; but in the end, being able to refuse her lady nothing, she gave way.

At length at the appointed hour of sunset Emlyn and Cicely stood in the chapel, whither the latter told the nuns she wished to go to return thanks for her deliverance from many dangers. They knelt before the altar, and while they made pretence to pray there heard knocks, which were the signal of the presence of Thomas Bolle. Emlyn answered them with other knocks, which told that all was safe, whereon the wooden image turned and Thomas appeared, dressed as before in Sir John Foterell's armour. So like did he seem to her dead father in this familiar mail that for a moment Cicely thought it must be he, and her knees trembled until he knelt before her, kissing her hand, asking after her health and that of the infant and whether she were satisfied with his service.

"Indeed and indeed yes," she answered; "and oh, friend! all that I have henceforth is yours should I ever have anything again, who am but a prisoned beggar. Meanwhile, my blessing and that of Heaven rest upon you, you gallant man."

"Thank me not, Lady," answered the honest Thomas. "To speak truth it was Emlyn whom I served, for though monks parted us we have been friends for many a year. As for the matter of the child and that spawn of hell, the Flounder, be grateful to God, not to me, for it was by mere chance that I came here that evening, which I had not intended to do. I was going about my business with the cattle when something seemed to tell me to arm and come. It was as though a hand pushed me, and the rest you know, and so I think by now does Mother Megges," he added grimly.

"Yes, yes, Thomas; and in truth I do thank God, Whose finger I see in all this business, as I thank you, His instrument. But there are other things whereof Emlyn has spoken to me. She said—ah! she said my husband, whom I thought slain and buried, in truth was only wounded and not buried, but shipped over-sea. Tell me that story, friend, omitting nothing, but swiftly for our time is short. I thirst to hear it from your own lips."

So in his slow, wandering way he told her, word by word, all that he had seen, all that he had learned, and the sum of it was that Sir Christopher had been shipped abroad upon the Great Yarmouth, sorely wounded but not dead, and that with him had sailed Jeffrey Stokes and the monk Martin.

"That's ten months gone," said Cicely. "Has naught been heard of this ship? By now she should be home again."

Thomas hesitated, then answered—

"No tidings came of her from Spain. Then, although I said nothing of it even to Emlyn, she was reported lost with all hands at sea. Then came another story—"

"Ah! that other story?"

"Lady, two of her crew reached the Wash. I did not see them, and they have shipped again for Marseilles in France. But I spoke with a shepherd who is half-brother to one of them, and he told me that from him he learned that the Great Yarmouth was set upon by two Turkish pirates and captured after a brave fight in which the captain Goody and others were killed. This man and his comrade escaped in a boat and drifted to and fro till they were picked up by a homeward-bound caravel which landed them at Hull. That's all I know—save one thing."

"One thing! Oh, what thing, Thomas? That my husband is dead?"

"Nay, nay, the very opposite, that he is alive, or was, for these men saw him and Jeffrey Stokes and Martin the priest, no craven as I know, fighting like devils till the Turks overwhelmed them by numbers, and, having bound their hands, carried them all three unwounded on board one of their ships, wishing doubtless to make slaves of such brave fellows."

Now, although Emlyn would have stopped her, still Cicely plied him with questions, which he answered as best he could, till suddenly a sound caught his ear.

"Look at the window!" he exclaimed.

They looked, and saw a sight that froze their blood, for there staring at them through the glass was the dark face of the Abbot, and with it other faces.

"Betray me not, or I shall burn," he whispered. "Say only that I came to haunt you," and silently as a shadow he glided to his niche and was gone.

"What now, Emlyn?"

"One thing only—Thomas must be saved. A bold face and stand to it. Is it our fault if your father's ghost should haunt this chapel? Remember, your father's ghost, no other. Ah! here they come."

As she spoke the door was thrown wide, and through it came the Abbot and his rout of attendants. Within two paces of the women they halted, hanging together like bees, for they were afraid, while a voice cried, "Seize the witches!"

Cicely's terror passed from her and she faced them boldly.

"What would you with us, my Lord Abbot?" she asked.

"We would know, Sorceress, what shape was that which spoke with you but now, and whither has it gone?"

"The same that saved my child and called the Sword of God down upon the murderess. It wore my father's armour, but its face I did not see. It has gone whence it came, but where that is I know not. Discover if you can."

"Woman, you trifle with us. What said the Thing?"

"It spoke of the slaughter of Sir John Foterell by King's Grave Mount and of those who wrought it," and she looked at him steadily until his eyes fell before hers.

"What else?"

"It told me that my husband is not dead. Neither did you bury him as you put about, but shipped him hence to Spain, whence it prophesied he will return again to be revenged upon you. It told me that he was captured by the infidel Moors, and with him Jeffrey Stokes, my father's servant, and the priest Martin, your secretary. Then it looked up and vanished, or seemed to vanish, though perhaps it is among us now."

"Aye," answered the Abbot, "Satan, with whom you hold converse, is always among us. Cicely Foterell and Emlyn Stower, you are foul witches, self-confessed. The world has borne your sorceries too long, and you shall answer for them before God and man, as I, the Lord Abbot of Blossholme, have right and authority to make you do. Seize these witches and let them be kept fast in their chamber till I constitute the Court Ecclesiastic for their trial."

So they took hold of Cicely and Emlyn and led them to the Nunnery. As they crossed the garden they were met by Mother Matilda and the nuns, who, for a second time within a month, ran out to see what was the tumult in the chapel.

"What is it now, Cicely?" asked the Prioress.

"Now we are witches, Mother," she answered, with a sad smile.

"Aye," broke in Emlyn, "and the charge is that the ghost of the murdered Sir John Foterell was seen speaking to us."

"Why, why?" exclaimed the Prioress. "If the spirit of a woman's father appears to her is she therefore to be declared a witch? Then is poor Sister Bridget a witch also, for this same spirit brought the child to her?"

"Aye," said the Abbot, "I had forgotten her. She is another of the crew, let her be seized and shut up also. Greatly do I hope, when it comes to the hour of trial, that there may not be found to be more of them," and he glanced at the poor nuns with menace in his eye.

So Cicely and Emlyn were shut within their room and strictly guarded by monks, but otherwise not ill-treated. Indeed, save for their confinement, there was little change in their condition. The child was allowed to be with Cicely, the nuns were allowed to visit her.

Only over both of them hung the shadow of great trouble. They were aware, and it seemed to them purposely suffered to be aware, that they were about to be tried for their lives upon monstrous and obscene charges; namely, that they had consorted with a dim and awful creature called the Enemy of Mankind, whom, it was supposed, human beings had power to call to their counsel and assistance. To them who knew well that this being was Thomas Bolle, the thing seemed absurd. Yet it could not be denied that the said Thomas at Emlyn's instigation had worked much evil on the monks of Blossholme, paying them, or rather their Abbot, back in his own coin.

Yet what was to be done? To tell the facts would be to condemn Thomas to some fearful fate which even then they would be called upon to share, although possibly they might be cleared of the charge of witchcraft.

Emlyn set the matter before Cicely, urging neither one side nor the other, and waited her judgment. It was swift and decisive.

"This is a coil that we cannot untangle," said Cicely. "Let us betray no one, but put our trust in God. I am sure," she added, "that God will help us as He did when Mother Megges would have murdered my boy. I shall not attempt to defend myself by wronging others. I leave everything to Him."

"Strange things have happened to many who trusted in God; to that the whole evil world bears witness," said Emlyn doubtfully.

"May be," answered Cicely in her quiet fashion, "perhaps because they did not trust enough or rightly. At least there lies my path and I will walk in it—to the fire if need be."

"There is some seed of greatness in you; to what will it grow, I wonder?" replied Emlyn, with a shrug of her shoulders.

On the morrow this faith of Cicely's was put to a sharp test. The Abbot came and spoke with Emlyn apart. This was the burden of his song—

"Give me those jewels and all may yet be well with you and your mistress, vile witches though you are. If not, you burn."

As before she denied all knowledge of them.

"Find me the jewels or you burn," he answered. "Would you pay your lives for a few miserable gems?"

Now Emlyn weakened, not for her own sake, and said she would speak with her mistress.

He bade her do so.

"I thought that those jewels were burned, Emlyn, do you then know where they are?" asked Cicely.

"Aye, I have said nothing of it to you, but I know. Speak the word and I give them up to save you."

Cicely thought a while and kissed her child, which she held in her arms, then laughed aloud and answered—

"Not so. That Abbot shall never be richer for any gem of mine. I have told you in what I trust, and it is not jewels. Whether I burn or whether I am saved, he shall not have them."

"Good," said Emlyn, "that is my mind also, I only spoke for your sake," and she went out and told the Abbot.

He came into Cicely's chamber and raged at them. He said that they should be excommunicated, then tortured and then burned; but Cicely, whom he had thought to frighten, never winced.

"If so, so let it be," she replied, "and I will bear all as best I can. I know nothing of these jewels, but if they still exist they are mine, not yours, and I am innocent of any witchcraft. Do your work, for I am sure that the end shall be far other than you think."

"What!" said the Abbot, "has the foul fiend been with you again that you talk thus certainly? Well, Sorceress, soon you will sing another tune," and he went to the door and summoned the Prioress.

"Put these women upon bread and water," he said, "and prepare them for the rack, that they may discover their accomplices."

Mother Matilda set her gentle face, and answered—

"It shall not be done in this Nunnery, my Lord Abbot. I know the law, and you have no such power. Moreover, if you move them hence, who are my guests, I appeal to the King, and meanwhile raise the country on you."

"Said I not that they had accomplices?" sneered the Abbot, and went his way.

But of the torture no more was heard, for that appeal to the King had an ill sound in his ears.

Chapter XI

Doomed

It was the day of trial. From dawn Cicely and Emlyn had seen people hurrying in and out of the gates of the Nunnery, and heard workmen making preparation in the guest-hall below their chamber. About eight one of the nuns brought them their breakfast. Her face was scared and white; she only spoke in whispers, looking behind her continually as though she knew she was being watched.

Emlyn asked who their judges were, and she answered—

"The Abbot, a strange, black-faced Prior, and the Old Bishop. Oh! God help you, my sisters; God help us all!" and she fled away.

Now for a moment Emlyn's heart failed her, since before such a tribunal what chance had they? The Abbot was their bitter enemy and accuser; the strange Prior, no doubt, one of his friends and kindred; while the ecclesiastic spoken of as the "Old Bishop" was well known as perhaps the cruelest man in England, a scourge of heretics—that is, before heresy became the fashion—a hunter-out of witches and wizards, and a time-server to boot. But to Cicely she said nothing, for what was the use, seeing that soon she would learn all?

They ate their food, knowing both of them that they would need strength. Then Cicely nursed her child, and, placing it in Emlyn's arms, knelt down to pray. While she was still praying the door opened and a procession appeared. First came two monks, then six armed men of the Abbot's guard, then the Prioress and three of her nuns. At the sight of the beautiful young woman kneeling at her prayers the guards, rough men though they were, stopped, as if unwilling to disturb her, but one of the monks cried brutally—

"Seize the accursed hypocrite, and if she will not come, drag her with you," at the same time stretching out his hand as though to grasp her arm.

But Cicely rose and faced him, saying—

"Do not touch me; I follow. Emlyn, give me the child, and let us go."

So they went in the midst of the armed men, the monks preceding, the nuns, with bowed heads, following after. Presently they entered the large hall, but on its threshold were ordered to pause while way was made for them. Cicely never forgot the sight of it as it appeared that day. The lofty, arched roof of rich chestnut-wood, set there hundreds of years before by hands that spared neither work nor timber, amongst the beams of which the bright light of morning played so clearly that she could see the spiders' webs, and in one of them a sleepy autumn wasp caught fast. The mob of people gathered to watch her public trial—faces, many of them, that she had known from childhood.

How they stared at her as she stood there by the head of the steps, her sleeping child held in her arms! They were a packed audience and had been prepared to condemn her—that she could see and hear, for did not some of them point and frown, and set up a cry of "Witch!" as they had been told to do? But it died away. The sight of her, the daughter of one of their great men and the widow of another, standing in her innocent beauty, the slumbering babe upon her breast, seemed to quell them, till the hardest faces grew pitiful—full of resentment, too, some of them, but not against her.

Then the three judges on the bench behind the table, at which sat the monkish secretaries; the hard-faced, hook-nosed "Old Bishop" in his gorgeous robes and mitre, his crozier resting against the panelling behind him, peering about him with beady eyes. The sullen, heavy-jawed Prior, from some distant county, on his left, clad in a simple black gown with a girdle about his waist. And on the right Clement Maldon, Abbot of Blossholme and enemy of her house, suave, olive-faced, foreign-looking, his black, uneasy eyes observing all, his keen ears catching every word and murmur as he whispered something to the Bishop that caused him to smile grimly. Lastly, placed already in the roped space and guarded by a soldier, poor old Bridget, the half-witted, who was gabbling words to which no one paid any heed.

The path was clear now, and they were ordered to walk on. Half-way up the hall something red attracted Cicely's attention, and, glancing round, she saw that it was the beard of Thomas Bolle. Their eyes met, and his were full of fear. In an instant she understood that he dreaded lest he should be betrayed and given over to some awful doom.

"Fear nothing," she whispered as she passed, and he heard her, or perhaps Emlyn's glance told him that he was safe. At least, a sign of relief broke from him.

Now they had entered the roped space, and stood there.

"Your name?" asked one of the secretaries, pointing to Cicely with the feather of his quill.

"All know it, it is Cicely Harflete," she answered gently, whereon the clerk said roughly that she lied, and the old wrangle began again as to the validity of her marriage, the Abbot maintaining that she was still Cicely Foterell, the mother of a base-born child.

Into this argument the Bishop entered with some zest, asking many questions, and seeming more or less to take her side, since, where matters of religion were not concerned, he was a keen lawyer, and just enough. At length, however, he swept the thing away, remarking brutally that if half he had heard were true, soon the name by which she had last been called in life would not concern her, and bade the clerks write her down as Cicely Harflete or Foterell.

Then Emlyn gave her name, and Sister Bridget's was written without question. Next the charge against them was read. It was long and technical, mixed up with Latin words and phrases, and all that Cicely made out of it was that they were accused of many horrible crimes, and of having called up the devil and consorted with him in the shape of a monster with horns and hoofs, and of her father's ghost. When it was finished they were commanded to answer, and pleaded Not Guilty, or rather Cicely and Emlyn did, for Bridget broke into a long tale that could not be followed. She was ordered to be silent, after which no one took any more heed of what she said.

Now the Bishop asked whether these women had been put to the question, and when he was told No, said that it seemed a pity, as evidently they were stubborn witches, and some discipline of the sort might have saved trouble. Again he asked if the witch's marks had been found on them—that is, the spot where the devil had sealed their bodies, on which, as was well known, his chosen could feel no pain. He even suggested that the trial should be adjourned until they had been pricked all over with a nail to find this spot, but ultimately gave up the point to save time.

A last question was raised by the beetle-browed Prior, who submitted that the infant ought also to be accused, since he, too, was said to have consorted with the devil, having, according to the story, been rescued from death by him and afterwards been carried in his arms and given to the nun Bridget, which was the only evidence against the said Bridget. If she was guilty, why, then, was the infant innocent? Ought not they to burn together, since a babe that had been nursed by the Evil One was obviously damned?

The legal-minded Bishop found this argument interesting, but ultimately decided that it was safer to overrule it on account of the tender age of the criminal. He added that it did not matter, since doubtless the foul fiend would claim his own ere long.

Lastly, before the witnesses were called, Emlyn asked for an advocate to defend them, but the Bishop replied, with a chuckle, that it was quite unnecessary, since already they had the best of all advocates—Satan himself.

"True, my Lord," said Cicely, looking up, "we have the best of all advocates, only you have mis-named him. The God of the innocent is our advocate, and in Him I trust."

"Blaspheme not, Sorceress," shouted the old man; and the evidence commenced.

To follow it in detail is not necessary, and, indeed, would be long, for it took many hours. First of all Emlyn's early life was set out, much being made of the fact that her mother was a gypsy who had committed suicide and that her father had fallen under the ban of the Inquisition, an heretical work of his having been publicly burned. Then the Abbot himself gave evidence, since, where the charge was sorcery, no one seemed to think it strange that the same man should both act as judge and be the principal witness for the prosecution. He told of Cicely's wild words after the burning of Cranwell Towers, from which burning she and her familiar, Emlyn, had evidently escaped by magic, without the aid of which it was plain they could not have lived. He told of Emlyn's threats to him after she had looked into the bowl of water; of all the dreadful things that had been seen and done at Blossholme, which no doubt these witches had brought about—here he was right—though how he knew not. He told of the death of the midwife and of the appearance which she presented afterwards—a tale that caused his audience to shudder; and, lastly, he told of the vision of the ghost of Sir John Foterell holding converse with the two accused in the chapel of the Nunnery, and its vanishing away.

When at length he had finished Emlyn asked leave to cross-examine him, but this was refused on the ground that persons accused of such crimes had no right to cross-examine.

Then the Court adjourned for a while to eat, some food being brought for the prisoners, who were forced to take it where they stood. Worse still, Cicely was driven to nurse her child in the presence of all that audience, who stared and gibed at her rudely, and were angry because Emlyn and some of the nuns stood round her to form a living screen.

When the judges returned the evidence went on. Though most of it was entirely irrelevant, its volume was so great that at length the Old Bishop grew weary, and said he would hear no more. Then the judges went on to put, first to Cicely and afterwards to Emlyn, a series of questions of a nature so abominable that after denying the first of them indignantly, they stood silent, refusing to answer—proof positive of their guilt, as the black-browed Prior remarked in triumph. Lastly, these hideous queries being exhausted, Cicely was asked if she had anything to say.

"Somewhat," she answered; "but I am weary, and must be brief. I am no witch; I do not know what it means. The Abbot of Blossholme, who sits as my judge, is my grievous enemy. He claimed my father's lands—which lands I believe he now holds—and cruelly murdered my said father by King's Grave Mount in the forest as he was riding to London to make complaint of him and reveal his treachery to his Grace the King and his Council—"

"It is a lie, witch," broke in the Abbot, but, taking no heed, Cicely went on—

"Afterwards he and his hired soldiers attacked the house of my husband, Sir Christopher Harflete, and burnt it, slaying, or striving to slay—I know not which—my said husband, who has vanished away. Then he imprisoned me and my servant, Emlyn Stower, in this Nunnery, and strove to force me to sign papers conveying all my own and my child's property to him. This I refused to do, and therefore it is that he puts me on my trial, because, as I am told, those who are found guilty of witchcraft are stripped of all their possessions, which those take who are strong enough to keep them. Lastly, I deny the authority of this Court, and appeal to the King, who soon or late will hear my cry and avenge my wrongs, and maybe my murder, upon those who wrought them. Good people all, hear my words. I appeal to the King, and to him under God above I entrust my cause, and, should I die, the guardianship of my orphan son, whom the Abbot sent his creature to murder—his vile creature, upon whose head fell the Almighty's justice, as it will fall on yours, you slaughterers of the innocent."

So spoke Cicely, and, having spoken, worn out with fatigue and misery, sank to the floor—for all these hours there had been no stool for her to sit on—and crouched there, still holding her child in her arms—a piteous sight indeed, which touched even the superstitious hearts of the crowd who watched her.

Now this appeal of hers to the King seemed to scare the fierce Old Bishop, who turned and began to argue with the Abbot. Cicely, listening, caught some of his words, such as—

"On your head be it, then. I judge only of the cause ecclesiastic, and shall direct it to be so entered upon the records. Of the execution of the sentence or the disposal of the property I wash my hands. See you to it."

"So spoke Pilate," broke in Cicely, lifting her head and looking him in the eyes. Then she let it fall again, and was silent.

Now Emlyn opened her lips, and from them burst a fierce torrent of words.

"Do you know," she began, "who and what is this Spanish priest who sits to judge us of witchcraft? Well, I will tell you. Years ago he fled from Spain because of hideous crimes that he had committed there. Ask him of Isabella the nun, who was my father's cousin, and her end and that of her companions. Ask him of—"

At this point a monk, to whom the Abbot had whispered something, slipped behind Emlyn and threw a cloth over her face. She tore it away with her strong hands, and screamed out—

"He is a murderer, he is a traitor. He plots to kill the King. I can prove it, and that's why Foterell died—because he knew—"

The Abbot shouted something, and again the monk, a stout fellow named Ambrose, got the cloth over her mouth. Once more she wrenched herself loose, and, turning towards the people, called—

"Have I never a friend, who have befriended so many? Is there no man in Blossholme who will avenge me of this brute Ambrose? Aye, I see some."

Then this Ambrose, and others aiding him, fell upon her, striking her on the head and choking her, till at length she sank, half stunned and gasping, to the ground.

Now, after a hurried word or two with his colleagues, the Bishop sprang up, and as darkness gathered in the hall—for the sun had set—pronounced the sentence of the Court.

First he declared the prisoners guilty of the foulest witchcraft. Next he excommunicated them with much ceremony, delivering their souls to their master, Satan. Then, incidentally, he condemned their bodies to be burnt, without specifying when, how, or by whom. Out of the gloom a clear voice spoke, saying—

"You exceed your powers, Priest, and usurp those of the King. Beware!"

A tumult followed, in which some cried "Aye" and some "Nay," and when at length it died down the Bishop, or it may have been the Abbot—for none could see who spoke—exclaimed—

"The Church guards her own rights; let the King see to his."

"He will, he will," answered the same voice. "The Pope is in his bag. Monks, your day is done."

Again there was tumult, a very great tumult. In truth the scene, or rather the sounds, were strange. The Bishop shrieking with rage upon the bench, like a hen that has been caught upon her perch at night, the black-browed Prior bellowing like a bull, the populace surging and shouting this and that, the secretary calling for candles, and when at length one was brought, making a little star of light in that huge gloom, putting his hand to his mouth and roaring—

"What of this Bridget? Does she go free?"

The Bishop made no answer; it seemed as though he were frightened at the forces which he had let loose; but the Abbot hallooed back—

"Burn the hag with the others," and the secretary wrote it down upon his brief.

Then the guards seized the three of them to lead them away, and the frightened babe set up a thin, piercing wail, while the Bishop and his companions, preceded by one of the monks bearing the candle—it was that Ambrose who had choked Emlyn—marched in procession down the hall to gain the great door.

Ere ever they reached it the candle was dashed from the hand of Ambrose, and a fearful tumult arose in the dense darkness, for now all light had vanished. There were screams, and sounds of fighting, and cries for help. These died away; the hall emptied by degrees, for it seemed that none wished to stay there. Torches were lit, and showed a strange scene.

The Bishop, the Abbot, and the foreign Prior lay here and there, buffeted, bleeding, their robes torn off them, so that they were almost naked, while by the Bishop was his crozier, broken in two, apparently across his own head. Worse of all, the monk Ambrose leaned against a pillar; his feet seemed to go forward but his face looked backward, for his neck was twisted like that of a Michaelmas goose.

The Bishop looked about him and felt his hurts; then he called to his people—

"Bring me my cloak and a horse, for I have had enough of Blossholme and its wizardries. Settle your own matters henceforth, Abbot Maldon, for in them I find no luck," and he glanced at his broken staff.

Thus ended the great trial of the Blossholme witches.

Cicely had sunk to sleep at last, and Emlyn watched her, for, since there was nowhere else to put them, they were back in their own room, but guarded by armed men, lest they should escape. Of this, as Emlyn knew well, there was little chance, for even if they were once outside the Priory walls, how could they get away without friends to help, or food to eat, or horses to carry them? They would be run down within a mile. Moreover, there was the child, which Cicely would never leave, and, after all she had undergone, she herself was not fit to travel. Therefore it was that Emlyn sat sleepless, full of bitter wrath and fear, for she could see no hope. All was black as the night about them.

The door opened, and was shut and locked again. Then, from behind the curtain, appeared the tall figure of the Prioress, carrying a candle that made a star of light upon the shadows. As she stood there holding it up and looking about her, something came into Emlyn's mind. Perhaps she would help, she who loved Cicely. Did she not look like a figure of hope, with her sweet face and her taper in the gloom? Emlyn advanced to meet her, her finger on her lips.

"She sleeps; wake her not," she said. "Have you come to tell us that we burn to-morrow?"

"Nay, Emlyn; the Old Bishop has commanded that it shall not be for a week. He would have time to get across England first. Indeed, had it not been for the beating of him in the dark and the twisting of the neck of Brother Ambrose, I believe that he would not have suffered it at all, for fear of trouble afterwards. But now he is full of rage, and swears that he was set upon by evil spirits in the hall, and that those who loosed them shall not live. Emlyn, who killed Father Ambrose? Was it men or—?"

"Men, I think, Mother. The devil does not twist necks except in monkish dreams. Is it wonderful that my lady—the greatest lady of all these parts and the most foully treated—should have friends left to her? Why, if they were not curs, ere now her people would have pulled that Abbey stone from stone and cut the throat of every man within its walls."

"Emlyn," said the Prioress again, "in the name of Jesus and on your soul, tell me true, is there witchcraft in all this business? And if not, what is its meaning?"

"As much witchcraft as dwells in your gentle heart; no more. A man did these things; I'll not give you his name, lest it should be wrung from you. A man wore Foterell's armour, and came here by a secret hole to take counsel with us in the chapel. A man burnt the Abbey dormers and the stacks, and harried the beasts with a goatskin on his head, and dragged the skull of drunken Andrew from his grave. Doubtless it was his hand also that twisted Ambrose's neck because he struck me."

The two women looked each other in the eyes.

"Ah!" said the Prioress. "I think I can guess now; but, Emlyn, you choose rough tools. Well, fear not; your secret is safe with me." She paused a moment; then went on, "Oh! I am glad, who feared lest the Fiend's finger was in it all, as, in truth, they believe. Now I see my path clear, and will follow it to the death. Yes, yes; I will save you all or die."

"What path, Mother?"

"Emlyn, you have heard no tidings for these many months, but I have. Listen; there is much afoot. The King, or the Lord Cromwell, or both, make war upon the lesser Houses, dissolving them, seizing their goods, turning the religious out of them upon the world to starve. His Grace sends Royal Commissioners to visit them, and be judge and jury both. They were coming here, but I have friends and some fortune of my own, who was not born meanly or ill-dowered, and I found a way to buy them off. One of these Commissioners, Thomas Legh, as I heard only to-day, makes inquisition at the monastery of Bayfleet, in Yorkshire, some eighty miles away, of which my cousin, Alfred Stukley, whose letter reached me this morning, is the Prior. Emlyn, I'll go to this rough man—for rough he is, they say. Old and feeble as I am, I'll seek him out and offer up the ancient House I rule to save your life and Cicely's—yes, and Bridget's also."

"You will go, Mother! Oh! God's blessing be on you. But how will you go? They will never suffer it."

The old nun drew herself up, and answered—

"Who has the right to say to the Prioress of Blossholme that she shall not travel whither she will? No Spanish Abbot, I think. Why, but now that proud priest's servants would have forbidden me to enter your chamber in my own House, but I read them a lesson they will not forget. Also I have horses at my command, but it is true I need an escort, who am not too strong and little versed in the ways of the outside world, where I have scarcely strayed for many years. Now I have bethought me of that red-haired lay-brother, Thomas Bolle. I am told that though foolish, he is a valiant man whom few care to face; moreover, that he understands horses and knows all roads. Do you think, Emlyn Stower, that Thomas Bolle will be my companion on this journey, with leave from the Abbot, or without it?" and again she looked her in the eyes.

"He might, he might; he is a venturous man, or so I remember him in my youth," answered Emlyn. "Moreover, his forefathers have served the Harfletes and the Foterells for generations in peace and war, and doubtless, therefore, he loves my lady yonder. But the trouble is to get at him."

"No trouble at all, Emlyn; he is one of the watch outside the gate. But, woman, what token?"

Emlyn thought for a moment, then drew a ring off her finger in which was set a cornelian heart.

"Give him this," she said, "and say that the wearer bade him follow the bearer to the death, for the sake of that wearer's life and another's. He is a simple soul, and if the Abbot does not catch him first I believe that he will go."

Mother Matilda took the ring and set it on her own finger. Then she walked to where Cicely lay sleeping, looked at her and the boy upon her breast. Stretching out her thin hands, she called down the blessing and protection of Almighty God upon them both, then turned to depart.

Emlyn caught her by the robe.

"Stay," she said. "You think I do not understand; but I do. You are giving up everything for us. Even if you live through it, this House, which has been your charge for many years, will be dissolved; your sheep will be scattered to starve in their toothless age; the fold that has sheltered them for four hundred years will become a home of wolves. I understand full well, and she"—pointing to the sleeping Cicely—"will understand also."

"Say nothing to her," murmured Mother Matilda; "I may fail."

"You may fail, or you may succeed. If you fail and we burn, God shall reward you. If you succeed and we are saved, on her behalf I swear that you shall not suffer. There is wealth hidden away—wealth worth many priories; you and yours shall have your share of it, and that Commissioner shall not go lacking. Tell him that there is some small store to pay him for his trouble, and that the Abbot of Blossholme would rob him of it. Now, my Lady Margaret—for that, I think, used to be your name, and will be again when you have done with priests and nuns—bless me also and begone, and know that, living or dead, I hold you great and holy."

So the Prioress blessed her ere she glided thence in her stately fashion, and the oaken door opened and shut behind her.

Three days later the Abbot visited them alone.

"Foul and accursed witches," he said, "I come to tell you that next Monday at noon you burn upon the green in front of the Abbey gate, who, were it not for the mercy of the Church, should have been tortured also till you discovered your accomplices, of whom I think that you have many."

"Show me the King's warrant for this slaughter," said Cicely.

"I will show you nothing save the stake, witch. Repent, repent, ere it be too late. Hell and its eternal fires yawn for you."

"Do they yawn for my child also, my Lord Abbot?"

"Your brat will be taken from you ere you enter the flames and laid upon the ground, since it is baptized and too young to burn. If any have pity on it, good; if not, where it lies, there it will be buried."

"So be it," answered Cicely. "God gave it; God save it. In God I put my trust. Murderer, leave me to make my peace with Him," and she turned and walked away.

Now the Abbot and Emlyn were face to face.

"Do we really burn on Monday?" she asked.

"Without doubt, unless faggots will not take fire. Yet," he added slowly, "if certain jewels should chance to be found and handed over, the case might be remitted to another Court."

"And the torment prolonged. My Lord Abbot, I fear that those jewels will never be found."

"Well, then you burn—slowly, perhaps, for much rain has fallen of late and the wood is green. They say the death is dreadful."

"Doubtless one day you will find it so, Clement Maldonado, here or hereafter. But of that we will talk together when all is done—of that and many other things. I mean before the Judgment-seat of God. Nay, nay, I do not threaten after your fashion—it shall be so. Meanwhile I ask the boon of a dying woman. There are two whom I would see—the Prioress Matilda, in whose charge I desire to leave a certain secret, and Thomas Bolle, a lay-brother in your Abbey, a man who once engaged himself to me in marriage. For your own sake, deny me not these favours."

"They should be granted readily enough were it in my power, but it is not," answered the Abbot, looking at her curiously, for he thought that to them she might tell what she had refused to him—the hiding-place of the jewels, which afterwards he could wring out.

"Why not, my Lord Abbot?"

"Because the Prioress has gone hence, secretly, upon some journey of her own, and Thomas Bolle has vanished away I knew not where. If they, or either of them, return ere Monday you shall see them."

"And if they do not return I shall see them afterwards," replied Emlyn, with a shrug of her shoulders. "What does it matter? Fare you well till we meet at the fire, my Lord Abbot."

On the Sunday—that is, the day before the burning—the Abbot came again.

"Three days ago," he said, addressing them both, "I offered you a chance of life upon certain conditions, but, obstinate witches that you are, you refused to listen. Now I offer you the last boon in my power—not life, indeed; it is too late for that—but a merciful death. If you will give me what I seek, the executioner shall dispatch you both before the fire bites—never mind how. If not—well, as I have told you, there has been much rain, and they say the faggots are somewhat green."

Cicely paled a little—who would not, even in those cruel days?—then asked—

"And what is it that you seek, or that we can give? A confession of our guilt, to cover up your crime in the eyes of the world? If so, you shall never have it, though we burn by inches."

"Yes, I seek that, but for your own sakes, not for mine, since those who confess and repent may receive absolution. Also I seek more—the rich jewels which you have in hiding, that they may be used for the purposes of the Church."

Then it was that Cicely showed the courage of her blood.

"Never, never!" she cried, turning on him with eyes ablaze. "Torture and slay me if you will, but my wealth you shall not thieve. I know not where these jewels are, but wherever they may be, there let them lie till my heirs find them, or they rot."

The Abbot's face grew very evil.

"Is that your last word, Cicely Foterell?" he asked.

She bowed her head, and he repeated the question to Emlyn, who answered—

"What my mistress says, I say."

"So be it!" he exclaimed. "Doubtless you sorceresses put your trust in the devil. Well, we shall see if he will help you to-morrow."

"God will help us," replied Cicely in a quiet voice. "Remember my words when the time comes."

Then he went.

Chapter XII

The Stake

It was an awful night. Let those who have followed this history think of the state of these two women, one of them still but a girl, who on the morrow, amidst the jeers and curses of superstitious men, were to suffer the cruelest of deaths for no crime at all, unless the traffickings of Emlyn with Thomas Bolle, in which Cicely had small share, could be held a crime. Well, thousands quite as blameless were called on to undergo that, and even worse fates in the days which some name good and old, the days of chivalry and gallant knights, when even little children were tormented and burned by holy and learned folk who feared a visible or at least a tangible devil and his works.

Doubtless their cruelty was that of terror. Doubtless, although he had other ends to gain which to him were sacred, the Abbot Maldon did believe that Cicely and Emlyn had practised horrible witchcraft; that they had conversed with Satan in order to revenge themselves upon him, and therefore were too foul to live. The "Old Bishop" believed it also, and so did the black-browed Prior and the most of the ignorant people who lived around and knew of the terrible things which had happened in Blossholme. Had not some of them actually seen the fiend with horns and hoofs and tail driving the Abbey cattle, and had not others met the ghost of Sir John Foterell, which doubtless was but that fiend in another shape? Oh, these women were guilty, without doubt they were guilty and deserved the stake! What did it matter if the husband and father of one of them had been murdered and the other had suffered grievous but forgotten wrongs? Compared to witchcraft murder was but a light and homely crime, one that would happen when men's passions and needs were involved, quite a familiar thing.

It was an awful night. Sometimes Cicely slept a little, but the most of it she spent in prayer. The fierce Emlyn neither slept nor prayed, except once or twice that vengeance might fall upon the Abbot's head, for her whole soul was up in arms and it galled her to think that she and her beloved mistress must die shamefully while their enemy lived on triumphant and in honour. Even the infant seemed nervous and disturbed, as though some instinct warned it of terror at hand, for although it was well enough, against its custom it woke continually and wailed.

"Emlyn," said Cicely towards morning, but before the light had come, after at length she had soothed it to rest, "do you think that Mother Matilda will be able to help us?"

"No, no; put it from your mind, dearie. She is weak and old, the road is rough and long, and mayhap she has never reached the place. It was a great venture for her to try such a journey, and if she came there, why, perhaps the Commissioner man had gone, or perhaps he will not listen, or perhaps he cannot come. What would he care about the burning of two witches a hundred miles away, this leech who is sucking himself full upon the carcass of some fat monastery? No, no, never count on her."

"At least she is brave and true, Emlyn, and has done her best, for which may Heaven's blessing rest upon her always. Now, what of Thomas Bolle?"

"Nothing, except that he is a red-headed jackass that can bray but daren't kick," answered Emlyn viciously. "Never speak to me of Thomas Bolle. Had he been a man long ago he'd have broken the neck of that rogue Abbot instead of dressing himself up like a he-goat and hunting his cows."

"If what they say is true he did break the neck of Father Ambrose," replied Cicely, with a faint smile. "Perhaps he made a mistake in the dark."

"If so it is like Thomas Bolle, who ever wished the right thing and did the wrong. Talk no more of him, since I would not meet my end in a bad spirit. Thomas Bolle, who lets us die for his elfish pranks! A pest on the half-witted cur, say I. And after I had kissed him too!"

Cicely wondered vaguely to what she referred, then, thinking it well not to inquire, said—

"Not so, a blessing on him, say I, who saved my child from that hateful hag."

Then there was silence for a while, the matter of poor Thomas Bolle and his conduct being exhausted between them, who indeed were in no mood for argument about people whom they would never see again. At last Cicely spoke once more through the darkness—

"Emlyn, I will try to be brave; but once, do you remember, I burnt my hand as a child when I stole the sweetmeats from the cooling pot, and ah! it hurt me. I will try to die as those who went before me would have died, but if I should break down think not the less of me, for the spirit is willing though the flesh be weak."

Emlyn ground her teeth in silence, and Cicely went on—

"But that is not the worst of it, Emlyn. A few minutes and it will be over and I shall sleep, as I think, to awake elsewhere. Only if Christopher should really live, how he will mourn when he learns—"

"I pray that he does," broke in Emlyn, "for then ere long there will be a Spanish priest the less on earth and one the more in hell."

"And the child, Emlyn, the child!" she went on in a trembling voice, not heeding the interruption. "What will become of my son, the heir to so much if he had his rights, and yet so friendless? They'll murder him also, Emlyn, or let him die, which is the same thing, since how otherwise will they get title to his lands and goods?"

"If so, his troubles will be done and he will be better with you in heaven," Emlyn answered, with a dry sob. "The boy and you in heaven midst the blessed saints, and the Abbot and I in hell settling our score there with the devil for company, that's all I ask. There, there, I blaspheme, for injustice makes me mad; it clogs my heart and I throw it up in bitter words, for your sake, dear, and his, not my own. Child, you are good and gentle, to such as you the Ear of God is open. Call to him; ask for light, He will not refuse. Do you remember in the fire at the Towers, when we crouched in that vault and the walls crumbled overhead, you said you saw His angel bending over us and heard his speech. Call to Him, Cicely, and if He will not listen, hear me. I have a means of death about me. Ask not what it is, but if at the end I turn on you and strike, blame me not here or hereafter, for it will be love's blow, my last service."

It seemed as though Cicely did not understand those heavy words, at the least she took no heed of them.

"I'll pray again," she whispered, "though I fear that heaven's doors are closed to me; no light comes through," and she knelt down.

For long, long she prayed, till at length weariness overcame her, and Emlyn heard her breathing softly like one asleep.

"Let her sleep," she murmured to herself. "Oh! if I were sure—she should never wake again to see the dawn. I have half a mind to do it, but there it is, I am not sure. If there is a God He will never suffer such a thing. I'd have paid the jewels, but what's the use? They would have killed her all the same, for else where's their title? No, my heart bids me wait."

Cicely awoke.

"Emlyn," she said in a low, thrilling voice, "do you hear me, Emlyn? That angel has been with me again. He spoke to me," and she paused.

"Well, well, what did he say?"

"I don't know, Emlyn," she answered, confused; "it has gone from me. But, Emlyn, have no fear, all is well with us, and not only with us but with Christopher and the babe also. Oh, yes, with Christopher and the babe also," and she let her fair head fall upon the couch and burst into a flood of happy tears. Then, rising, she took up the child and kissed it, laid herself down and slept sweetly.

Just then the dawn broke, a glorious dawn, and Emlyn held out her arms to it in an ecstasy of gratitude. For with that light her terror passed away as the darkness passed. She believed that God had spoken to Cicely and for a while her heart was at peace.

When about eight o'clock that morning the door was opened to allow a nun to bring them their food, she saw a sight which filled her with amazement. Her own eyes, poor woman, were red with tears, for, like all in the Priory, she loved Cicely, whom as a child she had nursed on her knee, and with the other sisters had spent a sleepless night in prayer for her, for Emlyn, and for Bridget, who was to be burned with them. She had expected to find the victims prostrate and perhaps senseless with fear, but behold! there they sat together in the window-place, dressed in their best garments and talking quietly. Indeed, as she entered one of them—it was Cicely—laughed a little at something that the other had said.

"Good-morning to you, Sister Mary," said Cicely. "Tell me now, has the Prioress returned?"

"Nay, nay, we know not where she is; no word has come from her. Well, at least she will be spared a dreadful sight. Have you any message for her ear? If so, give it swiftly ere the guard call me."

"I thank you," said Cicely; "but I think that I shall be the bearer of my own messages."

"What? Do you, then, mean that our Mother is dead? Must we suffer woe upon woe? Oh! who could have told you these sorrowful tidings?"

"No, sister, I think that she is alive and that I, yet living, shall talk with her again."

Sister Mary looked bewildered, for how, she wondered, could close prisoners know these things? Staring round to see that she was not observed, she thrust two little packets into Cicely's hand.

"Wear these at the last, both of you," she whispered. "Whatever they say we believe you innocent, and for your sake we have done a great crime. Yes, we have opened the reliquary and taken from it our most precious treasure, a fragment of the cord that bound St. Catherine to the wheel, and divided it into three, one strand for each of you. Perhaps, if you are really guiltless, it will work a miracle. Perhaps the fire will not burn or the rain will extinguish it, or the Abbot may relent."

"That last would be the greatest miracle of all," broke in Emlyn, with grim humour. "Still we thank you from our hearts and will wear the relics if they do not take them from us. Hark! they are calling you. Farewell, and all blessings be on your gentle heads."

Again the loud voices of the guards called, and Sister Mary turned and fled, wondering if these women were not witches, how it came about that they could be so brave, so different from poor Bridget, who wailed and moaned in her cell below.

Cicely and Emlyn ate their food with good appetite, knowing that they would need support that day, and when it was done sat themselves again by the window-place, through which they could see hundreds of people, mounted and on foot, passing up the slope that led to the green in front of the Abbey, though this green they could not see because of a belt of trees.

"Listen," said Emlyn presently. "It is hard to say, but it may be that your vision of the night was but a merciful dream, and, if so, within a few hours we shall be dead. Now I have the secret of the hiding-place of those jewels, which, without me, none can ever find; shall I pass it on, if I get the chance, to one whom I can trust? Some good soul—the nuns, perhaps—will surely shelter your boy, and he might need them in days to come."

Cicely thought a while, then answered—

"Not so, Emlyn. I believe that God has spoken to me by His angel, as He spoke to Peter in the prison. To do this would be to tempt God, showing that we have no trust in Him. Let that secret lie where it is, in your breast."

"Great is your faith," said Emlyn, looking at her with admiration. "Well, I will stand or fall by it, for I think there is enough for two."

The Convent bell chimed ten, and they heard a sound of feet and voices below.

"They come for us," said Emlyn; "the burning is set for eleven, that after the sight folk may get away in comfort to their dinners. Now summon that great Faith of yours and hold him fast for both our sakes, since mine grows faint."

The door opened and through it came monks followed by guards, the officer of whom bade them rise and follow. They obeyed without speaking, Cicely throwing her cloak about her shoulders.

"You'll be warm enough without that, Witch," said the man, with a hideous chuckle.

"Sir," she answered, "I shall need it to wrap my child in when we are parted. Give me the babe, Emlyn. There, now we are ready; nay, no need to lead us, we cannot escape and shall not vex you."

"God's truth, the girl has spirit!" muttered the officer to his companions, but one of the priests shook his head and answered—

"Witchcraft! Satan will leave them presently."

A few more minutes and, for the first time during all those weary months, they passed the gate of the Priory. Here the third victim was waiting to join them, poor, old, half-witted Bridget, clad in a kind of sheet, for her habit had been stripped off. She was wild-eyed and her grey locks hung loose about her shoulders, as she shook her ancient head and screamed prayers for mercy. Cicely shivered at the sight of her, which indeed was dreadful.

"Peace, good Bridget," she said as they passed, "being innocent, what have you to fear?"

"The fire, the fire!" cried the poor creature. "I dread the fire."

Then they were led to their place in the procession and saw no more of Bridget for a while, although they could not escape the sound of her lamentations behind them.

It was a great procession. First went the monks and choristers, singing a melancholy Latin dirge. Then came the victims in the midst of a guard of twelve armed men, and after these the nuns who were forced to be present, while behind and about were all the folk for twenty miles round, a crowd without number. They crossed the footbridge, where stood the Ford Inn for which the Flounder had bargained as the price of murder. They walked up the rise by the right of way, muddy now with the autumn rains, and through the belt of trees where Thomas Bolle's secret passage had its exit, and so came at last to the green in front of the towering Abbey portal.

Here a dreadful sight awaited them, for on this green were planted three fourteen-inch posts of new-felled oak six feet or more in height, such as no fire would easily burn through, and around each of them a kind of bower of faggots open to the front. Moreover, to the posts hung new wagon chains, and near by stood the village blacksmith and his apprentice, who carried a hand anvil and a sledge hammer for the cold welding of those chains.

At a distance from these stakes the procession was halted. Then out from the gate of the Abbey came the Abbot in his robes and mitre, preceded by acolytes and followed by more monks. He advanced to where the condemned women stood and halted, while a friar stepped forward and read their sentence to them, of which, being in Latin or in crabbed, legal words, they understood nothing at all. Then in sonorous tones he adjured them for the sake of their sinful souls to make full confession of their guilt, that they might receive pardon before they suffered in the flesh for their hideous crime of sorcery.

To this invitation Cicely and Emlyn shook their heads, saying that being innocent of any sorceries they had nothing to confess. But old Bridget gave another answer. She declared in a high, screaming voice that she was a witch, as her mother and grandmother had been before her. She described, while the crowd listened with intense interest, how Emlyn Stower had introduced her to the devil, who was clad in red hose and looked like a black boy with a hump on his back and a tuft of red hair hanging from his nose, also many unedifying details of her interviews with this same fiend.

Asked what he said to her, she answered that he told her to bewitch the Abbot of Blossholme because he was such a holy man that God had need of him and he did too much good upon the earth. Also he prevented Emlyn Stower and Cicely Foterell from working his, the devil's, will, and enabled them to keep alive the baby who would be a great wizard. He told her moreover that midwife Megges was an angel (here the crowd laughed) sent to kill the said infant, who really was his own child, as might be seen by its black eyebrows and cleft tongue, also its webbed feet, and that he would appear in the shape of the ghost of Sir John Foterell to save it and give it to her, which he did, saying the Lord's Prayer backwards, and that she must bring it up "in the faith of the Pentagon."

Thus the poor crazed thing raved on, while sentence by sentence a scribe wrote down her gibberish, causing her at last to make her mark to it, all of which took a very long time. At the end she begged that she might be pardoned and not burnt, but this, she was informed, was impossible. Thereon she became enraged and asked why then had she been led to tell so many lies if after all she must burn, a question at which the crowd roared with laughter. On hearing this the priest, who was about to absolve her, changed his mind and ordered her to be fastened to her stake, which was done by the blacksmith with the help of his apprentice and his portable anvil.

Still, her "confession" was solemnly read over to Cicely and Emlyn, who were asked whether, after hearing it, they still persisted in a denial of their guilt. By way of answer Cicely lifted the hood from her boy's face and showed that his eyebrows were not black, but light- coloured. Also she bared his feet, passing her little finger between his toes, and asking them if they were webbed. Some of them answered, "No," but a monk roared, "What of that? Cannot Satan web and unweb?" Then he snatched the infant from Cicely's arms and laid it down upon the stump of an oak that had been placed there to receive it, crying out—

"Let this child live or die as God pleases."

Some brute who stood by aimed a blow at it with a stick, yelling, "Death to the witch's brat!" but a big man, whom Emlyn recognized as one of old Sir John's tenants, caught the falling stick from his hand and dealt him such a clout with it that he fell like a stone, and went for the rest of his life with but one eye and the nose flattened on the side of his face. Thenceforward no one tried to harm the babe, who, as all know, because of what befell him on this day, went in after life by the nickname of Christopher Oak-stump.

The Abbot's men stepped forward to tie Cicely to her stake, but ere they laid hands on her she took off her wool-lined cloak and threw it to the yeoman who had struck down the fellow with his own stick, saying—

"Friend, wrap my boy in this and guard him till I ask him from you again."

"Aye, Lady," answered the great man, bending his knee; "I have served the grandsire and the sire, and so I'll serve the son," and throwing aside the stick he drew a sword and set himself in front of the oak boll where the infant lay. Nor did any venture to meddle with him, for they saw other men of a like sort ranging themselves about him.

Now slowly enough the smith began to rivet the chain round Cicely.

"Man," she said to him, "I have seen you shoe many of my father's nags. Who could have thought that you would live to use your honest skill upon his daughter!"

On hearing these words the fellow burst into tears, cast down his tools and fled away, cursing the Abbot. His apprentice would have followed, but him they caught and forced to complete the task. Then Emlyn was chained up also, so that at length all was ready for the last terrible act of the drama.

Now the head executioner—he was the Abbey cook—placed some pine splinters to light in a brazier that stood near by, and while waiting for the word of command, remarked audibly to his mate that there was a good wind and that the witches would burn briskly.

The spectators were ordered back out of earshot, and went at last, some of them muttering sullenly to each other. For here the company could not be picked as it had been at the trial, and the Abbot noted anxiously that among them the victims had many friends. It was time the deed was done ere their smouldering love and pity flowed out into bloody tumult, he thought to himself. So, advancing quickly, he stood in front of Emlyn and asked her in a low voice if she still refused to give up the secret of the jewels, seeing that there was yet time for him to command that they should die mercifully and not by the fire.

"Let the mistress judge, not the maid," answered Emlyn in a steady voice.

He turned and repeated the question to Cicely, who replied—

"Have I not told you—never. Get you behind me, O evil man, and go, repent your sins ere it be too late."

The Abbot stared at her, feeling that such constancy and courage were almost superhuman. He had an acute, imaginative mind which could fancy himself in like case and what his state would be. Though he was in such haste a great curiosity entered into him to know whence she drew her strength, which even then he tried to satisfy.

"Are you mad or drugged, Cicely Foterell?" he asked. "Do you not know how fire will feel when it eats up that delicate flesh of yours?"

"I do not know and I shall never know," she answered quietly.

"Do you mean that you will die before it touches you, building on some promise of your master, Satan?"

"Yes, I shall die before the fire touches me; but not here and now, and I build upon a promise from the Master of us all in heaven."

He laughed, a shrill, nervous laugh, and called out loud to the people around—

"This witch says that she will not burn, for Heaven has promised it to her. Do you not, Witch?"

"Yes, I say so; bear witness to my words, good people all," replied Cicely in clear and ringing tones.

"Well, we'll see," shouted the Abbot. "Man, bring flame, and let Heaven—or hell—help her if it can!"

The cook-executioner blew at his brands, but he was nervous, or clumsy, and a minute or more went by before they flamed. At length one was fit for the task, and unwillingly enough he stooped to lift it up.

Then it was that in the midst of the intense silence, for of all that multitude none seemed even to breathe, and old Bridget, who had fainted, cried no more, a bull's voice was heard beyond the brow of the hill, roaring—

"In the King's name, stay! In the King's name, stay!"

All turned to look, and there between the trees appeared a white horse, its sides streaked with blood, that staggered rather than galloped towards them, and on the horse a huge, red-bearded man, clad in mail and holding in his hand a woodman's axe.

"Fire the faggots!" shouted the Abbot, but the cook, who was not by nature brave, had already let fall his torch, which went out on the damp ground.

By now the horse was rushing through them, treading them under foot. With great, convulsive bounds it reached the ring and, as the rider leapt from its back, rolled over and lay there panting, for its strength was done.

"It is Thomas Bolle!" exclaimed a voice, while the Abbot cried again—

"Fire the faggots! Fire the faggots!" and a soldier ran to fetch another brand.

But Thomas was before him. Snatching up the brazier by its legs he smote downwards with it so that the burning charcoal fell all about the soldier and the iron cage remained fixed upon his head, shouting as he smote—

"You sought fire—take it!"

The man rolled upon the ground screaming in pain and terror till some one dragged the cage off his head, leaving his face barred like a grilled herring. None took further heed of what became of him, for now Thomas Bolle stood in front of the stakes waving his great axe, and repeating, "In the King's name, stay! In the King's name, stay!"

"What mean you, knave?" exclaimed the furious Abbot.

"What I say, Priest. One step nearer and I'll split your crown."

The Abbot fell back and Thomas went on—

"A Foterell! A Foterell! A Harflete! A Harflete! O ye who have eaten their bread, come, scatter these faggots and save their flesh. Who'll stand with me against Maldon and his butchers?"

"I," answered voices, "and I, and I, and I!"

"And I too," hallooed the yeoman by the oak stump, "only I watch the child. Nay, by God I'll bring it with me!" and, snatching up the screaming babe under his left arm, he ran to him.

On came the others also, hurling the faggots this way and that.

"Break the chains," roared Bolle again, and somehow those strong hands did it; indeed, the only hurt that Cicely took that day was from their hacking at these chains. They were loose. Cicely snatched the child from the yeoman, who was glad enough to be rid of it, having other work to do, for now the Abbot's men-at-arms were coming on.

"Ring the women round," roared Bolle, "and strike home for Foterell, strike home for Harflete! Ah, priest's dog, in the King's name—this!" and the axe sank up to the haft into the breast of the captain who had told Cicely that she would be warm enough that day without her cloak.

Then there began a great fight. The party of Foterell, of whom there may have been a score, captained by Bolle, made a circle round the three green oak stakes, within which stood Cicely and Emlyn and old Bridget, still tied to her post, for no one had thought or found time to cut her loose. These were attacked by the Abbot's guard, thirty or more of them, urged on by Maldon himself, who was maddened by the rescue of his victims and full of fear lest Cicely's words should be fulfilled and she herself set down henceforth, not as a witch, but as a prophetess favoured by God.

On came the soldiers and were beaten back. Thrice they came on and thrice they were beaten back with loss, for Bolle's axe was terrible to face and, now that they had found a leader and their courage, the yeoman lads who stood with him were sturdy fighters. Also tumult broke out among the hundreds who watched, some of them taking one side and some the other, so that they fell upon each other with sticks and stones and fists, even the women joining in the fray, biting and tearing like bagged cats. The scene was hideous and the sounds those of a sacked city, for many were hurt and all gave tongue, while shrill and clear above this hateful music rose the yells of Bridget, who had awakened from her faint and imagined all was over and that she fathomed hell.

Thrice the attackers were rolled back, but of those who defended a third were down, and now the Abbot took another counsel.

"Bring bows," he cried, "and shoot them, for they have none!" and men ran off to do his bidding.

Then it was that Emlyn's wit came to their aid, for when Bolle shook his red head and gasped out that he feared they were lost, since how could they fight against arrows, she answered—

"If so, why stand here to be spitted, fool? Come, let us cut our way through ere the shafts begin to fly, and take refuge among the trees or in the Nunnery."

"Women's counsel is good sometimes," said Bolle. "Form up, Foterells, and march."

"Nay," broke in Cicely, "loose Bridget first, lest they should burn her after all; I'll not stir else."

So Bridget was hacked free, and together with the wounded men, of whom there were several, dragged and supported thence. Then began a running fight, but one in which they still held their own. Yet they would have been overwhelmed at last, for the women and the wounded hampered them, had not help come. For as they hewed their path towards the belt of trees with the Abbot's fierce fellows, some of whom were French or Spanish, hanging on their flanks, suddenly, in the gap where the roadway ran, appeared a horse galloping and on it a woman, who clung to its mane with both hands, and after her many armed men.

"Look, Emlyn, look!" exclaimed Cicely. "Who is that?" for she could not believe her eyes.

"Who but Mother Matilda," answered Emlyn; "and by the saints, she is a strange sight!"

A strange sight she was indeed, for her hood was gone, her hair, that was ever so neat, flew loose, her robe was ruckled up about her knees, the rosary and crucifix she wore streamed on the air behind her and beat against her back, and her garb had burst open at the front; in short, never was holy, aged Prioress seen in such a state before. Down she came on them like a whirlwind, for her frightened horse scented its Blossholme stable, clinging grimly to her unaccustomed seat, and crying as she sped—

"For God's love, stop this mad beast!"

Bolle caught it by the bridle and threw it to its haunches so that, its rider speeding on, flew over its head on to the broad breast of the yeoman who had watched the child, and there rested thankfully. For, as Mother Matilda said afterwards with her gentle smile, never before did she know what comfort there was to be found in man.

When at length she loosed her arms from about his neck the yeoman stood her on her feet, saying that this was worse than the baby, and her wandering eyes fell upon Cicely.

"So I am in time! Oh! never more will I revile that horse," she exclaimed, and sinking to her knees then and there she gasped out some prayer of thankfulness. Meanwhile, those who followed her had reined up in front, and the Abbot's soldiers with the accompanying crowd had halted behind, not knowing what to make of these strangers, so that Bolle and his party with the women were now between the two.

From among the new-comers rode out a fat, coarse man, with a pompous air as of one who is accustomed to be obeyed, who inquired in a laboured voice, for he was breathless from hard riding, what all this turmoil meant.

"Ask the Abbot of Blossholme," said some one, "for it is his work."

"Abbot of Blossholme? That's the man I want," puffed the fat stranger. "Appear, Abbot of Blossholme, and give account of these doings. And you fellows," he added to his escort, "range up and be ready, lest this said priest should prove contumacious."

Now the Abbot stepped forward with some of his monks and, looking the horseman up and down, said—

"Who may it be that demands account so roughly of a consecrated Abbot?"

"A consecrated Abbot? A consecrated peacock, a tumultuous, turbulent, traitorous priest, a Spanish rogue ruffler who, I am told, keeps about him a band of bloody mercenaries to break the King's peace and slay loyal English folk. Well, consecrated Abbot, I'll tell you who I am. I am Thomas Legh, his Grace's Visitor and Royal Commissioner to inspect the Houses called religious, and I am come hither upon complaint made by yonder Prioress of Blossholme Nunnery, as to your dealings with certain of his Highness's subjects whom, she says, you have accused of witchcraft for purposes of revenge and unlawful gain. That is who I am, my fine fowl of an Abbot."

Now when he heard this pompous speech the rage in Maldon's face was replaced by fear, for he knew of this Doctor Legh and his mission, and understood what Thomas Bolle had meant by his cry of, "In the King's name!"

Chapter XIII

The Messenger

"Who makes all this tumult?" shouted the Commissioner. "Why do I see blood and wounds and dead men? And how were you about to handle these women, one of whom by her mien is of no low degree?" and he stared at Cicely.

"The tumult," answered the Abbot, "was caused by yonder fool, Thomas Bolle, a lay-brother of my monastery, who rushed among us armed and shouting 'In the King's name, stay.'"

"Then why did you not stay, Sir Abbot? Is the King's name one to be mocked at? Know that I sent on the man."

"He had no warrant, Sir Commissioner, unless his bull's voice and great axe are a warrant, and I did not stay because we were doing justice upon the three foulest witches in the realm."

"Doing justice? Whose justice and what justice? Say, had you a warrant for your justice? If so, show it me."

"These witches have been condemned by a Court Ecclesiastic, the judges being a bishop, a prior and myself, and in pursuance of that judgment were about to suffer for their sins by fire," replied Maldon.

"A Court Ecclesiastic!" roared Dr. Legh. "Can Courts Ecclesiastic, then, toast free English folk to death? If you would not stand your trial for attempted murder, show me your warrant signed by his Grace the King, or by his Justices of Assize. What! You do not answer. Have you none? I thought as much. Oho, Clement Maldon, you hang-faced Spanish dog, learn that eyes have been on you for long, and now it seems that you would usurp the King's prerogative besides—" and he checked himself, then went on, "Seize that priest, and keep him fast while I make inquiry of this business."

Now some of the Commissioner's guard surrounded Maldon, nor did his own men venture to interfere with them, for they had enough of fighting and were frightened by this talk about the King's warrant.

Then the Commissioner turned to Cicely, and said—

"You are Sir John Foterell's only child, are you not, who allege yourself to be wife to Sir Christopher Harflete, or so says yonder Prioress? Now, what was about to happen to you, and why?"

"Sir," answered Cicely, "I and my waiting-woman and the old sister, Bridget, were condemned to die by fire at those stakes upon a charge of sorcery. Although it is true," she added, "that I knew we should not perish thus."

"How did you know that, Lady? By all tokens your bodies and hot flame were near enough together," and he glanced towards the stakes and the scattered faggots.

"Sir, I knew it because of a vision that God sent to me in my sleep last night."

"Aye, she swore that at the stake," exclaimed a voice, "and we thought her mad."

"Now can you deny that she is a witch?" broke in Maldon. "If she were not one of Satan's own, how could she see visions and prophecy her own deliverance?"

"If visions and prophecies are proof of witchcraft, then, Priest, all Holy Writ is but a seething pot of sorcery," answered Legh. "Then the Blessed Virgin and St. Elizabeth were witches, and Paul and John should have been burnt as wizards. Continue, Lady, leaving out your dreams until a more convenient time."

"Sir," went on Cicely, "we have worked no sorcery, and my crime is that I will not name my child a bastard and sign away my lands and goods to yonder Abbot, the murderer of my father and perhaps of my husband. Oh! listen, listen, you and all folk here, and briefly as I may I will tell my tale. Have I your leave to speak?"

The Commissioner nodded, and she set out her story from the beginning, so sweetly, so simply and with such truth and earnestness, that the concourse of people packed close about her, hung upon her every word, and even Dr. Legh's coarse face softened as he heard. For the half of an hour or more she spoke, telling of her father's death, of her flight and marriage, of the burning of Cranwell Towers, and her widowing, if such it were; of her imprisonment in the Priory and the Abbot's dealings with her and Emlyn; of the birth of her child and its attempted murder by the midwife, his creature; of their trial and condemnation, they being innocent, and of all they had endured that day.

"If you are innocent," shouted a priest as she paused for breath, "what was that Thing dressed in the livery of Satan which worked evil at Blossholme? Did we not see it with our eyes?"

Just then some one uttered an exclamation and pointed to the shadow of the trees where a strange form was moving. Another moment and it came out into the light. One more and all that multitude scattered like frightened sheep, rushing this way and that; yes, even the horses took the bits between their teeth and bolted. For there, visible to all, Satan himself strolled towards them. On his head were horns, behind his back hung down a tail, his body was shaggy like a beast's, and his face hideous and of many colours, while in his hand he held a pronged fork with a long handle. This way and that rushed the throng, only the Commissioner, who had dismounted, stood still, perhaps because he was too afraid to stir, and with him the women and some of the nuns, including the Prioress, who fell upon their knees and began to utter prayers.

On came the dreadful thing till it reached the King's Visitor, bowing to him and bellowing like a bull, then very deliberately untied some strings and let its horrid garb fall off, revealing the person of Thomas Bolle!

"What means this mummery, knave?" gasped Dr. Legh.

"Mummery do you call it, sir?" answered Thomas with a grin. "Well, if so, 'tis on the faith of such mummery that priests burn women in merry England. Come, good people, come," he roared in his great voice, "come, see Satan in the flesh. Here are his horns," and he held them up, "once they grew upon the head of Widow Johnson's billy-goat. Here's his tail, many a fly has it flicked off the belly of an Abbey cow. Here's his ugly mug, begotten of parchment and the paint-box. Here's his dreadful fork that drives the damned to some hotter corner; it has been death to whole stones of eels down in the marsh-fleet yonder. I have some hell-fire too among the bag of tricks; you'll make the best of brimstone and a little oil dried out upon the hearth. Come, see the devil all complete and naught to pay."

Back trooped the crowd a little fearfully, taking the properties which he held, and handling them, till first one and then all of them began to laugh.

"Laugh not," shouted Bolle. "Is it a matter of laughter that noble ladies and others whose lives are as dear to some," and he glanced at Emlyn, "should grill like herrings because a poor fool walks about clad in skins to keep out the cold and frighten villains? Hark you, I played this trick. I am Beelzebub, also the ghost of Sir John Foterell. I entered the Priory chapel by a passage that I know, and saved yonder babe from murder and scared the murderess down to hell; yes, from the sham devil to the true. Why did I do it? Well, to protect the innocent and scourge the wicked in his pride. But the wicked seized the innocent and the innocent said nothing, fearing lest I should suffer with them, and—O God, you know the rest!

"It was a near thing, a very near thing, but I'm not the half-wit I've feigned to be for years. Moreover, I had a good horse and a heavy axe, and there are still true hearts round Blossholme; the dead men that lie yonder show it. Heaven has still its angels on the earth, though they wear strange shapes. There stands one of them, and there another," and he pointed first to the fat and pompous Visitor, and next to the dishevelled Prioress, adding: "And now, Sir Commissioner, for all that I have done in the cause of justice I ask pardon of you who wear the King's grace and majesty as I wore old Nick's horns and hoofs, since otherwise the Abbot and his hired butchers, who hold themselves masters of King and people, will murder me for this as they have done by better men. Therefore pardon, your Mightiness, pardon," and he kneeled down before him.

"You have it, Bolle; in the King's name you have it," replied Legh, who was more flattered by the titles and attributes poured upon him by the cunning Thomas than a closer consideration might have warranted. "For all that you have done, or left undone, I, the Commissioner of his Grace, declare that you shall go scot free and that no action criminal or civil shall lie against you, and this my secretary shall give to you in writing. Now, good fellow, rise, but steal Satan's plumes no more lest you should feel his claws and beak, for he is an ill fowl to mock. Bring hither that Spaniard Maldon. I have somewhat to say to him."

Now they looked this way and that, but no Abbot could they see. The guards swore that they had never taken eye off him, even when they all ran before the devil, yet certainly he was gone.

"The knave has given us the slip," bellowed the Commissioner, who was purple with rage. "Search for him! Seize him, for which my command shall be your warrant. Draw the wood. I'll to the Abbey, where perchance the fox has gone to earth. Five golden crowns to the man who nets the slimy traitor."

Now every one, burning with zeal to show their loyalty and to win the crowns, scattered on the search, so that presently the three "witches," Thomas Bolle, Mother Matilda, and the nuns, were left standing almost alone and staring at each other and the dead and wounded men who lay about.

"Let us to the Priory," said Mother Matilda, "for by the sun I judge that it is time for evening prayer, and there seem to be none to hinder us."

Thomas went to her horse, which grazed close at hand, and led it up.

"Nay, good friend," she exclaimed, with energy, "while I live no more of that evil beast for me. Henceforth I'll walk till I am carried. Keep it, Thomas, as a gift; it is bought and paid for. Sister, your arm."

"Have I done well, Emlyn?" Bolle asked, as he tightened the girths.

"I don't know," she answered, looking at him sideways. "You played the cur at first, leaving us to burn for your sins, but afterwards, well, you found the wits you say you never lost. Also your manners mended, and yonder captain knave learned that you can handle an axe, so we'll say no more about it, lad, for doubtless that Abbot and his spies were sore task-masters and broke your spirit with their penances and talk of hell to come. Here, lift my lady on to this horse, for she is spent, and let me lean upon your shoulder, Thomas. It's weary work standing at a stake."

Cicely's recollections of the remainder of that day were always shadowy and tangled. She remembered a prayer of thanksgiving in which she took small part with her lips, she whose heart was one great thanksgiving. She remembered the good sister who had given them the relics of St. Catherine assuring her, as she received them back with care, that these and these alone had worked the miracle and saved their lives. She remembered eating food and straining her boy to her breast, and then she remembered no more till she woke to see the morning sun streaming into that same room whence on the previous day they had been led out to suffer the most horrible of deaths.

Yes, she woke, and see, near by was Emlyn making ready her garments, as she had done these many years, and at her side lay the boy crowing in the sunlight and waving his little arms, the blessed boy who knew not the terrors he had passed. At first she thought that she had dreamed a very evil dream, till by degrees all the truth came back to her, and she shivered at its memory, yes, even as the weight of it rolled off her heart she shivered and whitened like an aspen in the wind. Then she rose and thanked God for His mercies, which were great.

Oh, if the strength of that horse of Thomas Bolle's had failed one short five minutes sooner, she, in whom the red blood still ran so healthily, would have been but a handful of charred bones. Or if her faith had left her so that she had yielded to the Abbot and shortened all his talk at the place of burning, then Bolle would have come too late. But it proved sufficient to her need, and for this also truly she should be thankful to its Giver.

After they had eaten, a message came to them from the Prioress, who desired to see them in her chamber. Thither they went, rejoiced to find that they were no longer prisoners but had liberty to come and go, and found her seated in a tall chair, for she was too stiff to walk. Cicely ran to her, knelt down and kissed her, and she laid her left hand upon her head in blessing, for the right was cut with the chafing of the reins.

"Surely, Cicely," she said, smiling, "it is I who should kneel to you, were I in any state to do so. For now I have heard all the tale, and it seems that we have a prophetess among us, one favoured with visions from on high, which visions have been most marvellously fulfilled."

"That is so, Mother," she answered briefly, for this was a matter of which she would never talk at length, either then or thereafter, "but the fulfilment came through you."

"My daughter, I was but the minister, you were the chosen seer, still let the holy business lie a while. Perhaps you will tell me of it afterwards, and meantime the world and its affairs press us hard. Your deliverance has been bought at no small cost, my daughter, for know that yonder coarse and ungodly man, the King's Visitor, told me as we rode that this Nunnery must be dissolved, its house and revenues seized, and I and my sisters turned out to starve in our old age. Indeed, to bring him here at all I was forced to petition that it might be so in a writing that I signed. See, then, how great is my love for you, dear Cicely."

"Mother," she answered, "it cannot be, it shall not be."

"Alas! child, how will you prevent it? These Visitors, and those who commission them, are hungry folk. I hear they take the lands and goods of poor religious such as we are, and if these are fortunate, give one or two of them a little pittance to get bread. Once I had moneys of my own, but I spent them to buy back the Valley Farm which the Abbot had seized, and of late to satisfy his extortions," and she wept a little.

"Mother, listen. I have wealth hidden away, I know not where exactly, but Emlyn knows. It is my very own, the Carfax jewels that came to me from my mother. It was because of these that we were brought to the stake, since the Abbot offered us life in return for them, and when it was too late to save us, a more merciful death than that by fire. But I forbade Emlyn to yield the secret; something in my heart told me to do so, now I know why. Mother, the price of those gems shall buy back your lands, and mayhap buy also permission from his Grace the King for the continuance of your house, where you and yours shall worship as those who went before you have done for many generations. I swear it in my own name and in that of my child and of my husband also—if he lives."

"Your husband if he lives might need this wealth, sweet Cicely."

"Then, Mother, except to save his life, or liberty or honour, I tell you I will refuse it to him, who, when he learns what you have done for me and our son, would give it you and all else he has besides—nay, would pay it as an honourable debt."

"Well, Cicely, in God's name and my own I thank you, and we'll see, we'll see! Only be advised, lest Dr. Legh should learn of this treasure. But where is it, Emlyn? Fear not to tell me who can be secret, for it is well that more than one should know, and I think that your danger is past."

"Yes, speak, Emlyn," said Cicely, "for though I never asked before, fearing my own weakness, I am curious. None can hear us here."

"Then, Mistress, I will tell you. You remember that on the day of the burning of Cranwell we sought refuge on the central tower, whence I carried you senseless to the vault. Now in that vault we lay all night, and while you swooned I searched with my fingers till I found a stone that time and damp had loosened, behind which was a hollow. In that hollow I hid the jewels that I carried wrapt in silk in the bosom of my robe. Then I filled up the hole with dust scraped from the floor, and replaced the stone, wedging it tight with bits of mortar. It is the third stone counting from the eastern angle in the second course above the floor line. There I set them, and there doubtless they lie to this day, for unless the tower is pulled down to its foundations none will ever find them in that masonry."

At this moment there came a knocking on the door. When it was opened by Emlyn a nun entered, saying that the King's Visitor demanded to speak with the Prioress.

"Show him here since I cannot come to him," said Mother Matilda, "and you, Cicely and Emlyn, bide with me, for in such company it is well to have witnesses."

A minute later Dr. Legh appeared accompanied by his secretaries, gorgeously attired and puffing from the stairs.

"To business, to business," he said, scarcely stopping to acknowledge the greetings of the Prioress. "Your convent is sequestrated upon your own petition, Madam, therefore I need not stop to make the usual inquiries, and indeed I will admit that from all I hear it has a good repute, for none allege scandal against you, perhaps because you are all too old for such follies. Produce now your deeds, your terrier of lands and your rent-rolls, that I may take them over in due form and dissolve the sisterhood."

"I will send for them, Sir," answered the Prioress humbly; "but, meanwhile, tell us what we poor religious are to do? I am turned sixty years of age, and have dwelt in this house for forty of them; none of my sisters are young, and some of them are older than myself. Whither shall we go?"

"Into the world, Madam, which you will find a fine, large place. Cease snuffling prayers and from all vulgar superstitions—by the way, forget not to hand over any reliquaries of value, or any papistical emblems in precious metals that you may possess, including images, of which my secretaries will take account—and go out into the world. Marry there if you can find husbands, follow useful trades there. Do what you will there, and thank the King who frees you from the incumbrance of silly vows and from the circle of a convent's walls."

"To give us liberty to starve outside of them. Sir, do you understand your work? For hundreds of years we have sat at Blossholme, and during all those generations have prayed to God for the souls of men and ministered to their bodies. We have done no harm to any creature, and what wealth came to us from the earth or from the benefactions of the pious we have dispensed with a liberal hand, taking nothing for ourselves. The poor by multitudes have fed at our gates, their sick we have nursed, their children we have taught; often we have gone hungry that they might be full. Now you drive us forth in our age to perish. If that is the will of God, so be it, but what must chance to England's poor?"

"That is England's business, Madam, and the poor's. Meanwhile I have told you that I have no time to waste, since I must away to London to make report concerning this Abbot of yours, a veritable rogue, of whose villainous plots I have discovered many things. I pray you send a messenger to bid them hurry with the deeds."

Just then a nun entered bearing a tray, on which were cakes and wine. Emlyn took it from her, and pouring the wine into cups offered them to the Visitor and his secretaries.

"Good wine," he said, after he had drunk, "a very generous wine. You nuns know the best in liquor; be careful, I pray you, to include it in your inventory. Why, woman, are you not one of those whom that Abbot would have burnt? Yes, and there is your mistress, Dame Foterell, or Dame Harflete, with whom I desire a word."

"I am at your service, Sir," said Cicely.

"Well, Madam, you and your servant have escaped the stake to which, as near as I can judge, you were sentenced upon no evidence at all. Still, you were condemned by a competent ecclesiastical Court, and under that condemnation you must therefore remain until or unless the King pardons you. My judgment is, then, that you stay here awaiting his command."

"But, Sir," said Cicely, "if the good nuns who have befriended me are to be driven forth, how can I dwell on in their house alone? Yet you say I must not leave it, and indeed if I could, whither should I go? My husband's hall is burnt, my own the Abbot holds. Moreover, if I bide here, in this way or in that he will have my life."

"The knave has fled away," said Dr. Legh, rubbing his fat chin.

"Aye, but he will come back again, or his people will, and, Sir, you know these Spaniards are good haters, and I have defied him long. Oh, Sir, I crave the protection of the King for my child's sake and my own, and for Emlyn Stower also."

The Commissioner went on rubbing his chin.

"You can give much evidence against this Maldon, can you not?" he asked at length.

"Aye," broke in Emlyn, "enough to hang him ten times over, and so can I."

"And you have large estates which he has seized, have you not?"

"I have, Sir, who am of no mean birth and station."

"Lady," he said, with more deference in his voice, "step aside with me, I would speak with you privately," and he walked to the window, where she followed him. "Now tell me, what was the value of these properties of yours?"

"I know not rightly, Sir, but I have heard my father say about £300 a year."

His manner became more deferential still, since for those days such wealth was great.

"Indeed, my Lady. A large sum, a very comfortable fortune if you can get it back. Now I will be frank with you. The King's Commissioners are not well paid and their costs are great. If I so arrange your matters that you come to your own again and that the judgment of witchcraft pronounced against you and your servant is annulled, will you promise to pay me one year's rent of these estates to meet the various expenses I must incur on your behalf?"

Now it was Cicely's turn to think.

"Surely," she answered at length, "if you will add a condition—that these good sisters shall be left undisturbed in their Nunnery."

He shook his fat head.

"It is not possible now. The thing is too public. Why, the Lord Cromwell would say I had been bribed, and I might lose my office."

"Well, then," went on Cicely, "if you will promise that one year of grace shall be given to them to make arrangements for their future."

"That I can do," he answered, nodding, "on the ground that they are of blameless life, and have protected you from the King's enemy. But this is an uncertain world; I must ask you to sign an indenture, and its form will be that you acknowledge to have received from me a loan of £300 to be repaid with interest when you recover your estates."

"Draw it up and I will sign, Sir."

"Good, Madam; and now that we may get this business through, you will accompany me to London, where you will be safe from harm. We'll not ride to-day, but to-morrow morning at the light."

"Then my servant Emlyn must come also, Sir, to help me with the babe, and Thomas Bolle too, for he can prove that the witchcraft upon which we were condemned was but his trickery."

"Yes, yes; but the costs of travel for so many will be great. Have you, perchance, any money?"

"Yes, Sir, about £50 in gold that is sewn up in one of Emlyn's robes."

"Ah! A sufficient sum. Too much indeed to be risked upon your persons in these rough times. You will let me take charge of half of it for you?"

"With pleasure, Sir, trusting you as I do. Keep to your bargain and I will keep to mine."

"Good. When Thomas Legh is fairly dealt with, Thomas Legh deals fairly, no man can say otherwise. This afternoon I will bring the deed, and you'll give me that £25 in charge."

Then, followed by Cicely, he returned to where the Prioress sat, and said—

"Mother Matilda, for so I understand you are called in religion, the Lady Harflete has been pleading with me for you, and because you have dealt so well by her I have promised in the King's name that you and your nuns shall live on here undisturbed for one year from this day, after which you must yield up peaceable possession to his Majesty, whom I will beg that you shall be pensioned."

"I thank you, Sir," the Prioress answered. "When one is old a year of grace is much, and in a year many things may happen—for instance, my death."

"Thank me not—a plain man who but follows after justice and duty. The documents for your signature shall be ready this afternoon, and by the way, the Lady Harflete and her servant, also that stout, shrewd fellow, Thomas Bolle, ride with me to London to-morrow. She will explain all. At three of the clock I wait upon you."

The Visitor and his secretaries bustled out of the room as pompously as they had entered, and when they had gone Cicely explained to Mother Matilda and Emlyn what had passed.

"I think that you have done wisely," said the Prioress, when she had listened. "That man is a shark, but better give him your little finger than your whole body. Certainly, you have bargained well for us, for what may not happen in a year? Also, dear Cicely, you will be safer in London than at Blossholme, since with the great sum of £300 to gain that Commissioner will watch you like the apple of his eye and push your cause."

"Unless some one promises him the greater sum of £1000 to scotch it," interrupted Emlyn. "Well, there was but one road to take, and paper promises are little, though I grudge the good £25 in gold. Meanwhile, Mother, we have much to make ready. I pray you send some one to find Thomas Bolle, who will not be far away, for since we are no longer prisoners I wish to go out walking with him on an errand of my own that perchance you can guess. Wealth may be useful in London town for all our sakes. Also horses and a packbeast must be got, and other things."

In due course Thomas Bolle was found fast asleep in a neighbour's house, for after his adventures and triumph he had drunk hard and rested long. When she discovered the truth Emlyn rated him well, calling him a beer-tub and not a man, and many other hard names, till at last she provoked him to answer, that had it not been for the said beer-tub she would be but ash-dust this day. Thereon she turned the talk and told them their needs, and that he must ride with them to London. To this he replied that good horses should be saddled by the dawn, for he knew where to lay hands on them, since some were left in the Abbot's stables that wanted exercise; further, that he would be glad to leave Blossholme for a while, where he had made enemies on the yesterday, whose friends yet lay wounded or unburied. After this Emlyn whispered something in his ear, to which he nodded assent, saying that he would bustle round and be ready.

That afternoon Emlyn went out riding with Thomas Bolle, who was fully armed, as she said, to try two of the horses that should carry them on the morrow, and it was late when she returned out of the dark night.

"Have you got them?" asked Cicely, when they were together in their room.

"Aye," she answered, "every one; but some stones have fallen, and it was hard to win an entrance to that vault. Indeed, had it not been for Thomas Bolle, who has the strength of a bull, I could never have done it. Moreover, the Abbot has been there before us and dug over every inch of the floor. But the fool never thought of the wall, so all's well. I'll sew half of them into my petticoat and half into yours, to share the risk. In case of thieves, the money that hungry Visitor has left to us, for I paid him over half when you signed the deeds, we will carry openly in pouches upon our girdles. They'll not search further. Oh, I forgot, I've something more besides the jewels, here it is," and she produced a packet from her bosom and laid it on the table.

"What's this?" asked Cicely, looking suspiciously at the worn sail- cloth in which it was wrapped.

"How can I tell? Cut it and see. All I know is that when I stood at the Nunnery door as Thomas led away the horses, a man crept on me out of the rain swathed in a great cloak and asked if I were not Emlyn Stower. I said Yea, whereon he thrust this into my hand, bidding me not fail to give it to the Lady Harflete, and was gone."

"It has an over-seas look about it," murmured Cicely, as with eager, trembling fingers she cut the stitches. At length they were undone and a sealed inner wrapping also, revealing, amongst other documents, a little packet of parchments covered with crabbed, unreadable writing, on the back of which, however, they could decipher the names of Shefton and Blossholme by reason of the larger letters in which they were engrossed. Also there was a writing in the scrawling hand of Sir John Foterell, and at the foot of it his name and, amongst others, those of Father Necton and of Jeffrey Stokes. Cicely stared at the deeds, then said—

"Emlyn, I know these parchments. They are those that my father took with him when he rode for London to disprove the Abbot's claim, and with them the evidence of the traitorous words he spoke last year at Shefton. Yes, this inner wrapping is my own; I took it from the store of worn linen in the passage-cupboard. But how come they here?"

Emlyn made no answer, only lifted the wrappings and shook them, whereon a strip of paper that they had not seen fell to the table.

"This may tell us," she said. "Read, if you can; it has words on its inner side."

Cicely snatched at it, and as the writing was clear and clerkly, read with ease save for the chokings of her throat. It ran—

"My Lady Harflete,

"These are the papers that Jeffrey Stokes saved when your father fell. They were given for safekeeping to the writer of these words, far away across the sea, and he hands them on unopened. Your husband lives and is well again, also Jeffrey Stokes, and though they have been hindered on their journey, doubtless he will find his way back to England, whither, believing you to be dead, as I did, he has not hurried. There are reasons why I, his friend and yours, cannot see you or write more, since my duty calls me hence. When it is finished I will seek you out if I still live. If not, wait in peace until your joy finds you, as I think it will.
"One who loves your lord well, and for his sake you also."

Cicely laid down the paper and burst into a flood of weeping.

"Oh, cruel, cruel!" she sobbed, "to tell so much and yet so little. Nay, what an ungrateful wretch am I, since Christopher truly lives, and I also live to learn it, I, whom he deems dead."

"By my soul," said Emlyn, when she had calmed her, "that cloaked man is a prince of messengers. Oh, had I but known what he bore I'd have had all the story, if I must cling to him like Potiphar's wife to Joseph. Well, well, Joseph got away and half a herring is better than no fish, also this is good herring. Moreover, you have got the deeds when you most wanted them and what is better, a written testimony that will bring the traitor Maldon to the scaffold."

Chapter XIV

Jacob and the Jewels

Cicely's journey to London was strange enough to her, who never before had travelled farther than fifty miles from her home, and but once as a child spent a month in a town when visiting an aunt at Lincoln. She went in ease, it is true, for Commissioner Legh did not love hard travelling, and for this reason they started late and halted early, either at some good inn, if in those days any such places could be called good, or perhaps in a monastery where he claimed of the best that the frightened monks had to offer. Indeed, as she observed, his treatment of these poor folk was cruel, for he blustered and threatened and inquired, accusing them of crimes that they had not committed, and finally, although he had no mission to them at the time, extracted great gifts, saying that if these were not forthcoming he would make a note and return later. Also he got hold of tale- bearers, and wrote down all their scandalous and lying stories told against those whose bread they ate.

Thus, long before they saw Charing Cross, Cicely came to hate this proud, avaricious and overbearing man, who hid a savage nature under a cloak of virtue, and whilst serving his own ends, mouthed great words about God and the King. Still, she who was schooled in adversity, learned to hide her heart, fearing to make an enemy of one who could ruin her, and forced Emlyn, much against her will, to do the same. Moreover, there were worse things than that since, being beautiful, some of his companions talked to her in a way she could not misunderstand, till at length Thomas Bolle, coming on one of them, thrashed him as he had never been thrashed before, after which there was trouble that was only appeased by a gift.

Yet on the whole things went well. No one molested the King's Visitor or those with him, the autumn weather held fine, the baby boy kept his health, and the country through which they passed was new to her and full of interest.

At last one evening they rode from Barnet into the great city, which she thought a most marvellous place, who had never seen such a multitude of houses or of men running to and fro about their business up and down the narrow streets that at night were lit with lamps. Now there had been a great discussion where they were to lodge, Dr. Legh saying that he knew of a house suitable to them. But Emlyn would not hear of this place, where she was sure they would be robbed, for the wealth that they carried secretly in jewels bore heavily on her mind. Remembering a cousin of her mother's of the name of Smith, a goldsmith, who till within a year or two before was alive and dwelling in Cheapside, she said that they would seek him out.

Thither then they rode, guided by one of the Visitor's clerks, not he whom Bolle had beaten, but another, and at last, after some search, found a dingy house in a court and over it a sign on which were painted three balls and the name of Jacob Smith. Emlyn dismounted and, the door being open, entered, to be greeted by an old, white-bearded man with horn spectacles thrust up over his forehead and dark eyes like her own, since the same gypsy blood ran strong in both of them.

What passed between them Cicely did not hear, but presently the old man came out with Emlyn, and looked her and Bolle up and down sharply for a long while as though to take their measures. At length he said that he understood from his cousin, whom he now saw for the first time for over thirty years, that the two of them and their man desired lodgings, which, as he had empty rooms, he would be pleased to give them if they would pay the price.

Cicely asked how much this might be, and on his naming a sum, ten silver shillings a week for the three of them and their horses, that would be stabled close by, told Emlyn to pay him a pound on account. This he took, biting the gold to see that it was good, but bidding them in to inspect the rooms before he pouched it. They did so, and finding them clean and commodious if somewhat dark, closed the bargain with him, after which they dismissed the clerk to take their address to Dr. Legh, who had promised to advise them so soon as he could put their business forward.

When he was gone and Thomas Bolle, conducted by Smith's apprentice, had led off the three horses and the packbeast, the old man changed his manner, and conducting them into a parlour at the back of his shop, sent his housekeeper, a middle-aged woman with a pleasant face, to make ready food for them while he produced cordials from squat Dutch bottles which he made them drink. Indeed he was all kindness to them, being, as he explained, rejoiced to see one of his own blood, for he had no relations living, his wife and their two children having died in one of the London sicknesses. Also he was Blossholme born, though he had left that place fifty years before, and had known Cicely's grandfather and played with her father when he was a boy. So he plied them with question after question, some of which they thought it was not to answer, for he was a merry and talkative old man.

"Aha!" he said, "you would prove me before you trust me, and who can blame you in this naughty world? But perhaps I know more about you all than you think, since in this trade my business is to learn many things. For instance, I have heard that there was a great trying of witches down at Blossholme lately, whereat a certain Abbot came off worst, also that the famous Carfax jewels had been lost, which vexed the said holy Abbot. They were jewels indeed, or so I have heard, for among them were two pink pearls worth a king's ransom—or so I have heard. Great pity that they should be lost, since my Lady there would own them otherwise, and much should I have liked, who am a little man in that trade, to set my old eyes upon them. Well, well, perhaps I shall, perhaps I shall yet, for that which is lost is sometimes found again. Now here comes your dinner; eat, eat, we'll talk afterwards."

This was the first of many pleasant meals which they shared with their host, Jacob Smith. Soon Emlyn found from inquiries that she made among his neighbours without seeming to do so, that this cousin of hers bore an excellent name and was trusted by all.

"Then why should we not trust him also?" asked Cicely, "who must find friends and put faith in some one."

"Even with the jewels, Mistress?"

"Even with the jewels, for such things are his business, and they would be safer in his strong chest than tacked into our garments, where the thought of them haunts me night and day."

"Let us wait a while," said Emlyn, "for once they were in that box how do we know if we should get them out again?"

On the morrow of this talk the Visitor Legh came to see them, and had no cheerful tale to tell. According to him the Lord Cromwell declared that as the Abbot of Blossholme claimed these Shefton estates, the King stood, or would soon stand, in the shoes of the said Abbot of Blossholme, and therefore the King claimed them and could not surrender them. Moreover, money was so wanted at Court just then," and here Legh looked hard at them, "that there could be no talk of parting with anything of value except in return for a consideration," and he looked at them harder still.

"And how can my Lady give that," broke in Emlyn sharply, for she feared lest Cicely should commit herself. "To-day she is but a homeless pauper, save for a few pounds in gold, and even if she should come to her own again, as your Worship knows, her first year's profits are all promised."

"Ah!" said the Doctor sadly, "doubtless the case is hard. Only," he added, with cunning emphasis, "a tale has just reached me that the Lady Harflete has wealth hidden away which came to her from her mother; trinkets of value and such things."

Now Cicely coloured, for the man's little eyes pierced her like gintlets, and her powers of deceit were very small. But this was not so with Emlyn, who, as she said, could play thief to catch a thief.

"Listen, Sir," she said, with a secret air, "you have heard true. There were some things of value—why should we hide it from you, our good friend? But, alas! that greedy rogue, the Abbot of Blossholme, has them. He has stripped my poor Lady as bare as a fowl for roasting. Get them back from him, Sir, and on her behalf I say she'll give you half of them, will you not, my Lady?"

"Surely," said Cicely. "The Doctor, to whom we owe so much, will be most welcome to the half of any movables of mine that he can recover from the Abbot Maldon," and she paused, for the fib stuck in her throat. Moreover, she knew herself to be the colour of a peony.

Happily the Commissioner did not notice her blushes, or if he did, he put them down to grief and anger.

"The Abbot Maldon," he grumbled, "always the Abbot Maldon. Oh! what a wicked thief must be that high-stomached Spaniard who does not scruple first to make orphans and then to rob them? A black-hearted traitor, too. Do you know that at this moment he stirs up rebellion in the north? Well, I'll see him on the rack before I have done. Have you a list of those movables, Madam?"

Cicely said no, and Emlyn added that one should be made from memory.

"Good; I'll see you again to-morrow or the next day, and meanwhile fear not, I'll be as active in your business as a cat after a sparrow. Oh, my rat of a Spanish Abbot, you wait till I get my claws into your fat back. Farewell, my Lady Harflete, farewell. Mistress Stower, I must away to deal with other priests almost as wicked," and he departed, still muttering objurgations on the Abbot.

"Now, I think the time has come to trust Jacob Smith," said Emlyn, when the door closed behind him, "for he may be honest, whereas this Doctor is certainly a villain; also, the man has heard something and suspects us. Ah! there you are, Cousin Smith, come in, if you please, since we desire to talk with you for a minute. Come in, and be so good as to lock the door behind you."

Five minutes later all the jewels, whereof not one was wanting, lay on the table before old Jacob, who stared at them with round eyes.

"The Carfax gems," he muttered, "the Carfax gems of which I have so often heard; those that the old Crusader brought from the East, having sacked them from a Sultan; from the East, where they talk of them still. A sultan's wealth, unless, indeed, they came straight from the New Jerusalem and were an angel's gauds. And do you say that you two women have carried these priceless things tacked in your cloaks, which, as I have seen, you throw down here and there and leave behind you? Oh, fools, fools, even among women incomparable fools! Fellow- travellers with Dr. Legh also, who would rob a baby of its bauble."

"Fools or no," exclaimed Emlyn tartly, "we have got them safe enough after they have run some risks, as I pray that you may keep them, Cousin Smith."

Old Jacob threw a cloth over the gems, and slowly transferred them to his pocket.

"This is an upper floor," he explained, "and the door is locked, yet some one might put a ladder up to the window. Were I in the street I should know by the glitter in the light that there were precious things here. Stay, they are not safe in my pocket even for an hour," and going to the wall he did something to a panel in the wainscot causing it to open and reveal a space behind it where lay sundry wrapped-up parcels, among which he placed, not all, but a portion of the gems. Then he went to other panels that opened likewise, showing more parcels, and in the holes behind these he distributed the rest of the treasure.

"There, foolish women," he said, "since you have trusted me, I will trust you. You have seen my big strong-boxes in my office, and doubtless thought I keep all my little wares there. Well, so does every thief in London, for they have searched them twice and gained some store of pewter; I remember that some of it was discovered again in the King's household. But behind these panels all is safe, though no woman would ever have thought of a device so simple and so sure."

For a moment Emlyn could find no answer, perhaps because of her indignation, but Cicely asked sweetly—

"Do you ever have fires in London, Master Smith? It seems to me that I have heard of such things, and then—in a hurry, you know—"

Smith thrust up his horned spectacles and looked at her in mild astonishment.

"To think," he said, "that I should live to learn wisdom out of the mouth of babes and sucklers—"

"Sucklings," suggested Cicely.

"Sucklers or sucklings, it means the same thing—women," he replied testily; then added, with a chuckle, "Well, well, my Lady, you are right. You have caught out Jacob at his own game. I never thought of fire, though it is true we had one next door last year, when I ran out with my bed and forgot all about the gold and stones. I'll have new hiding-places made in the masonry of the cellar, where no fire would hurt. Ah! you women would never have thought of that, who carry treasure sewn up in a nightshift."

Now Emlyn could bear it no longer.

"And how would you have us carry it, Cousin Smith?" she asked indignantly. "Tied about our necks, or hanging from our heels? Well do I remember my mother telling me that you were always a simple youth, and that your saint must have been a very strong one who brought you safe to London and showed you how to earn a living there, or else that you had married a woman of excellent intelligence—though it is plain now she has long been dead. Well, well," she added, with a laugh, "cling to your man's vanities, you son of a woman, and since you are so clever, give us of your wisdom, for we need it. But first let me tell you that I have rescued those very jewels from a fire, and by hiding them in masonry in a vault."

"It is the fashion of the female to wrangle when she has the worst of the case," said Jacob, with a twinkle in his eye. "So, daughter of man, set out your trouble. Perchance the wisdom that I have inherited from my mothers straight back to Eve may help that which your mothers lacked. Now, have you done with jests. I listen, if it pleases you to tell me."

So, having first invoked the curse of Heaven on him if ever he should breathe a word, Emlyn, with the help of Cicely, repeated the whole matter from the beginning, and the candles were lighted ere ever her tale was done. All this while Jacob Smith sat opposite to them, saying little, save now and again to ask a shrewd question. At length, when they had finished, he exclaimed—

"Truly women are fools!"

"We have heard that before, Master Smith," replied Cicely; "but this time—why?"

"Not to have unbosomed to me before, which would have saved you a week of time, although, as it happens, I knew more of your story than you chose to tell, and therefore the days have not been altogether wasted. Well, to be brief, this Dr. Legh is a ravenous rogue."

"O Solomon, to have discovered that!" exclaimed Emlyn.

"One whose only aim is to line his nest with your feathers, some of which you have promised him, as, indeed, you were right to do. Now he has got wind of these jewels, which is not wonderful, seeing that such things cannot be hid. If you buried them in a coffin, six foot underground, still they would shine through the solid earth and declare themselves. This is his plan—to strip you of everything ere his master, Cromwell, gets a hold of you; and if you go to him empty-handed, what chance has your suit with Vicar-General Cromwell, the hungriest shark of all—save one?"

"We understand," said Emlyn; "but what is your plan, Cousin Smith?"

"Mine? I don't know that I have one. Still, here is that which might do. Though I seem so small and humble, I am remembered at Court—when money is wanted, and just now much money is wanted, for soon they will be in arms in Yorkshire—and therefore I am much remembered. Now, if you care to give Dr. Legh the go-by and leave your cause to me, perhaps I might serve you as cheaply as another."

"At what charge?" blurted out Emlyn.

The old man turned on her indignantly, asking—

"Cousin, how have I defrauded you or your mistress, that you should insult me to my face? Go to! you do not trust me. Go to, with your jewels, and seek some other helper!" and he went to the panelling as though to collect them again.

"Nay, nay, Master Smith," said Cicely, catching him by the arm; "be not angry with Emlyn. Remember that of late we have learned in a hard school, with Abbot Maldon and Dr. Legh for masters. At least I trust you, so forsake me not, who have no other to whom to turn in all my troubles, which are many," and as she spoke the great tears that had gathered in her blue eyes fell upon the child's face, and woke him, so that she must turn aside to quiet him, which she was glad to do.

"Grieve not," said the kind-hearted old man, in distress; "'tis I should grieve, whose brutal words have made you weep. Moreover, Emlyn is right; even foolish women should not trust the first Jack with whom they take a lodging. Still, since you swear that you do in your kindness, I'll try to show myself not all unworthy, my Lady Harflete. Now, what is it you want from the King? Justice on the Abbot? That you'll get for nothing, if his Grace can give it, for this same Abbot stirs up rebellion against him. No need, therefore, to set out his past misdeeds. A clean title to your large inheritance, which the Abbot claims? That will be more difficult, since the King claims through him. At best, money must be paid for it. A declaration that your marriage is good and your boy born in lawful wedlock? Not so hard, but will cost something. The annulment of the sentence of witchcraft on you both? Easy, for the Abbot passed it. Is there aught more?"

"Yes, Master Smith; the good nuns who befriended me—I would save their house and lands to them. Those jewels are pledged to do it, if it can be done."

"A matter of money, Lady—a mere matter of money. You will have to buy the property, that is all. Now, let us see what it will cost, if fortune goes with me," and he took pen and paper and began to write down figures.

Finally he rose, sighing and shaking his head. "Two thousand pounds," he groaned; "a vast sum, but I can't lessen it by a shilling—there are so many to be bought. Yes; £1000 in gifts and £1000 as loan to his Majesty, who does not repay."

"Two thousand pounds!" exclaimed Cicely in dismay; "oh! how shall I find so much, whose first year's rents are already pledged?"

"Know you the worth of those jewels?" asked Jacob, looking at her.

"Nay; the half of that, perhaps."

"Let us say double that, and then right cheap."

"Well, if so," replied Cicely, with a gasp, "where shall we sell them? Who has so much money?"

"I'll try to find it, or what is needful. Now, Cousin Emlyn," he added sarcastically, "you see where my profit lies. I buy the gems at half their value, and the rest I keep."

"In your own words: go to!" said Emlyn, "and keep your gibes until we have more leisure."

The old man thought a while, and said—

"It grows late, but the evening is pleasant, and I think I need some air. That crack-brained, red-haired fellow of yours will watch you while I am gone, and for mercy's sake be careful with those candles. Nay, nay; you must have no fire, you must go cold. After what you said to me, I can think of naught but fire. It is for this night only. By to-morrow evening I'll prepare a place where Abbot Maldon himself might sit unscorched in the midst of hell. But till then make out with clothes. I have some furs in pledge that I will send up to you. It is your own fault, and in my youth we did not need a fire on an autumn day. No more, no more," and he was gone, nor did they see him again that night.

On the following morning, as they sat at their breakfast, Jacob Smith appeared, and began to talk of many things, such as the badness of the weather—for it rained—the toughness of the ham, which he said was not to be compared to those they cured at Blossholme in his youth, and the likeness of the baby boy to his mother.

"Indeed, no," broke in Cicely, who felt that he was playing with them; "he is his father's self; there is no look of me in him."

"Oh!" answered Jacob; "well, I'll give my judgment when I see the father. By the way, let me read that note again which the cloaked man brought to Emlyn."

Cicely gave it to him, and he studied it carefully; then said, in an indifferent voice—

"The other day I saw a list of Christian captives said to have been recovered from the Turks by the Emperor Charles at Tunis, and among them was one 'Huflit,' described as an English señor, and his servant. I wonder now—"

Cicely sprang upon him.

"Oh! cruel wretch," she said, 'to have known this so long and not to have told me!"

"Peace, Lady," he said, retreating before her; "I only learned it at eleven of the clock last night, when you were fast asleep. Yesterday is not this same day, and therefore 'tis the other day, is it not?"

"Surely you might have woke me. But, swift, where is he now?"

"How can I know? Not here, at least. But the writing said—"

"Well, what did the writing say?"

"I am trying to think—my memory fails me at times; perhaps you will find the same thing when you have my years, should it please Heaven—"

"Oh! that it might please Heaven to make you speak! What said the writing?"

"Ah! I have it now. It said, in a note appended amidst other news, for—did I tell you this was a letter from his Grace's ambassador in Spain? and, oh! his is the vilest scrawl to read. Nay, hurry me not—it said that this 'Sir Huflit'—the ambassador has put a query against his name—and his servant—yes, yes, I am sure it said his servant too—well, that they both of them, being angry at the treatment they had met with from the infidel Turks—no, I forgot to add there were three of them, one a priest, who did otherwise. Well, as I said, being angry, they stopped there to serve with the Spaniards against the Turks till the end of that campaign. There, that is all."

"How little is your all!" exclaimed Cicely. "Yet, 'tis something. Oh! why should a married man stop across the seas to be revenged on poor ignorant Turks?"

"Why should he not?" interrupted Emlyn, "when he deems himself a widower, as does your lord?"

"Yes, I forgot; he thinks me dead, who doubtless himself will be dead, if he is not so already, seeing that those wicked, murderous Turks will kill him," and she began to weep.

"I should have added," said Jacob hastily, "that in a second letter, of later date, the ambassador declares that the Emperor's war against the Turks is finished for this season, and that the Englishmen who were with him fought with great honour and were all escaped unharmed, though this time he gives no names."

"All escaped! If my husband were dead, who could not die meanly or without fame, how could he say that they were all escaped? Nay, nay; he lives, though who knows if he will return? Perchance he will wander off elsewhere, or stay and wed again."

"Impossible," said old Jacob, bowing to her; "having called you wife—impossible."

"Impossible," echoed Emlyn, "having such a score to settle with yonder Maldon! A man may forget his love, especially if he deems her buried. But as he stayed foreign to fight the Turk, who wronged him, so he'll come home to fight the Abbot, who ruined him and slew his bride."

There followed a silence, which the goldsmith, who felt it somewhat painful, hastened to break, saying—

"Yes, doubtless he will come home; for aught we know he may be here already. But meanwhile we also have our score against this Abbot, a bad one, though think not for his sake that all Abbots are bad, for I have known some who might be counted angels upon earth, and, having gone to martyrdom, doubtless to-day are angels in heaven. Now, my Lady, I will tell you what I have done, hoping that it will please you better than it does me. Last night I saw the Lord Cromwell, with whom I have many dealings, at his house in Austin Friars, and told him the case, of which, as I thought, that false villain Legh had said nothing to him, purposing to pick the plums out of the pudding ere he handed on the suet to his master. He read your deeds and hunted up some petition from the Abbot, with which he compared them; then made a note of my demands and asked straight out—How much?

"I told him £1000 on loan to the King, which would not be asked for back again, the said loan to be discharged by the grant to me—that is, to you—of all the Abbey lands, in addition to your own, when the said Abbey lands are sequestered, as they will be shortly. To this he agreed, on behalf of his Grace, who needs money much, but inquired as to himself. I replied £500 for him and his jackals, including Dr. Legh, of which no account would be asked. He told me it was not enough, for after the jackals had their pickings nothing would be left for him but the bones; I, who asked so much, must offer more, and he made as though to dismiss me. At the door I turned and said I had a wonderful pink pearl that he, who loved jewels, might like to see—a pink pearl worth many abbeys. He said, 'Show it;' and, oh! he gloated over it like a maid over her first love-letter. 'If there were two of these, now!' he whispered.

"'Two, my Lord!' I answered; 'there's no fellow to that pearl in the whole world,' though it is true that as I said the words, the setting of its twin, that was pinned to my inner shirt, pricked me sorely, as if in anger. Then I took it up again, and for the second time began to bow myself out.

"'Jacob,' he said, 'you are an old friend, and I'll stretch my duty for you. Leave the pearl—his Grace needs that £1000 so sorely that I must keep it against my will,' and he put out his hand to take it, only to find that I had covered it with my own.

"'First the writing, then its price, my Lord. Here is a memorandum of it set out fair, to save you trouble, if it pleases you to sign.'

"He read it through, then, taking a pen, scored out the clause as regards acquittal of the witchcraft, which, he said, must be looked into by the King in person or by his officers, but all the rest he signed, undertaking to hand over the proper deeds under the great seal and royal hand upon payment of £1000. Being able to do no better, I said that would serve, and left him your pearl, he promising, on his part, to move his Majesty to receive you, which I doubt not he will do quickly for the sake of the £1000. Have I done well?"

"Indeed, yes," exclaimed Cicely. "Who else could have done half so well—?"

As the words left her lips there came a loud knocking at the door of the house, and Jacob ran down to open it. Presently he returned with a messenger in a splendid coat, who bowed to Cicely and asked if she were the Lady Harflete. On her replying that such was her name, he said that he bore to her the command of his Grace the King to attend upon him at three o'clock of that afternoon at his Palace of Whitehall, together with Emlyn Stower and Thomas Bolle, there to make answer to his Majesty concerning a certain charge of witchcraft that had been laid against her and them, which summons she would neglect at her peril.

"Sir, I will be there," answered Cicely; "but tell me, do I come as a prisoner?"

"Nay," replied the herald, "since Master Jacob Smith, in whom his Grace has trust, has consented to be answerable for you."

"And for the £1000," muttered Jacob, as, with many salutations, he showed the royal messenger to the door, not neglecting to thrust a gold piece into his hand that he waved behind him in farewell.

Chapter XV

The Devil at Court

It was half-past two of the clock when Cicely, who carried her boy in her arms, accompanied by Emlyn, Thomas Bolle and Jacob Smith, found herself in the great courtyard of the Palace of Whitehall. The place was full of people waiting there upon one business or another, through whom messengers and armed men thrust their way continually, crying, "Way! In the King's name, way!" So great was the press, indeed, that for some time even Jacob could command no attention, till at length he caught sight of the herald who had visited his house in the morning, and beckoned to him.

"I was looking for you, Master Smith, and for the Lady Harflete," the man said, bowing to her. "You have an appointment with his Grace, have you not? but God knows if it can be kept. The ante-chambers are full of folk bringing news about the rebellion in the north, and of great lords and councillors who wait for commands or money, most of them for money. In short the King has given order that all appointments are cancelled; he can see no one to-day. The Lord Cromwell told me so himself."

Jacob took a golden angel from his pouch and began to play with it between his fingers.

"I understand, noble herald," he said. "Still, do you think that you could find me a messenger to the Lord Cromwell? If so, this trifle—"

"I'll try, Master Smith," he answered, stretching out his hand for the piece of money. "But what is the message?"

"Oh, say that Pink Pearl would learn from his Lordship where he can lay hands upon £1000 without interest."

"A strange message, to which I will hazard an answer—nowhere," said the herald, "yet I'll find some one to deliver it. Step within this archway and wait out of the rain. Fear not, I will be back presently."

They did as he bid them, gladly enough, for it had begun to drizzle and Cicely was afraid lest her boy, with whom London did not agree too well, should take cold. Here, then, they stood amusing themselves in watching the motley throng that came and went. Bolle, to whom the scene was strange, gaped at them with his mouth open; Emlyn took note of every one with her quick eyes, while old Jacob Smith whispered tales concerning individuals as they passed, most of which were little to their credit.

As for Cicely, soon her thoughts were far away. She knew that she was at a crisis of her fortune; that if things went well with her this day she might look to be avenged upon her enemies, and to spend the rest of her life in wealth and honour. But it was not of such matters that she dreamed, whose heart was set on Christopher, without whom naught availed. Where was he, she wondered. If Jacob's tale were true, after passing many dangers, but a little while ago he lived and had his health. Yet in those times death came quickly, leaping like the lightning from unexpected clouds or even out of a clear sky, and who could say? Besides, he believed her gone, and that being so would be careless of himself, or perchance, worst thought of all, would take some other wife, as was but right and natural. Oh! then indeed—

At this moment a sound of altercation woke her to the world again, and she looked up to see that Thomas Bolle was bringing trouble on them. A coarse fat lout with a fiery and a knotted nose, being somewhat in liquor, had amused himself by making mock of his country looks and red hair, and asking whether they used him for a scarecrow in his native fields.

Thomas bore it for a while, only answering with another question: whether he, the fat fellow, hired out his nose to London housewives to light their fires. The man, feeling that the laugh was against him, and noticing the child in Cicely's arms pointed it out to his friends, inquiring whether they did not think it was exactly like its dad. Then Thomas's rage burnt up, although the jest was silly and aimless enough.

"You low, London gutter-hound!" he exclaimed; "I'll learn you to insult the Lady Harflete with your ribald japes," and stretching out his big fist he seized his enemy's purple nose in a grip of iron and began to twist it till the sot roared with pain. Thereon guards ran up and would have arrested Bolle for breaking the peace in the King's palace. Indeed, arrested he must have been, notwithstanding all Jacob Smith could do to save him, had not at that moment a man appeared at whose coming the crowd that had gathered, separated, bowing; a man of middle age with a quick, clever face, who wore rich clothes and a fur- trimmed velvet cap and gown.

Cicely knew him at once for Cromwell, the greatest man in England after the King, and marked him well, knowing that he held her fate and that of her child in the hollow of his hand. She noted the thin-lipped mouth, small as a woman's, the sharp nose, the little brownish eyes set close together and surrounded by wrinkled skin that gave them a cunning look, and noting was afraid. Before her stood a man who, though at present he seemed to be her friend, if he chanced to become her enemy, as once he had been bribed to be her father's, would show her no more pity than the spider shows a fly.

Indeed she was right, for many were the flies that had been snared and sucked in the web of Cromwell, who, in his full tide of power and pomp, forgot the fate of his master, Wolsey, in his day a greater spider still.

"What passes here?" Cromwell said in a sharp voice. "Men, is this the place to brawl beneath his Grace's very windows? Ah! Master Smith, is it you? Explain."

"My Lord," answered Jacob, bowing, "this is Lady Harflete's servant and he is not to blame. That fat knave insulted her and, being quick- tempered, her man, Bolle, wrang his nose."

"I see that he wrang it. Look, he is wringing it still. Friend Bolle, leave go, or presently you will have in your hand that which is of no value to you. Guard, take this beer-tub and hold his head beneath the pump for five minutes by the clock to wash him, and if he comes back again set him in the stocks. Nay, no words, fellow, you are well served. Master Smith, follow me with your party."

Again the crowd parted as they walked after Cromwell to a side door that was near at hand, to find themselves alone with him in a small chamber. Here he stopped and, turning, surveyed them all narrowly, especially Cicely.

"I suppose, Master Smith," he said, pointing to Bolle, who was wiping his hands clean with the rushes from the floor, "this is the man that you told me played the devil yonder at Blossholme. Well, he can play the fool also. In another minute there would have been a tumult and you would have lost your chance of seeing his Grace, for months perhaps, since he has determined to ride from London to-morrow morning northwards, though it is true he may change his mind ere then. This rebellion troubles him much, and were it not for the loan you promise, when loans are needed, small hope would you have had of audience. Now come quickly and be careful that you do not cross the King's temper, for it is tetchy to-day. Indeed, had it not been for the Queen, who is with him and minded to see this Lady Harflete, that they would have burnt as a witch, you must have waited till a more convenient season which may never come. Stay, what is in that great sack you carry, Bolle?"

"The devil's livery, may it please your Lordship."

"The devil's livery, many wear that in London. Still, bring the gear, it may make his Grace laugh, and if so I'll give you a gold piece, who have had enough of oaths and scoldings, aye," he added, with a sour grin, "and of blows too. Now follow me into the Presence, and speak only when you are spoken to, nor dare to answer if he rates you."

They went from the room down a passage and through another door, where the guards on duty looked suspiciously at Bolle and his sack, but at a word from Cromwell let them through into a large room in which a fire burned upon the hearth. At the end of this room stood a huge, proud- looking man with a flat and cruel face, broad as an ox's skull, as Thomas Bolle said afterwards, who was dressed in some rich, sombre stuff and wore a velvet cap upon his head. He held a parchment in his hand, and before him on the other side of an oak table sat an officer of state in a black robe, who wrote upon another parchment, whereof there were many scattered about on the table and the floor.

"Knave," shouted the King, for they guessed that it was he, "you have cast up these figures wrong. Oh, that it should be my lot to be served by none but fools!"

"Pardon, your Grace," said the secretary in a trembling voice, "thrice have I checked them."

"Would you gainsay me, you lying lawyer," bellowed the King again. "I tell you they must be wrong, since otherwise the sum is short by £1100 of that which I was promised. Where are the £1100? You must have stolen them, thief."

"I steal, oh, your Grace, I steal!"

"Aye, why not, since your betters do. Only you are clumsy, you lack skill. Ask my Lord Cromwell there to give you lessons. He learned under the best of masters, and is a merchant by trade to boot. Oh, get you gone and take your scribblings with you."

The poor officer hastened to avail himself of this invitation. Hurriedly collecting his parchments he bowed himself from the presence of his irate Sovereign. At the door, about twelve feet away, however, he turned.

"My gracious Liege," he began, "the casting of the count is right. Upon my honour as a Christian soul I can look your Majesty in the face with truth in my eye—"

Now on the table there was a massive inkstand made from the horn of a ram mounted with silver feet. This Henry seized and hurled with all his strength. The aim was good, for the heavy horn struck the wretched scribe upon the nose so that the ink squirted all over his face, and felled him to the floor.

"Now there is more in your eye than truth," shouted the King. "Be off, ere the stool follows the inkpot."

Two ladies who stood by the fire talking together and taking no heed, for to such rude scenes they seemed to be accustomed, looked up and laughed a little, then went on talking, while Cromwell smiled and shrugged his shoulders. Then in the midst of the silence which followed Thomas Bolle, who had been watching open-mouthed, ejaculated in his great voice—

"A bull's eye! A noble bull! Myself cannot throw straighter."

"Silence, fool," hissed Emlyn.

"Who spoke?" asked the king, looking towards them sharply.

"Please, my Liege, it was I, Thomas Bolle."

"Thomas Bolle! Can you sling a stone, Thomas Bolle, whoever you may be?"

"Aye, Sire, but not better than you, I think. That was a gallant shot."

"Thomas Bolle, you are right. Seeing the hurry and the unhandiness of the missile, it was excellent. Let the knave stand up again and I'll bet you a gold noble to a brass nail that you'll not do as well within an inch. Why, the fellow's gone! Will you try on my Lord Cromwell? Nay, this is no time for fooling. What's your business, Thomas Bolle, and who are those women with you?"

Now Cromwell stepped forward, and with cringing gestures began to explain something to the King in a low voice. Meanwhile, the two ladies became suddenly interested in Cicely, and one of them, a pale but pretty woman, splendidly dressed, stepped forward to her, saying—

"Are you the Lady Harflete of whom we have heard, she who was to have been burnt as a witch? Yes? And is that your child? Oh! what a beautiful child. A boy, I'll swear. Come to me, sweet, and in after years you can tell that a queen has nursed you," and she stretched out her arms.

As good fortune would have it the child was awake, and attracted by the Queen's pleasant voice, or perhaps by the necklace of bright gems that she wore, he held out his little hands towards her and went quite contentedly to her breast. Jane Seymour, for it was she, began to fondle him with delight, then, followed by her lady, ran to the King, saying—

"See, Harry, see what a beautiful boy, and how he loves me. God send us such a son as this!"

The King glanced at the child, then answered—

"Aye, he would do well enow. Well, it rests with you, Jane. Nurse him, nurse him, perhaps the sex is catching. I and all England would see you brought to bed of that sickness, Sweet. What said you, Cromwell?"

The great minister went on with his explanations, till the King, wearying of him, called out—

"Come here, Master Smith."

Jacob advanced, bowing, and stood still.

"Now, Master Smith, the Lord Cromwell tells me that if I sign these papers, you, on behalf of the Lady Harflete, will loan me £1000 without interest, which as it chances I need. Where, then, is this £1000?—for I will have no promises, not even from you, who are known to keep them, Master Smith."

Jacob thrust his hand beneath his robe, and from various inner pockets drew out bags of gold, which he set in a row upon the table.

"Here they are, your Grace," he said quietly. "If you should wish for them they can be weighed and counted."

"God's truth! I think I had better keep them, lest some accident should happen to you on the way home, Master Smith. You might fall into the Thames and sink."

"Your Grace is right, the parchments will be lighter to carry, even," he added meaningly, "with your Highness's name added."

"I can't sign," said the King doubtfully, "all the ink is spilt."

Jacob produced a small ink-horn, which like most merchants of the day he carried hung to his girdle, drew out the stopper and with a bow set it on the table.

"In truth you are a good man of business, Master Smith, too good for a mere king. Such readiness makes me pause. Perhaps we had better meet again at a more leisured season."

Jacob bowed once more, and stretching out his hand slowly lifted the first of the bags of gold as though to replace it in his pocket.

"Cromwell, come hither," said the King, whereon Jacob, as though in forgetfulness, laid the bag back upon the table.

"Repeat the heads of this matter, Cromwell."

"My Liege, the Lady Harflete seeks justice on the Spaniard Maldon, Abbot of Blossholme, who is said to have murdered her father, Sir John Foterell, and her husband, Sir Christopher Harflete, though rumour has it that the latter escaped his clutches and is now in Spain. Item: the said Abbot has seized the lands which this Dame Cicely should have inherited from her father, and demands their restitution."

"By God's wounds! justice she shall have and for nothing if we can give it her," answered the King, letting his heavy fist fall upon the table. "No need to waste time in setting out her wrongs. Why, 'tis the same Spanish knave Maldon who stirs up all this hell's broth in the north. Well, he shall boil in his own pot, for against him our score is long. What more?"

"A declaration, Sire, of the validity of the marriage between Christopher Harflete and Cicely Foterell, which without doubt is good and lawful although the Abbot disputes it for his own ends; and an indemnity for the deaths of certain men who fell when the said Abbot attacked and burnt the house of the said Christopher Harflete."

"It should have been granted the more readily if Maldon had fallen also, but let that pass. What more?"

"The promise, your Grace, of the lands of the Abbey of Blossholme and of the Priory of Blossholme in consideration of the loan of £1000 advanced to your Grace by the agent of Cicely Harflete, Jacob Smith."

"A large demand, my Lord. Have these lands been valued?"

"Aye, Sire, by your Commissioner, who reports it doubtful if with all their tenements and timber they would fetch £1000 in gold."

"Our Commissioner? A fig for his valuing, doubtless he has been bribed. Still, if we repay the money we can hold the land, and since this Dame Harflete and her husband have suffered sorely at the hands of Maldon and his armed ruffians, why, let it pass also. Now, is that all? I weary of so much talk."

"But one thing more, your Grace," put in Cromwell hastily, for Henry was already rising from his chair. "Dame Cicely Harflete, her servant, Emlyn Stower, and a certain crazed old nun were condemned of sorcery by a Court Ecclesiastic whereof the Abbot Maldon was a member, the said Abbot alleging that they had bewitched him and his goods."

"Then he was pleader and judge in one?"

"That is so, your Grace. Already without the royal warrant they were bound to the stake for burning, the said Maldon having usurped the prerogative of the Crown, when your Commissioner, Legh, arrived and loosed them, but not without fighting, for certain men were killed and wounded. Now they humbly crave your Majesty's royal pardon for their share in this man-slaying, if any, as also does Thomas Bolle yonder, who seems to have done the slaying—"

"Well can I believe it," muttered the King.

"And a declaration of the invalidity of their trial and condemning, and of their innocence of the foul charge laid against them."

"Innocence!" exclaimed Henry, growing impatient and fixing on the last point. "How do we know they were innocent, though it is true that if Dame Harflete is a witch she is the prettiest that ever we have heard of or seen. You ask too much, after your fashion, Cromwell."

"I crave your Grace's patience for one short minute. There is a man here who can prove that they were innocent; yonder red-haired Bolle."

"What? He who praised our shooting? Well, Bolle, since you are so good a sportsman, we will listen to you. Prove and be brief."

"Now all is finished," murmured Emlyn to Cicely, "for assuredly fool Thomas will land us in the mire."

"Your Grace," said Bolle in his big voice, "I obey in four words—I was the devil."

"The devil you were, Thomas Bolle. Now, your meaning?"

"Your Grace, Blossholme was haunted, I haunted it."

"How could you do otherwise if you lived there?"

"I'll show your Grace," and without more ado, to the horror of Cicely, Thomas tumbled from his sack all his hellish garb and set to work to clothe himself. In a minute, for he was practised at the game, the hideous mask was on his head, and with it the horns and skin of the widow's billy-goat; the tail and painted hides were tied about him, and in his hand he waved the eel spear, short-handled now. Thus arrayed he capered before the astonished King and Queen, shaking the tail that had a wire in it and clattering his hoofs upon the floor.

"Oh, good devil! Most excellent devil!" exclaimed his Majesty, clapping his hands. "If I had met thee I'd have run like a hare. Stay, Jane, peep you through yonder door and tell me who are gathered there."

The Queen obeyed and, returned, said—

"There be a bishop and a priest, I cannot see which, for it grows dark, with chaplains and sundry of the lords of Council waiting audience."

"Good. Then we'll try the devil on these devil-tamers. Friend Satan, go you to that door, slip through it softly and rush upon them roaring, driving them through this chamber so that we may see which of them will be bold enough to try to lay you. Dost understand, Beelzebub?"

Thomas nodded his horns and departed silently as a cat.

"Now open the door and stand on one side," said the King.

Cromwell obeyed, nor had they long to wait. Presently from the hall beyond there rose a most fearful clamour. Then through the door shot the bishop panting, after him came lords, chaplains, and secretaries, and last of all the priest, who, being very fat and hampered by his gown, could not run so fast, although at his back Satan leapt and bellowed. No heed did they take of the King's Majesty or of aught else, whose only thought was flight as they tore down the chamber to the farther door.

"Oh, noble, noble!" hallooed the King, who was shaking with laughter. "Give him your fork, devil, give him your fork," and having the royal command Bolle obeyed with zeal.

In thirty seconds it was all over; the rout had come and gone, only Thomas in his hideous attire stood bowing before the King, who exclaimed—

"I thank thee, Thomas Bolle, thou hast made me laugh as I have not laughed for years. Little wonder that thy mistress was condemned for witchcraft. Now," he added, changing his tone, "off with that mummery, and, Cromwell, go, catch one of those fools and tell them the truth ere tales fly round the palace. Jane, cease from merriment, there is a time for all things. Come hither, Lady Harflete, I would speak with you."

Cicely approached and curtseyed, leaving her boy in the Queen's arms, where he had gone to sleep, for she did not seem minded to part with him.

"You are asking much of us," he said suddenly, searching her with a shrewd glance, "relying, doubtless, on your wrongs, which are deep, or your face, which is sweet, or both. Well, these things move Kings mayhap more than others, also I knew old Sir John, your father, a loyal man and a brave, he fought well at Flodden; and young Harflete, your husband, if he still lives, had a good name like his forebears. Moreover your enemy, Maldon, is ours, a treacherous foreign snake such as England hates, for he would set her beneath the heel of Spain.

"Now, Dame Harflete, doubtless when you go hence you will bear away strange stories of King Harry and his doings. You will say he plays the fool, pelting his servants with inkpots when he is wrath, as God knows he has often cause to be, and scaring his bishops with sham Satans, as after all why should he not since it is a dull world? You'll say, too, that he takes his teaching from his ministers, and signs what these lay before him with small search as to the truth or falsity. Well, that's the lot of monarchs who have but one man's brain and one man's time; who needs must trust their slaves until these become their masters, and there is naught left," here his face grew fierce, "save to kill them, and find more and worse. New servants, new wives," and he glanced at Jane, who was not listening, "new friends, false, false, all three of them, new foes, and at the last old Death to round it off. Such has been the lot of kings from David down, and such I think it shall always be."

He paused a while, brooding heavily, then looked up and went on, "I know not why I should speak thus to a chit like you, except it be, that young though you are, you also have known trouble and the feel of a sick heart. Well, well, I have heard more of you and your affairs than you might think, and I forget nothing—that's my gift. Dame Harflete, you are richer than you have been advised to say, and I repeat you ask much of me. Justice is your due from your Sovereign, and you shall have it; but these wide Abbey lands, this Priory of Blossholme, whose nuns have befriended you and whom you desire to save, this embracing pardon for others who had shed blood, this cancelling outside of the form of law of a sentence passed by a Court duly constituted, if unjust, all in return for a loan of a pitiful £1000? You huckster well, Lady Harflete, one would think that your father had been a chapman, not rough John Foterell, you who can drive so shrewd a bargain with your King's necessities."

"Sire, Sire," broke in Cicely in confusion, "I have no more, my lands are wasted by Abbot Maldon, my husband's hall is burnt by his soldiers, my first year's rents, if ever I should receive them, are promised—"

"To whom?"

She hesitated.

"To whom?" he thundered. "Answer, Madam."

"To your Royal Commissioner, Dr. Legh."

"Ah! I thought as much, though when he spoke of you he did not tell it, the snuffling rogue."

"The jewels that came to me from my mother are in pawn for that £1000, and I have no more."

"A palpable lie, Dame Harflete, for if so, how have you paid Cromwell? He did not bring you here for nothing."

"Oh, my Liege, my Liege," said Cicely, sinking to her knees, "ask not a helpless woman to betray those who have befriended her in her most sore and honest need. I said I have nothing, unless those gems are worth more than I know."

"And I believe you, Dame Harflete. We have plucked you bare between us, have we not? Still, perchance, you will be no loser in the end. Now, Master Smith, there, does not work for love alone."

"Sire," said Jacob, "that is true, I copy my masters. I have this lady's jewels in pledge, and I hope to make a profit on them. Still, Sire, there is among them a pink pearl of great beauty that it might please the Queen to wear. Here it is," and he laid it upon the table.

"Oh, what a lovely thing," said Jane; "never have I seen its like."

"Then study it well, Wife, for you look your last upon it. When we cannot pay our soldiers to keep our crown upon our head, and preserve the liberties of England against the Spaniard and the Pope of Rome, it is no time to give you gems that I have not bought. Take that gaud and sell it, Master Smith, for whatever it will fetch among the Jews, and add the price to the £1000, lessened by one tenth for your trouble. Now, Dame Harflete, you have bought the favour of your King, for whoever else may, I'll not lie. Ah! here comes Cromwell. My Lord, you have been long."

"Your Grace, yonder priest is in a fit from fright, and thinks himself in hell. I had to tarry with him till the doctor came."

"Doubtless he'll get better now that you are gone. Poor man, if a sham devil frights him so, what will he do at last? Now, Cromwell, I have made examination of this business and I will sign your papers, all of them. Dame Harflete here tells me how hard you have worked for her, all for nothing, Cromwell, and that pleases me, who at times have wondered how you grew so rich, as your learner, Wolsey, did before you. He took bribes, Cromwell!"

"My Liege," he answered in a low voice, "this case was cruel, it moved my pity—"

"As it has ours, leaving us the richer by £1000 and the price of a pearl. There, five, are they all signed? Take them, Master Smith, as the Lady Harflete is your client, and study them to-night. If aught be wrong or omitted, you have our royal word that we will set it straight. This is our command—note it, Cromwell—that all things be done quickly as occasion shall arise to give effect to these precepts, pardons and patents which you, Cromwell, shall countersign ere they leave this room. Also, that no further fee, secret or declared, shall be taken from the Lady Harflete, whom henceforth, in token of our special favour, we create and name the Lady of Blossholme, from her husband or her child, as to any of these matters, and that Commissioner Legh, on receipt thereof, shall pay into our treasury any sum or sums that Dame Harflete may have promised to him. Write it down, my Lord Cromwell, and see that our words are carried out, lest it be the worse for you."

The Vicar-General hastened to obey, for there was something in the King's eye that frightened him. Meanwhile the Queen, after she had seen the coveted pearl disappear into Jacob's pocket, thrust back the child into Cicely's arms, and without any word of adieu or reverence to the King, followed by her lady, departed from the room, slamming the door behind her.

"Her Grace is cross because that gem—your gem, Lady Harflete—was refused to her," said Henry, then added in an angry growl, "'Fore God! does she dare to play off her tempers upon me, and so soon, when I am troubled about big matters? Oho! Jane Seymour is the Queen to-day, and she'd let the world know it. Well, what makes a queen? A king's fancy and a crown of gold, which the hand that set it on can take off again, head and all, if it stick too tight. And then where's your queen? Pest upon women and the whims that make us seek their company! Dame Harflete, you'd not treat your lord so, would you? You have never been to Court, I think, or I should have known your eyes again. Well, perhaps it is well for you, and that's why you are gentle and loving."

"If I am gentle, Sire, it is trouble that has gentled me, who have suffered so much, and know not even now whether after one week of marriage I am wife or widow."

"Widow? Should that be so, come to me and I will find you another and a nobler spouse. With your face and possessions it will not be difficult. Nay, do not weep, for your sake I trust that this lucky man may live to comfort you and serve his King. At least he'll be no Spaniard's tool and Pope's plotter."

"Well will he serve your Grace if God gives him the chance, as my murdered father did."

"We know it, Lady. Cromwell, will you never have finished with those writings? The Council waits us, and so does supper, and a word or two with her Grace ere bedtime. You, Thomas Bolle, you are no fool and can hold a sword; tell me, shall I go up north to fight the rebels, or bide here and let others do it?"

"Bide here, your Grace," answered Thomas promptly. "'Twixt Wash and Humber is a wild land in winter and arrows fly about there like ducks at night, none knowing whence they come. Also your Grace is over-heavy for a horse on forest roads and moorland, and if aught should chance, why, they'd laugh in Spain and Rome, or nearer, and who would rule England with a girl child on its throne?" and he stared hard at Cromwell's back.

"Truth at last, and out of the lips of a red-haired bumpkin," muttered the King, also staring at the unconscious Cromwell, who was engaged on his writing and either feigned deafness or did not hear.

"Thomas Bolle, I said that you were no fool, although some may have thought you so, is there aught you would have in payment for your counsel—save money, for that we have none?"

"Aye, Sire, freedom from my oath as a lay-brother of the Abbey of Blossholme, and leave to marry."

"To marry whom?"

"Her, Sire," and he pointed to Emlyn.

"What! The other handsome witch? See you not that she has a temper? Nay, woman, be silent, it is written in your face. Well, take your freedom and her with it, but, Thomas Bolle, why did you not ask otherwise when the chance came your way? I thought better of you. Like the rest of us, you are but a fool after all. Farewell to you, Fool Thomas, and to you also, my fair Lady of Blossholme."

Chapter XVI

The Voice in the Forest

The four were back safe in their lodging in Cheapside, whither, after the deeds had been sealed, three soldiers escorted them by command.

"Have we done well, have we done well?" asked Jacob, rubbing his hands.

"It would seem so, Master Smith," replied Cicely, "thanks to you; that is, if all the King said is really in those writings."

"It is there sure enough," said Jacob; "for know, that with the aid of a lawyer and three scriveners, I drafted them myself in the Lord Cromwell's office this morning, and oh, I drew them wide. Hard, hard we worked with no time for dinner, and that was why I was ten minutes late by the clock, for which Emlyn here chided me so sharply. Still, I'll read them through again, and if aught is left out we will have it righted, though these are the same parchments, for I set a secret mark upon them."

"Nay, nay," said Cicely, "leave well alone. His Grace's mood may change, or the Queen—that matter of the pearl."

"Ah, the pearl, it grieved me to part with that beautiful pearl. But there was no way out, it must be sold and the money handed over, our honour is on it. Had I refused, who knows? Yes, we may thank God, for if the most of your jewels are gone, the wide Abbey lands have come and other things. Nothing is forgot. Bolle is unfrocked and may wed; Cousin Stower has got a husband—"

Then Emlyn, who until now had been strangely silent, burst out in wrath—

"Am I, then, a beast that I should be given to this man like a heriot at yonder King's bidding?" she exclaimed, pointing with her finger at Bolle, who stood in the corner. "Who gave you the right, Thomas, to demand me in marriage?"

"Well, since you ask me, Emlyn, it was you yourself; once, many years ago, down in the mead by the water, and more lately in the chapel of Blossholme Priory before I began to play the devil."

"Play the devil! Aye, you have played the devil with me. There in the King's presence I must stand for an hour or more while all talked and never let a word slip between my lips, and at last hear myself called by his Grace a woman of temper and you a fool for wishing to marry me. Oh, if ever we do marry, I'll prove his words."

"Then perhaps, Emlyn, we who have got on a long while apart, had best stay so," answered Thomas calmly. "Yet, why you should fret because you must keep your tongue in its case for an hour, or because I asked leave to marry you in all honour, I do not know. I have worked my best for you and your mistress at some hazard, and things have not gone so ill, seeing that now we are quit of blame and in a fair way to peace and comfort. If you are not content, why then, the King was right, and I'm a fool, and so good-bye, I'll trouble you no more in fair weather or in foul. I have leave to marry, and there are other women in the world should I need one."

"Tread on their tails and even worms will turn," soliloquized Jacob, while Emlyn burst into tears.

Cicely ran to console her, and Bolle made as though he would leave the room.

Just then there came a great knocking on the street door, and the sound of a voice crying—

"In the King's name! In the King's name, open!"

"That's Commissioner Legh," said Thomas. "I learned the cry from him, and it is a good one at a pinch, as some of you may remember."

Emlyn dried her tears with her sleeve; Cicely sat down and Jacob shovelled the parchments into his big pockets. Then in burst the Commissioner, to whom some one had opened.

"What's this I hear?" he cried, addressing Cicely, his face as red as a turkey cock's. "That you have been working behind my back; that you have told falsehoods of me to his Grace, who called me knave and thief; that I am commanded to pay my fees into the Treasury? Oh, ungrateful wench, would to God that I had let you burn ere you disgraced me thus."

"If you bring so much heat into my poor house, learned Doctor, surely all of us will soon burn," said Jacob suavely. "The Lady Harflete said nothing that his Highness did not force her to say, as I know who was present, and among so many pickings cannot you spare a single dole? Come, come, drink a cup of wine and be calm."

But Dr. Legh, who had already drunk several cups of wine, would not be calm. He reviled first one of them and then the other, but especially Emlyn, whom he conceived to be the cause of all his woes, till at length he called her by a very ill name. Then came forward Thomas Bolle, who all this while had been standing in the corner, and took him by the neck.

"In the King's name!" he said, "nay, complain not, 'tis your own cry and I have warrant for it," and he knocked Legh's head against the door-post. "In the King's name, get out of this," and he gave him such a kick as never Royal Commissioner had felt before, shooting him down the passage. "For the third time in the King's name!" and he hurled him out in a heap into the courtyard. "Begone, and know if ever I see your pudding face again, in the King's name, I'll break your neck!"

Thus did Visitor Legh depart out of the life of Cicely, though in due course she paid him her first year's rent, nor ever asked who took the benefit.

"Thomas," said Emlyn, when he returned smiling at the memory of that farewell kick, "the King was right, I am quick-tempered at times, no ill thing for it has helped me more than once. Forget, and so will I," and she gave him her hand, which he kissed, then went to see about the supper.

While they ate, which they did heartily who needed food, there came another knock.

"Go, Thomas," said Jacob, "and say we see none to-night."

So Thomas went and they heard talk. Then he re-entered followed by a cloaked man, saying—

"Here is a visitor whom I dare not deny," whereon they all rose, thinking in their folly that it was the King himself, and not one almost as mighty in England for a while—the Lord Cromwell.

"Pardon me," said Cromwell, bowing in his courteous manner, "and if you will, let me be seated with you, and give me a bite and a sup, for I need them, who have been hard-worked to-day."

So he sat down among them, and ate and drank, talking pleasantly of many things, and telling them that the King had changed his mind at the Council, as he thought, because of the words of Thomas Bolle, which he believed had stuck there, and would not go north to fight the rebels after all, but would send the Duke of Norfolk and other lords. Then when he had done he pushed away his cup and platter, looked at his hosts and said—

"Now to business. My Lady Harflete, fortune has been your friend this day, for all you asked has been granted to you, which, as his Grace's temper has been of late, is a wondrous thing. Moreover, I thank you that you did not answer a certain question as to myself which I learn he put to you urgently."

"My Lord," said Cicely, "you have befriended me. Still, had he pressed me further, God knows. Commissioner Legh did not thank me to-night," and she told him of the visit they had just received, and of its ending.

"A rough man and a greedy, who doubtless henceforth will be your enemy," replied Cromwell. "Still you were not to blame, for who can reason with a bull in his own yard? Well, while I have power I'll not forget your faithfulness, though in truth, my Lady of Blossholme, I sit upon a slippery height, and beneath waits a gulf that has swallowed some as great, and greater. Therefore I will not deny it, I lay by while I may, not knowing who will gather."

He brooded a while, then went on, with a sigh—

"The times are uncertain; thus, you who have the promise of wealth may yet die a beggar. The lands of Blossholme Abbey, on which you hold a bond that will never be redeemed, are not yet in the King's hands to give. A black storm is bursting in the north and, I say this in secret, the fury of it may sweep Henry from the throne. If it should be so, away with you to any land where you are not known, for then after this day's work here a rope will be your only heritage. More, this Queen, unlike Anne who is gone, is a friend to the party of the Church, and though she affects to care little for such things, is bitter about that pearl, and therefore against you, its owner. Have you no jewel left that you could spare which I might take to her? As for the pearl itself, which Master Smith here swore to me was not to be found in the whole world when he showed me its fellow, it must be sold as the King commanded," and he looked at Jacob somewhat sourly.

Now Cicely spoke with Jacob, who went away and returned presently with a brooch in which was set a large white diamond surrounded by five small rubies.

"Take her this with my duty, my Lord," said Cicely.

"I will, I will. Oh! fear not, it shall reach her for my own sake as well as yours. You are a wise giver, Lady Harflete, who know when and where to cast your bread upon the waters. And now I have a gift for you that perchance will please you more than gems. Your husband, Christopher Harflete, accompanied by a servant, has landed in the north safe and well."

"Oh, my Lord," she cried, "then where is he now?"

"Alas! the rest of the tale is not so pleasing, for as he journeyed, from Hull I think, he was taken prisoner by the rebels, who have him fast at Lincoln, wishing to make him, whose name is of account, one of their company. But he being a wise and loyal man, contrived to send a letter to the King's captain in those parts, which has reached me this night. Here it is, do you know the writing?"

"Aye, aye," gasped Cicely, staring at the scrawl that was ill writ and worse spelt, for Christopher was no scholar.

"Then I'll read it to you, and afterwards certify a copy to multiply the evidence."

"To the Captain of the King's Forces outside Lincoln.

"This to give notice to you, his Grace, and his ministers and all others, that we, Christopher Harflete, Knight, and Jeffrey Stokes, his servant, when journeying from the seaport whither we had come from Spain, were taken by rebels in arms against the King and brought here to Lincoln. These men would win me to their party because the name of Harflete is still strong and known. So violent were they that we have taken some kind of oath. Yet this writing advises you that so I only did to save my life, having no heart that way who am a loyal man and understand little of their quarrel. Life, in sooth, is of small value to me who have lost wife, lands and all. Yet ere I die I would be avenged upon the murderous Abbot of Blossholme, and therefore I seek to keep my breath in me and to escape.

"I learn that the said Abbot is afoot with a great following within fifty miles of here. Pray God he does not get his claws in me again, but if so, say to the King, that Harflete died faithful.

"Christopher Harflete.

"Jeffrey Stokes, & his mark."

"My Lord," said Cicely, "what shall I do, my Lord?"

"There is naught to be done, save trust in God and hope for the best. Doubtless he will escape, and at least his Grace shall see this letter to-morrow morning and send orders to help him if may be. Copy it, Master Smith."

Jacob took the letter and began to write swiftly, while Cromwell thought.

"Listen," he said presently. "Round Blossholme there are no rebels, all of that colour have drawn off north. Now Foterell and Harflete are good names yonder, cannot you journey thither and raise a company?"

"Aye, aye, that I can do," broke in Bolle. "In a week I will have a hundred men at my back. Give commission and money to my Lady there and name me captain and you'll see."

"The commission and the captaincy under the privy signet shall be at this house by nine of the clock to-morrow," answered Cromwell. "The money you must find, for there is none outside the coffers of Jacob Smith. Yet pause, Lady Harflete, there is risk and here you are safe."

"I know the risk," she answered, "but what do I care for risks who have taken so many, when my husband is yonder and I may serve him?"

"An excellent spirit, let us trust that it comes from on high," remarked Cromwell; but old Jacob, as he wrote vera copia for his Lordship's signature at the foot of the transcript of Christopher's letter, shook his head sadly.

In another minute Cromwell had signed without troubling to compare the two, and with some gentle words of farewell was gone, having bigger matters waiting his attention.

Cicely never saw him again, indeed with the exception of Jacob Smith she never saw any of those folk again, including the King, who had been concerned in this crisis of her life. Yet, notwithstanding his cunning and his extortion, she grieved for Cromwell when some four years later the Duke of Suffolk and the Earl of Southampton rudely tore the Garter and his other decorations off his person and he was haled from the Council to the Tower, and thence after abject supplications for mercy, to perish a criminal upon the block. At least he had served her well, for he kept all his promises to the letter. One of his last acts also was to send her back the pink pearl which he had received as a bribe from Jacob Smith, with a message to the effect that he was sure it would become her more than it had him, and that he hoped it would bring her a better fortune.

When Cromwell had gone Jacob turned to Cicely and inquired if she were leaving his house upon the morrow.

"Have I not said so?" she asked, with impatience. "Knowing what I know how could I stay in London? Why do you ask?"

"Because I must balance our account. I think you owe me a matter of twenty marks for rent and board. Also it is probable that we shall need money for our journey, and this day has left me somewhat bare of coin."

"Our journey?" said Cicely. "Do you, then, accompany us, Master Smith?"

"With your leave I think so, Lady. Times are bad here, I have no shilling left to lend, yet if I do not lend I shall never be forgiven. Also I need a holiday, and ere I die would once again see Blossholme, where I was born, should we live to reach it. But if we start to-morrow I have much to do this night. For instance, your jewels which I hold in pawn must be set in a place of safety; also these deeds, whereof copies should be made, and that pearl must be left in trusty hands for sale. So at what hour do we ride on this mad errand?"

"At eleven of the clock," answered Cicely, "if the King's safe-conduct and commission have come by then."

"So be it. Then I bid you good-night. Come with me, worthy Bolle, for there'll be no sleep for us. I go to call my clerks and you must go to the stable. Lady Harflete and you, Cousin Emlyn, get you to bed."

On the following morning Cicely rose with the dawn, nor was she sorry to do so, who had spent but a troubled night. For long sleep would not come to her, and when it did at length, she was tossed upon a sea of dreams, dreams of the King, who threatened her with his great voice; of Cromwell, who took everything she had down to her cloak; of Commissioner Legh, who dragged her back to the stake because he had lost his bribe.

But most of all she dreamed of Christopher, her beloved husband, who was so near and yet as far away as he had ever been, a prisoner in the hands of the rebels; her husband who deemed her dead.

From all these phantasies she awoke weeping and oppressed by fears. Could it be that when at length the cup of joy was so near her lips fate waited to dash it down again? She knew not, who had naught but faith to lean on, that faith which in the past had served her well. Meanwhile, she was sure that if Christopher lived he would make his way to Cranwell or to Blossholme, and, whatever the risk, thither she would go also as fast as horses could carry her.

Hurry as they would, midday was an hour gone ere they rode out of Cheapside. There was so much to do, and even then things were left undone. The four of them travelled humbly clad, giving out that they were a party of merchant folk returning to Cambridge after a visit to London as to an inheritance in which they were interested, especially Cicely, who posed as a widow named Johnson. This was their story, which they varied from time to time according to circumstances. In some ways their minds were more at ease than when they travelled to the great city, for now at least they were clear of the horrid company of Commissioner Legh and his people, nor were they haunted by the knowledge that they had about them jewels of great price. All these jewels were left behind in safe keeping, as were also the writings under the King's hand and seal, of which they only took attested copies, and with them the commission that Cromwell had duly sent to Cicely addressed to her husband and herself, and Bolle's certificate of captaincy. These they hid in their boots or the linings of their vests, together with such money as was necessary for the costs of travel.

Thus riding hard, for their horses were good and fresh, they came unmolested to Cambridge on the night of the second day and slept there. Beyond Cambridge, they were told, the country was so disturbed that it would not be safe for them to journey. But just when they were in despair, for even Bolle said that they must not go on, a troop of the King's horse arrived on their way to join the Duke of Norfolk wherever he might lie in Lincolnshire.

To their captain, one Jeffreys, Jacob showed the King's commission, revealing who they were. Seeing that it commanded all his Grace's officers and servants to do them service, this Captain Jeffreys said that he would give them escort until their roads separated. So next day they went on again. The company was not pleasant, for the men, of whom there were about a hundred, proved rough fellows, still, having been warned that he who insulted or laid a finger on them should be hanged, they did them no harm. It was well, indeed, that they had their protection, for they found the country through which they passed up in arms, and were more than once threatened by mobs of peasants, led by priests, who would have attacked them had they dared.

For two days they travelled thus with Captain Jeffreys, coming on the evening of the second to Peterborough, where they found lodgings at an inn. When they rose the next morning, however, it was to discover that Jeffreys and his men had already gone, leaving a message to say that he had received urgent orders to push on to Lincoln.

Now once more they told their old tale, declaring that they were citizens of Boston, and having learned that the Fens were peaceful, perhaps because so few people lived in them, started forward by themselves under the guidance of Bolle, who had often journeyed through that country, buying or selling cattle for the monks. An ill land was it to travel in also in that wet autumn, seeing that in many places the floods were out and the tracks were like a quagmire. The first night they spent in a marshman's hut, listening to the pouring rain and fearing fever and ague, especially for the boy. The next day, by good fortune, they reached higher land and slept at a tavern.

Here they were visited by rude men, who, being of the party of rebellion, sought to know their business. For a while things were dangerous, but Bolle, who could talk their own dialect, showed that they were scarcely to be feared who travelled with two women and a babe, adding that he was a lay-brother of Blossholme Abbey disguised as a serving-man for dread of the King's party. Jacob Smith also called for ale and drank with them to the success of the Pilgrimage of Grace, as their revolt was named.

In this way they disarmed suspicion with one tale and another. Moreover, they heard that as yet the country round Blossholme remained undisturbed, although it was said that the Abbot had fortified the Abbey and stored it with provisions. He himself was with the leaders of the revolt in the neighbourhood of Lincoln, but he had done this that he might have a strong place to fall back on.

So in the end the men went away full of strong beer, and that danger passed by.

Next morning they started forward early, hoping to reach Blossholme by sunset though the days were shortening much. This, however, was not to be, for as it chanced they were badly bogged in a quagmire that lay about two miles off their inn, and when at length they scrambled out had to ride many miles round to escape the swamp. So it happened that it was already well on in the afternoon when they came to that stretch of forest in which the Abbot had murdered Sir John Foterell. Following the woodland road, towards sunset they passed the mere where he had fallen. Weary as she was, Cicely looked at the spot and found it familiar.

"I know this place," she said. "Where have I seen it? Oh, in the ill dream I had on that day I lost my father."

"That is not wonderful," answered Emlyn, who rode beside her carrying the child, "seeing that Thomas says it was just here they butchered him. Look, yonder lie the bones of Meg, his mare; I know them by her black mane."

"Aye, Lady," broke in Bolle, "and there he lies also where he fell; they buried him with never a Christian prayer," and he pointed to a little careless mound between two willows."

"Jesus, have mercy on his soul!" said Cicely, crossing herself. "Now, if I live, I swear that I will move his bones to the chancel of Blossholme church and build a fair monument to his memory."

This, as all visitors to the place know, she did, for that monument remains to this day, representing the old knight lying in the snow, with the arrow in his throat, between the two murderers whom he slew, while round the corner of the tomb Jeffrey Stokes gallops away.

While Cicely stared back at this desolate grave, muttering a prayer for the departed, Thomas Bolle heard something which caused him to prick his ears.

"What is it?" asked Jacob Smith, who saw the change in his face.

"Horses galloping—many horses, master," he answered; "yes, and riders on them. Listen."

They did so, and now they also heard the thud of horse's hoofs and the shouts of men.

"Quick, quick," said Bolle, "follow me. I know where we may hide," and he led them off to a dense thicket of thorn and beech scrub which grew about two hundred yards away under a group of oaks at a place where four tracks crossed. Owing to the beech leaves, which, when the trees are young, as every gardener knows, cling to the twigs through autumn and winter, this place was very close, and hid them completely.

Scarcely had they taken up their stand there, when, in the red light of the sunset, they saw a strange sight. Along, not that road they had followed, but another, which led round the farther side of King's Grave Mount, now seen and now hidden by the forest trees, a tall man in armour mounted on a grey horse, accompanied by another man in a leathern jerkin mounted on a black horse, galloped towards them, whilst, at a distance of not more than a hundred yards behind them, appeared a motley mob of pursuers.

"Escaped prisoners being run down," muttered Bolle, but Cicely took no heed. There was something about the appearance of the rider of the grey horse that seemed to draw her heart out of her.

She leaned forward on her beast's neck, staring with all her eyes. Now the two men were almost opposite the thicket, and the man in mail turned his face to his companion and called cheerily—

"We gain! We'll slip them yet, Jeffrey."

Cicely saw the face.

"Christopher!" she cried; "Christopher!"

Another moment and they had swept past, but Christopher—for it was he—had caught the sound of that remembered voice. With eyes made quick by love and fear she saw him pulling on his rein. She heard him shout to Jeffrey, and Jeffrey shout back to him in tones of remonstrance. They halted confusedly in the open space beyond. He tried to turn, then perceived his pursuers drawing nearer, and, when they were already at his heels, with an exclamation, pulled round again to gallop away. Too late! Up the slope they sped for another hundred yards or so. Now they were surrounded, and now, at the crest of it, they fought, for swords flashed in the red light. The pursuers closed in on them like hounds on an outrun fox. They went down—they vanished.

Cicely strove to gallop after them, for she was crazed, but the others held her back.

At length there was silence, and Thomas Bolle, dismounting, crept out to look. Ten minutes later he returned.

"All have gone," he said.

"Oh! he is dead!" wailed Cicely. "This fatal place has robbed me of father and of husband."

"I think not," answered Bolle. "I see no bloodstains, nor any signs of a man being carried. He went living on his horse. Still, would to Heaven that women could learn when to keep silent!"

Chapter XVII

Between Doom and Honour

The day was about to break when at last, utterly worn out in body and mind, Cicely and her party rode their stumbling horses up to the gates of Blossholme Priory.

"Pray God the nuns are still here," said Emlyn, who held the child, "for if they have been driven out and my mistress must go farther, I think that she will die. Knock hard, Thomas, that old gardener is deaf as a wall."

Bolle obeyed with good will, till presently the grille in the door was opened and a trembling woman's voice asked who was there.

"That's Mother Matilda," said Emlyn, and slipping from her horse, she ran to the bars and began to talk to her through them. Then other nuns came, and between them they opened one of the large gates, for the gardener either could not or would not be aroused, and passed through it into the courtyard where, when it was understood that Cicely had really come again, there was a great welcoming. But now she could hardly speak, so they made her swallow a bowl of milk and took her to her old room, where sleep of some kind overcame her. When she awoke it was nine of the clock. Emlyn, looking little the worse, was already up and stood talking with Mother Matilda.

"Oh!" cried Cicely, as memory came back to her, "has aught been heard of my husband?"

They shook their heads, and the Prioress said—

"First you must eat, Sweet, and then we will tell you all we know, which is little."

So she ate who needed food sadly, and while Emlyn helped her to dress herself, hearkened to the news. It was of no great account, only confirming that which they had learnt from the Fenmen; that the Abbey was fortified and guarded by strange soldiers, rebellious men from the north or foreigners, and the Abbot supposed to be away.

Bolle, who had been out, reported also that a man he met declared that he had heard a troop of horsemen pass through the village in the night, but of this no proof was forthcoming, since if they had done so the heavy rain that was still falling had washed out all traces of them. Moreover, in those times people were always moving to and fro in the dark, and none could know if this troop had anything to do with the band they had seen in the forest, which might have gone some other way.

When Cicely was ready they went downstairs, and in Mother Matilda's private room found Jacob Smith and Thomas Bolle awaiting them.

"Lady Harflete," said Jacob, with the air of a man who has no time to lose, "things stand thus. As yet none know that you are here, for we have the gardener and his wife under ward. But as soon as they learn it at the Abbey there will be risk of an attack, and this place is not defensible. Now at your hall of Shefton it is otherwise, for there it seems is a deep moat with a drawbridge and the rest. To Shefton, therefore, you must go at once, unobserved if may be. Indeed, Thomas has been there already, and spoken to certain of your tenants whom he can trust, who are now hard at work preparing and victualling the place, and passing on the word to others. By nightfall he hopes to have thirty strong men to defend it, and within three days a hundred, when your commission and his captaincy are made known. Come, then, for there is no time to tarry and the horses are saddled."

So Cicely kissed Mother Matilda, who blessed and thanked her for all she had done, or tried to do on behalf of the sisterhood, and within five minutes once more they were on the backs of their weary beasts and riding through the rain to Shefton, which happily was but three miles away. Keeping under the lee of the woods they left the Priory unobserved, for in that wet few were stirring, and the sentinels at the Abbey, if there were any, had taken shelter in the guard-house. So thankfully enough they came unmolested to walled and wooded Shefton, which Cicely had last seen when she fled thence to Cranwell on the day of her marriage, oh, years and years ago, or so it seemed to her tormented heart.

It was a strange and a sad home-coming, she thought, as they rode over the drawbridge and through the sodden and weed-smothered pleasaunce to the familiar door. Yet it might have been worse, for the tenants whom Bolle had warned had not been idle. For two hours past and more a dozen willing women had swept and cleaned; the fires had been lit, and there was plenteous food of a sort in the kitchen and the store-room.

Moreover, in all the big hall were gathered about a score of her people, who welcomed her by raising their bonnets and even tried to cheer. To these at once Jacob read the King's commission, showing them the signet and the seal, and that other commission which named Thomas Bolle a captain with wide powers, the sight and hearing of which writings seemed to put a great heart into them who so long had lacked a leader and the support of authority. One and all they swore to stand by the King and their lady, Cicely Harflete, and her lord, Sir Christopher, or if he were dead, his child. Then about half of them took horse and rode off, this way and that, to gather men in the King's name, while the rest stayed to guard the Hall and work at its defences.

By sunset men were riding up from all sides, some of them driving carts loaded with provisions, arms and fodder, or sheep and beasts that could be killed for sustenance, while as they came Jacob enrolled their names upon a paper and by virtue of his commission Thomas Bolle swore them in. Indeed that night they had forty men quartered there, and the promise of many more.

By now, however, the secret was out, for the story had gone round and the smoke from the Shefton chimneys told its own tale. First a single spy appeared on the opposite rise, watching. Then he galloped away, to return an hour later with ten armed and mounted men, one of whom carried a banner on which were embroidered the emblems of the Pilgrimage of Grace. These men rode to within a hundred paces of Shefton Hall, apparently with the object of attacking it, then seeing that the drawbridge was up and that archers with bent bows stood on either side, halted and sent forward one of their number with a white flag to parley.

"Who holds Shefton," shouted this man, "and for what cause?"

"The Lady Harflete, its owner, and Captain Thomas Bolle, for the cause of the King," called old Jacob Smith back to him.

"By what warrant?" asked the man. "The Abbot of Blossholme is lord of Shefton, and Thomas Bolle is but a lay-brother of his monastery."

"By warrant of the King's Grace," said Jacob, and then and there at the top of his voice he read to him the Royal Commission, which when the envoy had heard, he went back to consult with his companions. For a while they hesitated, apparently still meditating attack, but in the end rode away and were seen no more.

Bolle wished to follow and fall on them with such men as he had, but the cautious Jacob Smith forbade it, fearing lest he should tumble into some ambush and be killed or captured with his people, leaving the place defenceless.

So the afternoon went by, and ere evening closed in they had so much strength that there was no more cause for fear of an attack from the Abbey, whose garrison they learned amounted to not over fifty men and a few monks, for most of these had fled.

That night Cicely with Emlyn and old Jacob were seated in the long upper room where her father, Sir John Foterell, had once surprised Christopher paying his court to her, when Bolle entered, followed by a man with a hang-dog look who was wrapped in a sheepskin coat which seemed to become him very ill.

"Who is this, friend?" asked Jacob.

"An old companion of mine, your worship, a monk of Blossholme who is weary of Grace and its pilgrimages, and seeks the King's comfort and pardon, which I have made bold to promise to him."

"Good," said Jacob, "I'll enter his name, and if he remains faithful your promise shall be kept. But why do you bring him here?"

"Because he bears tidings."

Now something in Bolle's voice caused Cicely, who was brooding apart, to look up sharply and say—

"Speak, and be swift."

"My Lady," began the man in a slow voice, "I, who am named Basil in religion, have fled the Abbey because, although a monk, I am true to the King, and moreover have suffered much from the Abbot, who has just returned raging, having met with some reverse out Lincoln way, I know not what. My news is that your lord, Sir Christopher Harflete, and his servant Jeffrey Stokes are prisoners in the Abbey dungeons, whither they were brought last night by a company of the rebels who had captured them and afterwards rode on."

"Prisoners!" exclaimed Cicely. "Then he is not dead or wounded? At least he is whole and safe?"

"Aye, my Lady, whole and safe as a mouse in the paws of a cat before it is eaten."

The blood left Cicely's cheeks. In her mind's eye she saw Abbot Maldon turned into a great cat with a monk's head and patting Christopher with his claws.

"My fault, my fault!" she said in a heavy voice. "Oh, if I had not called him he would have escaped. Would that I had been stricken dumb!"

"I don't think so," answered Brother Basil. "There were others watching for him ahead who, when he was taken, went away and that is how you came to get through so neatly. At least there he lies, and if you would save him, you had best gather what strength you can and strike at once."

"Does he know that I live?" asked Cicely.

"How can I tell, Lady? The Abbey dungeons are no good place for news. Yet the monk who took him his food this morning said that Sir Christopher told him that he had been undone by some ghost which called to him with the voice of his dead wife as he rode near King's Grave Mount."

Now when Cicely heard this she rose and left the room accompanied by Emlyn, for she could bear no more.

But Jacob Smith and Bolle remained questioning the man closely upon many matters, and, having learned all he could tell them, sent him away under guard and sat there till midnight consulting and making up their plans with the farmers and yeomen whom they called to them from time to time.

Next morning early they sought out Cicely and told her that to them it seemed wise that the Abbey should be attacked without delay.

"But my husband lies there," she answered in distress, "and then they will kill him."

"So I fear they may if we do not attack," replied Jacob. "Moreover, Lady, to tell the truth, there are other things to be thought of. For instance, the King's cause and honour, which we are bound to forward, and the lives and goods of all those who through us have declared themselves for him. If we lie idle Abbot Maldon will send messengers to the north and within a few days bring down thousands upon us, against whom we cannot hope to stand. Indeed, it is probable that he has already sent. But if they hear that the Abbey has fallen the rebels will scarcely come for revenge alone. Lastly, if we sit with folded hands, our own people may grow cold with doubts and fears and melt away, who now are hot as fire."

"If it must be, so let it be. In God's hands I leave his life," said Cicely in a heavy voice.

That day the King's men, under the captaincy of Bolle, advanced and invested the Abbey, setting their camp in Blossholme village. Cicely, who would not be left behind, came with them and once more took up her quarters in the Priory, which on a formal summons opened its gates to her, its only guard, the deaf gardener, surrendering at discretion. He was set to work as a camp servant, and never in his life did he labour so hard before, since Emlyn, who owed him many a grudge, saw to it that he did not lack for tasks that were mean and heavy.

Now that day Thomas and others spied out the Abbey and returned shaking their heads, for without cannon—and as yet they had none—the great building of hewn stone seemed almost impregnable. At but one spot indeed was attack possible, from the back where once stood the dormers and farm steadings which Emlyn had egged on Thomas to burn. These had been built up to the inner edge of the moat, making, as it were, part of the Abbey wall, but the fierce fire had so cracked and crumbled their masonry that several rods of it had fallen forward into the water.

For purposes of defence the gap this formed was now closed by a double palisade of stout stakes, filled in with faggots, the charred beams of the old buildings and other rubbish. Yet to carry this palisade, protected as it was by the broad and deep moat and commanded from the windows and the corner tower, was more than they dared try, since if it could be done at all it would certainly cost them very many lives. One thing they had learned, however, from the monk Basil and others, that in the Abbey there was but small store of food to feed so many: three days' supply, said Basil, and none put it at over four.

That evening, then, they held another council, at which it was determined to starve the place out and only attempt an onslaught if their spies reported to them that the rebels were marching to its relief.

"But," urged Cicely, "then my lord and Jeffrey Stokes will starve also," whereon they went away sadly, saying there was no choice, seeing that they were but two men and the lives of many lay at stake.

The siege began, just such a siege as Cicely had suffered at Cranwell Towers. The first day the garrison of the Abbey scoffed at them from the walls. The second day they scoffed no longer, noting that the force of the besiegers increased, which it did hourly. The third day suddenly they let down the drawbridge and poured out on to it as though for a sortie, but when they perceived the scores of Bolle's men waiting bow in hand and arrow on string, changed their minds and drew the bridge up again.

"They grow hungry and desperate," said the shrewd Jacob. "Soon we shall have some message from them."

He was right, since just before sunset a postern gate was opened and a man, holding a white flag above his head, was seen swimming across the moat. He scrambled out on the farther side, shook himself like a dog, and advanced slowly to where Bolle and the women stood upon the Abbey green out of arrow-shot from the walls. Indeed, Cicely, who was weak with dread and wretchedness, leaned against the oaken stake that had never been removed, to which once she was tied to be burned for witchcraft.

"Who is that man?" said Emlyn to her.

Cicely scanned the gaunt, bearded figure who walked haltingly like one that is sick.

"I know not—yes, yes, he puts me in mind of Jeffrey Stokes!"

"Jeffrey it is and no other," said Emlyn, nodding her head. "Now what news does he bear, I wonder?"

Cicely made no reply, only clung to her stake and waited, with just such a heart as once she had waited there while the Abbey cook blew up his brands to fire her faggots. Jeffrey was opposite to her now; his sunken eyes fell upon her, and at the sight his bearded chin dropped, making his face look even more long and hollow than it had before.

"Ah!" he said, speaking to himself, "many wars and journeyings, months in an infidel galley, three days with not enough food to feed a rat and a bath in November water! Well, such things, to say nothing of a worse, turn men's brains. Yet to think that I should live to see a daylight ghost in homely Blossholme, who never met with one before."

Still staring he shook the water from his beard, then added, "Lay- brother or Captain Thomas Bolle, whichever you may be now-a-days, if you're not a ghost also, give me a quart of strong ale and a loaf of bread, for I'm empty as a gutted herring, and floating heavenward, so to speak, who would stick upon this scurvy earth."

"Jeffrey, Jeffrey," broke in Cicely, "what news of your master? Emlyn, tell him that we still live. He does not understand."

"Oh, you still live, do you?" he added slowly. "So the fire could not burn you after all, or Emlyn either. Well, then, there's hope for every one, and perhaps hunger and Abbot Maldon's knives cannot kill Christopher Harflete."

"He lives, then, and is well?"

"He lives and is as well as a man may be after a three days' fast in a black dungeon that is somewhat damp. Here's a writing on the matter for the captain of this company," and, taking a letter from the folds of the white flag in which it had been fastened, he handed it to Bolle, who, as he could not read, passed it on to Jacob Smith. Just then a lad brought the ale for which Jeffrey had asked, and with it a platter of cold meat and bread, on which he fell like a famished hound, drinking in great gulps and devouring the food almost without chewing it.

"By the saints, you are starved, Jeffrey," said a yeoman who stood by. "Come with me and shift those wet clothes of yours, or you will take harm," and he led him off, still eating, to a tent that stood near by.

Meanwhile, Jacob, having studied the letter with bent and anxious brows, read it aloud. It ran thus—

"To the Captain of the King's men, from Clement, Abbot of Blossholme.

"By what warrant I know not you besiege us here, threatening this Abbey and its Religious with fire and sword. I am told that Cicely Foterell is your leader. Say, then, to that escaped witch that I hold the man she calls her husband, and who is the father of her base-born child, a prisoner. Unless this night she disperses her troop and sends me a writing signed and witnessed, promising indemnity on behalf of the King for me and those with me for all that we may have done against him and his laws, or privately against her, and freedom to go where we will without pursuit or hindrance or loss of land or chattels, know that to-morrow at the dawn we put to death Christopher Harflete, Knight, in punishment of the murders and other crimes that he has committed against us, and in proof thereof his body shall be hung from the Abbey tower. If otherwise we will leave him unharmed here where you shall find him after we have gone. For the rest, ask his servant, Jeffrey Stokes, whom we send to you with this letter.

"Clement, Abbot."

Jacob finished reading and a silence fell upon all who listened.

"Let us go to some private place and consider this matter," said Emlyn.

"Nay," broke in Cicely, "it is I, who in my lord's absence, hold the King's commission and I will be heard. Thomas Bolle, first send a man under flag to the Abbot, saying, that if aught of harm befalls Sir Christopher Harflete I'll put every living soul within the Abbey walls to death by sword or rope, and stand answerable for it to the King. Set it in writing, Master Smith, and send with it copy of the King's commission for my warrant. At once, let it be done at once."

So they went to a cottage near by, which Bolle used as a guard-house, where this stern message was written down, copied out fair, signed by Cicely and by Bolle, as captain, with Jacob Smith for witness. This paper, together with a copy of the King's commissions, Cicely with her own hand gave to a bold and trusty man, charged to ask an answer, who departed, carrying the white flag and wearing a steel shirt beneath his doublet, for fear of treachery.

When he had gone they sent for Jeffrey, who arrived clad in dry garments and still eating, for his hunger was that of a wolf.

"Tell us all," said Cicely.

"It will be a long story if I begin at the beginning, Lady. When your worshipful father, Sir John, and I rode away from Shefton on the day of his murder—"

"Nay, nay," interrupted Cicely, "that may stand, we have no time. My lord and you escaped from Lincoln, did you not, and, as we saw, were taken in the forest?"

"Aye, Lady. Some tricksy spirit called out with your voice and he heard and pulled rein, and so they came on to us and overwhelmed us, though without hurt as it chanced. Then they brought us to the Abbey and thrust us into that accursed dungeon, where, save for a little bread and water, we have starved for three days in the dark. That is all the tale."

"How, then, did you come out, Jeffrey?"

"Thus, my Lady. Something over an hour ago a monk and three guards unlocked the dungeon door. While we blinked at his lantern, like owls in the sunlight, the monk said that the Abbot purposed to send me to the camp of the King's party to offer Christopher Harflete's life against the lives of all of them. He told him, Harflete, also, that he had brought ink and paper and that if he wished to save himself he would do well to write a letter praying that this offer might be accepted, since otherwise he would certainly die at dawn."

"And what said my husband?" asked Cicely, leaning forward.

"What said he? Why, he laughed in their faces and told them that first he would cut off his hand. On this they haled me out of the dungeon roughly enough, for I would have stayed there with him to the end. But as the door closed he shouted after me, 'Tell the King's officers to burn this rats' nest and take no heed of Christopher Harflete, who desires to die!'"

"Why does he desire to die?" asked Cicely again.

"Because he thinks his wife dead, Mistress, as I did, and believes that in the forest he heard her voice calling him to join her."

"Oh God! oh God!" moaned Cicely; "I shall be his death."

"Not so," answered Jeffrey. "Do you know so little of Christopher Harflete that you think he would sell the King's cause to gain his own life? Why, if you yourself came and pleaded with him he would thrust you away, saying, 'Get thee behind me, Satan!'"

"I believe it, and I am proud," muttered Cicely. "If need be, let Harflete die, we'll keep his honour and our own lest he should live to curse us. Go on."

"Well, they led me to the Abbot, who gave me that letter which you have, and bade me take it and tell the case to whoever commanded here. Then he lifted up his hand and, laying it on the crucifix about his neck, swore that this was no idle threat, but that unless his terms were taken, Harflete should hang from the tower top at to-morrow's dawn, adding, though I knew not what he meant, 'I think you'll find one yonder who will listen to that reasoning.' Now he was dismissing me when a soldier said—

"'Is it wise to free this Stokes? You forget, my Lord Abbot, that he is alleged to have witnessed a certain slaying yonder in the forest and will bear evidence.' 'Aye,' answered Maldon, 'I had forgotten who in this press remembered only that no other man would be believed. Still, perhaps it would be best to choose a different messenger and to silence this fellow at once. Write down that Jeffrey Stokes, a prisoner, strove to escape and was killed by the guards in self-defence. Take him hence and let me hear no more.'

"Now my blood went cold, although I strove to look as careless as a man may on an empty stomach after three days in the dark, and cursed him prettily in Spanish to his face. Then, as they were haling me off, Brother Martin—do you remember him? he was our companion in some troubles over-seas—stepped forward out of the shadow and said, 'Of what use is it, Abbot, to stain your soul with so foul a murder? Since John Foterell died the King has many things to lay to your account, and any one of them will hang you. Should you fall into his hands, he'll not hark back to Foterell's death, if, indeed, you were to blame in that matter.'

"'You speak roughly, Brother,' answered the Abbot; 'and acts of war are not murder, though perchance afterwards you might say they were, to save your own skin, or others might. Well, if so, there's wisdom in your words. Touch not the man. Give him the letter and thrust him into the moat to swim it. His lies can make no odds in the count against us.'

"Well, they did so, and I came here, as you saw, to find you living, and now I understand why Maldon thought that Harflete's life is worth so much," and, having done his tale, once more Jeffrey began to eat.

Cicely looked at him, they all looked at him—this gaunt, fierce man who, after many other sorrows and strivings, had spent three days in a black dungeon with the rats, fed upon water and a few fingers of black bread. Yes; with the crawling rats and another man so dear to one of them, who still sat in that horrid hole, waiting to be hung like a felon at the dawn. The silence, with only Jeffrey's munching to break it, grew painful, so that all were glad when the door opened and the messenger whom they had sent to the Abbey appeared. He was breathless, having run fast, and somewhat disturbed, perhaps because two arrows were sticking in his back, or rather in his jerkin, for the mail beneath had stopped them.

"Speak," said old Jacob Smith; "what is your answer?"

"Look behind me, master, and you will find it," replied the man. "They set a ladder across the moat and a board on that, over which a priest tripped to take my writing. I waited a while, till presently I heard a voice hail me from the gateway tower, and, looking up, saw Abbot Maldon standing there, with a face like that of a black devil.

"'Hark you, knave,' he said to me, 'get you gone to the witch, Cicely Foterell, and to the recreant monk, Bolle, whom I curse and excommunicate from the fellowship of Holy Church, and tell them to watch for the first light of dawn, for by it, somewhat high up, they'll see Christopher Harflete hanging black against the morning sky!'

"On hearing this I lost my caution, and hallooed back—

"'If so, ere to-morrow's nightfall you shall keep him company, every one of you, black against the evening sky, except those who go to be quartered at Tower Hill and Tyburn.' Then I ran and they shot at me, hitting once or twice, but, though old, the mail was good, and here am I, unhurt except for bruises."

A while later Cicely, Jacob Smith, Thomas Bolle, Jeffrey Stokes, and Emlyn Stower sat together taking counsel—very earnest counsel, for the case was desperate. Plan after plan was brought forward and set aside for this reason or for that, till at length they stared at each other emptily.

"Emlyn," exclaimed Cicely at last, "in past days you were wont to be full of comfortable words; have you never a one in this extreme?" for all the while Emlyn had sat silent.

"Thomas," said Emlyn, looking up, "do you remember when we were children where we used to catch the big carp in the Abbey moat?"

"Aye, woman," he answered; "but what time is this for fishing stories of many years ago? As I was saying, of that tunnel underground there is no hope. Beyond the grove it is utterly caved in and blocked—I've tried it. If we had a week, perhaps—"

"Let her be," broke in Jacob; "she has something to tell us."

"And do you remember," went on Emlyn, "that you told me that there the carp were so big and fat because just at this place 'neath the drawbridge the Abbey sewer—the big Abbey sewer down which all foul things are poured—empties itself into the moat, and that therefore I would eat none of those fish, even in Lent?"

"Aye, I remember. What of it?"

"Thomas, did I hear you say that the powder you sent for had come?"

"Yes, an hour ago; six kegs, by the carrier's van, of a hundredweight each. Not so much as we hoped for, but something, though, as the cannon has not come—for the King's folk had none—it is of no use."

"A dark night, a ladder with a plank on it, a brick arched drain, two hundredweight, or better still, four of powder set beneath the gate, a slow-match and a brave man to fire it—taken together with God's blessing, these things might do much," mused Emlyn, as though to herself.

Now at length they took her point.

"They'd be listening like a cat for a mouse," said Bolle.

"I think the wind rises," she answered; "I hear it in the trees. I think presently it will blow a gale. Also, lanterns might be shown at the back where the breach is, and men might shout there, as though preparing to attack. That would draw them off. Meanwhile Jeffrey Stokes and I would try our luck with the ladder and the kegs of powder—he to roll and I to fire when the time came, for being, as you have heard, a witch, I understand how to humour brimstone."

Ten minutes later, and their plans were fixed. Two hours later, and, in the midst of a raving gale, hidden by the pitchy darkness and the towering screen of the lifted drawbridge, Emlyn and the strong Jeffrey rolled the kegs of powder over planks laid across the moat, into the mouth of the big drain and twenty feet down it, till they lay under the gateway towers! Then, lying there in the stinking filth, they drew the spigots out of holes that they had made in them, and in their place set the slow-matches. Jeffrey struck a flint, blew the tinder to a glow, and handed it to Emlyn.

"Now get you gone," she said; "I follow. At this job one is better than two."

A minute later she joined him on the farther bank of the moat. "Run!" she said. "Run for your life; there's death behind!"

He obeyed, but Emlyn turned and screamed, till, hearing her through the gale, all the guard hurried up the towers, flashing lanterns, to see what passed.

"STORM! STORM!" she cried. "UP WITH THE LADDERS! FOR THE KIND AND HARFLETE! STORM! STORM!"

Then she too turned and fled.

Chapter XVIII

Out of the Shadows

Through the black night sudden and red there shot a sheet of fire illumining all things as lightning does. Above the roaring of the gale there echoed a dull and heavy noise like to that of muffled thunder. Then after a moment's pause and silence the sky rained stones, and with them the limbs of men.

"The gateway's gone," shouted a great voice, it was that of Bolle. "Out with the ladders!"

Men who were waiting ran up with them and thrust them, four in all, athwart the moat. By the planks that were lashed along their staves they scrambled across and over the piles of shattered masonry into the courtyard beyond where none waited them, for all who watched here were dead or maimed.

"Light the lanterns," shouted Bolle again, "for it will be dark in yonder," and a man who followed with a torch obeyed him.

Then they rushed across the courtyard to the door of the refectory, which stood open. Here in the wide, high-roofed hall they met the mass of Maldon's people pouring back from the faggoted breach, where they had been gathered, expecting attack, some of them also bearing lanterns. For a moment the two parties stood staring at each other; then followed a wild and savage scene. With shouts and oaths and battle-cries they fought furiously. The massive, oaken tables were overthrown, by the red flicker of the pole-borne lanterns men grappled and fell and slew each other upon the floor. A priest struck down a yeoman with a brazen crucifix, and next moment himself was brained with its broken shaft.

"For God and Grace!" shouted some; "For the King and Harflete!" answered others.

"Keep line! Keep line!" roared Bolle, "and sweep them out."

The lanterns were dashed down and extinguished till but one remained, a red and wavering star. Hoarse voices shouted for light, for none knew friend from foe. It came; some one had fired the tapestries and the blaze ran up them to the roof. Then fearing lest they should be roasted, the Abbot's folk gave way and fled to the farther door, followed by their foes. Here it was that most of them fell, for they jammed in the doorway and were cut down there are on the stair beyond.

While Bolle still plied his axe fiercely, some one caught his arm and screamed into his ear—

"Let be! Let be! The wretch is sped."

In his red wrath he turned to strike the speaker, and saw by the flare that it was Cicely.

"What do you here?" he cried. "Get gone."

"Fool," she answered in a low, fierce voice, "I seek my husband. Show me the path ere it be too late, you know it alone. Come, Jeffrey Stokes, a lantern, a lantern!"

Jeffrey appeared, sword in one hand and lantern in the other, and with him Emlyn, who also held a sword which she had plucked from a fallen man, Emlyn still foul with the filth of the sewer and the mud of the moat.

"I may not leave," muttered Thomas Bolle. "I seek Maldon."

"On to the dungeons," shrieked Emlyn, "or I will stab you. I heard them give word to kill Harflete."

Then he snatched the light from Jeffrey's hand, and crying "Follow me," rushed along a passage till they came to an open door and beyond it to stairs. They descended the stairs and passed other passages which ran underground, till a sudden turn to the right brought them to a little walled-in place with a vaulted roof. Two torches flared in iron holders in the masonry, and by the light of them they saw a strange and fearful sight.

At the end of the open place a heavy, nail-studded door stood wide, revealing a cell, or rather a little cave beyond—those who are curious can see it to this day. Fastened by a chain to the wall of this dungeon was a man, who held in his hand a three-legged stool and tugged at his chain like a maddened beast. In front of him, holding the doorway, stood a tall, lank priest, his robe tucked up into his girdle. He was wounded, for blood poured from his shaven crown and he plied a great sword with both hands, striking savagely at four men who tried to cut him down. As Bolle and his party appeared, one of these men fell beneath the priest's blows, and another took his place, shouting—

"Out of the way, traitor. We would kill Harflete, not you."

"We die or live together, murderers," answered the priest in a thick, gasping voice.

At this moment one of them, it was he who had spoken, heard the sound of the rescuers' footsteps and glanced back. In an instant he turned and was running past them like a hare. As he went the light from the lantern fell upon his face, and Emlyn knew it for that of the Abbot. She struck at him with the sword she held, but the steel glanced from his mail. He also struck, but at the lantern, dashing it to the ground.

"Seize him," screamed Emlyn. "Seize Maldon, Jeffrey," and at the words Stokes bounded away, only to return presently, having lost him in the dark passages. Then with a roar Bolle leaped upon the two remaining men-at-arms as they faced about, and very soon between his axe and the sword of the priest behind, they sank to the ground and died still fighting, who knew they had no hope of quarter.

It was over and done and dreadful silence fell upon the place, the silence of the dead broken only by the heavy breathing of those who remained alive. There the wounded monk leaned against the door-post, his red sword drooping to the floor. There Harflete, the stool still lifted, rested his weight against the chain and peered forward in amazement, swaying as though from weakness. And lastly there lay the three slain men, one of whom still moved a little.

Cicely crept forward; over the dead she went and past the priest till she stood face to face with the prisoner.

"Come nearer and I will dash out your brains," he said in a hoarse voice, for such light as there was came from behind her whom he thought to be but another of the murderers.

Then at length she found her voice.

"Christopher!" she cried, "Christopher!"

He hearkened, and the stool fell from his hand.

"The Voice again," he muttered. "Well, 'tis time. Tarry a while, Wife, I come, I come!" and he fell back against the wall shutting his eyes.

She leapt to him, and throwing her arms about him kissed his lips, his poor, bloodless lips. The shut eyes opened.

"Death might be worse," he said, "but so I knew that we would meet."

Now Emlyn, seeing some change in his face, snatched one of the torches from its iron and ran forward, holding it so that the light fell full on Cicely.

"Oh, Christopher," she cried, "I am no ghost, but your living wife."

He heard, he stared, he stared again, then lifted his thin hand and stroked her hair.

"Oh God," he exclaimed, "the dead live!" and down he fell in a heap at her feet.

They thrust Cicely aside, Cicely who stood there shivering, she who thought he had gone again and this time for ever. With difficulty they broke the chain whereby he had been held like a kennelled hound, and bore him, still senseless, up the long passages, Bolle going ahead as guard and Jeffrey Stokes following after. Behind them came Emlyn supporting the wounded monk Martin, for it was he and no other who had saved the life of Christopher.

As they went up towards the stairs they heard a roaring noise.

"Fire!" said Cicely, who knew that sound well, and next instant the light of it burst upon them and its smoke wrapped them round. The Abbey was ablaze, and its wide hall in front looked like the mouth of hell.

"Did I not prophesy that it would be so—yonder at Cranwell burning?" asked Emlyn, with a fierce laugh.

"Follow me!" shouted Bolle. "Be swift now ere the roof falls and traps us."

On they went desperately, leaving the hall on their left, and well for them was it that Thomas knew the way. One little chamber through which they passed had already caught, for flakes of fire fell among them from above and here the smoke was very thick. They were through it, who even a minute later could never have walked that path and lived. They were through it and out into the open air by the cloister door, which those who fled before them had left wide. They reached the moat just where the breach had been mended with faggots, and mounting on them Bolle shouted till one of his own men heard him and dropped the bow that he had raised to shoot him as a rebel. Then planks and ladders were brought, and at last they escaped from danger and the intolerable heat.

Thus it was that Cicely who lost her love in fire, in fire found him once again.

For Christopher was not dead as at first they feared. They carried him to the Priory, and there Emlyn, having felt his heart and found that it still beat, though faintly, sent Mother Matilda to fetch some of that Portugal wine of hers which Commissioner Legh had praised. Spoonful by spoonful she poured it down his throat, till at length he opened his eyes, though only to shut them again in natural sleep, for the wine had taken a hold of his starved body and weakened brain. For hour after hour Cicely sat by him, only rising from time to time to watch the burning of the great Abbey church, as once she had watched that of its dormers and farm-steading.

About three in the morning the lead ceased to pour down in a silvery molten shower, its roofs fell in, and by dawn it was nothing but a fire-blackened shell much as it remains to-day. Just before daybreak Emlyn came to her, saying—

"There is one who would speak with you."

"I cannot see him," she answered, "I bide by my husband."

"Yet you should," said Emlyn, "since but for him you would now have no husband. The monk Martin, who held off the murderers, is dying and desires to bid you farewell."

Then Cicely went to find the man still conscious, but fading away with the flow of his own blood, which could not be stayed by any skill they had.

"I have come to thank you," she murmured, who knew not what else to say.

"Thank me not," he answered faintly, pausing often between his words, "who did but strive to repay part of a great debt. Last winter I shared in awful sin, in obedience, not to my heart, but to my vows. I who was set to watch the body of your husband found that he lived, and by my help he was borne away upon a ship. That ship was taken by the Infidels, and afterwards he and I and Jeffrey served together upon their galleys. There I fell sick, and your husband nursed me back to life. It was I who brought you the deeds and wrote the letter which I gave to Emlyn Stower. My vows still held me fast, and I did no more. This night I broke their bonds, for when I heard the order given that he should be slain I ran down before the murderers and fought my best, forgetting that I was a priest, till at length you came. Let this atone my crimes against my Country, my King and you that I died for my friend at last, as I am glad to do who find this world—too difficult."

"I will tell him if he lives," sobbed Cicely.

He opened his eyes, which had shut, and answered—

"Oh, he'll live, he'll live. You have had many troubles, but, save for the creep of age and death, they are over. I can see and know."

Again he shut his eyes and the watchers thought that all was done, till of a sudden once more he opened them and added in broken tones—

"The Abbot—show him mercy—if you can. He is wicked and cruel, but I have been his confessor and know his heart. He strove for a good end—by an evil road. Queen Catherine was the King's lawful wife. To seize the monasteries is shameless theft. Also his blood is not English; he sees otherwise, and serves the Pope as I do, and Spain, as I do not. As I have helped you, help him. Judge not, that ye be not judged. Promise!" and he raised himself a little on the bed and looked at her earnestly.

"I promise," answered Cicely, and as she spoke Martin smiled. Then his face turned quite grey, all the light went out of his eyes and a moment later Emlyn threw a linen cloth over his head. It was finished.

Cicely returned to Christopher to find him sitting up in bed drinking a bowl of broth.

"Oh, my husband, my husband," she said, casting her arms about him. Then she took her son and laid him upon his father's breast.

Three days had gone by and Christopher and Cicely were walking in the shrubbery of Shefton Hall. By now, although still weak, he was almost recovered, whose only sickness had been grief and famine, for which joy and plenty are wonderful medicines. It was evening, a pleasant and beautiful early winter evening just fading into night. Seated on a bench he had been telling her his adventures, and they were a moving tale worthy, as Cicely wrote afterwards in a letter to old Jacob Smith that is still extant in her fine, quaint handwriting, to be recorded in a book, though this it would seem was never done.

He told her of the great fight on the ship Great Yarmouth, when they were taken by the two Turkish pirates, and of how bravely Father Martin bore himself. Afterwards when they came to the galleys, by good fortune Martin, Jeffrey and he served on the same bench. Then Martin fell sick of some Southern fever, and being in port at Tunis at the time, where they could get fruit, they nursed him back to life and strength. Four months later the Emperor Charles attacked Tunis, and when it fell, through God's mercy, they were rescued with the other Christian slaves, after which Martin returned to England taking old Sir John's writings to be delivered to his next heir, for they all believed Cicely to be dead.

But Christopher and Jeffrey, having nothing to seek at home, stayed to fight with the Spaniards against the Turks, who had oppressed them so sorely. When that war was over they made their way back to England, not knowing where else to go and having a score to settle against the Spanish Abbot of Blossholme, and—well, she knew the rest.

Aye, answered Cicely, she knew it and never would forget it, but it was chill for him sitting on that bench, he must come in. Christopher laughed at her, and answered—

"Sweetheart, if you could have seen the bench on which it was my lot to sit yonder off the coast of Africa, but new recovered from the wound which I had of Maldon's men at Cranwell Towers, you would not be anxious for me here. There for six long months chained to Jeffrey and to Father Martin, for it pleased those heathen devils to keep the three of us together, perhaps that they might watch us better, through the hot days that scorched us, and the chill, wet nights, we laboured at our oars, while infidel overseers ran up and down the boards and thrashed us with their whips of hide. Yes," he added slowly, "they thrashed us as though we were oxen in a yoke. You have seen the scars upon my back."

"Oh, God! to think of it," she murmured; "you, a noble Englishman, beaten by those savage wretches like a brute? How did you bear it, Christopher?"

"I know not, Wife. I think that had it not been for that angel in man's form, the priest Martin—peace be to his noble soul—that angel who thrice at least has saved my life, I should have dashed out my brains against the thwarts, or starved myself to death, or provoked the Moors to kill me; I, who, thinking you dead, had no hope to live for. But Martin taught me otherwise; he preached patience and submission, saying that I did not suffer for nothing—of his own miseries he never spoke—and that he was sure that fearful as was my lot, all things worked together for good to me."

"And therefore it was that you lived on, Husband? Oh! I'll build a shrine to that saint Martin."

"Not altogether, dear. I'll tell you true; I lived for vengeance—vengeance on Clement Maldon, the man, or the devil, who wrought me all this ill, and, being yet young, made me old with grief and pain," and he pointed to his scarred forehead and the hair above, that was now grizzled with white, "and vengeance, too, upon those worshippers of Mohammed, my masters. Yes; though Martin reproved me when I made confession to him, I think it was for that I lived, and the saints know," he added grimly, "afterwards at the sack, and elsewhere, I took it on the Turks. Oh! you should have seen the last meeting of Jeffrey and myself with the captain of that galley and his officers who had so often beaten us. No, I am glad you did not see it, for it was fierce and bloody; even the hard-hearted Spaniards stared."

He paused, and perhaps to change the current of his mind—for during all his after-life, when Christopher brooded on these things he grew gloomy for hours, and even days—Cicely said hurriedly—

"I wonder what has chanced to our enemy, the Abbot. The search has been close, the roads are watched, and we know that he had none with him, for all his foreign soldiers are slain or taken. I think he must be dead in the fire, Christopher."

He shook his head.

"A devil does not die in fire. He is away somewhere, to plot fresh murders—perhaps our own and our boy's. Oh!" he added savagely, "till my hands are about his throat and my dagger is in his heart there's no peace for me, who have a score to pay and you both to guard."

Cicely knew not what to answer; indeed, when this mood was on him it was hard to reason with Christopher, who had suffered so fearfully, and, like herself, been saved but by a miracle or the mandate of Heaven.

Of a sudden a hush fell upon the place. The blackbirds ceased their winter chatter in the laurels; it grew so still that they heard a dead leaf drop to the ground. The night was at hand. One last red ray from the set sun struck across the frosty sky and was reflected to the earth. In the light of that ray Christopher's trained eyes caught the gleam of something white that moved in the shadow of the beech tree where they sat. Like a tiger he sprang at it, and the next moment haled out a man.

"Look," he said, twisting the head of his captive so that the glow fell on it. "Look; I have the snake. Ah! Wife, you saw nothing, but I saw him, and here he is at last—at last!"

"The Abbot!" gasped Cicely.

The Abbot it was indeed, but oh! how changed. His plump, olive- coloured countenance had shrunk to that of a skeleton still covered by yellow skin, in which the dark eyes rolled bloodshot and unnaturally large. His tonsure and jaws showed a growth of stubbly grey hair, his frame had become weak and small, his soft and delicate hands resembled those of a woman dead of some wasting disease, and, like his garments, were clogged with dirt. The mail shirt he wore hung loose upon him; one of his shoes was gone, and the toes peeped through his stockinged foot. He was but a living misery.

"Deliver your arms," growled Christopher, shaking him as a terrier shakes a rat, "or you die. Do you yield? Answer!"

"How can he," broke in Cicely, "when you have him by the throat?"

Christopher loosed his grip of the man's windpipe, and instead seized his wrists, whereon the Abbot drew a great breath, for he was almost choked, and fell to his knees, in weakness, not in supplication.

"I came to you for mercy," he said presently, "but, having overheard your talk, know that I can hope for none. Indeed, why should I, who showed none, and whose great cause seems dead, that cause for which I fought and lived? Let me die with it. I ask no more. Still, you are a gentleman, and therefore I beg a favour of you. Do not hand me over to be drawn, hanged and quartered by your brute-king. Kill me now. You can say that I attacked you, and that you did it in self-defence. I have no arms, but you may set a dagger in my hand."

Christopher looked down at the poor creature huddled at his feet and laughed.

"Who would believe me?" he asked; "though, indeed, who would question, seeing that your life is forfeit to me or any who can take it? Yet that is a matter of which the King's Justices shall judge."

Maldon shivered. "Drawn, hanged and quartered," he repeated beneath his breath. "Drawn, hanged and quartered as a traitor to one I never served!"

"Why not?" asked Christopher. "You have played a cruel game, and lost."

He made no answer; indeed, it was Cicely who spoke, saying—

"How came you in such a case? We thought you fled."

"Lady," he answered, "I've starved for three days and nights in a hole in the ground like an earthed-up fox; a culvert in your garden hid me. At last I crept out to see the light and die, and heard you talking, and thought that I would ask for mercy, since mortal extremity has no honour."

"Mercy!" said Cicely. "Of your treasons I say nothing, for you are not English, and serve your own king, who years ago sent you here to plot against England. But look on this man, my husband. Did he not starve for three days and nights in your strong dungeon ere you came thither to massacre him? Did you not strive to burn him in his Hall, and ship him wounded across the seas to doom? Did you not send your assassin to kill my babe, who stood between you and the wealth you needed for your plots, and bind me, the mother, to the stake—a food for fire? Did you not shoot down my father in the wood, fearing lest he should prove you traitor, and after rob me of my heritage? Did you not compel your monks to work evil and bring some of them to their deaths? Oh! have done! Worm dressed up as God's priest, how can you writhe there and ask for mercy?"

"I said I came to seek for mercy because the agony of sleepless hunger drove me, who now seek only death. Insult not the fallen, Cicely Foterell, but take the vengeance that is your due, and kill," replied the Abbot, looking up at her with his hollow eyes, adding, with a laugh that sounded like a groan, "Come, Sir Christopher; you have got a sword, and it is time you went to supper. The air is cold; your wife—if such she be—said it but now."

"Cicely," said Christopher, "go to the Hall and summon Jeffrey Stokes. Emlyn will know where to find him."

"Emlyn!" groaned the Abbot. "Give me not over to Emlyn. She'd torture me."

"Nay," said Christopher, "this is not Blossholme Abbey; though what may chance in London I know not. Go now, Wife."

But Cicely did not stir; she only stared at the wretched creature at her feet.

"I bid you go," repeated Christopher.

"And I'll not obey," she answered. "Do you remember what I promised Martin ere he died?"

"Martin dead! Is Martin, who saved your husband, dead?" exclaimed the Abbot, lifting his face and letting it fall again. "Happy Martin, to be dead."

"I was not there, and I am not bound by your promises, Cicely."

"But I am, and you and I are one. I vowed mercy to this man if he should fall into our power, and mercy he shall have."

"Then you spare him to destroy us. The wheels go round quick in England, Wife."

"So be it. What I vowed, I vowed. With God be the rest. He has watched us well heretofore, and I think," she added, with one of her bursts of triumphant faith, "will do so to the end. Abbot Maldon, sinful, fallen Abbot Maldon, you are as you were made, and Martin, the saint, said that there is good in your heart, though you have shown none of it to me or mine. Now, look you; yonder is a wooden summer-house, thatched and warm. Get you there, and I'll send you food and wine and new clothing by one who will not talk; also a pass to Lincoln. By to-morrow's dawn you will be refreshed, and then you will find a good horse tied to yonder tree, and so away to sanctuary at Lincoln, and, if aught of ill befalls you afterwards, know it is not our doing, but that of some other enemy, or of God, with Whom I pray you make your peace. May He forgive you, as I do, Who knows all hearts, which I do not. Now, farewell. Nay, say nothing. There is nothing to be said. Come, Christopher, for this once you obey me, not I you."

So they went, and the wretched man raised himself upon his hands and looked after them, but what passed in his heart at that moment none will ever learn.

Some months had gone by and Blossholme, with all the country round, was once more at peace. The tide of trouble had rolled away northward, whence came rumours of renewed rebellion. Abbot Maldon had been seen no more, and for a while it was believed that although he never took sanctuary at Lincoln, he had done a wiser thing and fled to Spain. Then Emlyn, who heard everything, got news that this was not so, but that he was foremost among those who stirred up sedition and war along the Scottish border.

"I can well believe it," said Cicely. "The sow must to its wallowing in the mire. Nature made him a plotter, and he will follow his heart to the end."

"Ere long he may find it hard to follow his head," answered Emlyn grimly. "Oh, to think that you had that wolf caged and turned him loose again to prey on England and on us!"

"I did but show mercy to the fallen, Nurse."

"Mercy? I call it madness. Why, when Jeffrey and Thomas heard of it I thought they would burst with rage, especially Jeffrey, who loved your father well and loved not the infidel galleys," answered the fierce Emlyn.

"Vengeance is mine, I will repay, saith the Lord," murmured Cicely in a gentle voice.

"The Lord also said that whoso sheddeth man's blood by man shall his blood be shed. Why, I've heard this Maldon quote it to your husband at Cranwell Towers."

"So will it be, Emlyn, if so it is to be, only let others shed that cruel blood. I would not have it on my hands or on those of any of my house, for after all he is an ordained priest of my own faith. Moreover, I had promised. Still, talk not of the matter lest it should bring trouble on us all, who had no right to loose him. Also these are ill thoughts for your wedding day. Go, deck yourself in those fine clothes which Jacob Smith has sent from London, since the clergyman will be at Blossholme church by four, and I think that Thomas has waited long enough for you."

Emlyn smiled a little, and shrugged her broad shoulders, muttering something that would have angered Thomas if he could have heard it, as Cicely went off to join Christopher, who called to her from another room.

She found him adding up figures on paper, a very different Christopher to the broken man they had rescued from the dungeon, though still much aged by the terrors of the past year and just now looking rueful.

"See, Sweet," he said, "we should give a marriage portion to Emlyn, who has earned it if ever woman did, but where it is to come from I know not. Those Abbey lands Jacob Smith bought from the King are not yours yet, nor Henry's either, though doubtless he will have them soon. Neither have any rents been paid to you from your own estates, and when they come they are promised up in London, while the Abbot's razor has shaved my own poor parsimony bare as a churchyard skull. Also Mother Matilda and her nuns must be kept till we can endow them with their lands again. One day we, or our boy yonder, may be rich, but till it comes there are hard times for all of us."

"Not so hard as some we have known, Husband," she answered, laughing, "for at least we are free and have food to eat, and for the rest we will borrow from Jacob Smith on the jewels that remain over. Indeed, I have written to him and he will not refuse."

"Aye, but how about Thomas and Emlyn?"

"They must do as their betters do. Though there is little stock on it, Thomas has the Manor Farm at low rent, which he may pay when he can, while Jacob put a present in the pocket of Emlyn's wedding dress. What's more, I think he will make her his heir, and if so she will be rich indeed, so rich that I shall have to curtsey to her. Now, go make ready for this marriage, and as you have no fine doublet, bid Jeffrey put on your mail, for you look best in that, or so at least I think, who to my mind look best in anything you chance to wear."

Then while he demurred, saying that there was now no need to bear arms in Blossholme, also that Jeffrey was away settling himself as landlord of the Ford Inn, the same that the Abbot had once promised to Flounder Megges, she kissed him, and seizing her boy, who lay crowing in the sunlight, danced with him from the room. For oh, Cicely's heart was merry.

There were many folk at the marriage of Emlyn Stower and Thomas Bolle, for of late Blossholme had been but a sorry place, and this wedding came to it like the breath of spring to the woods and meads around, a hint of happiness after the miseries of winter. The story of the pair had got about also. How they had been pledged in youth and separated by scheming men for their own purposes. How Emlyn had been married off against her will to an aged partner whom she hated, and Thomas, who was set down as a fool, forced to serve the monastery as a lay- brother, a strong hind skilled in the management of cattle and such matters, but half crazy, as indeed it had suited him to feign himself to be.

People knew the end of the thing also; that Emlyn had cursed the Abbot, and that her curse had been fulfilled. That Thomas Bolle had shaken off his superstitious fears and risen up against him and at last been given the commission of the King, and, as his Grace's officer, shown himself no fool but a man of mettle who had taken the Abbey by storm and rescued Sir Christopher Harflete from its dungeons. Emlyn also, like her mistress, had been bound to the stake as a witch, and saved from burning by this same Thomas, who with her had been concerned in many remarkable events whereof the countryside was full of tales, true or false. Now at last after all these adventures they came together to be wed, and who was there for ten miles round that would not see it done?

The monks being gone Father Roger Necton, the old vicar of Cranwell, he who had united Christopher and his wife Cicely in strange circumstances, and for that deed been obliged to fly for his life when the last Abbot of Blossholme burned Cranwell Towers, came to tie the knot before his great congregation. Notwithstanding that they were both of middle age, Emlyn in her grand gown and the brawny, red-haired Thomas in his yeoman's garb of green, such as he had worn when he wooed her many years before he put on the monk's russet robe, made a fine and handsome pair at the altar. Or so folk thought, though some friend of the monks, remembering Bolle's devil's livery and Emlyn's repute as a sorceress, cried out from the shadow that Satan was marrying a witch, and for his pains got his head broken by Jeffrey Stokes.

So the white-haired and gentle Father Necton, having first read the King's order releasing Thomas from his vows, tied them fast according to the ancient rites and blessed them both. At length it was finished, and the pair walked from the old church to the Manor Farm, where they were to dwell, followed, as was the custom, by a company of their friends and well-wishers. As they went they passed through a little stretch of woodland by the stream, where on this spring day the wild daffodils and lilies of the valley were abloom making sweet the air. Here Emlyn paused a moment and said to her husband, Captain Bolle—

"Do you remember this place?"

"Aye, Wife," he answered, "it was here that we plighted our troth in youth, and looked up to see Maldon passing us just beyond that same oak, and felt the shadow of him strike cold to our hearts. You spoke of it yonder in the Priory chapel when I came up by the secret way, and its memory made me mad."

"Yes, Thomas, I spoke of it," answered Emlyn in a rich and gentle voice, a new voice to him. "Well, now let its memory make you happy, as, notwithstanding all my faults, I will if I can," and swiftly she bent towards him and kissed him, adding, "Come on, Husband, they press behind us and I hope that we have done with perils and plottings."

"Amen," answered Bolle, and as he spoke certain strange men who wore the King's colours and carried a long ladder went by them at a distance. Wondering what was their business at Blossholme, the pair passed through the last of the woodland and reached the rise whence they could see the gaunt skeleton of the burnt-out Abbey that appeared within fifty paces of them. At this they paused to look, and presently were joined there by Christopher and Cicely, Mother Matilda and her good nuns, Jeffrey Stokes, and others. The place seemed grim and desolate in the evening light, and all of them stood staring at it filled with their separate thoughts.

"What is that?" said Cicely, with a start, pointing to a round black object new set over the ruin of the gateway tower.

Just then a red ray from the sunset struck upon the thing.

It was the severed head of Clement Maldon the Spaniard.

H. Rider Haggard – A Short Biography

Sir Henry Rider Haggard, KBE was born on June 22nd, 1856 at Bradenham in Norfolk, England.

More familiarly known as H. Rider Haggard, he was the eighth of ten children born to Sir William Meybohm Rider Haggard, a barrister (born, incidentally, in St Petersburg, Russia), and Ella Doveton, an author, poet and daughter of a merchant in the East India Trading Company.

Haggard was initially schooled at Garsington Rectory in Oxfordshire where he studied under the tutelage of Reverend H. J. Graham. His elder brothers, who seemed to find more favour with their father, graduated from various private schools whilst Haggard was sent to Ipswich Grammar School, saving his father a considerable sum in fees.

He failed his army entrance exam, and was therefore sent to a private crammer in London in preparation for the entrance exam to the British Foreign Office, which he appears never to have sat. However, it was during his two years in London that Haggard came into contact with a circle of people interested in the study of psychical phenomena and for which he too now developed a life-long interest together with a series of enduring friendships.

In 1875, Haggard's father used his family's connections to send him to Southern Africa to take up an unpaid position as assistant to the secretary to Sir Henry Bulwer, Lieutenant-Governor of the Colony of Natal. In 1876 he was transferred to the staff of Sir Theophilus Shepstone, Special Commissioner for the Transvaal. It was in this role that Haggard was present in Pretoria in April 1877 for the official announcement of the British annexation of the Boer Republic of the Transvaal. The official who had been nominated to read out the Proclamation lost his voice and Haggard was his replacement. It was a moment in history.

Haggard was to remain in the country for six years, during which time he served as Master of the High Court of the Transvaal and an adjutant of the Pretoria Horse.

It was here that he fell in love with Mary Elizabeth "Lilly" Jackson. He hoped to marry her once he obtained more certainty in his career path.

In 1878 he became Registrar of the High Court in the Transvaal and now the time seemed opportune to write to his father to tell him of his hope to marry. The reply from his father was uncompromising. He forbade it until his son had made a proper career for himself.

The following year, 1879, Lily married Frank Archer, a well-to-do banker.

Haggard returned briefly to England to marry a friend of his sister's, Marianna Louisa Margitson, a 21 year old, in 1880, and the couple travelled to Africa together. Haggard's years in Africa had proved, at least on a writing level, rich and inspirational for him, and while still in Natal he wrote two articles for The Gentleman's Magazine describing his experiences.

Moving back to England in (and accounts here differ as to whether it was 1881 or 1882) the couple settled in Ditchingham, Norfolk, Louisa's ancestral home. Later they moved to Kessingland and established connections with the church in Bungay, Suffolk. The marriage produced four children. A son named Jack (who tragically died at age 10 of measles) and three daughters, Angela, Dorothy and Lilias. (Lilias grew to become an author and her father's biographer.)

In England Law was to be the fulcrum of his career. However, although he studied, writing was growing in its appeal to him. His first book, Cetywayo and His White Neighbours, was an account and study of Britain's policies in South Africa.

From this point his career as a writer began to take substantial hold and with it a dramatic shift to fiction. Two years later he published his first fiction, Dawn followed in 1885 by arguably his most popular novel, King Solomon's Mines—detailing the life of the adventurer Allan Quatermain. This was followed the following year, 1886, by She: A History of Adventure, which introduced the female character Ayesha. Both characters, Quatermain and Ayesha, developed a series of books about their adventures.

The study of Law now fell away entirely. He appeared also to have a keen sense of his commercial appreciation. Rather than sell the copyright of his first best-seller, King Solomon's Mines, for a £100 fee he, instead, accepted a 10% royalty. This book is also generally accepted as the first of the Lost World writing genre.

Haggard obviously thought there were many further adventures to tell and it would be hard to find a publisher who would disagree given the start he had made. Sequels soon followed. Allan Quatermain continued his epic and swash-buckling adventures in Africa whilst the sequel to She entitled Ayesha played out her adventures in Tibet. Interestingly Haggard would later extend his characters adventures around the world with Eric Brighteyes, being the basis for an epic Viking romance.

The Haggard family lived at 69 Gunterstone Road in Hammersmith, London, from mid-1885 to mid-1888. It was here that he wrote his most famous works. His time in Africa had given him the experience and atmosphere as well as several observations and friendships of the people who would so influence his fictional characters. Chief among them were the larger-than-life adventurers Frederick Selous and Frederick Russell Burnham. Both were men of Empire and huge ambition as they helped uncover the great mineral wealth of Africa, as well as the ruins of ancient lost civilisations of the continent, such as Great Zimbabwe.

Three of Haggard's books, The Wizard (1896), Black Heart and White Heart; a Zulu Idyll (1896), and Elissa; the Doom of Zimbabwe (1898), are dedicated to Burnham's daughter Nada, the first white child born in Bulawayo; she had been named after Haggard's 1892 book Nada the Lily.

As is typical of the writing of the time his novels contain many of the stereotypes associated with colonialism, yet they also sympathise, to a degree, with the native populations. Africans often play heroic roles in the novels, although the protagonists are more often than not European. The time around the turn of the century was, after all, the great sprint to Empire by many European countries intent on gaining possessions of land, people and resources.

Three of Haggard's novels were written in collaboration with his friend Andrew Lang who shared his interest in the spiritual realm and paranormal phenomena and who was also a greatly admired editor.

Haggard's stories are still widely read today. Ayesha, the female protagonist of She, has been cited as a prototype by psychoanalysts such as Sigmund Freud (in The Interpretation of Dreams) and Carl Jung. Her epithet is, of course, "She Who Must Be Obeyed" and has for decades been used tongue-in-cheek to describe the presumed balance of influence between the sexes.

As a legacy it is easy to establish Haggard, and his pioneering work, as the author of the Lost World branch of writing and its influence of such other writers as Edgar Rice Burroughs, Robert E. Howard and Talbot Mundy. The Allan Quatermain character influenced many 'serials' in Hollywood during the 30s & 40s and can readily be seen as a template for Indiana Jones, the American archaeologist and explorer and huge box office film character.

Years later, when Haggard was a successful novelist, he was contacted by his former love, Lilly Archer, née Jackson. Lily had been deserted by her husband, who had embezzled funds and fled bankrupt to Africa. Haggard installed her and her sons in a house and saw to the children's education. Lilly eventually followed her husband to Africa, where he infected her with syphilis before dying of it himself. Lilly returned to England in late 1907, where Haggard again supported her until her death on April 22nd, 1909.

Haggard also wrote about agricultural and social reform, in part inspired by his experiences in Africa, but also based on what he saw in Europe. By the end of his life, he was adamantly opposed to Bolshevism, a position that he shared with his life-long friend Rudyard Kipling. The two had found friendship upon Kipling's arrival at London in 1889 largely on the strength of their shared opinions.

Haggard was extremely interested in the social affairs of the Country and eager to play a more active part in attempting reform. In 1895 he stood unsuccessfully for Parliament as a Conservative candidate for the Eastern division of Norfolk losing by 198 votes.

Also in 1895 he served on a government commission to examine Salvation Army labour colonies. This, and his heavy involvement in agriculture reform, led to him being a member of several further commissions on land use and related affairs, work that involved several trips to the Colonies and Dominions. This work, in part, helped lead to the passage of the 1909 Development Bill.

In 1911 he served on the Royal Commission examining coastal erosion.

He was an absorbed and dedicated writer of letters to The Times, nearly one hundred were published by them and the bibliography attached below reveals much in the range of subjects he wished to bring attention to.

He was made a Knight Bachelor in 1912 and a Knight Commander of the Order of the British Empire in 1919. Haggard was a member of several clubs including the Athenaeum, Savile, and Authors' clubs.

The district of Rider in British Columbia, Canada, was named in his honour.

Henry Rider Haggard died on May 14th, 1925 at the age of 68. His ashes were buried at Ditchingham Church. His papers are held at the Norfolk Record Office.

The first chapter of his book People of the Mist (1894) is credited with inspiring the 1912 motto of the Royal Air Force (formerly the Royal Flying Corps), Per ardua ad astra. "Through adversity to the stars" (or alternately "Through struggle to the stars") it is also used by other Commonwealth air forces such as the RAAF, RCAF, RNZAF, and the SAAF.

H. Rider Haggard – A Concise Bibliography

Novels
Dawn (1884) Published in three volumes
The Witch's Head (1884) Published in three volumes
King Solomon's Mines (1885) Allan Quatermain series
She: A History of Adventure (1886) Ayesha series
Allan Quatermain (1887) Allan Quatermain series
Jess (1887)
A Tale of Three Lions (1887) Allan Quatermain series
Maiwa's Revenge, or the War of the Little Hand (1888) Allan Quatermain series
Colonel Quaritch, VC (1889) Published in three volumes
Cleopatra (1889)
Beatrice (1890)
The World's Desire (1890) Co-written with Andrew Lang

Eric Brighteyes (1891)
Nada the Lily (1892)
An Heroic Effort (1893)
Montezuma's Daughter (1893)
The People of the Mist (1894)
Heart of the World (1895)
Joan Haste (1895)
The Wizard (1896)
Doctor Therne (1898)
Swallow: A Tale of the Great Trek (1899)
Lysbeth (1901)
Pearl Maiden (1903)
Stella Fregelius: A Tale of Three Destinies (1903)
The Brethren (1904)
Ayesha: The Return of She (1905) Ayesha series
The Way of the Spirit (1906)
Benita (1906)
Fair Margaret (1907)
The Ghost Kings(1908)
The Yellow God (1908)
The Lady of Blossholme (1909)
Morning Star (1910)
Queen Sheba's Ring (1910)
Red Eve (1911)
The Mahatma and the Hare (1911)
Marie (1912) Allan Quatermain series
Child of Storm (1913) Allan Quatermain series
The Wanderer's Necklace (1914)
The Holy Flower (1915) Allan Quatermain series
The Ivory Child (1916) Allan Quatermain series
Finished (1917) Allan Quatermain series]
Love Eternal (1918)
Moon of Israel (1918)
When the World Shook (1919)
The Ancient Allan (1920) Allan Quatermain series
She and Allan (1921) Allan Quatermain series / Ayesha series
The Virgin of the Sun (1922)
Wisdom's Daughter (1923) Ayesha series
Heu-Heu (1924) Allan Quatermain series]
Queen of the Dawn (1925)
The Treasure of the Lake (1926) Allan Quatermain series
Allan and the Ice-Gods (1927) Allan Quatermain series
Mary of Marion Isle (1929)
Belshazzar (1930)

Short Story Collections
Allan's Wife and Other Tales (1889)

Black Heart and White Heart: A Zulu Idyll (1900)
Smith and the Pharaohs (1920)

Publications in Periodicals and Newspapers
A Zulu War-Dance (July 1877) The Gentleman's Magazine
A Visit to the Chief (September 1877) The Gentleman's Magazine
Hydrophobia (letter) (3 November 1885) The Times
The Land Question (letter) (28 April 1886) The Times
About Fiction (February 1887) The Contemporary Review
Mr Rider Haggard and His Critics (letter) (27 April 1887) The Times
Our Position in Cyprus (July 1887) The Contemporary Review
American Copyright (letter) (11 October 1887) The Times
On Going Back (November 1887) Longman's Magazine
Delagoa Bay (letter) (17 December 1887) The Times
South African Policy (letter) (27 December 1887) The Times
Suggested Prologue to a Dramatised Version of She (March 1888) Longman's Magazine
Mr. Meeson's Will (18 June 1888) The Illustrated London News
The Wreck of the Copeland (18 August 1888) The Illustrated London News
Cleopatra (3 December 1888) The Illustrated London News
Hydrophobia and Muzzling (letter) (25 October 1889) The Times
The Annals of Natal (23 November 1889) The Saturday Review
Mummy at St Mary/Woolnoth's (letter) (25 December 1889) The Times
Mummies (letter) (27 December 1889) The Times
The Fate of Swaziland (January 1890) The New Review
In Memoriam (17 May 1890) Thompson's Seasons
American Copyright (letter) (5 June 1890) The Times
Mr Herbert Ward and Mr Stanley (10 November 1890) The Times
Nada the Lily (2 January 1892) The Illustrated London News
A New Argument Against Creation (19 December 1892) The Times
My First Book. Dawn. By H. Rider Haggard (April 1893) The Idler
The Tale of Isandlwana and Rorke's Drift (4 October 1893) The True Story Book
Lobengula (letter) (19 October 1893) The Times
The New Sentiment (letter) (6 November 1893) The Times
Wanted—Imagination   (25 December 1893) The Times
The Fate of Captain Patterson's Party (28 December 1893) The Times
The Three Volume Novel (letter) (27 July 1894) The Times
The Adventures of John Gladwyn Jebb (letter) (30 October 1894) The Times
Agriculture in Norfolk (letter) (30 October 1894) The Times
The Nelson Bazaar (letter) (16 February 1895) The Times
Everything is Peaceful (letter) (20 March 1895) The Times
Lord Kimberley in Norfolk (letter) (17 April 1895) The Times
The East Norfolk Election (letter) (23 July 1895) The Times
The East Norfolk Election (letter) (29 July 1895) The Times
Wilson's Last Fight (7 October 1895) The True Story Book
The Crisis in the Transvaal (letter) (2 January 1896) The Times
The Transvaal Crisis (letter) (13 January 1896) The Times
Jameson's Surrender (letter) (14 March 1896) The Times

The Rinderpest in South Africa (letter) (5 November 1896) The Times
Mr Rider Haggard and Dr Neufeld (letter) (9 January 1899) The Times
Shrinkage of Population in Agricultural Districts (letter) (9 May 1899) The Times
The South African Crisis—An Appeal (letter) (1 July 1899) The Times
Commandant-General Joubert and Mr H Rider Haggard (letter) (8 September 1899) The Times
Anglo-African Writers' Club (17 October 1899) The Times
The War (letter) (25 October 1899) The Times
Farming in 1899 (letter) (22 December 1899) The Times
Farming in 1899 (letter) (1 January 1900) The Times
Settlement of Soldiers in South Africa (letter) (5 May 1900) The Times
1881 and 1900 (letter) (2 October 1900) The Times
Farming in 1900 (letter) (1 January 1901) The Times
Central and Associated Chambers of Agriculture (letter) (6 November 1901) The Times
Small Holdings (letter) (8 November 1901) The Times
Rural England (letter) (4 February 1903) The Times
Mr Rider Haggard on Rural Depopulation (3 May 1903) The Times
Agricultural Distress (letter) (11 June 1903) The Times
The Motor Problem (letter) (24 June 1903) The Times
Fiscal Policy and Agriculture (letter) (16 December 1903) The Times
Telepathy Between a Human Being and a Dog (letter) (21 July 1904) The Times
Telepathy Between a Human Being and a Dog (letter) (9 August 1904) The Times
Mr Rider Haggard on Small Holdings (12 September 1904) The Times
Case L.1139 Dream (October 1904) Journal of the Society for Psychical Research
Mr Rider Haggard on Agriculture (22 October 1904) The Times
Mr Rider Haggard on Rural Housing (27 October 1904) The Times
The Deserted Village (letter) (25 August 1905) The Times
Decrease of Population and the Land (letter) (6 January 1906) The Times
Prevention of Cruelty to Children (3 February 1906) The Times
The New Land and Tenure Bill (letter) (12 March 1906) The Times
Garden City Association (17 March 1906) The Times
Mr H. Rider Haggard on the Zulus (19 May 1906) The Illustrated London News
To Be Proof against British Bullets: A Zulu Incantation (19 May 1906) The Illustrated London News
Housing of the Working Classes (26 June 1906) The Times
Mr Rider Haggard on Small Holdings (4 July 1906) The Times
The Unemployed and Waste City Lands (letter) (19 July 1906) The Times
Mr Rider Haggard on the Transvaal Constitution (7 August 1906) The Times
Vanishing East Anglia (1 September 1906) The Saturday Review
The Land Grabbing at Plaistow (5 September 1906) The Times
The Land Tenure Bill (22 November 1906) The Times
Publishers and the Public (letter) (19 February 1907) The Times
The Careless Children (2 March 1907) The Saturday Review
The Government and the Land (letter) (29 April 1907) The Times
Chambers of Agriculture (2 May 1907) The Times
The Government and the Land (letter) (8 May 1907) The Times
Miss Jebb on Small Holdings (15 June 1907) Country Life
Rural Housing and Sanitation Association (27 June 1907) The Times
St Thomas Hospital Medical School (28 June 1907) The Times
The Land Question (4 July 1907) The Times

A Plea for the Sitting Tennant (letter) (12 August 1907) The Times
A Literary Coincidence (letter) (19 October 1907) The Spectator
Town Planning Conference (26 October 1907) The Times
Dr Barnardo's Homes (16 November 1907) The Times
The Proposed Agricultural Party (5 December 1907) The Times
Mr Rider Haggard and Small Holdings (10 January 1908) The Times
Mr Haggard and Children's Legislation (13 March 1908) The Times
The Drink Trade and Common Sense (letter) (2 April 1908) The Times
The Zulus: The Finest Savage Race in the World (June 1908) The Pall Mall Magazine
Sparrows (letter) (18 August 1908) The Times
Sparrows, Rats and Humanity (letter) (5 September 1908) The Times
The Letters of Queen Victoria (letter) (26 November 1908) The Times
The Romance of the World's Greatest Rivers (December 1908) Travel Magazine
Afforestation. Mr Rider Haggard's View (1 March 1909) The Times
The Late Sir Marshal Clarke (letter) (13 April 1909) The Times
Mr Rider Haggard on Agriculture (27 November 1909) The Times
Mr Rider Haggard on South Africa (11 March 1910) The Times
Why? (letter) (25 April 1910) The Times
Mr Rider Haggard on Irish Agriculture (23 May 1910) The Times
Why Not? (letter) (12 July 1910) The Times
Mr Rider Haggard on Agriculture (16 September 1910) The Times
Mr Rider Haggard on Vermin (8 November 1910) The Times
Danish High Schools (21 December 1910) The Times
Sugar Beet Growing in Norfolk (6 March 1911) The Times
Rural Denmark (letter) (22 March 1911) The Times
Rural Denmark (letter) (3 April 1911) The Times
The Copyright Bill (letter) (6 June 1911) The Times
Mr Rider Haggard on Poverty. The Burden of Civilization (15 July 1911) The Times
Mr Rider Haggard and the Public Records (28 July 1911) The Times
The Farmers' Burden (1 December 1911) The Times
Egyptian Date Farm. The Financial Aspect (11 October 1912) The Times
Umslopogaas and Makokel. Sir H. Rider Haggard on Zulu Types (letter) (16 August 1913) The Times
The Death of Mark Haggard (letter) (10 October 1914) The Times
On the Land. Old Problems and New Ways. The War—and After. (15 March 1915) The Times
Soldiers as Settlers. After-War Problem for the Empire (20 August 1915) The Times
Raids by Air. Zeppelins and Zeppelins (letter) (22 October 1915) The Times
Women's Work on the Land. A Palliative in Hard Times (letter) (29 November 1915) The Times
Women on the Land. Town Girls' Unfitness for Farm Work (letter) (9 December 1915) The Times
Soldiers as Settlers. Sir Rider Haggard's Oversea Mission (2 February 1916) The Times
Soldiers as Settlers (letter) (7 February 1916) The Times
Soldier Settlers. The Future of Rural England (letter) (10 February 1916) The Times
Farewell Luncheon to Sir Rider Haggard (March 1916) United Empire
Soldier Settlers for the Empire. Offer from Victoria (18 April 1916) The Times
Sir R Haggard's Tour. Land for Ex-Service Men (22 July 1916) The Times
Sir H. Rider Haggard's Mission. Land for Ex-Soldiers (1 August 1916) The Times
Land for Ex-Soldiers. Outline of Sir R. Haggard's Report   (12 August 1916) The Times
Empire Land Settlement Deputation to the Secretary of State for the Colonies and the President of the
Board of Agriculture (September 1916) United Empire

Empire Land Settlement by Sir Rider Haggard (December 1916) United Empire
A Journey through Zululand by Sir H Rider Haggard (December 1916) The Windsor Magazine
Mr Wilson's Note. British Publicity (28 December 1916) The Times
Home Produce (letter) (22 February 1917) The Times
The Milk Supply (letter) (11 April 1917) The Times
Corn Production Bill. A National Measure (letter) (13 June 1917) The Times
A Protest and a Plea. Farmers and Meat (letter) (9 October 1917) The Times
Pig-Breeding. A Subject for Municipal Enterprise (letter) (22 February 1918) The Times
The German Colonies. Interests of the Dominions (letter) (5 November 1918) The Times
Light—More Light! (letter) (19 November 1918) The Times
A Great American. Tributes to the Late Mr Roosevelt (letter) (8 January 1919) The Times
Shut the Door (letter) (10 March 1919) The Times
Population and Housing. Emigration v Birth Control (25 March 1919) The Times
The Ex-Kaiser (letter) (11 April 1919) The Times
Empire Birth-Rate. Sir Rider Haggard on Emigration (17 April 1919) The Times
Ex-Service Men Abroad. Warnings from California (letter) (10 May 1919) The Times
Edith Cavell (letter) (16 May 1919) The Times
The Ex-Kaiser. Uncertainties of Trial (letter) (8 July 1919) The Times
Race Suicide Peril. Western Civilization Threatened (11 October 1919) The Times
The British Cinema. Production of Reputable Films (letter) (5 November 1919) The Times
Horrors on the Film. Limits of Publicity (letter) (19 November 1919) The Times
The British Museum (letter) (24 January 1920) The Times
Air Exploration and Empire (letter) (7 February 1920) The Times
The Liberty League. A Campaign Against Bolshevism (letter) (3 March 1920) The Times
Bolshevist Peril. Counter-Propaganda (4 March 1920) The Times
The Empire's Vacant Lands. Settlers and the Food Supply (14 April 1920) The Times
Films and Happy Endings. The Tyranny of a Convention (letter)   (21 April 1921) The Times
Land and its Burdens. Evil of Grinding Taxation (letter) (8 August 1921) The Times
Boy Emigrants (letter) (31 March 1922) The Times
Migration and Morals. Declining Birther Rate (7 April 1922) The Times
Labour Party's Programme. Confiscation and Class Hatred (letter) (28 October 1922) The Times
Efficient Denmark. Keeping the People on the Land (7 December 1922) The Times
The Egyptian Find. Tombs of Eighteenth Dynasty Queens (letter) (19 December 1922) The Times
King Tutankhamen. Reburial in Great Pyramid (letter) (13 February 1923) The Times
The Norfolk Dispute. A Truce while There is Time (letter) (3 April 1923) The Times
Rural Post and Telephone. Minister's Reply to Deputation (19 April 1923) The Times
Liberalism and Land Reform (letter) (1 May 1923) The Times
Small Holdings. Influence of Heredity (letter) (4 July 1923) The Times
Agricultural Parcel Post (26 July 1923) The Times
Country Houses for Sale. Empty East Anglian Mansions (letter) (14 June 1924) The Times
Plight of Agriculture (24 July 1924) The Times
Loans From the British Museum (letter) (30 July 1924) The Times
Zinovieff Letter. Mr MacDonald and a Political Plot (letter) (29 October 1924) The Times
Two Centuries of Publishing. Tributes to Messrs. Longmans (6 November 1924) The Times
Imagination and War (26 November 1924) The Times

Non-Fiction

Cetywayo and His White Neighbours (1882)
A Farmer's Year (1899)
The Last Boer War (1899)
A Winter Pilgrimage (1901)
Rural England (1902)
A Gardener's Year (1905)
The Poor and the Land (1905)
Regeneration (1910)
Rural Denmark (1911)
The Days of My Life (1926)

King Solomon's Mines
This novel has been adapted at least six times. The first version, King Solomon's Mines, directed by Robert Stevenson, premiered in 1937. The best known version premiered in 1950: King Solomon's Mines, directed by Compton Bennett and Andrew Marton, was followed in 1959 by a sequel, Watusi. In 1979 a low-budget version directed by Alvin Rakoff, King Solomon's Treasure, combined both King Solomon's Mines and Allan Quatermain in one story. The 1985 film King Solomon's Mines was a tongue-in-cheek parody of the story, with a 1987 sequel in the same vein, Allan Quatermain and the Lost City of Gold. Around the same time an Australian animated TV film came out, King Solomon's Mines. In 2008 a direct-to-video adaptation, Allan Quatermain and the Temple of Skulls, was released.

She
She has been adapted for the cinema at least ten times, and was one of the earliest films to be made, in 1899 as La Colonne de feu (The Pillar of Fire), by Georges Méliès. A 1911 version starred Marguerite Snow, a British-produced version appeared in 1916, and in 1917 Valeska Suratt appeared in a production for Fox which is lost. In 1925 a silent film of She, starring Betty Blythe, was produced with the active participation of Rider Haggard, who wrote the intertitles. This film combines elements from all the books in the series.

A decade later another cinematic version of the novels was released, featuring Helen Gahagan, Randolph Scott and Nigel Bruce. Unlike the book and the other films, this 1935 version was set in the Arctic, rather than Africa, and depicts the ancient civilisation of the story in an Art Deco style, with music by Max Steiner.

The 1965 film She was produced by Hammer Film Productions; it starred Ursula Andress as Ayesha and John Richardson as her reincarnated love, with Peter Cushing and Bernard Cribbins as other members of the expedition.

In 2001 another adaption was released direct-to-video with Ian Duncan as Leo Vincey, Ophélie Winter as Ayesha and Marie Bäumer as Roxane.

Dawn
The film Dawn was released in 1917, starring Hubert Carter and Annie Esmond.

Jess

This book was filmed in 1912, featuring Marguerite Snow, Florence La Badie and James Cruze, in 1914 with Constance Crawley and Arthur Maude, and in 1917 as Heart and Soul, starring Theda Bara in the title role.

Beatrice
The book was adapted into a 1921 Italian silent drama film called The Stronger Passion, directed by Herbert Brenon and starring Marie Doro and Sandro Salvini.

Swallow
The novel was adapted into a 1922 South African film.

Stella Fregelius
The book was adapted into a 1921 British film, Stella.

Moon of Israel
This novel was the basis of a script by Ladislaus Vajda, for film-director Michael Curtiz in his 1924 Austrian epic known as Die Sklavenkönigin (Queen of the Slaves).